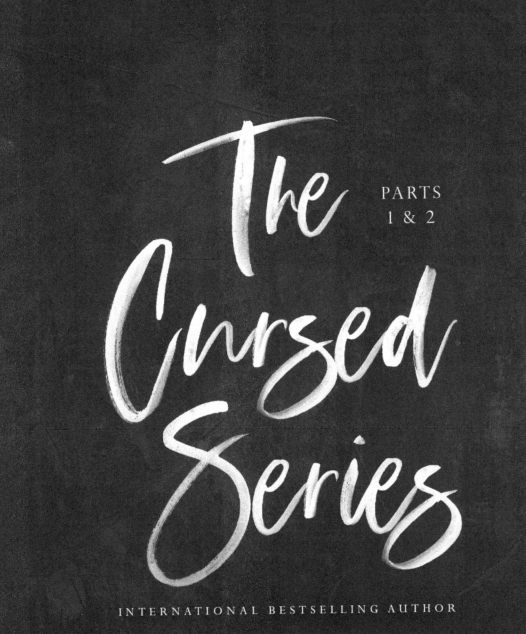

The Cursed Series

PARTS 1 & 2

INTERNATIONAL BESTSELLING AUTHOR

REBECCA DONOVAN

ISBN: 978-0-9995349-6-0

Dedicated to the Believers &

the Beautiful Souls in need of a screaming spot—

Your heart always knows the truth. You're worth fighting for.

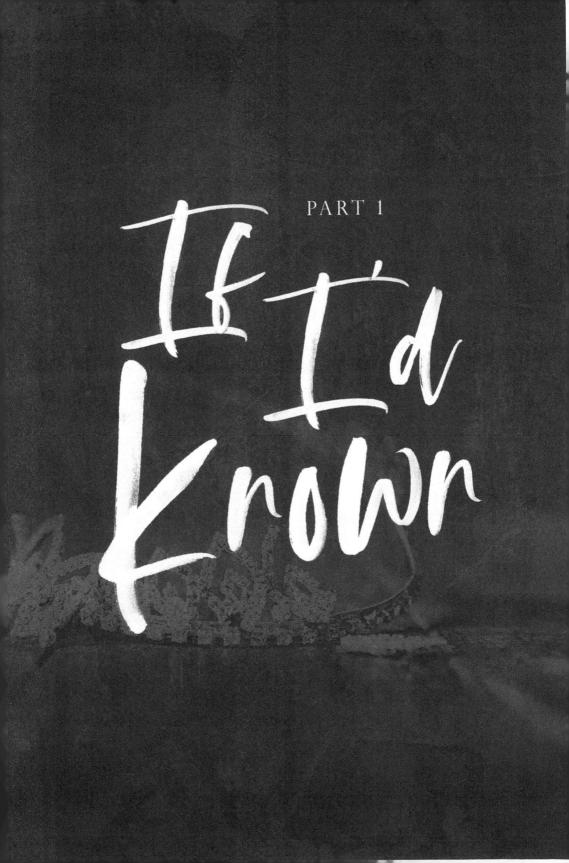

PART 1

If I'd Known

Prologue

We're all cursed—*every single one of us.*

It's not the compulsions or addictions that will take us down. It's not greed and lust that will bring us to our knees. Our curses are instilled in us as virtues, something we should attain and strive to become. Except it's these traits, the ones we deem to be the most honorable, that cause the most destruction.

I should know. I've been a witness to it my entire life. *Belief, Trust, Kindness* and *Boldness.* They sound like the best characteristics to possess. Except they're the reason for just about everything that's ever gone wrong.

My mother is lost to the *Belief* that love will find her. She still awaits the return of the man who, at the age of seventeen, vowed to always love her.

My grandmother was disappointed each time the *Trust* she had given was betrayed, causing her to be constantly wary of others' motives and intentions.

My aunt Allison allows the wrong people into her life—unable to understand that her *Kindness* doesn't mean others will be kind in return. Three kids with three different fathers later, she lives alone in South Carolina, pregnant with her fourth.

And the eldest, my aunt Helen, cannot advance in the world because her *Boldness* offends more than it inspires.

I wonder if I'm the only one who sees it—the weakness within us. I don't know if we're born cursed or if it's bestowed upon us at some pivotal moment in our lives, but it defines us and ultimately leads to our demise. So we can either accept it or live in denial.

Most live in denial, holding out hope for their "happily ever after."

Well, I hate to say it, but "happily ever after" is bullshit—an illusion concocted to sell books and movie tickets. Yet people want—no, they need to believe it exists. They prefer the lies.

Me? I'd rather know the truth, no matter how brutal.

Which is my curse right there...*Honesty*. I can't remember ever telling a lie, even when I was little. My grandmother was intolerant of anything other than the truth, and so that's all I ever spoke. And why would I want to lie? It's exhausting and takes way too much effort to keep the lies straight.

Every day, I see what lying can do. The false hope. Believing in something that was never real to begin with. Convinced of what will never be.

My curse has taught me how to decipher the bullshit. But telling the truth doesn't always work out so well.

Most of the time, I don't care who I offend. I'll say whatever's on my mind. Ask a question, and I'll give you an honest answer. If you don't really want to know, don't ask.

"Do these jeans make me look fat?"

Yes. But you are fat, so the jeans have nothing to do with it.

"Do you think he likes me?"

No. The fact that he had his tongue down another girl's throat last night should have been a clue.

"Can we still be friends?"

No. We were never friends to begin with. You annoy the hell out of me. And I'm totally okay if we never see each other again. Now go away.

I've come to accept that, regardless of how honest or silent I am, the truth is fated to destroy my life.

Chapter One

"Everyone lies, especially boys. You need to keep this"—my grandmother places her wrinkled finger on my small chest and thumps against my heart—"guarded like a fortress. Don't be fooled by sweet words and a handsome smile, no matter what he promises you. If it sounds too good to be true, it is."

I hate you. I really, really hate you," I tell the dirty clothes I shove into the Army bag.

I was supposed to go to the Laundromat last night, but I was too exhausted after my shift and chose sleep. I convinced myself as I collapsed in bed around midnight that I'd get up early and go before school—which was stupid because I'm not a morning person. So now, I'm exhausted and miserable.

I tuck the small pouch of quarters in the side pocket and set some textbooks on top before pulling the drawstring tight. Dragging the huge tube of clothes behind me, I lock my bedroom door with a click of the padlock and abandon the bag by the front door.

A dark suit is draped over the kitchen chair with a note.

Lana, would you be able to drop this off at the dry cleaners for me? If you can't, it's okay. — Nick

I toss the note onto the kitchen table and pick up the suit jacket. The weight of it and the silken threads feel expensive. I hold it in front of me, exposing the satin lining. It has to be tailor-made. I can't even imagine how much he paid for it.

I tell the suit, "You're lucky I like you," but, of course, I mean the man.

Nick met my mother when she was temping as a receptionist at a law firm in Boston about a year ago, but I didn't meet him 'til six months later. He's not the first guy in a suit to be tempted by her fair skin, long blond hair and youthful curves, but he's one of the few worthy of her. Nick's from New York, but he travels between there and Boston regularly. When he's here, he chooses to stay with us, despite the hour and a half commute. He wants to get a place together closer to the city. I think the only reason my mother hasn't given him an answer is because of me.

I've learned not to get involved in my mother's social life. We don't exactly have the same optimistic outlook on love. But it's obvious that Nick is dedicated to taking care of her. And I won't get in the way of my mother's happiness. She deserves to be happy. She deserves him.

I toss the jacket back on the chair. And, just as I begin to walk to the fridge, a clang reverberates against the floorboards. I stop and slowly turn, my stomach already reacting before I see what fell from his suit pocket. I stare at it for a moment, wishing I'd hated him just like the rest of them.

Now I do.

"Oh, you asshole," I say, bending to pick it up.

Nick's exotic spicy scent enters the room. My jaw clenches as I stand, keeping my back to him.

"Good morning," he says cheerily. "You're up early."

I turn to face him. He must have just taken a shower because his dark hair is still wet, combed neatly and slicked away from his face. Everything about him is expensive—from the crisp white shirt to his perfect, charming smile. He looks so out of place in this dilapidated kitchen. He rolls a suitcase next to him, resting it near the doorway.

I don't respond, only stare, wondering how I didn't see it. I have a gift for knowing when someone isn't who they appear to be—for seeing through the lies. But I never saw this coming. He was so convincing. I *believed* him!

The betrayal burns deep, or maybe it's just my pride that's singed. Regardless, now I want to punch him in the throat.

"Everything okay?" Nick asks, his brows furrowed in concern. "If it's about the suit, I can take it with me, ask the hotel to send it out. I just thought—"

"Or you could ask your wife," I say, cutting him off. I raise my middle finger to reveal the dark titanium band embedded with black diamonds. "Isn't she waiting for you in New York?"

"What... Lana, I—" he stutters.

"Don't." I shut him up before he can lie again. My voice is edged with venom. "Leave. Never come back. If you do, I'll murder you in your sleep. Understand?"

He remains frozen within the doorframe. His eyes flicker in panic. "It's not..."

"Piece of shit." I shove past him, causing him to stumble back a step.

I walk to the front door and hoist the straps of the Army bag over my shoulders with a grunt. Without looking back, I warn him, "Tell her the truth, or I will."

"Lana?" My mother's voice carries from her bedroom just before I slam the front door.

I look down at the wedding band on my finger, and my jaw flexes with unrelenting anger. This is going to kill her. Releasing a heavy breath, I trudge down the flight of stairs, the Army bag banging against my thighs with each step. It's practically as big as I am, and I fight not to fall face-first down the stairs.

The street is uncharacteristically quiet when I step outside, only because of the insane hour. The sun's rays peek between the neighborhood buildings, barely having risen itself. The cool morning air soothes my heated cheeks as I walk down the sidewalk.

We don't live in the best neighborhood, but there really isn't a *good* neighborhood in Sherling. At least we don't have gangs tagging every surface. Our street is a small side street, lined with about a dozen multifamily homes. Laundry hangs over porch railings. Broken-down cars take up space in pocked driveways. Most of the time, the sound of arguing or crying kids filters out the open windows, floating along the streets like white noise. I don't really hear it unless it's an overly dramatic fight. So now, with the street vacant of cars and everyone still asleep, the silence makes the anger in my head so much louder.

My mother doesn't belong here any more than he does. I know she's lived here most of her life, but she never quite fit in. She's a dreamer. A believer. A fragile bloom fighting for light in the middle of a landfill. He promised to take her away from all of this. He was supposed to save her from a life that continues to drain the color from her every day.

She sees the good in every person, regardless of who they are or what they've done in life. I always considered this naive. *But* she genuinely wants to believe every person is worthy. The liars. The cheats. The manipulators. The bastards who use her for their own self-serving needs. Not just the men, but the women too. Those who pretend to be a friend, until jealousy unveils their selfishness and insecurity. They're all the same. But she refuses to give up on them because, when my mother loves, she loves with everything. It's why *Belief* is her curse. It's that belief that will eventually break her.

My fingers curl into a fist, short nails digging into my palm. Oh, I hate him. Everything about him is a lie. I wish I'd seen through him. But he was so sincere. Maybe that's his curse and the reason I couldn't recognize his deception…*Sincerity*.

If Nick's curse is *Sincerity*, then he's the worst kind of human. Convincing people to believe him, to trust him, only to destroy them when they let him in.

The twenty-four-hour Laundromat at the end of the block is just as deserted as the street, except for the homeless man sleeping under the dryer vent in the alley.

After loading the washer, I sit on the chipped laminate counter and prop my best friend's textbook open on my crossed legs, trying to distract myself from the boiling rage that continues to churn in my stomach.

The distinct ting of a glass bottle rolling along the pavement draws my attention from Tori's algebra assignment. A woman in a leopard print skirt and black bustier stumbles across the street, running a hand through her disheveled dark hair. Smeared liner shadows her eyes, and her lips are smudged with faded red lipstick. I watch her zigzag across the desolate street. She falters when her stiletto heel catches the curb. I wince, expecting her to fall, but she corrects herself with a few stuttering steps.

I try to imagine what she looked like when the night began, confident and sexy. At some point in the night, her curse got the better of her, and this blur of a woman is all who's left.

I *finish my English lit assignment* just as the dryer rolls to a stop. After placing the folded clothes inside the Army bag, I start back to the house. The neighborhood has slowly begun to stretch its arms during the hour or so I was hidden in the Laundromat. Cars roll up to the intersections, waiting at the lights. Several women in need of their morning coffee stand at the bus stop, tote bags over their shoulders. Voices and music escape out of open windows as I walk past. Peaceful silence has lifted its veil, allowing chaos to resume its reign.

"I don't understand!" Her desperate wails reach me before I can see her. "Why didn't you tell me?"

I stop in front of the neighbor's house to find my distraught mother standing in the middle of our lawn and Nick next to his car with his suitcase in hand.

"I'm so sorry, Faye." His voice cracks in response. "I really am." He turns his back to her and tosses his suitcase in the passenger side of the shiny black BMW.

My mother collapses to her knees when he enters the driver's side without looking back. She covers her face to capture her tears. I can feel her heart breaking from here.

The tires spit out rocks as he tears out of the driveway, leaving a cloud of dust in his wake. Rubber connects with asphalt, and the squeal echoes down the street. I make eye contact with his green eyes and flash him my middle finger, still adorned with his wedding band, meaning every word the gesture signifies. He flinches.

"Asshole," I mutter, wishing I could hang him by his balls.

I turn back to the devastation he left behind—and I don't mean the driveway.

With a heavy sigh, I adjust the straps on my shoulders and approach the frail woman collapsed on the front lawn.

"What are you staring at?" I snap at our neighbor who's standing on her front porch with a coffee mug in her hand, fixated on the spectacle like she's watching a reality show.

She's wrapped in a torn terry robe, her hair a misshapen mass of curls, like she just crawled out of bed—which she probably has. Then again, I know she always looks like this, no matter what time of day. There's no reason to make an effort when she just has to sit at home to collect a paycheck.

"You really shouldn't be allowed out of your house looking like that, Gayle. You'll give the kids nightmares."

A couple of boys laugh as they pass by on their way to the bus stop. The middle-aged woman scowls at me. She glances at the broken heap on the front lawn with a judgmental shake of her head before disappearing inside. The screen door squeaks loudly before it crashes shut behind her.

I can sense others watching too, eyes peering out behind curtains.

I set the bag of clean clothes on the stoop and kneel down beside my mother, my hand on her back. "C'mon, Mom. Let's go inside."

"He…lied to me," she forces out between broken sobs. She lifts her head from her hands, her big blue eyes bloodshot. "Why…didn't…he tell me…he's still married?"

"Because he's a selfish prick," I tell her, filtering the honesty. If I were truly being honest with her, I would've used a lot more expletives. I wrap my arm around her thin waist and coax her up. "Let's get you inside, so the neighbors don't make money off you on YouTube."

8

She's not listening to me, but she lets me guide her to her feet. "Why? I don't...understand. I thought...he...loved me. I...believed him."

"I know you did," I soothe as we slowly move toward the front door. *I did too*, I finish in my head.

I bend down and pull on a strap of the duffel bag, slinging it over my shoulder. I keep one hand on my mother to keep her from toppling into the pit of despair and guide her up the stairs.

We somehow manage to climb to the second floor where the door was left ajar. I shut the marred door with the long, jagged crack down its center and secure the dead bolt.

"Why didn't I know? I should have known," my mother says in hiccupping gasps.

I don't have an answer for her because *I* should have known—which only lights up the fiery rage inside my chest.

"I'm so sorry, Lana," she whimpers, her slender shoulders rounding.

She disappears into her room, and I follow.

"You have nothing to apologize for, Mom," I say with a disheartened sigh.

She slowly sits on the edge of her bed, her shimmery eyes focused on the floor. "I loved him," she whispers, a tear glistening on her flushed cheek.

"I know."

Men with expensive suits and charming smiles have always asked her out when she temps. Understandably. My mother's beautiful and kind—and therefore viewed as an easy target. To them, she's a fling. A disposable hot piece to occupy their time until it hints at becoming serious. Then, they leave. It was a painful lesson. She was forced to learn to be careful with her heart and not fall for every jackass who winks at her.

I'm not the easiest person to get along with. I had to promise I'd back off after threatening too many boyfriends with missing body parts if they hurt her. Let her be the "adult" and make her own decisions. So I refused to acknowledge any of my mother's boyfriends again.

Then came Nick.

Nick was careful with her from the beginning. Asked her out for coffee for their first date and then lunch. Eventually, dinner and a movie. He slowly got close to her. And, in that time, I let him in too.

He was different. Until he wasn't.

I pull back the covers for her to climb in.

It's the same full bed she's slept in since she was a girl. This room is basically the same as when she shared it with her sisters, growing up. Dried flowers hanging from pins along the windowsill memorialize loves lost. Layers of time wallpaper every surface. Photos, art projects, yellowing band posters—constant reminders of the life we'll never escape. It's so…depressing.

Nick's soothing cologne lingers, at odds with the offensive herbal incense my mother burns—another indication that his presence was always a contradiction to everything within these walls.

"Lana, I'm—"

"Sorry. I know." Crimson stains blossom on the white pillow as blood begins to drip from her nose. "Shit, Mom."

I reach for the box of tissues and pull out a few. She takes them from me and presses the cluster under her nose. The hint of dark circles creeps beneath her eyes.

I fumble with the top of the prescription bottle. Dumping a small pill into my palm, I hand it to her along with the glass of water by her bedside. She takes it, swallowing it down.

"I'll get some ice."

By the time I return with ice wrapped in a kitchen towel, a scarlet pile of tissues has overtaken her nightstand. Blood trickles from beneath the tissue, staining her upper lip. I swap out the tissues for a damp facecloth and hand her the ice to apply to the bridge of her nose.

"You're going to be late for school," she mutters in a nasally voice, unable to open her eyes.

"I know." I was always going to be late, but she doesn't need to know that. There was no way I could have gotten the laundry done and still been on time. So now, I'll just be…later. "Will you be okay while I get ready?"

"Go," she urges quietly.

Hesitating a second, I leave the door cracked, so I can hear her if she calls for me.

When I return to check on her, she's asleep. But I know it's a troubled sleep by the way her brows pinch together, the pain apparent behind her lids. I brush the wisps of honey-blond hair away from her face. She's warm to the touch, a hint of a fever. She's been suffering from migraines for as long as I can remember, triggered by stress and…heartache. I don't know why her body betrays her every time someone else does. Maybe her heart can't handle being broken.

Over the past few months, despite being truly happy, the migraines have kept coming, accompanied by nosebleeds. Last week, she scared us when she grabbed hold of the counter to stay upright. Nick set up an appointment with her doctor for next week, even though she insisted it was nothing.

I watch her for a moment longer. Her face is pale, except for the fully formed shadows under her eyes and the flush of fever on her cheeks. Her lids twitch. This isn't nothing, and it's starting to freak me out.

I refill the glass of water at her bedside and leave a note, telling her I'll call her during lunch and that she has to pick up or else I'll come home. I leave her in her restless sleep as I slip out the front door.

My chest hurts and my whole body is weak with exhaustion. And I wasn't even the one who loved him.

Chapter Two

"He didn't love you!" I hear my grandmother yell.

I slowly crack my door, just enough so I can see without being caught.

"He did! And maybe he still does," my mother cries back, her face wet with tears. "Just let me call him."

My grandmother is holding my mom's phone. "If he loved you, then where is he?"

My mother's wide eyes are too stunned for words. A cry escapes her mouth as she runs out, slamming the front door behind her so hard, it cracks.

I hand the forged note, claiming I was at a doctor's appointment this morning, to Mrs. Kellerman in the front office. She gives it a suspicious glance as she scribbles on the tardy slip.

I'm about to walk out the office door when I hear, "Lana."

Maybe if I ignore him, he'll go away.

"I was just going to call you to my office."

I slowly turn, armed with an overly fake smile. "Mr. Garner. You know how much our visits mean to me, but I've had a really rough morning, and I need to get to geometry." It's not easy, being sarcastic and honest at the same time, but I've somehow mastered it.

My smile drops when I see Ms. Lewis in the doorway of his office, her hands on her hips. There's no need to fake anything with her. I can't stand her and she knows it…because I told her in front of the entire class last year when I had her for algebra.

"Sorry, this can't wait," Mr. Garner says, the apology sincere in his eyes. "Hopefully, it won't take long."

With my teeth clenched behind a stiff smile, I give in and walk into his office. I really don't need this. And I'm not exactly in the mood to hold anything back.

"Have a seat." Mr. Garner gestures to one of the thinly padded wooden chairs in front of his desk, closing the door behind me.

I drop my messenger bag on the floor and slouch in the chair with my arms crossed—all contrived pleasantries lost.

He walks around the desk and sits. "You're welcome to have a seat as well, Ms. Lewis."

She chooses to remain standing, sidling next to his desk with her hands still attached to her hips. Her face is pinched in a severe scowl. She's trying to look authoritative. Instead, she looks like she's eaten too many Toxic Waste candies. I ignore her and look to Mr. Garner for an explanation.

"Ms. Lewis is concerned that you may have helped Tori on her algebra test." The silent apology doesn't leave his eyes. He doesn't want to be here any more than I do.

"I'm not in Ms. Lewis's algebra class this year," I answer simply.

The veins protrude along Ms. Lewis's neck, sticking out like chicken bones. She purses her lips even more, struggling to keep from exploding.

"I know that," Mr. Garner says calmly. "I brought that up too. But Ms. Lewis is convinced that you—"

"Cheated!" Ms. Lewis snaps, unable to hold it in any longer. "You cheated! And I won't stand for it!"

"I'm not in your class, Ms. Lewis," I repeat calmly, like I'm talking to a child throwing a temper tantrum. "And didn't Tori take the test in front of you?

You were in the room, right?"

Her face reddens and her eyes twitch. It's hard to watch this woman coming apart. I raise an eyebrow in disapproval.

"She is not an A student. It's not possible she did that well on her own!"

"So you're saying you're not an effective teacher? You'd rather believe your students cheated than passed your class?" I question coolly. "Do you get off on flunking your students, Ms. Lewis?"

Ms. Lewis's mouth opens as she blinks repeatedly, a small squeak escaping.

"Lana," Mr. Garner warns. "Ms. Lewis, I know how hard you've worked to get Tori engaged in her classwork. Perhaps your commitment has finally paid off."

Ms. Lewis remains aghast. I think she's about to cry when she storms out of the office.

"I'm glad we cleared that up," I say cheerily, reaching for the strap of my bag as I stand. "Keep doing your thing, Mr. Garner."

"Lana," he calls to me before I can escape.

I slowly pivot to face him. He's wearing a ridiculous lime-green sweater-vest over a blue shirt with a yellow tie. He reminds me of an Easter egg. The man has no sense of fashion. When I look up at him, he's trying to hide an amused smile.

He adjusts the glasses on his face. "I'd really like to make it through the last three weeks of school without adding another page to your file." He rests his hand on top of the three-inch tattered file folder bound with a thick green elastic band.

"I will try to stay away, Mr. Garner. But they keep sending me back to you." I look around the small office, its walls covered with framed cliché posters of achievement and goals. "How can you sit in here all day and not want to break something?"

He lets out a breathy laugh.

Mr. Garner took over for Mrs. Colstrom after she had a heart attack at the beginning of the year. Not my fault, I swear! She was a naive, bubbly little thing who thought everyone could be saved by an inspirational slogan and a lollipop. Unfortunately, there weren't enough lollipops in the world to save me. Instead of wasting her breath on words of inspiration every time I was sent to the office, she'd let me work on my assignments in the library. I actually got more done there than if I'd stayed in class. And, sometimes, I even got to catch up on sleep.

In the short time Mr. Garner's been here, we've become well acquainted, considering I'm sent to his office at least once a week. I blame the *Honesty* curse and defensive educators. He knows I make decent enough grades. I get my assignments done—eventually. And I don't start fights on school property—mostly.

"Be good, Lana," Mr. Garner calls after me as I pass through the office.

My platform shoes clunk loudly on the linoleum as I continue down the hall in my pleated skirt, thigh-high tights and fitted tank. I pass by the dented and busted green lockers of the sophomore wing and reach mine just as the bell rings. The halls fill with a burst of voices.

"Please tell me you told that pruney bitch to sit and spin." Tori appears beside my open locker, sparkling in a strapless sequined top and skintight capris.

"You knew I was going to wear my platforms, didn't you?" I grin, eyeing her five-inch red pumps.

"I can't let you be taller than me when we walk down the hall," she says with a huff. "Besides, I look killer in these shoes."

"Until you start bitching about your feet hurting," I tease. "And, no, I didn't tell the bitch off. But I did question her dedication as a teacher. That didn't go over very well."

Tori laughs. "If she only knew."

"Not my fault she doesn't know how to hide her password."

I printed out the test in advance and helped Tori complete it. Tori pretended to work on the problems during the exam but passed in the correct one at the end—well, not *completely* correct. We didn't want to be that obvious.

"Speaking of"—I reach into my messenger bag and pull out her assignments—"here you go."

"I don't know why you bother. You know it's not important to me." She takes the books from me anyway.

"I'm not starting junior year without you," I tell her.

My motives for doing Tori's homework and papers are purely selfish. She's the only person I claim as a friend in this school, and I won't lose her because she doesn't give a shit about her future. Most of the students in this school don't have a future worth looking forward to—myself included. But being here is better than working a minimum wage job or dealing on the streets. Might as well show up for the next two years.

"It's not like I'll graduate."

"Shut up." I reply. "You *are* graduating."

I made a promise to her father that he'd see her graduate. She'll be the first in his family to actually hold a diploma, and well…I promised. And breaking a promise is worse than lying, so it's happening even if I have to hack into every teacher's computer and do all of her assignments for the next two years.

"Whatever," she says with a dramatic roll of her eyes. "You're coming over after school, right?"

I pause. Tori's eyes tighten.

"I have to go home first. I didn't bring my clothes for tonight."

Tori still appears suspicious. "We're going out. Friday night is *my* night."

"I know. Relax, okay?"

I close my locker, and we begin walking down the hall. We're not in the same class, but Tori has no problem with being late…ever.

"Nick left, and my mom's taking it pretty hard. I want to check on her before we go out." I stop in front of my classroom. "I'll explain at lunch."

Tori shoots me a death glare. "Sorry your mom's sad, but you're *not* bailing."

Tori does whatever she wants, when she wants, and she doesn't care who she has to shove out of the way to do it. I'm her best friend, and even I know she's a bitch. Admittedly, I'm one too. Obviously, *Consideration* isn't her curse. But, ironically, *Loyalty* is.

Somehow, I survive geometry and American government without shoving a pen through my temple.

What are you up to tonight?"

I try to ignore the voice coming from beside my locker, but sadly, he's still standing there when I close it.

"Nothing with you," I respond. Then I turn and walk away.

But he's persistently annoying. I don't look at him as I strut purposely down the hall, hoping he'll take the not-so-subtle hint.

"There's a party—"

"Not going," I finish before he can tell me where.

"C'mon, Lana. Don't be like that," he pleads, catching up to me.

I continue walking. I think he disappears into the cafeteria as I pass it. But I'd have to be paying attention to him to know. I enter the darkened chemistry lab and pull a key out of my purse. With a quick glance around the empty room, I unlock the closet door and slip inside.

The small space is filled with rows of bottles neatly alphabetized on shelves. This is the period Mr. Tilman "eats lunch" with Miss Hall in the librarian's office, so I know I won't get caught. They're not eating lunch, trust me. I'd pour one of these chemicals into my eyes before sneaking in on that again. But it was worth the lifetime of psychological trauma so I could copy his key to the supply closet.

I didn't steal Mr. Tilman's key for the chemicals, although I could probably make some serious money selling certain ingredients to the right people. I swiped it so I'd have a place to get away from the bullshit that is high school. It's like my own private office…that smells like sulfur. There are trade-offs for everything in life.

Sitting at the small desk in the corner, I dig for my phone in my bag. I dial my mother twice before she picks up.

"How are you feeling?" I ask her.

"I'm, uh…okay."

"You're not," I counter. Her hesitation makes the lie obvious. "Any more nosebleeds?"

"No."

"Did you eat anything?"

"Not yet. I've been sleeping," she replies, a sob escaping. "Lana, I'll be fine. I'm just...upset. It's nothing you have to worry about."

"Go back to sleep. I'll see you when I get home."

I rest my head in my hand, rubbing my forehead. I *am* worried. I could sit here and curse Nick for convincing my mother he was in love with her. And I do. But there's something going on other than hurt feelings.

I close my eyes against the roiling heat in my gut. I look down at the ring and pull it off, rolling it between my fingers. There's a date etched on the inside—*October 7, 2000.* He's been married for more than sixteen years. My stomach turns at the betrayal.

I slide the ring onto my thumb where it fits perfectly. Good luck explaining this to your wife, asshole.

I *find Tori outside the* cafeteria, sitting on the stone wall with some girl. I sit next to Tori, opening the yogurt I picked up on my way.

"Hey, Lana," the girl says. "I was just talking about you. I can't believe you turned Cody down. I don't think he's ever heard the word *no.*"

"Or maybe he chooses not to," Tori adds sharply.

"Who's Cody?" I ask, completely lost. I insert a spoonful of yogurt into my mouth.

The girls look at each other and then at me.

"Cody Walker. The captain of...everything," the girl explains in disbelief. "He asked you to a party tonight, and you totally shut him down."

I shake my head, not following, and continue to eat my yogurt.

Tori laughs. "You're unbelievable," she says with a shake of her head.

"Whatever," I reply dismissively. "Is Nina meeting up with us tonight?"

"She has to work the early shift, so she'll be out by eleven thirty," Tori replies.

"What are we doing? The Basement?"

"You get into The Basement?" the girl interrupts, her mouth hanging open.

"Who are you?" I ask, taking a moment to focus on her.

She's thin and angular with her hair pulled up in a messy bun that I know firsthand takes way more time to get right than it looks. She has this European thing about her with the almond shape of her eyes and the thin slope of her nose. She's pretty in an I'm-starving-myself kind of way.

"Emory. I'm in your English lit class."

I nod like it means something. It doesn't.

"Lana doesn't *participate* in high school," Tori explains.

"But she's in class every day—mostly," Emory says, baffled. "You weren't there this morning."

Tori laughs. "I mean, she doesn't get involved in all the gossip bullshit. She has no idea who anyone is. Status means nothing to her."

"And it matters to you?" I question.

"Not really," Tori replies with a shrug. "But I know what's going on. Who's who. It's…entertaining, like a Latin soap opera—overly dramatic and predictable. But you're completely oblivious."

"Because it doesn't matter," I say simply. "We're here for four years. This shit means nothing in the real world, where we actually have to survive."

"Not to us. But to them"—she nods toward Emory—"it defines them."

"That's pathetic."

Emory's face reddens, and I realize I was a bit too honest. I don't apologize for being too honest, otherwise that's all I'd be doing.

"We haven't been to a high school party since…well, it's been a while," Tori delicately explains to Emory.

"But…you're sophomores?" Emory questions, clueless. "I mean, I've *heard*

19

about you, but I just thought…" She doesn't finish. She must realize that what she heard was closer to the truth than most rumors.

I know we have a reputation. I'm not exactly sure what it is, but it's obvious something's being said.

I stand. All the questions are annoying me. Tori stands with me.

"We've gotta go. Thanks for your help earlier," Tori tells her before we walk away.

"Why were you sitting with her?" I ask. "She's—"

"I know," Tori cuts me off with a sigh before I can find an appropriate—or inappropriate—word for the girl. "She let me copy off her earlier today. We had a pop quiz in biology. So you might have to put up with her for a little while until I can ditch her."

I nod, getting it. "Or I can stay away and let you deal with her. She asks too many questions."

"She's just trying to figure out what's true. There are so many stories going around about us; we're practically fictional."

"It's no one's business what we do when we leave here."

"Right. But that's what makes them talk more."

I roll my eyes. "Why do you even bother listening?"

"Because it's funny. There's one rumor that we're involved with the Russian Mafia."

"The Russian Mafia? Seriously? We're in the middle-of-nowhere Massachusetts. I don't think the Russian Mafia even knows this shit town exists. And neither of us is Russian. *You're* Puerto Rican. That's so dumb."

Tori laughs. "Told you it's funny."

I groan. "People are stupid."

"Stupid people have made us legends in this school. Haven't you noticed how everyone acts when we walk by?" Recognizing the unamused look on my face, she adds, "It's not like I care. But again, it makes me laugh."

Just for a second, I look around and watch them follow us with their eyes, whispering. I notice the sidesteps to clear the way. It's not funny; it's sad.

I stop in front of an open door. "You're staying 'til the end of school, right?"

Tori sighs dramatically. "I guess. If I skip technology again, I'll get detention, and there's no way I'm staying in this building longer than I have to. I'll find you after."

I walk into French class and take my usual seat at the back of the room.

"Want to be my partner again today?"

I glance over at Lincoln, opening my notebook. "Sure."

Lincoln's one of the few people I can stand. He doesn't ask dumb questions and focuses on the classwork. He's smart, and he cares about his grades.

There are a select group of students who are actually *trying* to get out of this town. They're the ones who give this building some semblance of a high school, organizing their after-school clubs, participating in sports and driven to make the Honor Roll.

I don't participate in anything, despite Mr. Garner's persistent efforts. Hell, I barely participate in class. The only reason I even know we have sports teams is because I see the players wearing their jerseys on game days. And I know I can skip out early on the days we have pep rallies.

Lincoln's ambitious. I've seen him wear a couple of different game jerseys. I *think* one is basketball. Or it should be since he's so fricken tall. He always has his assignments done for class. He's even helped me finish mine when I've gotten stuck. And I'm pretty sure he's our class president or vice president or something like that. I have no idea what that means exactly, but there were posters up at the beginning of the school year, asking us to vote for people, and I remember seeing his name. I'm not sure if he won, but I hope he did. He's a nice guy.

Halfway through our conjugation assignment, Lincoln leans forward and whispers, "Do you think I have a chance with Tori?"

"What do you mean?" I ask. That question could easily mean so many things. I'm surprised. I would never have guessed she was his type, because he's definitely not hers.

"There's this party tonight in Oaklawn. I was hoping she'd go with me."

"We have plans," I tell him.

"Oh." He lowers his eyes, uncomfortable.

I sigh, recognizing that I sounded like a bitch. "Ask her. I don't actually know what we're doing. If she says yes, then we'll be there."

Lincoln's eyes light up. "Good. A friend of mine was talking about going too."

"Don't set me up."

"Right. No. I'm not," he fumbles. "I was just saying…we can all…hang out."

"Sure." I shrug. "Ask Tori first. I'll do whatever she wants."

I *walk into chemistry*. I hate this class. Not only because trying to reconfigure molecules makes me want to scorch my brain with a Bunsen burner, but because it's the last class before freedom. It's the worst kind of torture, which means it feels like the longest class of the day. And, to make today even worse, the persistent douche takes a seat on the stool next to mine.

"Why are you sitting here?" I look around and find Paola two tables back, sitting next to a guy wearing a backward baseball cap.

She shrugs her shoulders in apologetic confusion.

"Thought we could be partners today," he says, leaning in and running a finger along my arm. "You know we're good together."

I scoff. "Excuse me?"

"C'mon, baby," he purrs, a pathetic attempt at sounding sexy. "Your hot little body up against mine—now that's chemistry."

I close my eyes and bite my lip, trying so hard not to laugh. But I can't stop it from bubbling up and bursting out of my mouth.

"What?" he asks, grinning without really knowing why.

"Go away," I tell him.

He appears confused. "What did you say?"

"Get off the stool. Go back to your table. And leave me alone." I glare at him, all humor gone. "I'm serious. Get the fuck away from me."

His eyes tighten like he can't believe I just said that to him. "So you're going to be like that, huh?" He smirks like he knows something I don't. "See ya."

Wearing a cocky grin, he stands from the stool and struts back to his table. Paola sits down next to me just as Mr. Tilman walks in the door, flushed and disheveled. Guess he took a long lunch.

"**What do you think** about checking out a party in Oaklawn? At least until Nina gets out of work," Tori asks me as I shove books into my messenger bag.

I stop what I'm doing and stare at her in shock. "Lincoln asked you? And you said yes?"

"You knew?"

"He asked if I thought you'd go. But I didn't think you'd say yes." I really didn't.

Tori tends to go for the older, bad-boy types. And there are definitely plenty of those in Sherling. Lincoln doesn't really fit into that mold. He honestly doesn't fit in here at all now that I think about it.

"He's sweet. And *hot*." She offers this like it explains everything.

"You don't do sweet," I remind her.

Tori laughs. "I know. That's what's going to make this so fun."

"Oh no. Are you going to destroy this poor guy?" I ask, suddenly worried for him.

I don't know much about Lincoln, but he doesn't deserve to be one of Tori's clawing posts.

"I'm not like that."

I give her a knowing look.

"All the time," she finishes, trying to look innocent. I laugh just as she informs me, "You're going too."

"He's not interested in me."

"He said something about a friend."

"Don't even," I warn her.

She knows how I feel about being forced to be with a guy because my friend is hooking up with his friend. I'm the worst wing-girl.

"I know. I know. But you'll do this for me, right?" she pleads, batting her thick lashes.

"I guess," I reply reluctantly.

She reveals a wicked smile. "We haven't been to a high school party in a couple years. And never in Oaklawn. No matter what happens, this is going to be a night we'll never forget."

I can't argue with that.

"How are we getting there?" I ask. "Let's not go with Lincoln and his friend. I don't want to be stuck with them if you lose interest or if they want to stay and we don't."

"I'll figure something out. Tony might be able to drive us."

"I doubt your brother will want to drive us all the way to Oaklawn."

"He will if you flirt with him." Tori grins suggestively.

"You're awful," I say with a laugh.

It's obvious her brother has a thing for me. I've thought about it. But he's Tori's *brother*, and when it ends—because it *will* end—I don't want it to be awkward every time I go over to their house. So we just flirt because flirting's innocent—mostly.

"What time are you coming over?"

"I'm not sure. But I shouldn't be long. I just have to pick up a change of clothes and check on my mom. I'll text you when I leave my house."

"Oh shit. I don't have Lincoln's number to let him know. I'm going to go find him. Meet me outside?"

"Sure," I reply, closing my locker.

"And maybe I'll find out more about his *friend*."

"Please don't," I beg.

Tori just smiles before walking away.

I *lean against the* massive stone banister along the front steps of the school, searching for Tori, as everyone floods out through the doors in a mad rush. A red Jeep Wrangler parked along the curb catches my attention—or I should say, the guy leaning against it, who keeps staring at me, does. He looks just like—

"So he *does* exist," Tori says from beside me.

We watch Lincoln approach the Jeep, and the two guys greet each other with a hand clasp and a pound-on-the-back guy embrace.

"Shit. *He's* Lincoln's friend? Are all the Harrison boys that perfect?" When I don't respond, she says, "Lana? You know who that is, right?"

She knows I do, even if he's only ever been talked about like some sort of mystical being.

"This is definitely going to be an unforgettable night."

"Yes, it is," I reply, unable to look away.

Like he knows we're talking about him, he looks up at us, wearing an enchanting smile. I can't force myself to look away, even though I know I should. I continue to watch as he and Lincoln get into his Jeep. I find myself smiling at him when he looks back over his shoulder one more time before driving away.

Chapter Three

"If I can tell you one thing," my aunt Helen says, one of the few times she decides to talk to me, "it's don't think that anyone's ever going to give you anything in this life. If you want it, you have to fight for it, even if that means drawing blood."

*M*om?" *I call out as I shut the door* and drop my messenger bag to the floor.

There's only silence in return.

"Mom?" I say softly, peeking into her room. I'm struck by the potent fragrance of the incense. My eyes water in protest as it burns my nostrils. There's no getting used to that smell.

I quietly enter her room when she still doesn't respond. I find her curled up on her side under the blankets, asleep. Her face is drained of color, except for the ruddy patches on her cheeks. Without touching her, I know she still has a fever. Placing my hand on her forehead only confirms it. She doesn't stir with my touch, which concerns me more.

"Mom?" I say gently, but she doesn't move.

I pick up the water glass and carry it into the kitchen, filling it with cold water from a pitcher in the fridge. Before I bring it back to her room, I glance at her work schedule posted on the side.

Tori's going to kill me.

"**I have to work tonight.**" I close my eyes, braced for her reaction.

"What the fuck?" She doesn't filter the anger in her voice. "You're covering for *her*, aren't you?"

I ignore the spite in her tone. I don't know what Tori's issue is with my mother, but this isn't the time to get into it.

"I get off at ten. What time did you tell Lincoln we'd meet him?"

"I didn't. Lana, this is bullshit, and you know it."

"She's sick, Tori. There's nothing I can do about it. You know that."

And she does, which is why she doesn't tell me to get someone else to cover for her. We can't afford to miss a shift.

"I'm picking your ass up right at ten o'clock. Be ready."

"I'll need to shower before we go out."

There's silence.

"Tori, I can't smell like the diner. It's disgusting."

After another dramatic moment of silence, she finally says, "Fine. I'll ask Tony to pick you up. But we have to leave my house by ten thirty. Tony's going out, and he's our ride to the party."

"I'll be so quick, I promise," I assure her. It's not like she's giving me any other choice. "I've gotta go. But I'll see you tonight."

I sort through the bag of clean clothes, pulling out my hideous hunter-green polyester uniform. I swear the dress was made out of a leisure suit. It might even be flame retardant. The only good thing about it is that grease, ketchup and beer wash right out of it, and it never needs to be ironed.

Unlike my favorite jeans that got ruined last weekend when Nina threw up on me. If she'd eaten, she might've been able to hold down whatever that bright pink drink was. So gross. Now they will have to become my favorite cutoffs. But I don't have time to mess with cutting them right now.

I opt to pack a pair of fitted white lace-trimmed shorts, a low-cut bright sea-blue halter top and wedge sandals that wrap around my ankles. I drape my cropped black leather jacket over the tote and proceed to dress in the hideousness that is my uniform.

Luckily, *my mother* has the dinner shift, so I don't have to deal with the *totally* obnoxious drunks. Stella's is technically a diner. But, really, it's a bar…that serves horrible food. The people who frequent Stella's aren't here for the menu. They're here for the cheap beer and strong well drinks. They'll eat anything to sop up the puddle of liquor in their stomachs. The greasier, the better.

I have no idea who *Stella* is. Margo owns the place. Jim runs it. No one ever mentions Stella or why the place is named after her. All that's left of her is a black-and-white photo of a blonde sitting on the back of an old convertible, blowing a kiss at the camera with *Stella* scrawled in smeared blue ink on the white border. She's surrounded by pictures of motorcycles and muscle cars along with a framed dollar bill. Whoever she was, the sentiment is now lost in the chaos.

I've been working here since before it was legal for me to have a job. I started two years ago when my mother was sick for a week and we couldn't afford the lost wages. It's not like this place offers sick days or vacation. One day, I came in and clocked in under her name. No one cared as long as I could balance plates and not spill beers.

"Lana, hook us up with a pitcher?"

I take a moment to actually look at the acne-faced guy who thinks he knows me. I sure as hell don't know him, although I have a feeling we go to the same high school.

"Why should I?" I ask him. "What do you got that I want? And *think* before you answer that because I definitely don't want you." I eye his scrawny frame critically.

The acne victim's mouth drops as his friends start laughing.

"Uh, how about this?" He reaches into a pocket and pulls out a small sealed plastic bag filled with pills of various colors, another smaller bag of white powder and a joint.

"What are you doing, man?" the guy across from him questions sternly.

With a quick warning glance, he continues, "We call it 'party in a bag.'" He smiles like he's clever.

I don't change my bored expression, although I like the sound of it.

I take the bag from his hand before he can react and slip it into my apron pocket. I turn and walk away without a word, returning with a pitcher of beer and a stack of glasses.

I drop their check.

"You charged us for the pitcher?" he asks incredulously. "I thought—"

"Don't," I threaten. "If this is any good, I can hook you up with *partiers*."

He shuts his mouth, knowing I could easily triple his business just by dropping a few words to the right people.

"Hey, sweetness, can we get another round?" a guy calls, his face hidden behind a shrubbery of facial hair.

He raises his hand to swat my ass. I can feel the gesture before I see it. Since I started working here, I've adapted a sixth sense for sexual advances. And these scumbags have tried just about everything.

"Touch my ass, and I'll make sure there's shards of glass in your beer," I warn him.

His hand lowers under the table.

I drop their ticket. "If you're just staying for drinks, you can walk the three feet to the bar to get them yourselves."

"Lana, can you take that table of guys who just sat down?" Marisa asks as I walk by her, dumping plates on the metal counter for the dishwasher.

"That's not my table," I tell her, not about to be nice at nine forty-five. "I'm off soon anyway. Sorry."

I don't stick around to hear her complain. I pick up the plates waiting for me on the raised stainless counter, hiding the shit show that is the kitchen. If people saw what happened back there, they'd never eat here again. I shuffle around the bodies hanging out at the counter…or bar. Whatever it is, it's the worst setup ever.

I drop the plates on the table, not caring if the correct order is in front of the right person. They're my last table. I need them to eat and settle up, so I can get the hell out of here. Tony should be here soon, and I know Tori won't let me hear the end of it if we don't leave her house by ten thirty.

"Anything else?" I ask, leaving the check without waiting for an answer. "If you need another drink, you can get it at the bar."

Technically, I'm not supposed to serve alcohol. I'm only fifteen. But Jim and Margo ignore the law. And the police are too preoccupied with what happens in the parking lot to notice what happens *inside* this metal Twinkie.

It's a job. I can't afford *not* to be here. And, believe me, I *constantly* remind myself of this too.

I clear my other tables and make sure they've all paid before returning to the table I just fed. "Ready to pay?" I ask.

They're interfering with my night. If they don't like the not-so-friendly service, they came to the wrong place. Besides, I'm not counting on the crappy tip they never planned to leave me.

A guy with tattoos covering his thick arms pulls out two twenties and drops them on top of the bill without looking at it.

"Need change?"

He shakes his head. I try to hide the surprise that flashes across my face with a blink. Maybe he can't count. I'm not about to offer a math lesson. I hand the cash to Margo at the register and wait for the change. All she does is handle the money. She doesn't trust anyone. Not even Georgia or Mal, who've worked the bar since before I was born. No one touches the cash other than Margo, who remains perched on her wooden stool, watching everyone with her beady blue eyes.

She reminds me of a bird, frail and thin, with wrinkled skin hanging off her, scowling at everyone like she's tempted to peck their eyes out. She sees *everything*. I try not to talk to her. I try not to even look at her if I can help it. She creeps me out.

I duck into the back, past the counter where plates of food are waiting to be picked up. "Jim, I'm clocking out."

"No you're not," he bellows. "You have five minutes left in your shift. Go check the bathrooms."

I stop, wishing I had kept my mouth shut and just clocked out. He would never have known.

As soon as I push open the red metal door, I'm forced to cover my mouth and nose. The stench is overwhelming. One of the toilets isn't working. Jim knew and didn't want to deal with it himself. Bastard. Well, I'm definitely not going to unclog it. Women are disgusting. I'm convinced we're grosser than men— throwing who knows what into the toilets, pissing all over the seats, littering the floor with shreds of toilet paper that are destined to stick to the bottom of someone's shoe. There's no way I can get away with leaving it like this. I'll get reamed the next time I work.

I pull on latex gloves and pick up the fragments of paper towels and toilet paper scattered on the floor, shoving them into the overflowing trash. I wipe down the chipped porcelain sinks and step down on the trash to compact it.

Taking the trash bag with me, I walk out the back door to toss it in the dumpster. When I try to go back in, the door's locked. I groan. Of course it is. I'm *never* getting out of here. I'm forced to walk all the way around to the front where there's a line to get in.

A car honks. I turn my head just as Tori pulls herself out the passenger window, sitting on the edge of the door.

"Why are you here? I thought I was coming to your house?" I question, recognizing she's dressed to go out.

"Change of plans. Tony's meeting friends, so we have to go now or else we won't have a ride."

31

Tony nods with a subtle grin in the driver's seat. I smile back, biting my lip to keep it from being too big.

I look down at my hideous, stained uniform that smells like grease and beer, knowing the rest of me pretty much smells the same. "But I'm repulsive."

"Put on extra perfume. Besides, guys love the smell of this place. You may even get licked tonight," Tori teases wickedly.

I shoot her a disgusted look.

My skin feels like I have a layer of oil clinging to it, and I don't even want to know what my hair is doing.

"Seriously, Tori?" I gripe. With a frustrated sigh, I turn toward the line blocking the front door.

"Hurry up!" Tori hollers in return.

I push my way through the bodies, not bothering to excuse myself. It wouldn't help. This crowd responds better to brute force. And I desperately need to get out of here.

And *now* there's suddenly a line to get into the bathroom. The clogged toilet's probably not helping.

I grit my teeth in frustration. "You've got to be kidding me." This night just keeps getting better and better. Hell, this entire day has been shit. Might as well keep it coming.

I slip into the kitchen without being seen by Jim and past the grill where Carlos is flipping hockey pucks. Some of them, I know, are supposed to be pancakes. I glance at him, and he winks at me.

"Going out tonight, beautiful?"

"Trying," I respond.

Carlos is a flirt but harmless. A guy who feels compelled to compliment Margo's bug eyes is pathetic, not threatening. I seriously doubt he's ever had a girlfriend in his life. I kinda feel sorry for him. Until I catch him staring at my ass and have to fight the urge to punch him.

I clock out at five past ten, grab my bag and try Jim's office door so I can change. It's locked. Why is it impossible to get out of here tonight? I hide myself in the corner the best I can and slip my shorts on under my dress. I unzip the green monster and let it fall to the floor, quickly pulling the halter top over my head and removing my bra beneath it. When I turn around, Carlos is staring with his brows raised and a spatula hanging limp in his hand.

"What?!" I question accusingly, trying not to think about what he might've seen.

He just stares at me dumbly.

I ignore him and pick up my crumpled uniform, shoving it into my bag. I exchange my black sneakers for the strappy wedge sandals. I don't have a mirror, so I use the camera on my phone to check my makeup. Running a finger under my eyes to capture the smears only makes it worse, so I add dark liner and smudge it for a smoky effect and finish with shiny pink gloss on my lips. I gather my hair into a knot on top of my head and slide on a sparkly crystal headband to hold back my bangs. Despite the effort, I still *feel* like a mess. I'm just hoping *hard* I don't look it.

I exit the back door without saying anything to Jim. I clocked out. I'm done.

I spritz perfume on my neck and wrists then spray it in the air to walk through it, desperate to conceal the *eau de Stella's*. As long as I don't act like a mess, no one will know. Right? That's what Tori always tells me.

"Act the way you want everyone to see you, no matter how you're really feeling."

I haven't quite mastered it. I tend to be way too expressive. My feelings are always evident all over my face, even when I try to hide them.

"Fake it 'til you make it." Great. Now I'm quoting posters from Mr. Garner's office.

I open the back door of Tony's car and throw my bag across the seat before sliding in. "Okay, bitch, let's go to this fucking party."

Chapter Four

"Never let a boy lay a hand on you," my grandmother says sternly, pointing a finger in my face. She looks angry. But I don't remember doing anything wrong. And a boy definitely didn't touch me. "Do you understand me? Not ever."

I nod, too scared to ask what she means.

House party in Oaklawn, huh?"** Tony pulls into the circular driveway lined with cars.

"Hey," Tori declares defensively, "we *never* go to house parties."

"Maybe because no one we know owns a house." I eye the people wearing plaid and jeans, standing outside the house, holding red Solo cups. It's like walking onto the set of a CW show. I had no idea that these kinds of parties really existed.

"You'd never catch me at one of these white-boy parties," Tony says with a chuckle.

"We're not staying. I told Lincoln I'd meet him here; that's all. Nina's picking us up after she gets off work," Tori explains, as if she has to keep defending why we're here.

I don't know why she's so sensitive about it. Maybe because she always wants her four older brothers to think she's badass, and this party is anything but.

"Don't call me if you get stuck," Tony tells his sister. "Lana, call me if you need a ride."

His dark eyes find me in the rearview mirror and I wink.

"Asshole," Tori throws at him, getting out of the car. "C'mon, Lana."

I grab my bag and slide out.

"Don't have too much fun without me," Tony says to me, flashing a devilish smile before driving away.

"You two need to get it over with," Tori grumbles, walking toward the open front door of the huge white house.

"He's hot, but I'm *not* hooking up with your brother," I tell her *again*.

"The flirting is making me nauseous."

"Too bad," I say with a laugh. "It's better than hearing me scream his name in the room next to yours."

"Ew," she groans, scrunching her nose in disgust.

"Exactly," I reply, smiling.

"Fine. I get it," Tori snaps, nudging through the packed bodies in search of alcohol—or at least, I hope she is.

Without warning, Tori turns around and faces me. I stop short.

"What?" I try to look over her shoulder, thinking she saw someone she doesn't want to run into.

"Be nice," she instructs, almost threatening.

"You're telling *me* to be nice?" I let out a short laugh at the irony.

"Whatever," she says with an eye roll. "I just mean that I know these aren't exactly our people, but I want to see what Lincoln's all about. He's…different. And I don't want you ruining it with your *honesty*."

I laugh. "I will *try*," I assure her. "But I make no promises."

She sighs and turns back around, leading us through a huge crowded room where everyone's drinking and laughing. We finally emerge into a large open kitchen, but I still don't see any alcohol, only abandoned red cups and half-eaten bowls of chips and pretzels.

"Where do we get a drink?"

I'm suddenly nervous. Maybe we needed to bring our own, even though Tori promised me they'd have plenty here. We never go to parties where the alcohol is free. It always costs something.

Tori scans the crowd until a smile emerges on her face. I follow her gaze and find Lincoln. It's actually hard to miss him since he towers over everyone…and he's like the only black guy here.

"I need alcohol," I tell her as she starts in his direction.

She doesn't respond. Maybe she didn't hear me, but I can't stay at this party and remain sober. I squeeze through the crowd and spot a keg on the back porch.

"Of course there's a keg," I mumble, feeling stupid for doubting that *this* party wouldn't supply drinks.

The apartment parties we've been to, you have to fend for yourself—bring your own and then guard it for the night, so no one steals your stash. Girls usually flirt—or some loose interpretation of that word—to get drinks, but that also means being stuck with that guy for the rest of the party.

I always make sure we come stocked with our own alcohol. There's no way I'm going to be dependent upon a guy for drinks, and I'm definitely *not* owing him for my buzz.

I tug on my bag and struggle to get through the crowd until I'm finally outside in the open space of the deck, slightly annoyed. I don't usually carry big purses, and getting caught on everyone who walks by is driving me crazy. I need to hide it somewhere. I'm not worried about it being taken. It's not like anyone here is going to care about a beaten-up tote. I'm wearing the leather jacket with my tip money hidden in the inside pocket, and my phone's zipped in the outer one. I pat the other pocket to make sure I put the "party in a bag" in there. I walk down the steps and around the side of the deck, tucking my things in the darkest corner underneath. If anyone really wants the hideous uniform and shitty sneakers, they can have them.

"What're you doing over here?" I hear as soon as I stand back up. "Are you getting sick?"

"Uh, no," I reply sharply. "What are you doing over here? Looking for a victim?" I walk past the gargantuan dude who stares after me silently.

As I wait in line at the keg, I can *feel* the eyes on me. From everywhere. I scan the crowd and curse Tori under my breath. Of course they're staring—with my ass cheeks peeking out of my lacy shorts and the cleavage revealed within the cowl of the low-cut halter. Where we usually go out, no one would think twice about what I'm wearing. Not here. I'm getting scanned up and down, like they're trying to decide if they should threaten me to stay away from their boyfriends or offer me fifty for twenty minutes in the backseat.

"Who are you, and why are you at my party?"

There's a guy in a blue polo shirt and khaki shorts next to me. He looks like most of the guys here—throw in a baseball hat here or there or a random button-down hanging over a T-shirt.

"I'm here for the free beer," I tell him with a sardonic smile.

He smiles back. "Then let's make that happen. Excuse me, guys," he tells everyone waiting ahead of me in line. "The lady needs a beer."

A moment later, he hands me a filled red Solo cup. "Here you go."

"Thank you." I take it from him and offer a small smile, not enough to encourage him to stick around.

"My name's Blake. Let me know if you need anything, okay?" And, just like that, he's rushing off to help some other girl in need of a shot. "Whitney, I have Fireball for you!"

"Who are you anyway?" a girl asks from behind me. "Who'd you come here with?"

It's not a friendly let-me-introduce-myself question. It's a total territorial you-have-some-nerve-showing-up-here question.

"It's not about who I came here with," I tell her with a smirk. "You should be worried about who I *leave* with."

She gasps in mock horror. I fight the urge to roll my eyes.

I enter the house and find an empty spot in the corner of the kitchen. I don't bother looking for Tori and Lincoln. I'm *not* third-wheeling it. I'm prepared to hang out here, lean against the counter and observe the spectacle happening around me 'til it's time to go.

"Where are you from?"

"Can you believe she even thinks she has a chance with him?"

"You're not from Oaklawn, right? I know I'd remember you."

"And did you see what she's wearing? That diet's definitely *not* working."

"Oh shit!"

Girls scream as a drunken ass collides with them, barely making it in time to throw up in the sink.

I'm a captive audience to the Middle America drama. The gossip. The terrible pop music blaring through the speakers. The amateurs who can't handle what's in their cups. The couple pressed against the wall, making out, his hand up her shirt. And, yes, I'm aware a guy's standing next to me, trying to get me to talk to him.

"What did you say your name was?"

When he refuses to take a hint after I continue to blatantly ignore him, I release an impatient breath and say to his face, "Go away."

He looks offended. I laugh at him.

"Bitch."

"Undeniably," I agree.

He scowls and shoves a path to the living room where a group of girls are failing to make dancing happen.

And then...I see his bright blue eyes. The same captivating shade as his brother. And, most likely, their father's. The eyes that wouldn't look away when he saw me at school earlier today and that hold me in place now.

He smiles, and a deep dimple creases his right cheek.

"Shit," I breathe out.

He remains focused on me as he navigates the crowd. People talk to him along the way. He responds but doesn't take his eyes off me and never stops moving in my direction. I am pinned to this spot, anticipating his approach until he's finally in front of me. And I mean *right* in front of me. His hand rests on the counter next to my waist as he bends down, and his lips brush my ear.

"Hey, Lana."

A shiver shoots down my spine.

"How do you know me?"

He doesn't pull away. My mouth is so close to his skin, I could easily suck on his neck.

"Who doesn't know you?" he says, his voice a low rumble that sends a jolt through my heart. He leans away to look me in the eye.

I laugh. "Just about everyone here."

"This isn't usually your scene." There's an ease rolling off him, like he's comfortable with the attention. He's definitely getting plenty of that from just about everyone around us—for completely different reasons than I am.

"No, it isn't." I nod toward Tori, who's laughing flirtatiously at something Lincoln said, placing her hand on his arm. "Being a good friend. So you're *the* Joey Harrison? I thought you were a myth."

He laughs, standing to his full height. And I'm regretfully aware of the distance between us.

"Yeah, I don't come home much anymore."

"Where do you hide?" I take a gulp of the chilled beer, needing to cool down.

"I go to a private school up north."

I smirk. "Of course you do."

He narrows his eyes, confused by my response.

"I'm glad you're here." He hasn't glanced around once.

I can't say I'm uncomfortable with his unwavering attention, but it's definitely intense.

"Are you now?" I tease with a grin, trying to appear unaffected.

He flashes a devilish smile before taking a sip of his beer. "Want to get out of here? We were thinking of trying another party."

"Who's 'we'?" I've learned that committing to leaving with a group of guys can lead to complications later.

"Lincoln, me and Vic." He nods to the guy leaning against the counter across from us.

I hadn't noticed him before now. He stands out worse than I do in his leather jacket with his clean-shaven head and a large tattoo scrawled up his neck and etched across his skull. He looks like sunshine walking. By that I mean, depressing as hell.

"I'm not sure what we're doing, but we're leaving as soon as our friend gets here." I scan the kitchen and locate the clock on the microwave. "Which should be soon."

Joey pulls his phone from his pocket, examining the screen. "Excuse me a second?"

"Take all the seconds you need," I tell him, impressed by the request.

He has more manners than most adults I know. But then again, I work at a dive bar.

Joey exits the sliding door onto the deck, his phone to his ear.

I glance over at the scowling mass across from me and try to figure out how that friendship happened. Vic doesn't make eye contact, but I can almost hear him growling. Charming.

"Where's Joey? I saw him talking to you," Tori asks, appearing out of nowhere. "Please don't tell me you pissed him off already."

"I'm not *that* big of a bitch," I reply defensively.

Tori shoots me a look, silently challenging my statement.

I roll my eyes. "He's outside on the phone."

"That must be where Lincoln went," she tells me. "So, do you mind if we hang out with them tonight?"

"Tori, did you meet Vic?" I grin wickedly and nod toward him. "He's with the guys."

Tori turns with a huge smile to greet him, but before she can open her mouth to say anything, she takes him in, and the smile vanishes. "Oh no," she says, eyeing him up and down, openly judging. She turns back to me. "Seriously? Nina is not going to be okay with"—she eyes him and makes a face like he smells foul—"*him.*"

I keep wearing my wicked grin, amused by her reaction.

"This is bullshit," she complains loud enough for Vic to hear her.

"When is Nina getting here?"

"I was about to text her," she says, opening her purse and pulling out her phone.

"Hey, ladies," Joey greets us, a beautiful smile spread across his face. "Wanna come to The Point with us? I got on the list."

"You did?" Tori's brows rise. "I thought The Point was exclusive and impossible to get into?"

Joey shrugs with a confident grin. A smile blooms on Tori's face, her eyes lit. Tori knows I've been dying to get into a Point party for forever but haven't been able to get access. She doesn't even have to ask if I want to go; she already knows the answer.

"The only problem is, we need a ride. My brother took my Jeep, and I have to get it from him when we get there."

"Umm…let me see if I can make that happen," Tori says, lifting her phone to her ear and walking out onto the deck, away from the noise.

"How did you get on the list?" I ask Joey, beyond impressed.

"My brother owes me," he explains vaguely.

"We have a ride!" Tori announces a minute later. "Nina hooked us up. She'll be here in thirty."

I consider for a second who Nina could be getting a ride from. Maybe one of the girls at the club? I hope so because I don't want her to feel like she needs to entertain Doom and Gloom all night.

"Play a round of beer pong with me while we wait?" Joey takes my hand like he's about to lead me away.

"Uh, no," I respond, not moving.

"You've never played before," he accuses with a smirk.

I open my mouth to deny it, bothered by his assumption. But I can't lie. "No."

He pulls me after him, not allowing me to resist. "C'mon. We're doing this."

After filling our keg cups, Joey leads me downstairs to the finished basement where a small crowd surrounds a ping-pong table. There's a couple standing at either end of the table with a cluster of cups spread out in front of them. A girl takes aim with a ping-pong ball before tossing it, landing it in a cup. Everyone chants, "Drink," as the other couple takes gulps from their beers and then removes the cup from the table.

Resting his free hand on my hip, Joey bends down to explain the rules, speaking directly into my ear, the way he did earlier. At the low murmur of his voice, I catch myself inadvertently leaning into him as I listen. When I feel his chest against my back, I stand up straighter, pulling away. I don't let guys touch me, not so intimately anyway. I need to know they're worth my time before I get close. But I keep gravitating toward Joey. His hands feel like they belong on my body. I step away from him, and his hand falls away. With the release of his touch, I'm snapped awake—once again very aware of the vacant space between us.

"Harrison, do you have a partner yet? You play winner," a guy in a pink polo shirt calls to Joey from across the room.

Joey grins and points to me. The pink polo shirt guy smiles wide, like he approves of Joey's choice. I fight back the urge to roll my eyes—oh-so glad I have his approval.

Within a few minutes, one cup remains on the farthest side of the table, and the guy on the opposite end sinks the ball. Everyone hollers and cheers while the losing couple chugs their beers.

"This is a stupid game," I observe out loud.

Joey laughs and takes my hand to lead me to the losers' end.

"Think of it as one of those carnival games," Joey says from behind me so that only I can hear. "You know, the ones where you have to toss a ring around a bottle or throw darts at balloons. Except we need to get a ping-pong ball into a bunch of cups and force people to drink."

"Do I get a prize if we win?" I ask sarcastically, realizing too late that he could easily misinterpret that question.

Joey laughs, revealing the deep dimple with his beautiful smile. "If we win, I'll make sure you go home with a prize," he promises, "even if I have to buy you a stuffed monkey."

I grin, grateful that he didn't turn the comment into an invitation to get in my shorts. "I'd prefer a zebra."

This makes him laugh again.

"Ready?" the guy at the other end calls to us impatiently.

"Let's win me a zebra," I say, earning strange looks from the spectators who heard me.

And *we do win*. It may have helped that the other team just played three games and were kinda drunk. Or it could have had something to do with the fact that I'm pretty damn good at this stupid game. Not bragging or anything, but I'm impressive, sinking the ping-pong ball in cup after cup, earning cheers and high fives from the onlookers. And a bear squeeze of a hug from Joey when I nailed the winning shot, which made it difficult to breathe for more than one reason. Wow, he's built.

Who knew that the best way to fit in at a party was to kill them at their own game?

"Who's up next?" one of the losers asks. They have names, but I don't remember them.

"We've gotta go." Joey's announcement is met with groans.

That's when I notice the same bitchy girl from earlier glaring at me from across the room. When he takes ahold of my hand, like we're meant to be together, I can't help but smirk at her, which only makes her angrier. So, of course, I laugh.

"What?" Joey asks, looking in their direction. He must catch on before I say anything because he pulls me closer, settling his hand on the small of my back as he guides me away.

I check my phone while we climb the stairs and find a text from Tori from two minutes ago. *Nina's out front. Waiting.*

"They're out front," I tell Joey, abandoning my empty beer cup next to some expensive-looking sculptures on a table in the hallway.

As soon as we step outside, I remember, "Oh. My bag."

"Where'd you leave it?" Joey asks.

"I'll be right back," I tell him, releasing his grasp to rush along the side of the house. I duck down in the shadows and reach under the deck for my bag.

When I stand, there's someone behind me.

"Got it," I say, assuming it's Joey.

Except this guy's much bigger.

"Knew you'd show up to find me," he says, hovering a little too close.

"You're delusional," I tell him, moving to walk past him.

He grabs my arm, whipping me around to face him. "Where do you think you're going?"

I stare up at the same annoying guy from earlier today at school. The guy who obviously *won't* take no for an answer. I search for his name but can't bring it to the surface. God, I really suck with names.

"Don't touch me." I slip my free hand into my jacket pocket.

"You think you're too good for me?"

"Yes," I say, realizing too late that the answer should've remained in my head. "But don't take it personally. I'm too good for most guys."

That didn't help. His grip on my arm tightens as his cockiness turns bitter. "You're such a fucking bitch."

"I should really have that tattooed somewhere," I say, removing my hand from my pocket and pressing the button. "Now let go of me or I'm going to carve my name on your balls."

He glances down at the blade glistening between his legs.

"Lana?"

I don't redirect my eyes from the douche who's cutting off the circulation in my arm.

I gently tap the crotch of his jeans with the flat part of the blade. He jolts away like I've shocked him. I don't hesitate to escape, finding Joey waiting for me at the front corner of the house. I ease the blade back into the handle and conceal it in my pocket just as I reach him.

Joey eyes me curiously, glancing behind me. "Everything okay?"

I provide the most honest answer I can offer at this second. "I need a drink."

Nina, Tori and Lincoln are standing beside a car I don't recognize. It's huge and old. It looks like a tan tank with a black canvas top. When I look more closely, I notice Gary, Nina's boss from the strip club, in the driver's seat. What the hell? He's the biggest perv in existence. Way too many hands touching girls who are barely legal. I met him once and had to shower immediately after from just being molested by his eyes. Why is he here?

"Finally!" Tori exclaims when she sees us approaching. She grabs my arm and pulls me away from everyone. "Where have you been? You didn't get in a fight or anything, right? I was getting worried when I couldn't find you. I had a bad feeling because half of these girls are skanks, and I was about to claw someone if I had to stay at this party a single second longer, so I knew you were probably on the edge of taking someone out. Is everything okay?"

"Take a breath, Tor." I raise my hands for her to see that they're blood-free. There's obvious relief in her eyes.

When we turn back to the car, everyone's seated inside, not leaving us many options. Tori glares at Vic, who is sitting in the middle of the backseat, between Joey and Lincoln. I know she wanted to be the one sitting near Lincoln. She opens the passenger door and slides in beside Nina.

I'm about to squeeze in after her when she looks up at me and says, "Sit in the back," followed by a wink.

She closes the door before I can respond.

When I open the back door, Joey is smiling up at me.

"Hey," I say, unable to hide my smile.

He pats his lap. "C'mon in, pretty girl."

Chapter Five

"Lying is the worst kind of betrayal."

I watch the tear drip from my mother's nose onto the pillow as I lie across from her in bed, her hand holding mine tightly.

"Don't ever lie to protect someone from the truth. Untrue words hurt as much as a knife to the heart."

"*Are you comfortable?" Joey asks*, leaning in so that his voice hums in my ear.

I'm beginning to think this is his way of unraveling me. It's more intimate than the hand he has resting on my hip. I tilt my head toward him, my cheek brushing against his freshly shaven skin. He smells so good. I almost close my eyes to inhale him.

"I am," I reply, leaning a little farther back into the corner of the car, my legs draped across his, so I have a better view of him.

"I'm impressed with your beer pong skills." His mouth quirks, revealing a hint of a dimple. "You sure you haven't played before?"

"I'm sure." I smile wryly. "You owe me a zebra."

"I do."

He's slowly moved closer, so now he only has to lean his gorgeous head in just a little to kiss me. Lost in his attentive gaze and seduced by the low rumble of his voice, I *want* him to kiss me. I brush my hand along his neck, transfixed.

"Want some?"

It's like someone shook me and I'm awakened from a trance, dropped back into the middle of reality with music blaring and bodies squeezed in next to us. I catch Nina's scrutinizing eyes in the rearview mirror. Whatever she sees, she isn't happy about it. I remove my hand from Joey's neck and sit up a little straighter.

Tori leans over with the bottle in her hand. "Lana?"

"Sure," comes out way too wistful. I clear my throat. Not bothering to look at what I'm drinking, I hold my breath and take two long gulps, breathing out against the astringent peppermint burn.

I offer the bottle to Joey. After taking his share, he passes it to Vic.

"Hey," I say when Vic makes eye contact.

"Vic, this is Lana." Joey nods toward me. "Vic and I go to school together in Vermont."

"What's up?" Vic nods with a quick lift of the thick black eyebrows that shadow his sunken grey eyes.

After he takes a long swig from the bottle, he hands it to Lincoln and crosses his arms. The energy rolling off him is dark and brooding. I can tell he's going to be as much fun to have around as the plague. I haven't wanted anything to do with him since I first saw him at the party, and that hasn't changed.

"How you doin', Lana?" Lincoln asks, his long legs bent uncomfortably behind the front seat.

I never know how to respond to that question. People don't really *want* to know the miserable truth. And I can't lie and tell them what they expect to hear, so I offer an ambiguous shrug.

Even though I saw him at the party, this is the first time Lincoln and I have spoken tonight.

"I didn't know you and Joey were friends."

"You and I don't exactly talk about things like that," he replies.

That's true. I've been his partner in French just about all year, and I don't know much about him other than he plays sports and has a scholarship to go…somewhere. Oh, and that he apparently has a thing for Tori.

Most guys do.

Tori isn't exactly girlfriend material. So I wouldn't have encouraged him if I had known he was seriously into her. She's never been exclusive with a guy for as long as I've known her, which is practically forever. She's distant but flirty. Something about her aloofness comes across as untouchable. And predictably, guys want what they can't have, making her that much more alluring. Tori takes advantage, taunting and teasing. Manipulating to get what she wants before dropping them.

I feel bad for Lincoln, watching him as he's unable to keep his eyes off her. He's not like the guys we usually go out with. She could really mess him up if he's not careful.

"*Hello*, Lana," Nina calls to me from the front seat, annoyed.

"Uh, sorry," I respond, realizing I haven't even acknowledged her since getting in the car. "How was your night?"

Nina shrugs. "The usual."

Nina's nineteen. She dropped out of school last year to work at a local strip club. She's tall and thin with straight dark hair that touches her ass, and blessed with breasts that men pay to see and pray to touch. She keeps saying she's planning to get her GED. Not sure I believe it.

Nina parties with us when she's not working. She's the type of girl who attracts attention everywhere she goes—supermarket included. Guys are pathetic around her. But she's just as standoffish as we are when it comes to getting serious with anyone. Nina's curse is *Respect*. She demands it from everyone—her friends, her patrons, and especially, her men.

If they disrespect her, she can throw a punch unlike anyone I know. I was surprised the first time I saw it. She nailed some guy in the face for feeling her up while we were at the movies. I'm pretty sure she broke his nose. Nina taught me how to defend myself. Even gave me the small pink switchblade that I have in my pocket.

Nina moved in with Tori after sticking a fork in her mother's boyfriend's thigh. He tried to slide his hand under her skirt while they were eating dinner—*with her mother sitting across the table!* Her mother kicked her out, swearing the man she loved would never have done that. The boyfriend is lucky she didn't aim a little higher. As for her mother…I have no words.

I'm still not sure why we're in the ogre's car.

Then Nina explains, "So Gary offered to give us a ride and hooked us up with a couple partials." Which means he took some nearly empty bottles of liquor from the club's bar. She raises her eyebrows and forces a smile.

Now I know. Gary was our only option, which totally sucks because I'm really not in the mood to put up with his creepy-hand-roaming thing.

"So explain how we got on the list tonight?" Nina asks, still speaking to us through the rearview mirror.

"My brother, Parker," Joey explains.

His fingers casually skim the exposed skin along my waistline. I draw in a quick breath. He must notice because the side of his mouth quirks up, even while he remains focused on Nina's reflection.

Nina whips around in her seat. "Parker Harrison?" Her eyes flit over Joey's face intently, earning a curious look in return.

"You know my brother?" he asks, surprised.

I didn't realize Nina hadn't been told Joey's last name, and she must not have gotten a good look at him 'til now because the relation is pretty obvious.

Nina flashes me a quick glance before turning back around in her seat, composed once again. "We see him out every once in a while," she says, her voice indifferent.

But I know better. Truth is, *everyone* knows who Parker Harrison is. It's hard not to. He's an older, more refined version of Joey. But, unlike Joey, Parker is everywhere—bars, parties, basically anywhere people are having a good time.

Tucking his cell phone in his pocket, Vic leans forward to talk to Gary. "Can we make a stop?"

"This isn't a taxi," Gary gripes. "I didn't know I'd be driving all of *you*." He glares over the seat.

"Aw, Gary," Nina coos, rubbing her slender, manicured fingers on the back of his bulbous head.

I repress a gag. I don't know how she fakes it. There's probably more grease in his slicked hair than in the drip bucket at Stella's.

"You know they're my friends." She leans in close so her shiny red lips are almost touching his ear. "Be nice, please."

Gary sighs in contentment as she pets his huge ogre head. "Where do you want to go?"

"I need to pick up some smokes. Next convenience store works," Vic tells him, sitting back against the seat, his fists clenched within his crossed arms.

What's up with this guy?

"You smell good," Joey says, his nose brushing against my shoulder.

"Thanks," I reply, hoping it's the perfume he's attracted to and not Stella's stench. Thinking back to what Tori said earlier, I try not to laugh. Apparently, grease *is* sexy. That's so wrong.

"I've been wanting to meet you for a while." He squeezes my waist.

I jump and my shoulder knocks him in the jaw.

I cannot believe that just happened.

"I'm so sorry." I cringe, mortified.

"It's okay," he assures me, rubbing his chin. "Didn't realize you were ticklish."

"Very."

"Everywhere?" he asks, a teasing grin spreading on his gorgeous face.

Oh, I wish I could lick that dimple. Yup, I really did just think that.

His other hand grips my thigh. I jump again—without assaulting him this time.

"Guess so," he says with a laugh, gently rubbing the traitorous spot.

If I could whip around and straddle him right now, I would. Slutty, I know. But I swear I'm not usually this pathetic. A guy has *never* affected me like this before.

"I wish we were alone right now," I whisper in his ear, tucking my hand between his knees and running a thumb over his leg.

I know we haven't even had a full conversation. But I don't care. I'm sitting on top of the muscular thighs of one of the hottest guys I've ever met, and all I want to do is give in to every urge pulsing through my hormonal teenage body. It's like I have no control.

Joey pulls me in a little closer. "Me too."

"Need another drink?" Tori asks, leaning so far over the front seat that she's practically in my face. "You know, take the edge off?"

She eyes Joey's hand on my bare leg and glares at him. He drops it by his side. I sober with the release of his touch.

"Yeah," I reply guiltily.

She knows this isn't me. I'm not the girl who spreads my legs for any guy who looks my way. She usually gives me shit for being so cold and bitchy. Then again, *she's* not sitting on Joey's lap right now, leaning against his firm chest.

Actually, *she's* the reason I'm sitting here!

Tori's almost as small as I am. I could've fit in the front seat of this boat with her and Nina. But she told me to sit in the back with that stupid wink she gave me. So I'm totally blaming my sluttiness on her.

I grab the bottle from her and guzzle until I can't. If tearing off Joey's clothes isn't an option, then I'm going to need a lot of sedation.

I hand the bottle to Joey, who draws in several mouthfuls. I guess I'm not the only one fighting to behave.

We turn into the parking lot of a convenience store with crooked cardboard signs plastered to its grimy windows, advertising cigarettes, milk and lottery tickets. Lincoln slides out of the car after Gary puts it in park. Tori gets out at the same time.

"Why don't I sit in the back? Vic, you can sit up front."

"Whatever," he grumbles, stalking past her toward the store.

Tori smiles seductively up at Lincoln, brushing her hand along his chest as he holds the door open with the dumbest smile on his face. She's torturing him. And when she ducks into the car, the glint in her eyes tells me she knows it too. Poor guy.

As soon as she scoots next to Joey, she flips my dangling legs up so my feet are on her thighs. "Hey, Lana."

I'm in trouble. And when she clutches my ankle, I know she's definitely not happy with me. Again, this is *her* fault.

"Hey, Tori," I respond, forcing a smile.

Joey looks between us and sinks back into the seat like he's trying to get out of the way.

"You look really cute tonight." She directs her attention to Joey. "Doesn't she look really cute tonight?"

"Uh, yeah," Joey responds, obviously confused and not wanting to be in the middle of whatever this is.

"Thanks," I reply shortly.

Tori is fierce. Not a physical threat like Nina. She and I are barely over five feet. But she has a temper and a vocabulary that makes grown men cower. And when she goes off, her long black curls whip around her head like a raging storm. Her neck flips from side to side, and a finger topped with a sharp nail is in the face of whoever she's telling off. Spanglish snaps from her tongue like a whip, leaving a guy looking for his balls and the most confident girl whimpering. It's like she verbally skins them alive. I've only been on the other end of that Latina finger twice. And neither time ended well.

I watch her hand now, waiting. She keeps it resting on my ankle.

"You should know she's my best friend, Joey." She sounds like one of the guys from the *Godfather* before he pulls out a gun and blows the head off of whoever's across the table from him.

"I *do* know that," Joey replies carefully.

"Then you should know I'm really protective of my friends. Especially my best friend."

He nods. My eyes narrow. I don't get it. Where's this coming from?

"And being with my best friend is *earned*." Tori stares him down. I reach for her hand before she can point the finger. "She's not a prize that lands on your lap. Got it?"

"Of course," he replies, unable to look away from her blazing brown eyes.

"Um, can I talk to you a minute?" I request, squeezing Tori's hand.

She blinks away from Joey and looks to me with a brilliant smile. "Yeah, sure."

I open the door and ease off Joey's lap. Joey moves to get out, and Tori presses her hand into his chest, pushing him back against the seat.

"I got it," she says, crawling around him. She steps out and shuts the door in his face.

"What's up with you? Why are you acting like this?" I ask as soon as we're alone.

"Why are you letting him touch you like that?" she demands. "Lana, that's not you."

"Hey! You're the one who has me sitting on his lap, and if you felt what I felt, you wouldn't be so judgy right now." I clamp my mouth shut, realizing how wrong that sounded.

"You're right. It's my fault," she admits, leaning back against the car with her arms crossed. "I set you up. I should have known you'd be an easy lay for him."

"Yeah, it is your fault! Wait…what? Easy? I'm *not* easy," I say, completely offended. Then I notice the gleam in her eye. She's fucking with me. "You're a bitch, Tori."

"Just needed you to wake up and stop acting like a slut." Tori smiles and steps toward me, pulling me into a hug. "Remember, he's a dumbass guy. He has to deserve you first. You're not a trophy, Lana."

"Right," I reply, suffocated by her mane.

Tori and I made a pact when we were in fifth grade to always be honest and protect each other, no matter what. And then, in sixth grade, after a stupid argument over who could like Justin Walker, we added that no guy is worth fighting over. Ever. Joey Harrison included.

We're interrupted when the back door opens.

"Your phone beeped." Joey has it in his hand.

I take it from him. "Thanks." I pat my jacket pocket and find it open. Thankfully, the switchblade didn't fall out too.

I enter my passcode to read the text from my mother. *Could you pick up some flu medicine while you're out?*

The flu? I hesitate before responding. We both know this *isn't* the flu. But maybe she just needs something for the symptoms.

I type back, *Okay.*

Then I slip the phone back in my pocket and zip it up.

"Everything alright?" Joey asks, his brows drawn together in concern.

"Uh"—I force a smile— "I just need to pick up something for my mother. I'll be right back."

I can tell he's about to ask me a question, so I turn away quickly, leaving him standing outside the car, watching me walk away.

I pull open the grime-covered door and freeze after taking just three steps.

I stare at the small silver gun. I don't know what make it is, but it's one of those kinds where the barrel opens up, and the bullets are loaded one at a time. Holding the gun is a big guy wearing a black leather jacket with a cloth face shield pulled up over his nose and a hoodie covering his head.

"What the hell are you doing in here?!" Vic yells at me.

I look from the gun to the skinny man with the bushy mustache behind the counter, his hands raised. I don't say anything.

The guy behind the counter anxiously flips his unblinking eyes between us. I look from him back to Vic. Vic shakes his head at me before focusing on the cashier.

"Hurry up!" Vic yells at the guy, who grabs cash from the register and shoves it across the counter. "And pull out a bunch of lottery tickets too!" Vic forces his voice to be deeper than it is. "Slowly!" he warns the man.

The cashier's shaking hands reach out and pull at the lottery tickets hanging on the wall behind the counter. He tears off a long string and offers them to Vic.

"Give them to her," Vic demands, waving the gun toward me.

"What?!" I yell. "I don't want anything to do with your dumbass robbery! I'm not touching them."

Vic aims the gun at my chest. "Take the fucking tickets."

I'm not nervous or scared. I'm more annoyed than anything. Why did I have to walk in on this dipwad robbing the convenience store? I bet he's going to walk away with barely two hundred dollars. He's such a fricken idiot.

"Fine." I snatch the trail of tickets from the clerk and fold them up, grumbling, "Asshole," under my breath. I shove them in my inside pocket. "Can we leave now?"

Vic stuffs the bills in his jacket pocket and starts walking backward, keeping the gun pointed at the cashier. I shove the door open and stomp to the car.

"Hurry up and get in the car!" Vic growls at me, hiding the gun in the back of his pants. He pulls down the scarf and shoves back the hood in one quick motion. He's opening the passenger door as I'm sliding back onto Joey's lap. "Drive. Now."

"What just happened?" Gary demands. He's the only one who seems to have noticed our odd exit.

"Nothing," Vic replies, agitated. "Just fucking drive." He looks at me over his shoulder.

I want to punch him in the face. He's beyond stupid! I cross my arms and lean back against the arm Joey has loosely draped around me. I stare Vic down, imagining my hands wrapped around his throat, strangling him.

"Lana, what happened?" Tori asks, easily picking up on my hostile mood.

I don't take my eyes off the contagion that is Vic. I'm certain disdain is written all over my face as I silently curse him with a thousand deaths. I'm not even trying to hide it. But I know, if I say something, everything will go to shit.

"Nothing," Vic snaps.

I don't say a word.

Chapter Six

"Lana, why did you punch the boy at school today?" my grandmother asks.

"I didn't," I answer honestly.

"Who did?"

I scrape my foot on the floor, not looking up at her. "My friend."

"Why?"

"Because he was trying to lift up my skirt." My words are quiet.

"Why didn't you say anything when your teacher asked what happened?"

"Because I didn't want her to get in trouble."

"But you told me."

I look up, suddenly afraid. "Is she in trouble?"

My grandmother sighs. "No. I would have punched him too."

After driving maybe five minutes, two cop cars fly by with their lights flashing. I twist around to follow them, my heart racing. When I turn back, Vic is glaring at me.

"Fuck off."

Tori and Lincoln look between us and then at each other. Joey's arm encircles me protectively.

"Vic, did something happen at the store?" Lincoln asks cautiously.

I'm not sure how well the two of them know each other. But since Joey's not saying anything, Lincoln must feel the need to step up.

"No," Vic grunts.

"Then let me have a cigarette," Gary demands. "You guys are driving me crazy."

Vic remains silent.

"Where are the cigarettes you bought, Vic?" Tori tosses a suspicious look my way before sharing a silent exchange with Lincoln.

"They didn't have my brand," Vic grumbles, his attention directed out the window.

I clench my fists, fighting the urge to scream. This asshat is about to ruin my life, and I need him gone. Now.

"We need to ditch him at the party," I tell Joey, only because his ear is right next to my mouth and Tori's too far away.

"Why?" Joey asks.

I can only shake my head, afraid to say too much and have Vic overhear. As much as I'm not afraid of the douche, he does have a gun. And he's obviously stupid enough to hold up a convenience store with it. He's probably dumb enough to use it too. As much as my life blows, I'm not looking to die tonight.

Everyone knows something's up. The tension in the car is as thick as Gary's neck…which is a tree trunk. Tori keeps staring at the back of Vic's head like she's waiting for him to make a move. Nina starts messing with the music. She may act unfazed, but she'd willingly push him out of the moving car if it came to it.

Lincoln's fighting to remain calm with his hands pressed against his thighs. But the tendons straining in his neck give away just how close he is to losing it.

The only one who seems oddly relaxed is Joey, whose hand has found the skin along my waistband again. Obviously something very wrong is going on, and he hasn't reacted even a little. He's either oblivious or he's brilliant at the whole calm-under-pressure thing.

I'm stiff against him, his touch unable to soothe the tension.

"Can I have the bottle?" I ask Nina.

She slides around and hands me a different bottle of something darker, passing it off with a wink. She's trying to keep me relaxed too. Except I'm not. When I reach for the bottle, my hand is shaking. I resist the urge to crash it over Vic's asinine head.

I swallow down the cinnamon-flavored whiskey until it sends me into a coughing fit. Then I pass the bottle back.

"Someone needs to tell me what the fuck is going on right now, or I'm pulling over and dumping your asses on the side of the road!" Gary bellows over the music, making me flinch.

Joey's grip tightens on my waist.

"No you're not." Vic's voice is low and threatening, like an approaching storm. "Keep driving."

"What did you just say, you little fuck?" Gary's face is redder than raw hamburger, and his skin doesn't look much better.

"Easy, baby," Nina murmurs seductively in his ear.

I shudder when she soothingly runs her hand along the stubble coating the folds of his triple chin.

Joey pulls me back against him. "Don't worry about them." His voice melts me against his hard chest.

I nuzzle into his neck so it looks like I'm kissing him. "How well do you know Vic?"

Joey turns toward me, brushing his fingers along my cheek, our mouths almost touching. His breath tickles as he says, "We're not exactly friends. I told my dad I'd take him out, as a favor."

He pauses and smooths a thumb over my lower lip. Despite this crazy-ass situation, I'm actually getting turned on right now. What is wrong with me?!

"It's…complicated. Why? Did he do something?"

I breathe out slowly, unable to respond.

"Forget about him." He leans in until our lips brush, and I quiver.

"You're fogging up the car," Tori stretches over and says so close, she could join us.

Joey pulls away.

"Tori!" I exclaim, glaring at her.

Tori smirks and sits back again.

I glance behind us, expecting lights to appear at any second. They don't. Or not yet anyway.

"Vic, tell me what you did!" Lincoln suddenly yells, slamming his palm on Vic's headrest.

I jump and Joey presses me against him. He opens his mouth to say something to Lincoln, but then closes it wordlessly.

"I'm sick of your shit. I'm not going down for whatever the fuck you just did! So talk. *Now*."

I've never heard Lincoln raise his voice before. He's always so calm and put together. But I guess everyone has their limit. And Lincoln's sword is drawn. It's pretty impressive. Tori must think so too because she gives him a once-over with a raised brow.

Vic turns abruptly, leaning over the seat. "Everyone needs to calm the fuck down! Okay? Nothing happened. When Lana walked in, I was yelling at the clerk. He was trying to sell me this shit brand of cigarettes because he didn't have what I wanted. Wouldn't shut up about how they're all the same, and that they'll kill me. I wasn't up for the lecture, so I told him to go fuck himself. When Lana came in, I grabbed her and told her we were leaving. That's why she's acting like she has something stuck up her ass." He directs his attention to me. "Sorry I touched you, okay? Will you just fucking relax?"

Oh, I want to kick him in the face. And I could too, easily, since my foot is dangling off Joey's leg, right below Vic's chin. But before I can, he twists back around and returns to his angry, pouting posture.

"Little boy, you dropped your toy," Nina sings mockingly, displaying the gun on her flat palm.

Just as Vic grabs for it, she flips it in her hand and points it at his forehead.

"Nina!" Tori calls out.

But Nina doesn't react. Her full attention is pinned on Vic.

"You don't know what the fuck you're doing," Vic challenges her.

Nina cocks the hammer.

No one moves. I don't even think we're breathing. Gary may be screaming. But I can't hear him. The entire world is on mute. I'm staring at the silver muzzle indenting the flesh on Vic's skull.

"How do you know it's loaded?" Vic questions, sounding way too cocky for a guy who might have his brains splattered against the window at any second.

"I don't. But you do," she says, her shiny red lips parting to reveal a big white smile.

"You know I could take that from you, right?"

Nina just smirks wickedly. I grimace with a silent groan. Vic better shut his mouth. He has no idea who he's talking to.

Nina's a fighter. I'm convinced she came into the world that way so she could survive the shit she's been dealt her entire life. She may look super girlie and have a figure to die for, but she's ferocious. Without hesitation, she's had my back in a fight more times than I can count. Even when I'm the one who started it.

So I know, if Vic makes a move, I'm going to want to block my ears.

The car stops. At least it doesn't feel like we're moving anymore. I'm afraid to look away to find out.

"Nina, honey, would you please put down the gun?" Gary asks her so gently, it doesn't even sound like him.

My eyes remain glued to the point where the gun is attached to Vic's head. His jaw tenses. Nina smiles wider, a menacing glint in her dark eyes.

"What did you do in the store?" Nina asks calmly.

Vic swallows. "Nothing. Ask Lana."

"I'm not asking her. I'm asking *you*. She's a sweet girl, and she shouldn't be involved in this. She might actually go to college. I'm not fucking with that. I'm not going to let *you* fuck with that either. So, one more time. What did you do in that convenience store?"

Vic sneers. "Nothing."

"Okay, I'm going to shit myself if you don't put down the gun, Nina! Please!" Gary whimpers.

I steal a glance his way. Beads of sweat are covering his forehead and streaking down the sides of his face. He may even be crying. My nose scrunches in disgust. I know this is intense, but...really?

"Fine," Nina huffs and tips the gun back, easing the hammer in place.

The entire car exhales.

"Give me my gun," Vic demands, holding out his hand.

Nina laughs. "Uh. No."

"Get out!" Gary screams. "Get out of my car! Now!" He opens his door.

The next thing I know, my door is open and he's yanking me out.

"Hey!" I holler, trying to pull my arm out of his clammy grip.

"All of you, out! I'm not putting up with this shit!"

I yank free, but the force of the motion sends me tripping over my four-inch wedges, and I topple onto my ass. Joey is out a second later, followed by Tori, both of them in Gary's face. The finger is out, and Spanish flies from Tori's mouth.

"Keep your hands off her!" Joey yells, practically bumping against Gary's gut. He's taller than Gary by a few inches, but Gary wins with three times the girth.

A large black hand is in my face. I look up. It takes me a couple seconds to realize that Lincoln is offering to help me up.

"Thanks."

His hand completely swallows mine as he lifts me off the ground. I swipe at the dirt on my butt, still watching the three go at it. It's all words. Nothing about their posture has me concerned that someone's about to swing.

We're in the middle of nowhere. There's maybe a streetlight every quarter mile on this forgotten road, lighting it just enough to make it creepy. Gary pulled off into one of those gravel turnouts on the side of the road—the ideal location when you're desperate to relieve your bladder or throw your door open just in time to vomit. So not the ideal location to be dumped with a psycho and his gun.

"Where's Nina and Vic?" I ask in a rush, frantically searching the darkness.

"I don't know," Lincoln answers, his voice as concerned as mine.

We creep toward the front of the car. Nina's back is to us. She's leaning against the fender on the other side of the car. Vic is in his signature angry stance, scowling at her.

Nina has the barrel of the gun open and is *throwing* bullets at Vic.

"Tell me what you did, Vic," she says in a taunting tone. "C'mon. You want your toy back, don't you?"

Vic grunts something.

"Then tell me. Quit being a bitch." There's a sadistic lilt in Nina's voice, like she's enjoying this.

She's starting to scare me a little. I put a big star on that mental note I already had, reminding me to never piss her off.

Vic bares his teeth. "Give me my gun, or I'm going to—"

"To what?" Lincoln challenges, straightening a few inches taller, like he might jump over the car.

Vic looks up and spots us across the hood. Nina snaps the barrel shut with a flick of her wrist and stuffs the gun into her purse.

Vic breathes out audibly, like he can't believe he has to repeat himself. "This is a fucking joke. I don't know why you won't drop it. *Nothing* happened."

At least he's persistent with the nothing-happened story. I have to give him that. And I'm not going to contradict it. If I do, everyone in the car could be considered accomplices after the fact. And I won't let that happen. Right now, only Vic and I know what went down in that store. And we're the only ones who will ever know. Unless he does something else stupid.

Nina approaches us with a hip-swaying saunter. The dark purple dress hugs her curves perfectly as she balances on heels that bring her to supermodel height.

She looks completely unfazed by everything that just transpired. A lethal goddess.

If only I were that composed…and tall.

"Screw this," Gary declares loudly. "Nina, let's go."

Nina shakes her head with an insincere apology. "Sorry, baby. I'm staying."

"But you said—"

"I lied," she interrupts.

Gary growls, furious. "Don't bother showing up tomorrow."

Nina doesn't flinch.

Before any of us can react, Gary is in the car, reversing with the gas pedal pressed to the floor. Joey jumps out of the way to avoid getting clipped. Shifting to drive, Gary tears off down the street, covering us in a spray of gravel.

Waving my hand to clear the dust storm, I watch the taillights disappear in disbelief. "What the hell?! My bag's in his car."

Which means my house keys are too. I reach into my open jacket pocket, relieved to find I still have my phone and switchblade.

"I can't believe he just left us here." Tori has her hands on her hips. Looking around the dark, deserted road, she asks, "Where are we?"

"I think we're still a few miles away." Lincoln lifts his hand as if to touch her back, then stops himself and lowers it.

"There's no way I'm walking in these," she says, gesturing to her knee-high boots. She whips around and points a bladed nail at Vic. "Why do you have to be such an asshole? I swear—"

"What? She's the one who held the gun to my head." Vic jerks his chin aggressively toward Nina. "I didn't do anything wrong."

"Except have a gun to begin with!" Tori screams, her curls flailing.

"I brought it for protection," Vic argues.

"From *us*? You're fucking unbelievable."

Nina wraps an arm around Tori's shoulders, coaxing her away before it can escalate further. I turn my back to them, needing to escape the drama.

"You okay?" Joey asks, coming up beside me.

"Not even a little," I reply, taking a few steps toward the edge of the road.

He slips his arm around my waist, easing my back against him to shield me from everyone behind us. Tucking his thumb into the top of my shorts, he rests his chin on the top of my head. "Let's work on that. What do you think?"

I laugh lightly. "Go for it. Anything you can do to make this night better, I'm in." But I already feel better leaning into him. I'm convinced I could block out bombs going off—all he has to do is touch me and whisper in my ear.

I'm suddenly spun around, Joey's hands firmly gripping my hips. As aggressive as the move was, his lips don't crash down on mine. Instead they tease, barely touch. I'm breathless. I grab him by the back of the neck to pull him into me.

"Joey, give your brother a call. Maybe he can send someone to pick us up."

Yup. We're still not alone.

I ease away, my breath caught in my chest. I look around to find everyone staring at us.

Tori tilts her head to the side, not amused. "Stop groping her and get us a ride."

"There isn't a signal at The Point," Joey tells them.

Lincoln releases a heavy breath. "Shit, that's right."

"So what do we do?" I ask. I turn at the sound of a car approaching.

"Screw this," Tori says, striding out past the white line and halfway into the lane with her hip thrust out.

The headlights illuminate her fitted black shorts and sheer top over a hot-pink bra. She waves her arms in the air. They're either going to hit her or...

They swerve, missing her, and then slow to a stop along the side of the road.

"Nice," Lincoln says, impressed.

Actually, so am I.

The red pickup truck backs up, braking a few feet away.

"How do we know they're not psychos?" I ask.

"We don't," Tori says. "But we have our own psycho, so if anything, *they* should be worried." She looks toward Vic. Except he's not here. "Where'd our psycho go?"

"Vic!" Lincoln calls out.

But he doesn't appear from within the shadows of the trees where he was sulking only a moment ago.

The driver's window rolls down, and a guy with super gelled dark blond hair leans out. "Need a lift?"

Lincoln steps forward. "Yeah, man, that'd be great. Our ride ditched us. We're trying to get to The Point."

"Us too!" a voice squeals excitedly.

That's when I notice the girl with a hot-pink bobbed wig sticking her head out the small window in the back of the cab. Her face is speckled with glitter, and she's smiling so big, she's making my cheeks hurt looking at her.

"You can jump in the back," the guy tells us.

Lincoln looks around again as we near the truck. "Vic!"

"Leave him," Nina says, pulling out a bottle from her satchel of a purse. She approaches the passenger side and waves the liquor at the girl. "Can I sit up here with you?"

"Sure!" the girl exclaims. "Wow. You're so nice. Look, Seth, she's sharing with us." She scoots over to make room for Nina. "I'm Allie."

"Great," Nina replies. She tips the bottle back and chugs, preparing herself to sit next to the happiest girl on the planet.

Joey and Lincoln lower the tailgate and hop into the back before offering to help Tori and me up.

Just as Lincoln reaches to close it again, Vic's fingers curl around the metal, forcing it back down. "Hey!"

"Where were you?" Lincoln asks him in alarm. "Didn't you hear me calling you?"

"What the hell, man? Were you going to leave me?" Vic jumps up onto the truck and shoves Lincoln.

Joey leaps forward to get between them. "Don't start." His voice is low and authoritative.

No one moves. Joey looks between the two guys. Their eyes lock, silently challenging each other.

"Sit down."

Lincoln backs away and sits, resting against the cab without taking his eyes off Vic. Joey lowers himself beside me, prepared to jump back up if necessary. Vic stands defiantly, glaring at Lincoln with his fists clenched.

"Vic, sit your ass down," I tell him.

He directs his attention to me, trying to intimidate me with his scary stare. I roll my eyes. He grabs the edge of the tailgate to close it.

Tori knocks on the window. "We can go."

Vic stumbles and falls on his ass when the truck takes off. I snicker. If only he'd fallen out.

Chapter Seven

"Don't lose yourself to anyone," my aunt Allison says to me, lying on her bed, staring up at the ceiling with a funny-smelling cigarette dangling between her fingers, "not a boy or a friend or even your family. You can't care what anyone thinks of you, Lana, because as soon as you do, you're lost."

*J*oey leans back against the cab and eases me onto his lap. "I like you here."

"I like me here too," I admit, relaxing against his chest.

"How are you doing now?" he asks, his breath tickling my neck.

"Better." I smile.

He smiles back, revealing the dimple. I lean over and kiss it. I can't help myself. Joey turns his head and his lips barely brush across mine. Shooting stars surge through my entire body.

He hasn't truly kissed me yet, and the anticipation is causing my pulse to beat erratically. Seriously, I need ten minutes…twenty alone with him and we'll both be soaring. All the crazy that's happened tonight will instantly be forgotten.

Joey presses his forehead against mine. "What do you think about starting over? You know, have tonight start right now?"

"I think I like that," is released within a breath.

Joey caresses my cheek with his thumb, eliciting a shiver.

Out of the corner of my eye, I notice big blue eyes right next to my head. I lean back to find Allie's face poking through the cab window, her chin resting on her hand, staring at us dreamily.

"You two are so cute."

Tori snorts loudly. I flip her the finger.

"Here." Allie offers me the nearly depleted bottle of liquor.

I take it from her, down a shot and pass it off. I've been waiting for the buzz to kick in, to mellow me out. But this night has been anything but chill. Hopefully it will finally overtake me when we get to The Point.

"You guys know that The Point parties are exclusive, right?" Joey announces to everyone in the bed of the truck. "We're not really supposed to have access, so keep it between us. Okay?" He focuses on Vic, receiving an affirming grunt in return.

"Of course," Tori assures him.

"We won't say anything," I promise. "How do people usually get on the list?"

"All I know is that everyone on the list has to be approved. I'm not sure how they request to get on it. But they have to pay crazy money for the privilege, basically ensuring their silence, or else they're blackballed—which, in this group, is social suicide."

"How do they find out about the parties?" I ask.

I've been *dying* to go since I first found out about The Point parties two years ago. We've only ever heard whispers *after* they've happened—the secrecy heightening my obsession.

"Everyone on the list receives a text with a code on it. When they sign in, the location is revealed along with a bar code that gets them in. They can pay to bring up to six of their friends." As an afterthought, Joey adds, "Oh, phones aren't allowed inside. You have to check them in as you enter."

"Who came up with this? It's insane," I ask, impressed.

"No one knows. The organizers don't want anyone knowing their identities so they can't be influenced, or busted. This isn't exactly legal," Joey explains. "I heard they've expanded it to six different spots in three towns. I think they're trying to make it a legit business."

Tori eyes him suspiciously. "How do you know so much about it?"

Joey only shrugs with a grin that convinces me he knows someone involved.

I sink back against the side of the truck, groaning. "Wait. How much does it cost to get in? I don't have a ton of money on me." I can't waste my tip money on a party, not if I want to keep our lights on.

"You're with me tonight," Joey says, taking ahold of my hand. "Don't worry about it."

"You sure?" I ask, uncomfortable with him paying.

"Very." Joey pulls me closer to him and lowers his voice, his mouth next to my ear. "But this isn't our first date, Lana. I want to save that for another night, okay? Because I definitely want to see you again."

It sounds like a line. I should totally blow him off like I do any other guy who tries too hard. Except it doesn't *feel* like a line. Everything about him makes my heart race, causing me to do and say things I never would.

I press my lips together to hide the huge smile that wants to explode onto my face. "I want to see you again too." I am *so* pathetic tonight.

We pull through the open gates of the chain-link fence a few minutes later, entering The Point—which is a collection of old brick factory buildings and warehouses in the middle of nowhere. Some of the buildings are abandoned. Others have businesses in them. It's hard to tell the difference because they all look like they should be torn down.

The truck stops at the first building. "We'll let you off here since we have to park out back."

"Thanks for the ride," Lincoln tells him as Nina gets out of the cab and shuts the door.

"Not a problem."

"We'll look for you inside." Allie pops out of the open window and sits on the door. "Love you guys!" She remains hanging out of the truck when Seth pulls away, thrusting her arms in the air and screaming with excitement.

"What is she on?" Tori asks.

"Sunshine and fucking rainbows," Nina says, grabbing the bottle away from Lincoln.

I laugh.

"Girl talk," Tori says to Joey and Lincoln.

They nod in understanding and start walking down the alley between the first and second buildings. Vic remains behind us…somewhere. I should probably be more aware of where he is. I should also be more afraid of him than I am. But I'm not.

Tori nudges me with her shoulder to get my attention. "About earlier…I know how weird you can get about keeping your mouth shut, especially if you think it might take us down too. I won't ask. But know you have nothing to worry about. Okay?"

"We've got you," Nina pledges, passing me the bottle. "And I'll get your bag from Gary tomorrow because you know he can't fire me."

I look between her and Tori. "Thanks."

"Now what's up with you and Joey?" Nina asks with unexpected enthusiasm.

"I'm not sure. I don't know how to explain it. But whatever it is, it's…intense."

"Yeah. Anyone within ten feet of you two can smell the *intensity*." Tori shoots me a side-eyed look loaded with judgment. She takes the bottle from me.

"Ew, Tori," Nina says with a laugh.

"Stop. I'm not going to hook up with him. But let me have a little fun, okay?" I implore.

Tori lifts a shoulder in resignation.

"Speaking of fun"—I reach into my pocket and pull out the plastic bag— "look what I got us for tonight. It only cost me…well, nothing."

Nina squeals. "Let me see." She examines the bag in her palm. "There's a little of everything in here. They sell it like this?"

"They call it, 'party in a bag.'"

"That's kind of a stupid and genius name at the same time," she says, pulling the seal apart and selecting a tiny foil square labeled with a smiling mushroom sticker. "Do you trust them?"

"Can you really trust anyone with a pocketful of drugs?"

"True," Nina replies. "Well, here goes nothing." She chews the chocolate and swallows. "Let the party begin."

"Don't get lost on your trip," Tori tells Nina, taking the bag from her. She removes the small blue pill with an *X* stamped on it before handing the bag back to me.

I inspect the contents, select the brown powder capsule of Molly and toss it back with a swig from the bottle, finally starting to feel the mellowing effects of the alcohol.

"This night is going to be ridiculous!" Nina exclaims, thrusting her arms in the air with an exaggerated sway of her hips.

"Now how do we get rid of Psycho?" I tip my head slightly in Vic's direction.

"We'll lose him inside," Tori assures me. "But don't go anywhere alone. I don't trust him."

Joey and Lincoln have stopped at the end of the next building, waiting for us.

"It's insane how much he looks like Parker." Nina scans Joey, eyeing him like he's candy.

"Which is why I'm a little creeped out about you two together," Tori says to me. "But I'll lay off, I promise."

Tori hands Lincoln the bottle when we reach them. The guys finish off the last of it and toss it in a dumpster across the alley.

I notice a group of people enter a blue door farther down.

"Is that where we're going?" Nina asks.

"Yeah, that's our entrance," Joey tells us.

"There's more than one?" I'm still trying to wrap my head around this setup.

"They don't want lines outside to give away the location, so there are five entrances, and everyone's given a block of time to show up. They also need to keep us hidden from the cops."

"You seriously know a lot about this for someone who's never been," Tori notes, studying him warily.

Joey doesn't respond.

When we reach the door, Joey takes my hand. "I don't want to lose you."

I give him a gentle squeeze back, not planning on being lost.

The door cracks open, revealing a hint of the broad figure behind it. Joey releases my hand long enough to pull out his phone and bring up the code. The guy scans it with another phone, and the image disappears.

"How many?"

"Five."

"Six," Vic corrects him.

Joey's back stiffens. It's the first time I've seen him react to Vic or any of the fucked-up-ed-ness that's happened tonight.

Joey shakes his head in annoyance and says, "Six."

The door opens and we're ushered into a tight hallway. The guy locks the outside door behind us.

"Phones." He holds out a black plastic bag.

Reluctantly, I drop mine inside, followed by everyone else. A token is handed to Joey, who slips it into his front pocket.

"Hands," the doorman demands.

Joey holds out his hand, turning it over. The guy presses a stamp against the inside of his wrist. I do the same, letting him brand me with ultraviolet ink.

Once he's marked everyone, he unlocks the black door at the other end of the hallway and silently holds it open. The whole man-of-a-few-words thing he has going on is intimidating. It could also be the six-ish feet of bulging muscle. I doubt anyone's stupid enough to mess with him. And just as the thought enters my head, Vic tries to push past us, practically knocking me over.

The doorman shoves him against the wall. "Cut the shit or you're out."

Joey's hands are on my waist, steadying me. "You okay?"

I nod.

"Vic, stay the fuck away from us," Nina threatens.

We move past him, his dark eyes following us as we enter a dimly lit stairwell. A giant pink neon arrow points up, so we do as instructed and climb the stairs. I feel the bass pounding above us before I can hear the music. On the next level, a green neon star marks a red door. As soon as Joey opens it, we're engulfed by electronic beats and lasers cutting across the room.

We step inside. The door falls shut behind us as we stare in wordless wonder. I've never been to anything like this before. I can't move for a minute, needing to take it all in. The entire space is surrounded by large screens, displaying images and colors pulsing to the music. The DJ is at the far end on an elevated stage—a bouncing silhouette between a lit booth and a wall of screens. It's what I imagine a club in Vegas or LA would be like. And to think they set this up for one night in an abandoned building is beyond insane.

"I can't believe I'm here," I utter in awe.

Everywhere I look, people are dancing, even along the mezzanine that wraps around the upper level.

Joey turns to me, his eyes lit with excitement. "Ready?" He offers me his hand, eager to get lost in the crowd.

I laugh. "Yes." Taking his outstretched hand, I let him navigate us toward the stage.

I glance over my shoulder to make sure Nina, Lincoln and Tori are behind us.

"Go!" Nina yells after me, still by the door.

When I realize they aren't following, I pull Joey back toward them.

"We'll find you after we go to the bar."

"Will you hold my jacket then?" I ask her, already feeling too warm. Shrugging out of it, I toss it to Nina before they disappear in the opposite direction.

Joey clasps my hand again, and within a few feet, we're swallowed up by the crowd of jumping, swaying and grinding bodies.

When we're completely immersed somewhere in the middle of the madness, he turns to me and places his hands on my hips, drawing me to him. "We'll get a drink in a little while. I've needed this all night."

I drape my hands over his shoulders and lose myself to the bass, rolling with the wave of intoxication that has finally taken over. With his hands gripping my hips, Joey guides our bodies until they're moving in unison. He's really good at this. Maybe *too* good because I'm so overwhelmed by the feel of him against me that everyone else disappears. His hands glide from my hips to the small of my back, pressing me firmly against him. If we were any closer, we'd dissolve into each other.

I've never wanted a guy this badly before. Then again, a guy's never made me *feel* like this before. My body responds to his slightest touch. My pulse quickens every time his voice rumbles low in my ear. I'm held captive by him—willingly. I could seep into his skin and lose myself.

Joey dips his head down and slides his mouth along my neck. I draw in a quick breath. When he reaches my lips, he breathes against them, continuing to tease and torment me. I close my eyes, needing to taste him, but he refuses to kiss me. I exhale slowly, unraveling.

A few songs later, a tap on the shoulder wakes me from my Joey-induced haze. Tori is standing next to us with Lincoln and Nina dancing behind her. We separate to include them. Nina hands me a bottle of water with a knowing wink, and I could kiss her. My mouth is so dry, it's like I've swallowed sand.

Every so often Joey brushes his hand against mine, playfully interlacing our fingers. I know he's trying not to give Tori a reason to throw her drink on him. But it's too hard for us to resist. We're overcome with a compulsion to touch. Within a song, he surrenders to the pull, moving in close behind me. I wrap my arms around his neck, and he trails his hand down my side. Our bodies ease together in a fluid, singular motion.

"I think I need a drink," Joey murmurs in my ear before tasting the sweat on my neck.

I squeeze his hands on my hips. "Yeah, me too." I look to Tori and Nina. "Bar?"

They nod and we cut through the crowd to the other end of the open space.

Just when the dancers start to thin out, we run into a wall of people waiting to order drinks at the glowing square bar.

"There you are!" I look back to see a hand on Joey's shoulder. "I thought I told you to stay downstairs when you got here and I'd come give you your keys."

I turn to find Parker Harrison standing before us.

Parker and Joey may look alike in many ways, but while Joey's disheveled and sexy, Parker's polished and powerful. Joey's hair is displaced from raking his fingers through it, and Parker's is trimmed and neatly parted to the side. Joey's boyishly charming in an untucked button-down while Parker's jaw-droppingly kempt in a sports jacket. He looks…important.

I find myself captivated by eyes the same shade of electric blue as the boy I've been grinding against for the past hour. But I don't expect the betrayal I see reflected back in them. Whatever lecture he was about to give his brother about being here is lost.

"Lana? What are you doing here?"

"Hi, Parker." My stomach twists when his focus darts from Joey to me in confusion.

"You know each other?" Joey asks.

"Yeah," Parker replies, sounding distant as he pins me with a questioning stare.

I don't say anything. There isn't anything to say. But I don't look away either, even though I should.

"Lana's here with me tonight."

I can feel the weight of Joey's arm around my shoulder, claiming me.

Parker tears his attention away from me and gives his brother a pitying look. Then he laughs this amused, almost maniacal laugh. "Are you sure about that?"

"Hey, Parker." Nina steps between us, stopping directly in front of him, her chest brushing against his. "Buy me a drink?"

Parker eases his hand along her waist and places a ghost of a kiss on her cheek. "Hey, gorgeous. Maybe later? I have to go take care of something."

Nina visibly deflates but recovers quickly. "No problem."

Lengthening her spine, she turns and walks briskly away. I almost shiver from the ice rolling off her.

I step out from under Joey's territorial limb and follow after her. Tori comes up beside me and makes a pained face when I look at her.

"I know, right?! What the hell was that about?" I huff.

But Tori's expression doesn't change. Clearly she wasn't listening. She runs a knuckle under her eye, indicating I should do the same.

I swipe my finger to remove the smeared makeup. "Better?"

Tori shakes her head with a grimace, like it hurts her to see me like this. "You're a mess."

I glance down at the rivulets of sweat running down my chest, disappearing into my cleavage, forming dark blue wet marks under my boobs. Tori's right. I'm a disaster.

"I'll be right back," I tell her, needing to disappear immediately.

She nods, hurrying me past her.

"Lana!" Joey calls after me.

"Relax. She's just going to the bathroom," I hear Tori tell him. "You can live without her for ten minutes."

I spot flashing neon lights in the left corner, animating a girl dancing. There's one of a guy fist-pumping directly across from it. They have to be the bathrooms.

I swipe my fingers under my eyes again and keep my head down, not wanting anyone to see the mascara melting down my face.

An arm wraps around my waist and I'm swept into the darkness under the stairs.

"Why are you here with my brother?"

"Holy shit, Parker!" I exclaim breathlessly, lowering the elbow that was inches from smashing his nose.

"Tell me," he demands impatiently, remaining way too close. I attempt to take a step back, but his arm tightens around my waist. "You've refused to go out with me every time I've asked. My brother's home for a day and you're here with *him?*"

"Really?" I huff, pushing at his chest to separate us.

Parker releases me and gestures impatiently when I don't continue.

"Lincoln asked Tori to a party tonight. And it turns out, Lincoln and Joey are friends, which I'm sure you know. We're all here together. But it's not like you have any claim. You know that."

"Why do you have to be so difficult?"

Parker takes a step toward me, and I mimic it with a step back.

"You know why." It's a conversation we've had too many times over the past year, and my answer's not going to change.

"I don't have to see her again. You know what it's like with her. We're not *together*," he pleads. "We use each other. That's it."

"And that makes it better? She's one of my best friends. You became untouchable to me the moment you touched her. You know my rule."

I know what the two of them have doesn't mean anything. Nina pretty much repeats the same thing Parker just said. But they still get together, no matter how toxic whatever they have is. *Respect* and *Confidence*—like fire and an accelerant, their curses are a dangerous combination. They're constantly tearing each other apart—when they're not...well, tearing each other apart.

He growls in frustration. "Don't start anything with my brother." His words have an underlying threat to them.

"What?! You don't have a say in that either!"

"Lana, don't..." Before he can finish whatever asinine thing he's about to say, I clench my teeth to keep from screaming and stalk past him. "Lana!"

"Stay away from me, Parker!" I yell over my shoulder, hurriedly squeezing by people to increase the distance between us. My shoulder collides with a body.

"Lana?"

I slowly look up to find a guy with wavy brown hair and big dark eyes looking down at me. I scan the mold of the navy T-Shirt over his sculpted chest and the way his snug jeans fit perfectly. He's hot. Then I meet his eyes again and realize who he is. Holy shit.

"Mr. Garner?"

I instantly want to die. I just thought my guidance counselor was *hot*. But, in my defense, he looks way different without the glasses and tie. *Way* different.

"Isaac," he corrects quickly, looking around like we might get caught doing something wrong. "What are you doing here?" Before I can answer, he says, "Forget it. Where's Tori?"

I tip my head toward the line at the bar. He looks in her direction and nods, even though she's hidden within the crowd.

"I can't believe you're here," he says, shaking his head. "Actually, if any of my students could get into this place, it'd be you and Tori. I swear it'll be a miracle if you two graduate in one piece."

I often think the same thing. "Wasn't expecting to see *you* either."

"You probably don't know, but I grew up in Oaklawn. I went to school with a lot of people here."

"How old are you?" I ask automatically.

I always thought he was old, like thirty or something. Maybe it's the tie…or seeing him sitting behind a desk, surrounded by inspirational quotes. But tonight, dressed like a normal guy, he doesn't look much older than…Parker.

"Old enough to know I shouldn't be caught drinking with you," he replies. "I didn't see you tonight. And you didn't see me."

"I don't even know who you are," I say, which isn't far from the truth.

Isaac laughs. Even thinking his first name feels wrong. "Be good, Lana. Don't get into trouble." Then he walks off.

Talk about weird. This night cannot get any more twisted. And just as I think it, I wish I hadn't. The last thing I want to do is tempt Fate. We don't have a good history.

"Hey! There you are! I thought I'd lost you. Wait. Where are the rest of your friends? Are you lost? Do you need me to help you find them?"

I remain still, staring up at the willowy girl with bright pink hair in a turquoise bandeau and matching sequined miniskirt.

"It's Allie!"

"Umm, yeah. I remember." Like there's any way I could possibly forget. "They're in line at the bar. I have to use the bathroom."

"Me too!" she exclaims. "I found this super-secret bathroom upstairs that doesn't have a line. Wanna come?!"

I eye the football field length line waiting to get in the girls' bathroom. "Sure."

Allie takes my hand and leads me up the stairs. Looking down from here, I can see how big this place truly is. It's crazy-huge. The entire mezzanine is lined with black curtains, making it feel more private and…sinister. I watch a girl in a metallic dress disappear into the dark with a bottle and glasses on her tray. It takes a moment for my eyes to adjust before I see the groups of people on lush couches concealed within the shadows. I can only imagine what they're doing back there.

"So there's this office or something hidden up here with a bathroom in it. Another girl showed me earlier," Allie tells me.

She pulls back a section of the heavy curtain next to a black door, casting light into the dark space. I quickly duck through the opening and she follows, concealing us behind the fabric wall.

Light shines through a window-lined office where four girls wait to use the bathroom. When we enter, the first thing I notice is an oversized ornate mirror propped on a metal desk. A girl's leaning in close to it, lining her eyes. When I approach it, I immediately cringe at my reflection. No wonder Joey hasn't kissed me.

I slide my headband off and let my hair down, shaking out the sweat-soaked strands. I rake my fingers through the length that extends to my lower back before sweeping it up into a large twisted bun and securing it on top of my head, sliding the crystal headband back in place. That's a *little* better.

"Is your hair white?" Allie asks.

I turn with a start, unaware she was hovering.

"It's blond. It's just really light."

She's not the first to mistake my hair for being white. Although it's usually little kids I'm correcting.

"You should totally color it white," she says to my reflection, stepping closer to the mirror without blinking her eyes. "You would look like a frost princess. But you really *do* look like a princess." She reaches out to touch me, the reflected me, running a finger along my headband. "It's so sparkly."

"Uh, thanks. My mother gave it to me." I watch her curiously. She's definitely…unique.

Allie spins around to face me, the real me, and throws her arms around my neck. "You're *so* beautiful," she says, hugging me tight. She steps back, holding me at arm's length, and just stares at me like she's trying to decide if I'm real. "I'm so high."

I nod. Really? I mean, the wide, unblinking eyes pretty much gave that away. And for the first time, I recognize I'm feeling pretty floaty myself—but definitely not lost in the stratosphere like Allie.

"You gotta go?" a thin brunette in boy shorts and a bikini top asks, motioning toward the bathroom that just opened up.

"I do," I answer. And I also need the sink to clean off the black streaks running down my face. I look like I've been crying mud.

I ease out of Allie's grip and enter the bathroom.

When I come back out, Allie's still there. I'm not sure why. Maybe she thinks we're friends now. Except…we're not.

I inspect the sweat marks on my top in the mirror. Pulling the fabric away from my skin, I flap it gently, hoping it'll dry.

"Want to go outside?" Allie asks. "It's so hot in here." She plops down on the desk, like she's too weak to stand. "I need some air."

She looks out of it. I'm worried she may pass out, and there's no way I can hold her up.

"Where can we go?"

"This way," she says, crisscrossing her long legs as she weaves toward the door. "Why am I so hot? This is so not good, my princess."

"It's okay," I assure her, taking her by the elbow to steer her through the curtain so that she doesn't grab on to it and pull it down. "Which way?"

"That way." Allie points right.

I direct us through the black door, entering a stairwell.

"That way again." Her finger indicates a blue door with *Exit* lit above it.

I push through and find a small group of people smoking on a fire escape suspended above the alley between two buildings.

Allie stumbles out of my grasp and trots down a few feet before collapsing on a grated metal step. "Omigod. My skin needed this so bad." She flops her arms over the railing in blissful relief.

"Water?" some guy asks, offering her a bottle.

"You are so super sweet," she says, looking up at him with her big blue eyes and thousand-watt smile.

I grab the bottle from him first to make sure it's sealed before letting her have it.

When she dumps half of it in her mouth, she releases an obnoxiously loud moan. "Best. Water. Ever."

"Glad I could make you happy," the guy says with a creepy, predator smile.

I turn to him, knowing he's lingering because he thinks he has a chance with her. "Get lost."

He scowls and goes back into the building. That's when I notice the black boots on the steps next to my head. And, of course, I find Vic, the master scowler, doing exactly that down at me.

I let out a disgusted breath and focus on Allie, pointedly ignoring him. "How are you feeling?"

"I'm so happy," she responds, beaming. "Here, have some." She hands me the bottle of water before taking ahold of the railing to pull herself up.

I easily finish it and abandon the empty bottle on the step. "Thanks."

Allie stares at me with that same doe-eyed expression she wore in the truck. "You could be a fairy, you know. You have the biggest black eyes."

"They're brown."

"A little, tiny nose, kissed with stardust."

"Or freckles."

"And super-pointy cheekbones. Do you have pointy ears too?"

She tips her head to look, like she expects they might be.

"I don't."

"All you need are wings and you'd be my fairy princess." She places her palms on my cheeks and speaks in a high-pitched voice, "I wish I could shrink you and put you in my pocket."

I have no idea what she's talking about. She's delusional. I need to get her back to her boyfriend.

"Where's Seth? Let's go find him. I'm sure my friends are wondering where I am too." Or at least I hope they are.

"You do have wings! They're just hiding!" Allie declares when I turn to walk toward the door. She traces a finger along my right shoulder blade. "You *are* my fairy princess!"

"Yup, you're right," I say with a sigh.

When I glance at her over my shoulder, I realize Vic is gone—which is a good and bad thing. Good because I can't stand to be within two feet of him. Bad because now I have no idea where he is again, and I still don't trust him not to do something stupid.

I reach for the door at the same time it pushes open. A girl steps out and I slide by her.

"Allie!" I hear her screech in excitement right before the door clicks shut behind me.

I groan into the empty stairwell, knowing Allie's no longer following me. I'd much rather be drinking and dancing with my friends, but I can't leave her. She's a disaster. I have to help her find Seth. I'm blaming the drugs for my uncharacteristic kindness.

I set my hand on the release bar. As the door cracks open, I'm forcefully yanked from behind and slammed against the wall. Pain floods my head when it collides with the concrete. I blink to clear the spots from my eyes, disoriented. Something hard pokes my ribs and a forearm presses against my chest, pinning me. I pull at the arm, then grunt when the object jabs into me. It's a gun.

How many guns does he have? Did he get this back from Nina? Why am I thinking about this right now?

"You're not going to say anything about what happened tonight," Vic demands, his rank breath invading my senses.

I stab him a thousand times with my glare. When I refuse to answer, he thrusts his weight against me, crushing my chest. I grit my teeth in pain.

"Right?"

"I'm not going to say anything," I growl. "Now get off me!"

I try to push him, but he shoves me back against the concrete, banging my head again. I cry out, overcome with blinding pain.

"If you do, I'll hurt you," he threatens. "I mean, *really* hurt you."

"Hey! Get off my fairy princess!" Before I can react, Allie jumps on Vic's back. "Leave her alone!"

"What the— Get off me, you psycho!" Vic bellows as she wraps an arm around his neck and pounds his back with her fist.

Vic steps back. I move to get out from under his arm, but he lunges forward, trapping me again. He whips the hand holding the gun over his shoulder and hits Allie on the side of the head.

"Ow!" she yelps, releasing him and landing with a hard thud on her feet. She staggers backward, her hand cradling her head. "That hurt."

"You asshole!" I jam my knee between his legs.

Vic moans in pain and bends in half, cupping himself. Clasping my hands together, I swing up as hard as I can, colliding with his jaw. Vic's head flips up with a howl. He stumbles back, slamming into Allie.

REBECCA DONOVAN

Allie pounds his arm with the sides of her fists. "You're so mean!"

Vic reaches out and clutches Allie by the throat. She claws at his hand, making gurgling noises. As I rush toward him, he stares at me, his dark brows dipping to shadow his eyes. A malevolent, bloody smile creeps across his face, causing me to falter in my steps. If evil has a face, he's staring at me right now. I know exactly what he's about to do the second before he does it.

"No!"

I reach for Allie…just as Vic tosses her down the stairs.

Chapter Eight

"Where's my daddy?" I ask.

Everyone stops eating. My aunt Allison's fork clangs on her plate. I look at my mom. She doesn't say anything.

"He's gone, baby girl," my grandmother tells me, running her hand over my head.

A sharp cry escapes and my mom cups a hand over her mouth to trap it as tears fill her eyes. She looks like she's in so much pain.

I never ask about my dad again.

Allie's scream echoes throughout the stairwell 'til it's abruptly cut off when she collides with the first step. Her body continues to haphazardly tumble with thuds and clangs down the metal stairs, coming to a violent stop on the concrete landing.

I remain frozen with my mouth gaping open in a silent scream.

Allie doesn't make a sound—not a groan or a cry, despite the awkward angle her leg is bent beneath her. Her arms are splayed above her head. Blood slowly seeps out from under her short blond hair, pooling into a crimson halo around her head.

"Allie?" My voice is weak, like I've been screaming this whole time.

She doesn't move.

I take a step, about to go to her, when a hysterical voice turns me around. "What did you do?"

I stare into the frantic wide eyes of the girl from the fire escape, the one Allie hugged.

"Did you...did you push her?" But it's not really a question. It's an accusation.

I can see the blame in her glassy-eyed stare. But she's not focused on my face; she's looking down...at my hand clutching Allie's pink wig. I drop it like it's burning my skin. Panic begins to creep over me like crawling vines.

"You did. You pushed her." Her words are thorns, penetrating my flesh.

I take a step back, shaking my head. My lungs constrict, and I can't draw in enough air. This can't be happening. She stares at me like I'm some kind of monster, and I want to shrink into nothing. I take another step backward. She opens her mouth. I shake my head faster, silently begging. I continue to increase the distance between us, moving farther away from her. I need to disappear before she—

A horrific, bloodcurdling scream vibrates throughout my bones.

Doors click open. Two large bodies in black rush by from behind, brushing past me. Several more people enter from the fire escape. Their faces blur. I'm unable to focus. Color and voices move around me. But no one goes to her. Allie's still lying in her blood, needing someone to save her. My heart is beating so fast, I have to press my hand to the wall to stay on my feet.

"What's wrong?" a girl asks, her attention drawn to the screaming girl, yet to notice the broken body at the bottom of the stairs.

But the massive bouncer who first entered sees Allie and his stature changes, taking on an authoritative stance. His voice bellows, "Get them out of here!"

The other body in black forces the small group back onto the fire escape, keeping the devastation hidden behind him. The screaming girl is sobbing now, the only one left in the stairwell...other than me. But no one seems to notice me, except for her. She grasps the muscular arm of the bouncer closest to her, pointing... directly at me. But he's too busy locking the door leading to the fire escape.

The bouncer in charge lowers his voice and speaks into the cuff of his shirt, "I need the E team to stairwell five. Now."

Air moves around me as the door behind me is shoved open again. A different guy dressed in black hurries by me.

I slip through the opening just as I hear the lead bouncer shout orders at him, "Lock down all entrance points into this stairwell. Don't let anyone come or—"

And then the door clicks shut, cutting him off.

A tall, thinner, but no less intimidating, male moves in front of the closed door with his arms crossed in front of him.

I turn and take a step into the dark, my senses overwhelmed with the sudden inundation of strobing lights and pounding bass. I stare, unfocused, and release a quivering breath. I can't feel a thing other than the frantic beat of my heart. Bodies dance seductively along the railing, arms floating in the air, hands gripping hips. I remain paralyzed by the twisting vines of panic around my limbs.

Hands grip my shoulders. I blink up into bright blue eyes.

"Lana? Are you okay?" Parker examines my face with concern.

I can't find the words to respond to his question. Am I okay? No. I'm not. I am so far from being okay that I am nothing.

He calls to me again, "Lana?"

I fight to break free from the suffocating panic holding me mute.

"Parker?" I utter feebly.

None of this feels real. I'm stuck in a slow-moving dream.

"Are you hurt?" he asks when I continue to stand there, staring into his eyes.

He scans my body, searching for injuries. His inspection comes to a sudden halt. Parker wraps his hands around my wrists and holds them up. A spray of blood glistens along the back of my left hand, and pink hairs are entangled around the fingers of my right. I yank free from his grip, my pulse firing rapidly.

Parker reaches into his pocket and hands me a pressed handkerchief. I take it from him and frantically scrub at my hands, smearing red stains on the pristine white cloth.

Raising his right cuff to his mouth, Parker talks into it, "Find my brother. Tell him I need him on the mezzanine. Now."

I inspect my trembling hands, turning them over to make sure I'm rid of all the evidence. Parker eases the cloth from my grip, stuffing it into his pants pocket.

He gently cups my face. "Everything's going to be okay."

I'm lost to my hyperventilating breaths, unable to connect with what he's telling me.

"Lana?" He forces me to focus on him. "I've got this. But you need to leave. Okay?"

Panic wraps around me again, squeezing tighter and tighter.

"Don't say anything to anyone about what happened," Parker instructs.

"But I didn't—" I begin in a rush.

"Don't," he interrupts firmly. "Not a word."

He thinks I did it, that I pushed her—just like the screaming girl in the stairwell.

Parker leans in and presses a kiss to my forehead, murmuring, "I'll take care of everything."

I take a step back, at a loss. He truly believes I'm capable of *that?*

"What's going on?" Joey asks from behind Parker. "Some guy said…"

Parker turns to face his brother.

"Lana?" Joey looks from me to Parker. "Everything okay?"

"No," Parker responds, his spine lengthening with his cursed *Confidence*. "A girl fell down the stairs. The EMTs are taking her to the hospital, but I need you and Lana to leave in case the cops show up." He reaches into his pocket and pulls out a car key. "There's a door on the opposite side, downstairs. Go through it. Take the elevator to the first level. Your Jeep will be there along with your phone. I'll get her friends and meet you"—he hesitates for a moment— "at the golf course. Wait for me."

Parker looks to me again, caressing my cheek, "Say nothing."

Joey takes hold of my hand. "I've got her."

Parker looks down at our clasped hands and scowls.

In the next second, Joey is guiding me along the mezzanine. I look back just as Parker disappears through the black door leading to the stairwell, talking into his cuff.

Joey navigates us down the stairs and around the perimeter of the crowded dance floor. Bodies brush by in a streak of color and jostling of flesh. I can't focus on anything other than the hand holding mine and the blue shirt in front of me.

When we reach the black door concealed in the dark corner, Joey knocks and an unseen hand immediately opens it. It falls closed behind us after we pass through. A tall guy with a blond buzz cut stands behind it silently. He struts over to what looks like a closed garage door and pulls on a strap, revealing a freight elevator. We enter and the door comes crashing down behind us, shutting us off from the booming music and chattering voices.

Within the quiet box, the inner chaos overtakes me—Vic's threats, Allie's fall, the girl's screaming, Parker's warning... I collapse against the wall, my unfocused eyes trained on the floor. My mind is whirling. My pulse is thrumming. I clench my shaking fists and concentrate on breathing, trying to free myself of panic's strong hold.

"Lana." Joey's voice finds me, deep and soothing.

I lift my head.

Joey has the elevator control in his hand, his eyes steadied on me. He doesn't say anything for a moment, just holds me in his brilliant blue gaze.

"Nothing bad's going to happen to you, I promise." He sounds so certain, like he has the ability to control our fate. "Do you believe me?"

I blink away the tears stinging my eyes and swallow against the lump lodged in my throat. "It's too late."

I cover my eyes with a hand, wanting to hide from the cruel reality. Images too real and graphic to ever forget... Allie sprawled motionless, her blood seeping into the concrete around her. The cold disconnect in Vic's eyes just before he shoved her. And me, standing above Allie with her bright pink wig clenched in my fist, unable to move. Then there's that scream…that high-pitch, horror-movie scream. I swear it's still ringing in my ears.

And I *left* Allie…at the bottom of those stairs. I abandoned her. I should have stayed with her. I don't even know if she was still breathing.

"We need to go back. I need to make sure she's still alive," I plead, strangling a sob.

"The girl? You were there?" His tone is gentle.

I nod. "It was Allie, the girl from the truck. I tried…" My voice breaks as I struggle to speak. "I tried to reach her before he pushed her, but I couldn't."

"Who pushed her?" Joey asks cautiously.

"Vic." His name escapes before I can capture it. I bite my lip to keep from saying more.

I'm not usually this careless. I blame my chemically altered state for allowing the honesty to slip out. This isn't me. I don't overreact like this. I'm the one who holds it together when shit gets bad. But right now, I don't have control over my mind or my body, no matter how hard I fight for it.

Joey's quiet. I watch him carefully, attempting to read the contemplation reflected in his eyes. I try to convince myself that this wasn't a secret I needed to keep. Vic isn't someone I need to protect. But Joey is. And now that he knows the truth, I'm not sure what he'll do with it.

Joey drops the elevator control and slowly walks to me, encircling me in his arms. As soon as he touches me, my breath evens out and the crushing sensation in my chest releases. I squeeze him tight, burying my face in his shoulder, but I don't allow myself to cry. He holds me until the tension in my muscles dissipates and the shaking subsides. His lips press against my temple, and the last tendrils of panic fall away.

I tip my head up.

Joey brushes a strand of hair from my cheek. "There's nothing you can do if we go back. Parker said they were taking her to the hospital. Let's wait and find out if she's okay before we decide what to do, alright?"

I nod, convinced leaving is the best option. He wraps his arms around me one more time, giving me the strength I need to stand on my own before he lets go.

"Ready to get out of here?"

"Yeah," I breathe out, feeling calmer.

Joey pushes the button to lower the elevator, and when he opens it, we step out into a kind of parking lot on the ground floor, presumably for everyone working here. Joey's red Jeep is at the far end, parked in front of the large sliding doors. Holding my hand, he weaves through the maze of cars until we reach it. Joey's cell phone is on the driver's seat. Mine isn't here. I hope Parker will know to bring it with him. I can't afford to lose it.

Two guys in black slide the giant barnlike metal doors open. Joey starts up the Jeep. I half-expect to see red and blue strobes flashing from an ambulance or a police car, but I'm not really surprised when I don't.

Just before Joey pulls forward, a black van flies by the entrance. Joey and I exchange a silent glance, knowing that Allie must be in that van.

Just like the door we entered in the corner of the club, the private garage entrance slides shut behind us as soon as we pull out. We drive through The Point in the dark. Joey doesn't turn on the headlights until we pass the gates and reach the road.

We don't say anything as we drive along the deserted, winding road. I stare out at nothing. The Jeep's top is off and the wind whips loose strands of hair around my head. Joey hands me a sweatshirt when I shiver. I take it from him and slip it on, inhaling the detergent combined with his distinct scent—a mixture of grass and rain.

I lean my forehead against the window, my thoughts continuing to jump around. I close my eyes and inhale deeply. This day should never have happened.

I can sit here and dissect everything I could have done differently from the moment I woke up. But I know everything that's gone wrong tonight is because of Vic.

I clench my jaw so tight, my teeth feel like they might shatter. If I ever see him again, I'm going to *kill* him.

"Why was Vic with you tonight?"

Joey glances at me quickly before looking back to the road. "You don't have to worry. Parker won't bring him to the country club."

"That's not why I'm asking."

Joey shifts uncomfortably. "We're not friends, like I said. We go to the same boarding school. His mother died of cancer a few months ago, and my father asked me to...I don't know, make sure he's okay. My family knows his family. Our fathers went to college together."

"Did you know he was a psychopath?"

"No!" Joey answers adamantly, turning his head to me. "He's not the nicest guy, but I never would've believed he'd push a girl down the stairs. Or that he'd bring a gun. I'm really sorry, Lana, for everything he's done."

"It's not your fault," I reply quietly, sinking into the seat. "His father...is he...powerful?" I have to know what I'm up against since I seem to be the only witness to the truth.

"Vic lives with his grandfather," Joey responds carefully.

When he doesn't say more, I silently urge him to answer the question.

Joey nods regretfully. "He has a lot of connections. He'll cover this up before Vic is accused of anything. That's why I said we should wait to see what happens with Allie before we decide what to do. If it comes down to his word against yours, it won't be good."

I laugh humorlessly. "Of course, because the truth *never* wins." I say this more to myself than to Joey. I turn away from him, the muscles in my jaw knotting up again.

The engine whirring and the tires crunching along the dirt road fill the silence. Staring out the side window, I attempt to focus on our surroundings for the first time since we veered off Sherling's paved roads. I have no idea where we are. It's dark. There aren't any streetlights...or houses. Just woods. The forest appears endless. The tall silhouettes feel like they're closing in around us.

I've never been outside of Sherling before tonight. That town has a way of trapping people within its borders. They're deceived into believing their miserable existence is an inescapable sentence of minimum wage jobs and child support payments.

I can't say I'm convinced there's something better waiting for me outside Sherling, but I refuse to be another one of its stories—predictable and meaningless, doomed to repeat itself. Always the same ending. But, after tonight, I don't think I'll have a say in what happens to me. Maybe I never did.

Parker's words find their way back to me in the quiet. *"Say nothing."*

I know he didn't tell me this to protect me. If Parker really believes I pushed Allie, then he *knows* I'd never admit to it. And Vic isn't the reason either. He didn't even know Vic was with us. And then I remember how he took charge of everything. Insisting Joey leave with me. Confident Allie would be taken to the hospital. Securing our quick exit with just a few words spoken into his cuff.

Parker needs my silence to protect himself.

"Parker's one of the organizers, isn't he?"

Joey hesitates before responding. "You know I can't say anything," he says, concern evident on his face.

But I don't need Joey to confirm it. I know. Parker's always been one to take risks in the name of success. He's cursed with *Confidence*. Failure has never been an option for him. He was our source of amphetamines a couple summers ago when we first started doing everything our parents told us not to. I've heard he's had his hands in other recreational habits as well. He's discreet, so I don't know anything for certain. He's been good at keeping a low profile while being successful at whatever he does. Apparently, he's been busy moving up in the world—fast.

"I won't tell anyone," I promise. "But if the police find out he's one of the people running an illegal club, then…"

"It would be *really* bad for him, especially if someone got seriously hurt," Joey finishes, his meaning understood.

"Right."

A dark pit opens up in the bottom of my stomach. There isn't anything I can do to make this right. The one person who deserves to go down for this is evidently untouchable—and not just because his grandfather would pay to cover it up, but because everyone I remotely care about would suffer, myself included, if I told the truth. I clench my jaw, fighting the urge to scream.

Joey clears his throat, drawing my attention away from all the ways my life sucks right now. "I probably don't want to know this, but how do you know my brother?"

I stop breathing with the question, not sure how honest I should be. I'm not about to tell him that Parker was my first kiss. I don't think Parker even knows he was my first kiss. It was two summers ago. I was thirteen, almost fourteen— don't want it to sound *that* bad. Parker and Joey are from Oaklawn, so Parker didn't know anything about me. He thought I was sixteen—not because I told him. He assumed, and I didn't correct him.

Tori and I learned the art of dressing a certain way and applying makeup just right so that we appeared older. I started covering shifts for my mother at Stella's around that time, so I'd also acquired the attitude to back it up. No one's ever questioned my age, even if I can barely see over the bar. It's all in how you present yourself to the world, and I had no fucks to give...until tonight. It helps that I possess an ID that says I'm twenty-two. None of the bars we go to ever blink twice at it. But we live in Sherling. They'd rather have the bodies in the bar and money in their tills.

The first party Tori and I crashed was this high school party at a two-family house a few streets over from Tori's place. Parker was there on "business," just stopping in on his way to a party of his own. But he ended up staying. I may have had something to do with that. He was smooth—still is—saying all the right things and focused on me like I was the only girl in the room. As aloof as I may have tried to act, I was jumping around and screaming with excitement on the inside. Here I was, at my first party, and this absolutely gorgeous guy was hitting on me. I wanted to die!

I did my best to play hard to get. I didn't give him my number when he asked for it. Actually, he *still* doesn't have my number. But when he leaned over in that dark corner I was pressed against, his arm resting on the wall above my head, I didn't move. I didn't push him away. I didn't turn my head. I stood there, perfectly still, and let him press his lips to mine. He teased with slow, playful kisses. And when his tongue entered my mouth, he was slow and gentle. It was…perfect. I think my knees would have given out if the wall hadn't been holding me up.

That was the first and last time Parker Harrison ever kissed me. And it's *the* kiss I will never forget.

Parker must have asked around about me after that because the next time we saw him out, he was pissed. Kissing a thirteen-year-old wasn't exactly good for his reputation, no matter how old he *thought* I was. He had just graduated and wouldn't have been caught dead with a junior, forget about a girl who hadn't even entered high school. Then he saw Nina with us…

Once *they* happened, he was completely off-limits to me. Even when he came around again and got to know me better.

I refuse to give him a chance, no matter how many times he asks.

I must have been quiet too long because Joey suddenly says, "Forget it. Don't tell me."

"It's not like that. We just…see him around," I assure him, trying to sound casual. "He and Nina have a thing. Or whatever. And he sometimes goes to the same bars we do in Sherling."

"You have a fake ID?" Joey asks in surprise.

"You don't?"

Joey shrugs. "I don't really use it. It's one of Parker's old ones. I've never tried to get into bars. The town where I go to school is too small. I'm afraid I'd get busted with it. But I buy beer outside of town sometimes." He shifts uncomfortably again. "So…he and Nina, not…" Joey shakes his head. "Never mind."

"Nothing's going on between me and Parker."

"Sorry," he says with a weak smile. "It's happened before…"

I laugh. "You and your brother have hooked up with the same girl?"

"No," he replies adamantly. "This girl and Parker had a…*thing*, and when he ended it, she thought I could be the perfect revenge. Except, I couldn't stand to talk to her, let alone kiss her."

"If I remember right, you don't need to talk to kiss," I tease.

I swear his cheeks redden. "You know what I mean."

I've been trying to figure out Joey's curse since the party. But whatever it is, it isn't obvious. As much as he looks like a mussed, youthful version of Parker, he is *nothing* like him. And so…I guess I should stop comparing them.

"I wouldn't use you as revenge," I tell him sincerely. "I'm not interested in your brother. Most of the time, I wish I didn't know him."

"Me too."

I roll my head against the seat to face him, my cheek pressed against the cool leather, expecting him to be joking. But he just stares out the windshield, his expression a bit solemn. When Joey looks over at me, he offers a half-smile, just enough to give a hint to the dimple on his right cheek.

"This night…" He lets out a dry laugh before looking back out the windshield with a shake of his head. "I'd say I wish it was over, except…" He looks at me again, peering right into my eyes. "I keep thinking it'll get better."

"It did. For a couple hours," I say with a weak smile.

The Jeep slows and Joey turns down a dark drive. The headlights shine on a large wooden sign—*Oaklawn Country Club*. We follow a long road that splits the golf course in half, eventually reaching an expansive building with a wall of windows.

A small *Clubhouse* sign is posted in the middle of a dimly lit circular drive where a chandelier glows above carved wooden doors. The building is dark with no signs of movement behind the glass. Joey continues to the left side of the clubhouse where a *Deliveries* sign beckons us into the shadows.

Parking the Jeep on the far side of the dumpster, Joey shuts off the engine.

We're not completely concealed here, but at least the Jeep won't be obvious if someone drives by. Unbuckling his seat belt, Joey shifts to face me. He doesn't say anything. We just look at each other, a thousand words confessed within a few seconds of silence.

"You going to be okay?" he asks. The question he's asked so much tonight.

"If I'd known—"

The ringing of his phone keeps the truth from leaping off the tip of my tongue.

Joey looks from me to his beckoning phone, hesitant. He lifts it from the cup holder. "It's Parker," he says apologetically, sliding his thumb across Parker's face to answer it.

Panic rushes in like it never left, quickening my heartbeat, stealing my breath and tying my stomach into intricate knots. I fight the urge to rip the phone out of his hand and demand to know if Allie's okay…if she's alive.

I stare at Joey as he listens, trying to read the expression on his face with each nod. But he won't look at me, and his eyes give nothing away. I'm about ready to scream when he shifts and holds out the phone.

"Parker wants to talk to you."

I stare at it without making a move to take it, suddenly afraid to know the truth. I glance at Joey. His brows rise in encouragement. I smile weakly and accept it, slowly bringing it to my ear.

"Yeah?" My voice is weak.

Music blasts through the speaker. I can hear Tori and Nina singing out of tune at the top of their lungs.

"Hello?" I say louder when no one responds.

"You have nothing to worry about." Parker's distinct voice cuts through the noise.

"What do you mean?" I can feel Joey watching me. "Is she—"

"She's fine, Lana. A broken leg and a concussion. But she'll recover," Parker assures me. "And no one saw you. The guys who found her are contracted not to disclose anything. Keep quiet, and all's good. Nothing's going to happen to you. *I've* got you."

"Okay," I respond quietly, trying to let it all sink in, ignoring the fact that he still thinks I'm the reason she ended up at the bottom of the stairs. And he obviously doesn't know about the screaming girl who thinks the same thing.

"Who are you talking to?" Nina demands impatiently, her voice slurred.

"I'll see you in a bit," Parker says, hanging up before I can ask which hospital she's at.

I slowly lower the phone and hand it back to Joey.

"She's going to be okay." Joey reaches for my hand, enveloping it in his warmth.

Tension immediately seeps from my muscles. Just like that…I can breathe again, my chest visibly collapsing with the release of air.

"Would Parker lie? Do you think she's really okay?" I ask, knowing how much trouble this could mean for Parker. I've learned to never underestimate what someone is capable of when they're desperate and have everything to lose.

Joey hesitates thoughtfully. "I don't know how he could cover it up. He's done some questionable things to protect himself, but…he's not a bad guy."

"How can he keep someone from talking?" Regardless of whatever influence Parker has over people, I strongly doubt his weak threats of denied access to a party or social suicide would keep mouths shut.

"I don't think he can," Joey answers simply. "But what can they say other than a girl fell? No one knows, not even the people working there, that he's one of the organizers. And only you and Vic know the truth. They'll have to change locations just in case, but I don't think Parker has anything to worry about. Neither do you."

"Nothing to worry about," I tell myself. Is that true?

Allie's alive. That's a good thing. And she's the only other person who knows what really happened.

Chapter Nine

"But he told me he loved me." My mother's words come out muffled with her face buried in the pillow.

I stand by the door, peeking in. I'm supposed to be in bed, but my mom's crying woke me up.

"And why would you believe him?" my grandmother asks, scowling down at her daughter with her arms crossed. "How many times do I have to tell you, those words are the most poisonous lies ever spewed from a man's mouth?"

ant to sit on the green with me while we wait for them?" Joey asks, taking my hand and kissing my palm.

I smile gently. "Sure." I watch him get out of the Jeep. Maybe this day doesn't have to be a *total* nightmare.

Joey meets me at the back of the Jeep. His sweatshirt hangs low on me, creating the illusion that it's the only thing I'm wearing. He fights to hide a grin when he sees me. If he says something stupid like, *I like you in my clothes*, I'm going to throw it at him and get back in the Jeep. Wearing a guy's clothes has this weird effect on them, like it's some twisted sign of ownership. And I'm *not* a possession. Joey offers me his hand instead. I accept it, relieved he keeps whatever comment I saw flash across his face to himself.

We pass between a line of small evergreen trees that separate the delivery area from the golf course and carefully tread down a steep embankment until we're on the finely groomed green. Joey leads us to a circular area where the grass is even shorter before letting go of my hand to sit with his legs stretched out in front of him.

I untie my wedges and sink my feet into the lush, cool grass. Sitting down next to him, I pull my knees up to my chest and stretch the sweatshirt over them.

"Are you cold?" Joey asks, wrapping an arm around me and tucking me against his side.

"No, I'm good." I lean into him, resting my head on his chest.

It's so quiet here, it's almost unsettling.

"What colleges are you considering?"

The question seems so out of nowhere. I lean back to look up at him. "What?"

"When we were in the car, Nina said you were going to college. Where are you looking?"

"She was holding a gun to Vic's head, and you remember *that*?" I ask, laughing.

Joey shrugs with a lopsided grin. I laugh again.

"I have no idea why she said that," I tell him. "My guidance counselor keeps sending me home with brochures. But I haven't really thought about it."

"Why not?"

"Why should I? Having a college degree doesn't mean I won't end up working at a coffee shop when I graduate, except I'll have a shitload of student loans to pay off on top of it."

"Don't you have dreams of becoming something...more?" He studies me intently, waiting. I don't know what makes me more uncomfortable, the question or that he's honestly interested in my answer.

"More than what? College won't change who I am," I say, shifting my focus away from his scrutinizing gaze and leaning back against his side. "I'm not sure what the point is...wanting more from life than I've already been given. Money doesn't make you happy. I can't see how working eighty hours a week will either."

"Then what will…make you happy?"

"What's with these questions?" I counter evasively, sitting up straight so that his arm falls away.

"Hey," he soothes, scooting closer and setting his hand on my waist, "I'm just trying to get to know more about you."

"Why?"

"Uh…because I like you," he offers carefully. "We don't have to talk about you, if you don't want to."

"Let's not."

I know I'm being a bitch and should feel bad, but honestly, I don't trust anyone who wants to know more than my name. And I'm not sure how to explain that to him without making it awkward.

"Would you rather ask me questions? Or…we can just sit here. They should be here soon."

And now…it *is* awkward. Crap. Why do I suck at this so much?

I search for something, *anything*, to say so it's not so tense. I've never dated a guy or even been out on a date. We go to parties and bars where small talk is just that. Stupid, mindless conversation that leads to making out or getting felt up in a dark corner. Even the guy I regularly hook up with keeps the pillow talk to a minimum. It's just about the sex, and that's completely fine with me. I don't *want* anyone to get to know me.

"Tell me something embarrassing," I blurt.

Joey lets out a short laugh. "We can't talk about you, but I have to reveal something embarrassing? That's fair."

"Maybe if you share something vulnerable, I'll feel more comfortable."

I bat my eyes at him dramatically. He chuckles.

"Umm…" He searches the sky in contemplation.

"Don't think too much about it. The first thing that comes to mind."

"The first time I had an erection, I was in church."

"Wha—" I can't even get the word out before I burst out laughing. "Details."

I know that if I could see him clearly his face would be bright red.

He continues, "This really pretty girl was sitting in front of me—I think she went to school with Parker actually—and during the greet-your-neighbor part of the sermon, she turned around, and when she bent over to hug me, I got a face full of boobs. Let's just say, I held on tight until my grandmother swatted me with her purse."

"What'd the girl do?" I ask, still chuckling.

"She laughed, especially when she saw the tent in my khakis. My grandmother was mortified, and my mother yelled, 'William!' so loud that half the church turned around and stared at me cupping my crotch. I had no idea what was happening or how to make it go away. It was undeniably the most embarrassing moment of my life."

My stomach's hurting I'm laughing so hard "That's amazing!" I finally catch my breath. "Why'd she call you William?"

"My full name is three first names, and everyone calls me something different. It even confuses *me* sometimes."

"Joseph William Harrison?"

He nods slowly. "That's it."

I raise my eyebrows. "Add some Roman numerals to the end and you could be royalty."

Joey laughs. "I'm the furthest thing from honorable."

"Really?" I question, leaning in until we're a breath apart. "I don't know if I believe that," I say, tempting him with a salacious grin.

I watch his mouth part. His eyes don't leave mine. He wraps a hand around the back of my neck and pulls me to him.

I close my eyes, anticipating the touch of his lips. And when they finally find me, my whole world stills. A lightness overtakes me, swirling in my head. His mouth caresses mine, stealing my breath. A small moan escapes at the caress of his tongue. I can't breathe, but I don't want to. I grip the front of his shirt, needing to get closer. Needing him. His arm tightens around my waist. I am lost in him, in this kiss.

Joey slowly pulls away, our breaths mingling in quick pants. His hand still cups my neck as he gently presses his forehead to mine. "I can't tell you how long I've wanted to do that."

Before we can connect again, his phone chimes.

With an apologetic groan, he leans away and pulls it out of his pocket. He reads the screen, then looks across the golf course to the far side of the clubhouse. "They're here. Told us to meet them at the pool."

Four silhouettes approach the waist-high fence surrounding the pool and climb over. I only have a second to process what they're planning before I see someone, who I assume to be Nina, pull her dress over her head.

I turn back to Joey. "Not yet. Okay?"

He grins and nods before texting a reply and setting the phone beside him on the grass.

Without hesitating, he pulls me onto his lap and I straddle him, our lips crashing together. We are not gentle—groping, groaning and grinding. Our breathing is as frantic as our heartbeats. My fingers tangle in his hair. His hands slide under the sweatshirt and grip my bare back. I don't pull away to breathe. I could seriously die kissing him.

Joey pulls the sweatshirt roughly over my head and flips me so I'm lying on top of it, his body pressed to me. His mouth tastes down the lines of my neck and into the revealing slope of the halter. I wrap my legs around him and tilt my head back, consumed by his touch. I tug at the edges of his shirt, desperate to run my hands along his skin. He separates long enough to yank it over his head and toss it on the grass.

His body crushes me in the best possible way and I gasp.

"You feel so good," he murmurs against my neck, sucking the skin below my ear.

I grip him tighter, moving beneath him.

He groans with a heavy breath. "Oh god, Lana, I love you."

I freeze.

Joey begins to lift my shirt, and I grab his hands, stopping him.

"Get off me."

He looks down at me, confusion surfacing beneath the lust. "What?"

I shove hard at his chest. "Get off me!"

Joey rolls to the side, not resisting. Realization and shock flash across his face. His mouth drops open, but nothing comes out. I stand, adjusting my shirt and snatching my shoes.

"Lana!" Joey calls to me, his tone laden with panic. "Don't go!"

But I'm already storming away, rage pulsing through my veins. I clamp my teeth so tight, I can feel the muscles in my neck constricting.

"Lana!"

I focus on the pool, blocking him out. He'd better stay the fuck away from me. If he follows me or tries to touch me, I swear I will castrate him.

"Hey!"

My footsteps stumble. The voice is deeper, not Joey's. I turn and am blinded by a bright spotlight.

"Stay right there."

I don't have to see to know he's a police officer. So…I run.

"Stop!"

The pool seems so fricken far away right now. And when I'm halfway there, I watch Parker, Lincoln, Tori and Nina scramble up and out of the pool. They grab their clothes as they run for the fence. The spotlight veers away from me for just a moment to illuminate them. It gives me the second I need to push into the hedges along the side of the clubhouse.

I hear the police car pull out of the delivery area. I consider running for it, but by this time, the four of them are already disappearing into the trees. I can't see what's on the other side, but I have to assume it's where Parker left his car.

As much as I don't want to, I look back to where I left Joey, but I don't see him. A second later, I hear the Jeep start up and pull away. Where's he going?

I'm about to step out of the hedges, not sure where to go, when the police car comes into view again at the pool side of the clubhouse, its spotlight shining on the blue water. I shove back into the hedges, scraping my arms against the prickly branches, just as the light swings up, sweeping along the golf course toward where Joey and I were on the green.

I hug my knees to my chest, trying to make myself as small as possible when the light passes in front of the hedges. I close my eyes, afraid to even breathe. When I open them again, the light is gone and I exhale. I wait for what feels like an eternity before poking my head out. The police car is pulling away, its spotlight still searching the area as it turns onto a road on the other side of the trees. It doesn't stop. Parker must have driven off, which means…they left me.

I stay in the hedges another couple minutes in case the cops decide to circle back. This is pathetic. They really have nothing better to do than to chase after skinny-dippers on a Friday night? Considering we're in Oaklawn, that's probably a major offense.

When I finally emerge from the confines of the hedges, my legs and arms are streaked with fine red scratches, and I'm covered in green needles. Pulling the elastic free, I shake out my hair, tiny green slivers raining down. When I secure it back on top of my head, I realize my headband's missing.

"Shit," I grumble.

That's one of the few nice things I own—an heirloom from my mother that my grandmother gave to her. I try to retrace my steps, searching for it, but it's too dark to see anything in the grass. Giving up, I decide to walk back toward the pool, just in case Joey is parked somewhere near the delivery area or comes back there to get me. I'd rather walk back to Sherling than get in the car with him.

"I love you?" I growl, the words inciting a rush of riotous fury. "What the fuck?"

I can't believe he said that. *Those* words. The worst of all lies.

I clench my fists with my shoes dangling between my fingers. "I love you?!" My stomach rolls and bile rises in the back of my throat.

I can't believe I let him touch me. That I thought for a second that he was actually a decent guy. So stupid!

When I reach the road on the other side of the trees, it's deserted. The street is lined with huge houses with lanterns lit on either side of their doors and at the end of their driveways. The front lawns and hedges are perfectly trimmed, just like the golf course, but no one's on the street. I walk in the direction of the road leading to the main street. The entire time, I'm hexing Joey and every other guy who has ever used those words to seduce or manipulate a girl.

I'm halfway down the road that divides the golf course when headlights flood the dark. I am completely exposed with nowhere to hide. But right now, I don't care if I'm picked up by the police. My feet hurt. I'm cold. And the anger has drained all the life out of me. This night honestly can't get any worse.

The car slows as it nears. It's a gold or tan-colored Land Rover. I keep my head down and continue walking past it when it stops across from me and the driver's window rolls down.

"Lana."

I pause and lift my head.

"Get in."

I stare at Parker for a second before crossing the street toward him, my shoulders slumped in defeat. I open the back door, expecting to find the car full, but it's empty.

"Sit in the front," he instructs.

I close the back door and climb into the passenger seat. "Where is everyone?"

"With Joey. I met him on the side of the road. He said you were still here." Parker comes to a stop at the intersection with the main road and looks at me. "He said it'd be better if I came to get you. The girls were starving, so they went with him. They said to meet them at Stella's."

"If he's going to be there, then just take me home," I tell Parker.

Parker pulls onto the main street, his car still the only one on the road. "What happened?"

I stare at the same encroaching dark forest as before, unable to look at him. "I don't want to talk about it."

"He didn't hurt you, right?" Parker says this like even the idea of it is impossible.

"No," I huff. "He's a liar. Just like everyone else."

Parker doesn't respond. Neither of us speaks as he drives through Oaklawn, eventually crossing into Sherling.

"You don't lie."

I turn my head, his words cutting through the prolonged silence. "How do you know?"

"I remember you telling me once that you don't lie—ever. And…I believe you. You've never lied to me, even when I wished you had." He releases a low chuckle. "You really don't, do you?"

"No, I don't," I reply simply.

"Then can I ask you one question that you promise to answer?"

I shift in my seat so I'm angled toward him, intrigued by the request. This could be dangerous. But Parker doesn't exactly seem like the kind of guy who wants to explore the depths of my soul. If Joey had asked this, my answer would have been an automatic no. I narrow my eyes, considering Parker's motive.

He grins when I hesitate. "It's just one question, Lana. How bad could the truth be?"

I lean back against the seat. "If I agree, what do I get in return?"

Parker laughs. "What do you want?"

"Stop hooking up with Nina," I tell him without thinking. And I'm not sure *why* this is my demand. I don't want him, and I'm not jealous of them. But it's something that's always bothered me. Perhaps because I know how toxic they are together, and I want better for Nina. And maybe for Parker too.

"Done," he answers immediately. "I'd actually already decided that earlier tonight, so your wish was kind of a waste. So that means I get to ask you anything, and you have to tell me the truth."

I exhale in resignation. "What do you want to know?"

Parker flashes me a wily grin. "I didn't say I was going to ask you now. I think I'll save it."

I roll my eyes. "You're so dramatic."

Parker laughs. "Always."

The streetlights of Sherling fill the darkness. Cars and buses pass on either side of us. Exhausted, I half-focus on the closed storefronts hidden by graffiti-tagged gates and the people loitering outside of the few bars that are still open.

Parker pulls into Stella's pocked dirt parking lot. I scan the cars in search of Joey's Jeep.

"He's not here," Parker assures me. "I texted him to go."

"Thanks," I say softly, unclicking the seat belt. "Well, I'd say it was fun, but it wasn't."

Parker gives me a sympathetic smile. "I was serious earlier when I said I got you, Lana. I do. Anytime you need me, I'm here." He opens up his console and pulls out my phone. "You have my number now. Use it anytime."

"You hacked into my phone?" I narrow my eyes. He smiles wickedly. "You're trouble."

Parker smiles wider, not denying it. I realize a second too late that I'm staring at him, lost in his seductive smile. His hand brushes against my cheek, tucking loose strands of hair behind my ear. I pull away when his thumb caresses my lower lip.

He grins. "We will happen, you know."

I release an exasperated sigh. "Really, Parker?"

I shove open the passenger door with an annoyed grunt and slam it behind me. It's not until my bare feet make contact with the rocky ground that I remember my shoes are in his car. But he's already pulling away. I hold my hand up to stop him just as a truck pulls out and blocks me from view.

I tap on my screen to call him; it's dead. "Of course."

I delicately navigate the terrain on the balls of my feet, grimacing in pain with each stone-ridden step. I squeeze past the drunks waiting in line to get in and pop out on the other side with a heavy breath.

Tori and Nina are easy to find halfway down in a booth, giggling uncontrollably.

Nina has her wet hair braided to the side while Tori's is pulled back in a knot at the nape of her neck. They look like they've had the best night. Their table is littered with a half-dozen plates of pie slices in various stages of consumption and a large red plastic cup of Coke in front of each of them. I consider leaving, not wanting to ruin it.

Tori stops laughing when I come to a stop next to their table.

"Lana! Holy shit, where the fuck have you been?" she exclaims, jumping out of the booth and wrapping me in a quick, tight embrace.

I hug her back, inhaling the sharp chlorine scent on her skin.

She steps back and scans me. "You look…horrible!"

I blink.

"Omigod," Nina gasps. "What happened to you? Did you get in a fight?"

I stare at her, confused. She's staring at my chest.

I look down, unable to see what she's focused on. But I do see the angry red scratches marring my arms and legs. "What?"

"You have a bruise," she says, gently touching my collarbone. It's tender but not bad. It must be from when Vic pinned me against the wall. "Seriously, what happened to you?"

"Can we sit?" I ask, so tired, I feel like I might fall over.

The girls slide back into the booth, and I slip in next to Tori, slumping down against the cracked vinyl.

"So?" Tori demands when I don't start talking right away.

I open my mouth, but nothing comes out. I have no idea where to even start.

"What happened with Joey?" Nina blurts.

I close my eyes and groan between clenched teeth. "I never want to see another Harrison ever again. Not a single one of them. Ever."

"He didn't do that to you, did he?" Tori asks, ready to be just as pissed off as I am.

"No. This is courtesy of Vic." I focus on Nina. "Did you give him back his gun?"

"What?!" Nina replies, shocked. "No way. It's right…" She shuffles through her satchel. Her eyes narrow in confusion as she starts dumping items on the table. "I swear it was in here." She looks up, at a loss. "I have no idea where it is."

"He has it," I tell them. "Stupid fuck. Did you see him when you left?"

They both shake their heads.

"What did he do to you?" Tori asks.

I grind my teeth together, knotting the muscles in my jaw. With a shake of my head, I rake a hand through my loose bangs.

"Lana," Nina implores, "you have to tell us. You know we'll protect you no matter what."

"Let me think about it," I tell them, needing to figure out what could potentially happen if they knew.

I don't want to risk them being involved if it goes to shit. I have no idea if Allie really is okay. Or if that screaming girl told anyone what she saw. Hell, Vic could claim to be a witness to me pushing her, and I have no way of proving that I didn't. Telling Nina and Tori could put them at risk. I don't trust Vic not to go after them, especially if he thinks they may be a threat.

"Can we go home?" I ask with a heavy sigh. "Every inch of me either hurts or is covered with dirt."

"Lana, where are your shoes?" Nina exclaims with a laugh.

"In Parker's car. I took them off when I started walking back from the country club."

"You really are having the worst night ever," Tori declares.

"You have no idea."

Chapter Ten

"She isn't your curse." I keep my eyes shut at the sound of my grandmother's voice. "You can love her."

"I'm trying," my mother whispers. "But every time I look at her, I see the truth, and I know I've lost him."

"Not because of her," my grandmother says gruffly.

"Yes," my mother counters sadly, "because of her."

"Here," **Nina says, holding** out a pair of sparkly black flip-flops.

"You have flip-flops in your purse?" I ask incredulously.

"You try wearing stilettos for hours. Of course I carry around a pair of flip-flops. They've saved me more times than I can count, and now, they're saving you. So, you're welcome."

"Thank you," I say, apology in my tone. I slide my feet into them and am grateful for the gargantuan purse Nina lugs around with her everywhere.

We step out of Stella's and start walking across the parking lot.

"My place?" I confirm.

The girls nod, knowing I'm within walking distance. The walk isn't nearly as shady as a bus ride at two o'clock in the morning.

Tori hands me my leather jacket, and I happily put it on. "Thanks."

"Parker says we're done," Nina announces.

I try to read the emotion behind the declaration but can't. At least *Parker* told me the truth.

"Are you okay with this?" I ask delicately.

She shrugs indifferently. "You know he doesn't mean it. But whatever. He's kind of a slut, and he definitely doesn't respect me. So he can go to hell."

I laugh.

"What did Joey do?" Tori asks. "He a slut too?"

"I don't know," I tell them, "but he *is* a liar."

Tori sighs, shaking her head. "So no more Harrisons." She pauses and bites her lip. "Except…I'm going out with Lincoln again…so you may have to tolerate Joey. But I'll try to make sure it's from a distance."

I study her curiously. "You're serious about Lincoln? You really like him?"

A girlish smile emerges. "He's *so* nice. And his body? Un-be-lievable."

"At least one of us ended up with a good one," Nina says. We round the corner and start down my street. "I think we need to visit the 'party in a bag.' I remember seeing a joint in there, and we could definitely use it."

"Definitely," I agree adamantly, searching my pockets. I pull out the switchblade, wishing I'd had it earlier in the stairwell with Vic. And then I pat the inside pocket and reach for the small plastic bag. Before I can put the switchblade back in my pocket, a car pulls up beside us.

"Lana Peri?" a deep booming voice confirms.

Instinctively, Nina rolls her hand beneath mine, removing the knife from it and slipping it in her purse. A beam of light blinds me just as I drop the bag of drugs to the ground and step on them.

"What was that?" a female voice asks. A car door shuts.

I raise my hands in the air to show that they're empty, familiar with the routine.

"Are you Lana Peri?" the guy asks again.

"Yes," I tell him, shielding my eyes from the flashlight.

"Take a step this way."

With a sigh, I do.

The female officer snaps a pair of rubber gloves over her hands and picks up the plastic bag. "Looks like you've been having an eventful night, Lana."

"Step behind the vehicle," the male officer instructs.

"Are you ladies with her?" the female asks Nina and Tori.

I silently connect with them, and they know what I want them to do.

"We just got here," Nina tells them.

"What are your names?" she asks, setting the drugs on the trunk and pulling out paper and a pen to write them down.

I don't hear what else they say because the male officer's voice is too loud in my ear.

"Place your hands on the trunk. We're arresting you for possession of narcotics. Do you understand?"

I nod.

The female officer comes around behind me while the male officer drops the drugs into an evidence bag. "Do you have anything sharp on your body before I pat you down?"

"No," I answer flatly, staring at the back window, shutting every emotion down.

My face doesn't flinch with the slightest expression. I don't move when her hands pat down my body, tucking her fingers along my waistline. This part is never fun. She grips my wrist and brings it behind my back.

The weight of the cool metal settles around my wrists as the handcuffs click, tightening. I turn my head away from the flashing lights as the male officer grips my arm, moving me toward the open door of the police car.

Tori stands next to Nina, biting her lip. Nina has her arms crossed, wearing a defiant scowl. I want to assure them that I've got this. That everything's going to be okay. But I don't know if that's true. I have no idea what I'm being brought in for, other than possession. There could be so many reasons they were looking for me—theft, assault, armed robbery, trespassing or, depending on who's been talking, attempted murder.

The officer places his hand on the top of my head as I duck down. And that's when I see the red Jeep pull up in front of the house next to us. A phone to his ear, he stands up on his seat so I can see him.

He mouths the words, *Keep your mouth shut.*

Not a problem. I don't plan on confessing to anything. Even if I did do it.

I watch Nina and Tori disappear in the distance with Lincoln and Joey by their sides, staring after the police car. Usually they'd be asked a lot more questions. Thankfully, the cops are only interested in me and chose not to call backup to bring the girls in too. I don't dwell on it, although their rush to take me in should concern me.

The ride to the station is uneventful. As is the booking process.

I don't know how long I've been in the holding cell, shivering on the slab that's meant to be a bed, when a balding male cop finally unlocks the door.

"The detectives have some questions for you," he tells me.

He takes hold of my arm and escorts me to a small interrogation room with gloomy gray walls. I sit in a hard metal chair at a dented wooden table and glance up at the two-way mirror in front of me.

Things just got serious. This has nothing to do with possession.

I take a breath, trying to steady my pulse. But it continues to pick up speed.

A few minutes later, the door opens and two men in suits walk in, nodding toward the cop, who leaves us. They say something, probably their names, but I'm not listening. I'm staring at the small figure behind them, clutching a rose-colored duster sweater around her body.

I stand up in a sudden movement, the chair scraping against the floor. "What is she doing here?"

"Lana," my mother says gently, "it's okay. They said I needed to be here."

A lanky, bald detective points to a chair in the corner of the room, near the door. She smiles at him nervously and sits.

"Have a seat," the detective with the horrible complexion and bushy mustache instructs firmly.

Keeping my eyes on my mother, I lower myself onto the chair again. She's ghostly pale, and her eyes are rimmed red. I know she's not well, and she shouldn't have to be here.

The detective with the mustache—Freddy, I'll call him since I missed his name and his skin reminds me of a nightmare—sits across from me with a file in his hand. He proceeds to recite my Miranda rights and has me sign the paper stating I understand them. The other detective leans against the wall next to the door with his arms folded.

"Want to let you know that we're recording this right now," he tells me, tilting his head toward the two-way mirror. A red light is faintly visible on the other side.

I flip it off with an obnoxious smile.

"Nice," he mutters.

I give him a let's-get-on-with-this look of impatience as I lean back in the chair with my arms crossed. If they actually did their homework and looked me up, they know they're about to waste a lot of time because I don't talk. Ever. No matter how long they keep me in this depressing room.

I watch him flip open the file folder on the table between us, and he spreads a couple grainy photos in front of me. Now I know why I'm here. It's next to impossible to make out the faces, the imagery is so poor, but my blinding blond hair is hard to miss, as is the gun in the hand of the guy dressed in black.

"What have you been up to tonight, Lana?"

I raise my eyes to look at him, my face expressionless. And that's how I remain for the next hour or two. It's hard to tell since there isn't a clock in this oppressive room. They ask questions. I don't answer.

"Tell us who the male with the gun is, Lana. Make it easier on yourself," the detective with the pockmarks along his jawline asks me for the hundredth time. "If you didn't do anything wrong, then you have nothing to worry about."

The corner of my mouth quirks. His eyes narrow into a glower. I know better. The truth won't save me. There's a reason *Honesty*'s my curse.

My mother continues to look frailer with each passing second. I don't want her in here, but I'm a minor, and they don't want to worry about my rights being violated if they question me without a parent present. It's worse for her than it is for me. And I'm concerned she's about to pass out.

"Could you get my mother some water?" I ask the detective who's remained standing by the door with his arms crossed. I think he's supposed to look intimidating. It's not working.

The detective glances at my stricken mother and back to Freddy.

Freddy gives him a subtle nod and glances at the two-way glass, making sure the red light is on and the camera's still recording this pathetic interview.

"Lana, we have you on tape at the convenience store. We have the statement from the clerk. We recovered the stolen lottery tickets from your possession. You know who the guy is holding the gun. All you have to do is tell us; otherwise, it looks like you're his accomplice. Either way, you're obstructing the investigation."

I glance at my mother again. She wipes a tear from her cheek with a shaky hand. I try to reassure her with a small smile. She bites her lip to keep from crying.

"Does she really need to be in here?" I ask again for the tenth time.

The door opens. The wall art reappears with a bottle of water. Once he's through the door, I notice someone's behind him. A tall, regal-looking man in a suit. His salt-and-pepper hair is slicked back—not in a slimy mob-boss way, but in a distinguished I-have-money-and-power kind of way. His vibrant blue eyes take in the room with an assessing glance, from my mother to Freddy, and then steady on me. His face is expressionless, but his eyes tell me everything I need to know. He's confident, intelligent, and he gets exactly what he wants…just like his son.

"This interview is over," he announces.

My mother stands, her crystal-blue eyes wide. "Niall?"

The man's face softens when he turns toward her, a small, sad smile on his face. "Faye," he acknowledges solemnly, like he's silently apologizing for something.

Her eyes flood with tears that she blinks back, gratitude and relief dancing in them. The relief confuses me—like she knows he *will* fix this.

"Don't worry. I'll take care of her. Why don't you wait out in the hall for me?"

My mother nods, quickly glancing at me before slipping out of the room. With the click of the door closing, Niall focuses back on us—or I should say, on me. He stares at me stoically, his face not giving anything away.

Freddy's jaw clenches. "Niall, *you're* her lawyer? I didn't think you took these kind of cases."

Niall Harrison doesn't respond to his question. "I need a moment alone with my client."

PART 2

Knowing
You

Prologue

he truth is the truth. It is never wrong. It's not always what you want it to be. It can be profound and enlightening. Or it can be ugly and brutal. But it will always be the truth.

But it's not. Not really.

We each have our own twisted version of the truth, tainted by perception. And sometimes, it's all we have. So we guard and protect it with unwavering belief, even if it's a lie.

And *my* truth is *Trust* killed my grandmother.

My grandmother raised me. My mother had just graduated high school when I was born, and she still lived at home with her sisters. She didn't need to take care of me all of the time. Or even some of the time. My grandmother was going to have a say in how I was raised no matter what. She had an opinion about everything, and let anyone know it. So, maybe my mother just gave up and let her have me.

In my grandmother's house, you either needed to shut up and do what you were told or be as stubborn and loud as she was. My aunt Helen and my grandmother could be heard halfway down the street in a rage of stubbornness. Whereas my mother and Aunt Allison slammed a lot of doors in their silent obedience. I'm a blend of the two. My words were never shouted but were definitely damaging. My stubbornness had every crack in the corner of the kitchen memorized by the time I was seven, having been forced to stare at the wall for hours at a time—my grandmother's favorite punishment when I openly expressed my will.

Despite everything, she was the most important person in my life. There was something about us being cursed with *Trust* and *Honesty*. We needed each other. She knew I'd always tell her the truth, regardless of how brutally delivered. And I trusted her with my life. But beyond our walls, the world was filled with liars, thieves and murderers. Every life experience held a lesson to be learned. And my grandmother was the most passionate of teachers. No matter how many times I'm forced to learn the hard way, the lesson is always the same.

Trust **no one**.

Everyone lies.

You can only save **yourself**.

Chapter One

There once was a girl named Thaylina who lived in a tower. And even though it was old, and the frigid air seeped in through its cracked stones, she loved the tower because it was home.

The girl was watched over and protected by a wise and powerful sorceress, who raised her as her own. The sorceress instilled Thaylina with wisdom so she would not be fooled by the ways of the world.

'm already awake when they come in for morning call. Sleep is next to impossible in a room filled with girls tossing on squeaky springs. Besides, I was too wired from the night before to sleep. Watching a girl being pushed down a flight of stairs and getting arrested for something you didn't do can make anyone fear closing their eyes.

I climb off my bunk, pulling the covers over the pillow in one motion. After sliding on my issued flip-flops, I shuffle toward the bathrooms with the rest of the groggy girls, mumbling and yawning.

I can feel her slide in step next to me before I see her.

"Look who it is."

I keep my eyes on the spindly hairs sticking out the braid on the head in front of me. It's too fricken early for this bullshit.

"Can't stay away, Lana?" And her mouth just won't stay shut. "Did you finally kill someone?"

I whip around just as her claw reaches out to grab my hair. My fingers wrap around her wrist, and a foot sweeps her legs out from under her. My knee is on her chest before she can inhale. Panic sweeps across her dark eyes as she fights for her next breath.

"Stay the fuck away from me, Sienna," I growl, an inch away from her teary face.

I'm up and walking away in less than a minute, blending in with the line of girls who didn't give us a second glance. A guard hollers, "Hey, what's going on up there?" I'm already in the bathroom by the time she reaches Sienna.

After a brief shower, I'm ushered to the cafeteria for breakfast. I'm not hungry, so I grab a plastic cup and fill it with water. I find a table in the far corner and sit. And because I'm so welcoming, not a single person sits next to me. Exactly how I prefer it.

I watch. Figure out who's in charge. Who's afraid. And who's a bitch just to be a bitch. I recognize a few faces, besides Sienna's. But they ignore me. The only ones who pay me any attention are the curious ones. The ones who haven't been told who I am or why they should stay away.

The first time I was here two years ago, I learned quickly that the only way to stay out of the drama is to be bigger than the drama. To let them know I don't give a shit what anyone thinks about me. But if anyone touches me, I will retaliate. And it will be painful…for one of us.

I only had to send a couple of girls to the hospital in need of stitches and a splint to be left alone. I also earned a certain amount of respect when it became obviously apparent that I'd never say a word or give anyone up. I can't believe I'm back here, having to deal with all of this bullshit again. All because I couldn't risk revealing the truth.

I hate my curse.

I sense someone standing across from me, and lift my head to find one of the counselors looking down at me from the other side of the empty table. "Your lawyer's here."

Wordlessly, I stand and follow her. Halfway down a long corridor, she opens the door to the visitors' room. The lines of rectangular tables and seats are vacant. The tall man draped in a finely tailored dark gray suit stands in the middle of the room, waiting for me. After he demanded I be transported to juvie last night, he told me he'd see me in the morning. But I never really expected him to show up.

Niall Harrison offers a gentle smile, his eyes creasing in concern. "Hi, Lana." This man doesn't belong in this room. It feels as wrong as finding a sleek Mercedes in a used car lot.

I don't move closer as the door clicks shut and the lock slides in place behind me.

"Where's Dwight?" I ask, referring to my court-appointed lawyer who's been representing me since my "public disturbance" a couple years ago.

"Home, I assume."

"Why are you here?"

"To help you."

"Why?" I can't help but be cynical. There's no reason for him to be here. Not one.

"I want to," Niall states plainly.

"I can't afford you."

"That's not an issue."

"*Why* are you doing this?" His evasiveness is starting to get to me.

"My sons are concerned about you. They came to me separately and asked that I represent you. As did your mother."

I don't move. "How do you know my mother?"

"Why don't we talk?" He pulls out a chair. When I remain still, he says, "At least sit down so we can review the charges."

My flip-flops slap against the linoleum with each step. He waits 'til I'm seated across from him before lowering into the blue plastic bucket chair across from me. I slump back, pressing my knees against the table with my arms crossed over the red jumpsuit.

"As of right now, they're only charging you with possession and trespassing."

"Trespassing?"

"You were identified at the Oaklawn Country Club."

I roll my eyes. Of course I was.

"I feel certain I can get those charges dismissed. I'm most concerned about the potential obstruction charge in relation to the armed robbery of the convenience store. I was informed that they may also charge you as an accomplice. I haven't been provided with the police report yet, so I need you to fill in the details and tell me what happened."

I sink farther into the chair and silently stare at him.

"Please, Lana. Let me help you."

I don't say a word.

Niall presses his lips together and inhales deeply through his nose.

I know I'm testing his patience, but the last person I want representing me is Parker and Joey's father. Not just because it's *them*, but because they're so wrapped up in the truth of this that I *can't* confide in their father. I don't even think it'd be legal for him to represent me if he knew of their indirect involvement.

"Dwight can handle this."

"Dwight still represents you. He and I are working together on your case. But right now, I'm the one who's here," Niall explains calmly. "I was able to fast track your case and get the probable cause hearing moved to this Tuesday. I'm going to request that the court release you into your mother's custody, but with your previous arrests, and the pending armed robbery charges, that's very unlikely." Hardened lines form around his mouth as he contemplates his next words.

"What?" I demand, dreading the worst.

"A girl called into the station last night, claiming that a friend of hers was pushed down a flight of stairs."

My feet fall to the floor with a heavy thump. Niall's brow creases at my inadvertent reaction.

"Why are you telling me this?"

"An officer I know personally informed me that the suspect described sounds a lot like you. The detectives assigned to the case want you to come in for questioning."

I don't respond. I try not to react. But his bright blue eyes stay on me, absorbing the tension in my jaw and flicker in my eyes. I can't risk letting this man see through me.

"Do you know anything about it? I would hate to be blindsided by this later if I agree to bring you in."

"What happened to the girl? The one who was pushed down the stairs?" I ask, my chest tightening.

"She's in a coma," he explains solemnly. "They're not sure if she'll make it."

All of the air is sucked out of my lungs as I fold forward, setting my hands on the table to keep myself upright. Parker said she was okay. Did he lie? Or did he not know how badly she was hurt?

"She regained consciousness briefly after she was brought in and started calling out for…" Niall reads directly from his notes, annunciating each word with a hint of confusion. "My. Fairy. Princess."

He glances at my shaking hands. I yank them off the table and cross my arms tightly against my chest again.

"I won't tell them anything if you bring me in. So don't even bother."

"They don't have much to go on. The caller never came in. So I'll decline the interview request for now." Niall's voice is careful and calm. "Lana, you have to tell me *something* about the armed robbery. I promise that everything you say will remain between us. Dwight doesn't even have to know if you don't want him to. *No one* will hear the truth if that's what's best."

I study him as he studies me, wondering if he'll still hold this promise if his loyalty is tested. Loyalty to his family. Loyalty to Vic's family. All to save me, a girl he doesn't even know. He focuses on me with fierce sincerity, a sort of intense protectiveness that I've never had directed at me before.

"I can tell you what happened at the convenience store, but I can't tell you the name of the guy with the gun."

"It's going to be difficult to prove you didn't have anything to do with it if I can't give them the name of the person who did," he explains, frustrated by my terms. "Why do you insist on protecting him?"

"It's not *him* I'm protecting. It's everyone who was with me that night."

Niall leans back and stares at the papers in front of him, a contemplative expression on his face. The conviction reflected in his eyes when they turn back up to me makes me very aware of why he can afford that suit. It's the look of a man who knows exactly where the lines are and how to cross them without taking a step.

"Tell me what happened inside the store. Nothing about before you entered. Or after. Only the details of the robbery itself."

I take a deep breath and do something I've only done a few times in my life—and I don't mean tell the truth, because that's the only thing I *can* do. This time, I tell the *entire* truth, and only because it won't make a difference. I'm so used to keeping the details to myself because most of the time, people can't handle unabridged honesty. But today, Niall Harrison hears exactly what happened inside the dingy convenience store…every second.

And when I'm done, he steeples his fingers and presses them against his lips, contemplating my options.

"You left together?" he asks.

"Yes."

"Got into the same vehicle?"

I hesitate before answering, but since he doesn't know who else was in the car, I respond. "Yes."

"He still had the gun while you were in the vehicle?"

"Uh," I stumble, not sure how to respond since Nina ended up taking it from him. I shrug evasively. "He had it when we entered the car."

Niall's mouth turns up slightly, aware of my creative truth. "Okay." He's quiet for a long time, his thoughts trapped behind the unwavering stare directed at his notepad. Niall lowers his hands and takes a breath before fixating on me with the same intensity. "Without a name, you'll most likely be found guilty of obstruction. But, we can make an offer to plead that out."

The next thing he says lights a fire in my gut. "You should name him, Lana."

"Why?"

"To protect yourself," he says firmly. "Especially since you weren't a participant in the robbery."

Anger lashes up my throat and out my mouth. "And what about everyone else who was in that car with me? Am I supposed to just forget about how this could screw up their lives? To what? Snitch on someone who will never be convicted?"

"Why would you say that?" he asks, his brows furrowing. "We have him on tape. You're a witness. Everyone in the car saw you leave together, so they can confirm his identity as well."

"But we all covered it up. Even if no one knew exactly what happened, they knew *something* did. I won't bring them into this." I clench my fists. "So no, I won't name him."

Niall lets out a long breath. "You're not making this easy on me or yourself."

"What are you getting out of this?" I implore impatiently. "Does it have to do with my mother? How do you know her?"

Niall's face remains expressionless. "I *want* to help you, Lana. The life you've been given…It's not your fault. You don't belong in here."

"What does *that* mean?" I demand.

Niall continues as if he didn't hear me. "I made a few calls this morning, and if the judge agrees, you may be transferred out of here." I lean forward in anticipation. "But you won't be going home." My head cocks to the side, like I didn't quite hear him right. "You should be allowed the opportunity for a better life, away from all of this. A chance you won't be given in a detention facility."

"What are you talking about?" I ask. "Where are you planning to send me?"

"I still need to work out the details, so I'd rather not say right now."

I eye him suspiciously, hoping I didn't just make a mistake by allowing him to represent me.

"It's your only option, Lana…if you want any sort of a life outside of prison." Niall closes the file and slides it into a leather attaché case. "In regards to Allison Pixley, the girl in a coma, say nothing. If you're formally charged, that'll mean they have more evidence, and then you'll *have to* talk to me. But only then."

I consider nodding but fear the small movement could be taken as a sign of admission.

Niall pushes his chair back and stands. He's quiet, looming over me, focused on my face for a second too long. I notice a small muscle tick in his jaw.

"I promise to continue doing everything I can to protect you." And without another word, he walks away and knocks on the window of the metal door, letting the guard know we're done.

Chapter Two

Beneath the tower lived a beast with silver eyes and long sharp fangs. His true form could only be seen at night. For when he stepped out into the daylight, he was wrapped in an enchanted cloak, disguised as a man. A falsehood that attracted women with sweet words and alluring charm.

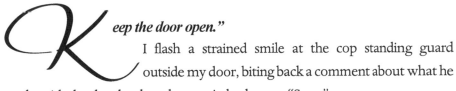

"Keep the door open."

I flash a strained smile at the cop standing guard outside my door, biting back a comment about what he can do with the doorknob and a certain body part. "Sure."

"You have fifteen minutes," he tells Nina and Tori before they enter. It comes out as a directive like they just walked into boot camp.

"What's with the babysitter?" Nina asks, winking at him.

Tori blatantly ignores him, too focused on the half-packed bags splayed out on my floor. "Why are you packing?"

"Are you seriously going to stand right there?" I bark at Officer I-Still-Live-With-My-Mother, making a point to fold a pair of lacy thongs that don't really need folding. His face flushes. He takes a few steps into the living room, out of view, as I knew he would.

"They're sending me away, as part of my plea agreement," I explain, continuing to pack—more to keep from having to look at them than to rush to get out of here. I haven't seen or spoken with either of them since I was arrested over three weeks ago. I wasn't allowed contact with anyone other than my mother and the lawyers. It was honestly the fastest court process ever. It usually takes months to go through what Niall made happen in just a couple of weeks. I'm grateful, but I'd also rather not be packing my bags right now.

"Where are you going?" Nina asks, slowly scanning the disarray.

"Some private school." I shut the empty drawer and open the one below it.

"Stop." Tori takes the stack of clothes from my hands and tosses them on the bed. "What the hell's going on? We haven't seen you since that night, and every time we asked your mother, she'd say your lawyer was taking care of everything. This was supposed to be for possession. So, what is this?" Tori holds up her hands to present the disaster that is my room being packed away. "Because it doesn't feel right."

I let out a long breath, my eyes tracing the floorboards before facing my friends' worried expressions. "The charges were…complicated. The police tried to get me to talk, and I wouldn't. Not without making a mess of everything. You would've been charged just for being there. I couldn't let that happen." I look from Nina to Tori. "I pled to obstruction and aiding and abetting. Niall arranged to have me sent to a private school instead of juvie. The judge said it's an opportunity to straighten out my life, away from *bad influences*." I roll my eyes. "I wasn't given a choice."

"For how long?"

"Where's the school?"

The girls ask in unison.

"I don't know. They haven't told me where. I'm due back in court in six months, so I hope they'll let me come home by Christmas."

"This is bullshit," Tori proclaims through gritted teeth, collapsing onto my bed. "I cannot believe you covered for that asshole. He's the one who should be sent away. Not you."

Nina stops flipping through the hangers in my closet long enough to connect with me. "We would've told them who he was if we knew what happened. You shouldn't have pled out for him... or us." She looks away and selects a pink fur jacket to model in front of the full-length mirror hung on the back of the door. I know she's avoiding, finding a way to focus her anger by doing something menial. She forgets that I know her and can easily see that she's just as pissed as I am. But emotions aren't her thing. I wish they weren't mine.

"This was the only option," I tell them, having already accepted whatever fate awaited since the night I was arrested, knowing I had to protect my friends. But I never expected to be sent away to a new school. It feels much more permanent than a stint at some state-run program. "I'll tell you where I am once I'm there." I start packing again, resigned.

Niall prepared me before today's court date. I knew that he was going to request to have me transferred out of juvie. But he *didn't* say anything about a private school! It's so much worse than I could've prepared for. How is this the best thing for me? I've already raged through anger and frustration, screaming at Niall in the halls of the courthouse this morning. I felt betrayed. Now, I'm too spent and defeated, the anger simmering in my gut. Packing is the only thing I can do, or else, I was told, that it'll be done for me by Officer Dickhead. And the last thing I want is for him to pocket a pair of my thongs while he shoves only sweats and T-shirts into a bag.

"Your mom has to know where you're going," Tori says, keenly watching me pack just about everything I own. "We'll find out from her."

I shrug. "I guess."

Tori stands and blocks my way to the closet where Nina's buttoning up a blouse she stole for me for my birthday last year.

"Why are you acting like this? Like you don't care?" she demands passionately, the only one of us who has no issue displaying her fury.

"So I won't cry." I bite my lip to keep it from trembling. There's an ache that won't let me go. I slowly meet her eyes. "I'm afraid that I'm never coming back.

I don't know why. I just am." I've experienced so many emotions the past few weeks, I can feel them fighting to get out. A tear drops off my lash and slowly draws a line down my cheek.

Tori closes the distance and wraps her arms around me. "No one's going to keep you from us. It doesn't matter where they send you. You understand? You're our girl. We *will* find you. Hell, we'll break you out if you need us to."

I release a choked laugh into her shoulder, holding her just as tightly, knowing they would.

"None of this 'I'm never going to see you again' bullshit," Nina says from over Tori's shoulder, hands on her hips. "Alright?"

I nod, wiping the moisture from my cheeks, and force a smile. But there's more to it than just missing my friends. I hate thinking about what might happen while I'm away. How can I keep the promise I made to make sure Tori graduates? And who will have Nina's back when her need for respect gets the better of her? Then there's my mom…

"Can I have this?" Nina asks, swirling in a yellow empire dress that still has the tag on it.

"Go for it," I reply, my voice thick with emotion. "Yellow isn't my color."

I grip Tori by her shoulders so she can see how serious I am. "Promise me you'll graduate." She rolls her eyes. "Promise me."

"Whatever."

Her answer isn't convincing, so I make sure mine is.

"I'll never forgive you if you don't."

"I'll graduate," she drones with a heavy sigh. "But you'll be here. So stop. Okay?" I nod slightly. "I'll make Lincoln do my work while you're away."

I grin. I can already see it, Tori painting her nails while Lincoln patiently tries to explain the Pythagorean theorem. Good luck, Lincoln.

"And you," I say to Nina, who is pulling her shirt back on. "Don't put up with anything less than you deserve. Not in men, or in life. Please, get out of this soul-sucking town."

With a mischievous gleam in her eye, Nina promises, "We're not going anywhere without you."

"Stop worrying about us," Tori says dismissively. "We'll be fine. Just do whatever you have to do to get back to us."

I'm zipping up my last bag when a knock draws our attention. Niall fills the doorway dressed in a dark suit. His presence stills the room. "Girls." Niall nods politely to Nina and Tori before directing his attention to me. "Are you ready, Lana?"

I shrug.

"Why don't you go ahead and say goodbye. We need to get on the road." He steps away, giving us privacy.

"Holy fuck, they *are* all perfect," Nina exhales. "I still can't believe he's your lawyer."

"Me neither," I reply bitterly, still feeling the sting of betrayal.

"Text as soon as you get there," Tori says, pulling me into another suffocating hug.

When she lets go, I look between them. "While I'm gone, can you check in on my mom?"

Tori avoids my gaze. But Nina nods. "Of course."

"Thanks."

I don't watch them leave. I can't. Instead, I busy myself with double checking my drawers, so they don't see that I'm fighting to hold it together. They're the only friends I've ever had, and they've always been there for me, especially every time things got bad. I can't shake the feeling crawling around inside me that I won't see them again. And I didn't want the fear in my eyes to be the last thing they saw before they left.

I'm surprised to find the cop gone when I drag my bags into the living room. In his place is a tall, military-looking guy standing by the door dressed in a black suit and a pressed white button-down.

"Jax will take your bags to the car," Niall tells me as the man approaches.

Reluctantly, I step aside to allow him access to my belongings. He easily slings the four bags and my backpack over his shoulders before disappearing down the stairs.

My mother rises from the couch, wearing an overly wide smile to conceal the tears shining in her eyes. She opens her arms and I step into her hug. She squeezes me tight. We've never been an overly affectionate family, so I savor this moment for as long as I can, inhaling the jasmine scent of her hair.

I step back and look at her, pleading. "Please go to your doctor's appointment next week." She smooths away the tears on my cheeks. She rescheduled the appointment a few weeks ago, making some excuse about needing to work or be at my court appearance. "Please tell me you'll go?"

"I'll go," she says softly, her eyes flickering to meet mine briefly before fussing with my hair. She's lying.

I open my mouth to tell her…so many things. To protect herself. Not to let anyone break her heart. To pay the gas bill that's due next week. That I'll be back as soon as I can. But I don't say any of the thousand thoughts that rush through my mind. Instead, I look into her shimmering translucent blue eyes and smile, trying to silently reassure her that we'll get through this—that she has nothing to worry about—because I can't force the lies through my lips.

I turn toward Niall, who's waiting by the door. He smiles gently at my mother. "I'll take care of her."

"Thank you," she says, her voice a rasp of emotion.

I walk down the stairs with Niall behind me. I don't look back. I can't. Seeing her fragile and tormented face is not what I want to hold on to as I leave her behind. I have to believe she'll be okay. That she *will* go to the doctor, and he'll figure out what's wrong and fix her. That she will become a strong, independent woman, who realizes she doesn't need a man to be happy. That true love is an illusion, and she's better off surrounding herself with loyal friends, ending her search for *him*. I know none of this will ever happen, but I'd rather hold on to the delicate stem of hope.

I step out into the bright June sunshine and exhale, releasing the emotions that have stormed through me all day. That's when I see the shiny black sedan parked in our pitted driveway. I truly thought I'd be transported to the school in a police car, so I'm not expecting Niall Harrison's Jaguar and Mr. Crew-Cut standing beside it holding the back door open. I hesitate just a moment before entering, glancing around the neighborhood, absorbing its chaos as if for the last time. Then I duck my head and crawl inside, letting Jax block it all out with the click of a door.

Niall enters on the other side. There's plenty of room on the expansive leather, so it doesn't feel too awkward sharing the backseat with him.

"How long is the drive?" I ask.

"About four hours." Niall pulls papers out of his briefcase.

"Do you have my phone? I was told they gave you my personal property bag when we left court today."

"I do, but not with me. I'll be sure to bring it to you when I come by on Sunday."

Which means I won't have my phone the entire weekend. I cross my arms in annoyance and slump against the door. "When can I come back?"

"I'll try to arrange a visit for Thanksgiving." My mouth drops in protest, but he cuts me off. "You're still a person of interest in the Pixley case. It's best if you aren't in Sherling during the investigation. We don't want to draw any more attention to you. Hopefully they'll do their jobs, start looking at the evidence and stop relying on some anonymous phone call."

I clench my jaw in silent defiance, instead of complaining about being sent away to begin with. I redirect my attention out the window, watching the town I grew up in, the only place I've ever been for nearly sixteen years, disappear. I won't miss it. But I don't want to be forced to leave. At the town line, I feel a shift in the air as if we've driven through an invisible barrier. And then it's gone. My life. My friends. My family. Everything that was mine is no longer.

I'm on my own.

I press my head against the cool glass and close my eyes. I don't open them again until I hear Niall's low voice. "Lana, we're here."

I blink awake, my neck sore from the awkward angle it was bent while I slept. The door opens, and I look up at G.I. Jax, who stares down at me expectantly. I unbuckle the seatbelt and step out of the car. I have no idea where I am, but I'm definitely not prepared for *this*.

Chapter Three

Thaylina wasn't like most girls. She had a gift. At times, she even considered it a curse. She possessed the power to see beneath the mask of anyone she met—straight into their hearts, detecting their deepest desires and true intentions. All she had to do was peer into their eyes.

The first thing I notice, standing outside the car, is how quiet it is. The shuffling of my feet on the gravel drive as I make a slow turn and the birds chirping in the trees are the only sounds I hear. Silence makes me uncomfortable, like I'm waiting for something to happen. And that something is usually unexpected, which is never good.

The next thing I notice is that I'm surrounded by nothing. Behind me is a long driveway leading to a scrolling iron gate that is much too tall to climb and a guard booth monitoring everyone who comes and goes. In front of me is a huge campus with a sprawling lawn that goes on for so long that I cannot see its end, only hints of other buildings spread across it. On either side of this massive campus are wrought iron fences that keep us protected from whatever is hidden in the dense forest with its endless rows of trees that eventually fade to black.

Finally, I focus on what I can no longer avoid. I tilt my head up to take in the floors upon floors of stone topped by severely angled eaves, pointing dramatically to the sky. The building is grand and impressive while feeling cold and confining at the same time. Tall rectangular windows mirror the grass and woods below and the clouds and sky above, obscuring what's hidden behind them. I cup my eyes and squint against the glare to focus on what looks like a person standing in front of a window peering down at me from an upper floor. But with a blink, they're gone. Or maybe they were never really there.

The yawn of the large, intricately carved wooden doors swinging open draws my attention. Revealed within the massive arched frame is a woman in a white tweed skirt-suit with a black silk blouse beneath, the collar tied in a large bow on the side of her neck. The vintage attire reminds me of one of Niall's suits, tailored to fit her perfectly.

"Welcome to Blackwood," she announces with a blinding white smile that makes me want to shield my eyes like I did when looking up at the windows.

"Lana?" Niall beckons, waiting for me to join him on the walkway.

"I'll make sure your bags get delivered to your room," Jax tells me, encouraging me forward with a nod of his head.

I let out a breath and force my legs to move.

"Good Afternoon, Dr. Kendall," Niall says when we reach the petite woman with the neon smile. He offers her his hand, which she cups in both of hers.

I study her with fascination and abhorrence. There isn't a wrinkle on her suit…or her face. She doesn't have a hair out of place on her fiery red head. And that smile—that fabricated smile that just won't quit—never reaches her eyes. And that's all that I need to know without her saying a word.

She's a liar.

"Mr. Harrison, it's always a pleasure to see you." She flutters her fake lashes at him, the smile a permanent fixture on her face. I feel myself instinctively step back when she redirects her attention my way. "Lana, it's so wonderful to have you with us at Blackwood. I know you're going to find your experience here transformative."

"I doubt it," I mumble. I haven't even entered the building, and I already want to get back in the car and drive away.

If she heard me, she doesn't react. "Let's get you settled in. There are only a few other students here right now. The rest arrive on Sunday for the summer session, so it'll be quiet around here this weekend." We follow her into the foyer, which triggers thoughts of Hogwarts with its enormous stone staircase wrapping around the towering foyer in a progression of angles. In the center, an elaborate, three-tiered chandelier is suspended, as if floating. The walls are adorned with Renaissance-style paintings and tapestries. It feels more like a medieval castle than a private school.

We enter a pair of French doors to the left of the foyer and step into the administration office. A large wooden counter separates the waiting area from the three empty desks on the other side—each in front of a corresponding dark, wooden door. It's disturbingly pristine, with every piece of paper and pen in its place. I fight the urge to scream to prove this isn't some twisted nightmare.

"Usually, your introductory meeting is performed by your life advisor, but he doesn't arrive until Monday. So I decided to personally welcome you. This is a big adjustment for you, Lana, and I want to impress upon you that we all want you to succeed. Don't we, Mr. Harrison?"

Niall clears his throat, taken off guard. "Yes. Of course."

The warden, dean, headmistress, or whatever the hell they call her, pauses in front of the door closest to the windows. "There's no need for you to stay, Mr. Harrison. I'm sure you are expected elsewhere. Lana and I can get along perfectly from here."

Niall hesitates, looking to me. I glance away, still unable to meet his traitorous eyes. "Lana?"

"It's fine. Go," I grumble.

I can sense that he's reluctant to leave, even without looking at him. "Okay. Well, I'll check in on you this Sunday. Call me if you need anything."

I want to tell him not to bother. That I don't need or want anything from him. But he's my only connection to the outside world. To my mother. To Allie's case.

Niall hasn't asked me more about that night, but he's kept me updated regularly on the investigation and Allie's condition. As of three days ago, she was still in a coma. I don't expect the police to make any progress in finding out who pushed her. I won't reveal the truth without Allie's account to support mine. I can't. Not as long as it's my word against Vic's.

I look over my shoulder just as Niall disappears into the foyer, dread sinking like lead into the pit of my stomach. I want to yell, "Take me with you!" But swallow the panic.

I follow the Warden into her office—because as of right now, this is my prison.

The door makes a definitive click when she closes it behind me. She gestures to the white Victorian-style chairs with black velvet padding, positioned in front of her elaborately carved, white, wooden desk. "Please have a seat, Lana." She lowers onto a black, high-back chair on the other side. It's more reminiscent of a throne than an office chair. How fitting.

Her office is just as immaculate as the previous room. Everything in its place, like it's never used or touched, and all in black and white, from the abstract art on the wall to the white bookcase and black filing cabinet in each corner. Even the carpet is a dizzying pattern of black and white fleur-de-lis. The only color is her vibrant red hair pulled up into smoothed barrel curls on top of her head, like a crown. I feel washed out in this setting, like all of my color has been drained away.

"This won't take long. Your life advisor will review what's expected of you in more detail, but I'd like to go over the most important guidelines."

"Um, what's a life advisor?" I ask, having heard her say it twice now.

"Every student is assigned someone to guide them. Your life advisor will help you make the best possible choices while you're here. But more importantly, he'll provide you with the confidence and skills to continue to make positive life decisions long after you've left us. We want you to succeed. To Thrive. To be your absolute best self. And we're here to make sure that happens. We pride ourselves on educating and transforming young people into responsible and contributing members of society."

I may have just thrown up in my mouth because it's all bullshit. Every word. This woman's only concern is making sure her checks clear to cover her Botox injections. She sure as hell doesn't give a damn what happens to me, while I'm here or long after I'm gone.

And this is when I disconnect. Everything that flies out of her smiling mouth becomes a buzz of rhetoric. I watch her lips move with a pained expression, my cheeks ache just looking at her. Not a single line moves on her face other than her mouth. Maybe the smile is surgically altered. A facelift gone wrong. She's like a Disney character on crack. Overly sweet and unbelievably fake. I guarantee there isn't a single authentic thing about this woman. Not her personality. Her gleaming white teeth. Her perky boobs. Or her emblazoned red hair.

The sourness in my stomach intensifies the longer I sit here, watching her shiny pink lips stretch and contort. With every word, the disingenuousness is revealed, like peeling an apple to find it's rotting underneath its shiny red flesh. It's all a façade. The truth is concealed within the twist of her words.

"To help you focus and be in the moment, we don't allow students to have their own personal cell phones or computers. You may use the computers in the study hall and library, but they do not grant access to social media sites or personal email accounts. We want you to be fully present in your studies and engage with your peers at Blackwood.

"I know it's a bit of an adjustment, but soon, you won't even miss the distractions." She says this without pause, as if she was prepared for me to have some sort of adverse reaction. I'm sure most students do when they learn they'll be disconnected from the rest of the world. But I wouldn't have access to a phone or a computer in juvie either. It's not that big of an adjustment for me. It just sucks that I can't contact Tori and Nina to let them know where I am.

She sets a small black phone on the desk. "We offer our own phone service so that we may communicate with you and support your positive choices. These phones will contact the administrative office, the security team and your approved contacts. We'll periodically check in. It's part of our exceptional security protocol.

We want to keep you safe and will make certain the choices you make do just that."

What? I almost say it out loud, but catch myself. Why are they concerned about my safety? We're in the middle of the fricken woods! Why do they need to stalk my every move? What kind of trouble could I possibly get into? Who *needs* this much supervision?

"Can the phones call out?"

"Yes. But they're monitored and can only call your approved contacts." She drags her mouse and makes a few clicks. "You're able to call Faye Peri or Niall Harrison."

"What about my friends?" I'm doubtful they're listed, but I have to ask.

"They aren't approved right now. But they may be added at a later time, once we've all agreed they're not going to deter from your success."

My success? What exactly are they expecting? This is sounding more like a reprogramming facility where they feed everyone bullshit and convince them it's candy. Exactly how do they plan to bring out our *best selves*? I'm actually afraid to find out. Especially when she keeps talking about how transformative this will be. This place is starting to freak me out.

The Queen Warden continues, but I'm lost in my head, trying to calm the cataclysm of emotions roiling inside of me. When she finally stands, handing me the phone that I left untouched on her desk, I can't look at her. I'm too busy chanting, *it's just six months*, over and over in my head. It'll be painful, like electroshock therapy, but it won't last forever. I can do this. What other choice do I have? But thinking that only pisses me off all over again.

A knock turns me around.

"Perfect timing." She walks to the door. "Sophia, thank you for being so prompt."

"Of course," a pleasant voice says from the other side.

"Please, come in." The Queen Warden takes a step to the side and a girl with shoulder-length black hair held back by a floral scarf greets me. She has big, round grey eyes that are striking against the light brown of her skin. Even though she's a few inches taller than me, she seems more delicate, like a doll, wearing a powder blue gingham skirt, a short-sleeved white blouse and sandals.

"Lana, this is Sophia," the Warden says. "I've asked her to give you a tour of the campus and to accompany you to dinner."

Sophia smiles so wide I can see *all* of her teeth. "Hi."

I nod without saying anything, not feeling very friendly right now.

"You girls enjoy the rest of this beautiful day."

I brush past Sophia without a glance.

"Hold up," she calls, following after me into the foyer.

I begin pacing in front of the main doors, trying to wrap my head around why Niall would send me to this messed up school.

"It's different than you were expecting, huh?" she asks calmly, but with a tone of understanding. "It is for everyone when they first get here."

I stop and stare at her. "Where is *here*? I have no idea where I am."

Her eyes tighten in confusion. "They didn't tell you?"

I shake my head. "I didn't even know the name of the school until I arrived. I know I'm not in Massachusetts. But where? New York? Connecticut?"

"Vermont," she answers. "In a town called Kingston. It's not a large town. The students from the two private schools and the skiers in the winter months bring in more people than probably live here year-round. But we pretty much keep to ourselves." She motions toward another set of doors on the opposite side of the foyer. "Want to take a walk around?"

I shrug in indifference.

When we're through the doors, I'm struck by an overwhelmingly sweet fragrance. Across the small rectangle of grass is what appears to be a tunnel formed by wisteria vines.

"We call this the Court. I suppose it's meant to be short for courtyard. It connects all of the buildings together."

The emerald green lawn stretches the length of the building, interrupted by hedges that are a story tall. We're caged in by the shrubbery and the only way out, other than going back into the building, is through the flowers.

I look over the top of the hedges and wisteria at the surrounding buildings. The one directly opposite of us is so far away, I can barely see it. The rest are evenly spaced to form a perfect circle around the Court.

"Straight across are the dorms. It's difficult to see them from here. I'll show you once we get farther in." We walk through the arching purple blooms. Bees whir overhead. "It can get pretty confusing once you enter because all the buildings are exactly the same, but each one has its own distinct entrance into the Court. I have a map of the buildings that I'll give to you. But I don't have one of the Court. It changes a little all the time; there isn't an accurate map."

I'm about to ask what she means when we emerge on the other side of the wisteria tunnel, only to walk into a small forest of birch trees. This is weird.

"Is this some kind of maze?"

"They call it 'an intricate architectural landscape,' but essentially, yes, it's—"

"Fucked up."

I spin around. Within the spotted white trunks is a girl sitting on a framed white swing. The kind that belongs on a front porch, not in a tiny forest of birch trees.

"Ashton!" Sophia scolds her.

"Aw. Did I scare you?" Ashton asks with a Cheshire smile. A cloud of smoke seeps out of her full lips. She takes another hit from the vape dangling from her fingers. She looks like she belongs in a rock magazine in her leather pants and neon pink bandeau, lounging casually on the swing with one leg dangling, an arm draped over the back. The bare feet are a little strange though. "I'm Ashton." She smiles again, her attention focused on me. "Is Sophia being the perfect tour guide?"

"We just started," I tell her.

"Oh, good." She hops up from her perch and leaves the swing rocking in her wake as she weaves between the trees to join us. "There's still time."

"For what?" I ask, finally getting a good look at the odd girl. Her sapphire blue eyes inspect me in return. Chestnut hair falls in thick, wavy layers over her shoulders. She's stunning and could easily be a model with her long legs wrapped in skin-tight leather. She's practically an Amazon next to me, even in bare feet.

"Let me translate for you," Ashton offers, unable to suppress the drug-induced grin.

"I speak English," I tell her with an amused laugh. This girl must be seriously high.

"Not for *you*." Ashton looks to Sophia. "For you, because someone needs to tell her how it really is around here. Not the propaganda of lies the administration makes you memorize."

Sophia's mouth opens in offense.

"Don't get all pissy." Ashton half-heartedly pacifies her. "It's not your fault you try to paint a positive coat of bullshit over everything. I blame your parents for demanding perfection. And since my parents are narcissistic asshats who don't give a fuck, I'm…me. The complete opposite of you. Which is why I'm the translator." Ashton looks to me. "Ready?"

"Translate away." Everything she just said sounded like a distorted riddle. This should be entertaining.

Sophia huffs in annoyance but doesn't stop Ashton from joining us when we begin walking again.

"So what's with this place?" I ask. I'm hoping one of them reveals something about this school that will help me understand why the hell I'm here. My bet is on Ashton. Sophia seems wound too tight and may snap if forced to break from her script.

"The Court or the school?" Ashton clarifies.

"Both."

"What do you already know?" She spins around in front of us, brushing her hands along the branches of the willow tree that drape over the path.

"Only what I was told when I arrived. No phones. No computers. That they do random check-ins. All to make sure we're *safe* and being our *best selves*. Whatever that's supposed to mean."

Ashton chuckles. "Oh, you had the Dr. Kendall welcome package. Nice."

"It's not a bad message," Sophia says, in an attempt to defend...the school? Dr. Kendall? Seriously? If Sophia's proper and reserved self is the example of "transformed" then I'm all set.

"The school is an elite institution that helps us reach our best potential. With an education at Blackwood, students become some of the most sought-after collegiate candidates," Sophia explains as if reciting from a teleprompter that I can't see.

"Translation," Ashton interjects before Sophia can continue. "We're here because our parents failed at being parents and needed someone else to step in and take over. Every single one of us is at Blackwood because no one else wanted us." Sophia opens her mouth as if to argue, but Ashton stops her with, "Even *your* parents couldn't handle the pressure." This shuts Sophia's mouth with an irritated snap.

Ashton turns to me. "Privacy's a big deal around here. No one will ask who your parents are, or why you're here. At least most won't. You can tell us if you want. But we get it if you don't. Whatever you did, it doesn't matter. Not to us."

As much as I appreciate her candor, Ashton still isn't making complete sense. Obviously this isn't a typical boarding school. I guess I never thought it would be.

"Okay," I reply in contemplation, taking it in as best as I can without prying even though I want to. "So explain the Court. How the hell do they expect people to get around without getting lost?"

I've already lost my way. We've passed three different gardens. One featuring a fountain with a mermaid shooting water out of her mouth. Another with a white wooden gazebo in the center of a patch of daisies. And another with hammocks hung within caves of hedges. It's like I've tripped into Wonderland. And I'm apparently surrounded by its main characters. Just waiting for the Mad Hatter to make an appearance, but I suspect there's plenty of crazy to go around this place.

"Look toward the building you want to get to, and don't lose track of it as you follow the paths that will take you there," Sophia instructs.

"The dumbasses who designed this didn't make a circular path along the perimeter that connects all of the buildings. Not on the Court side anyway. But walking around the drive on the outside takes forever. It's like they *want* us to get lost. Sick fucks."

"You shouldn't walk in here by yourself until you get used to it," Sophia advises.

"And never alone after dark," Ashton adds dramatically, her brows raised in emphasis.

"Why?" I practically scoff at her ominous tone. Everyone is seriously overreacting with this staying safe bullshit. We're in a garden, granted it's a twisted and messed up garden. But it's not like we're in Detroit.

"It's just easy to lose your way." Sophia dismisses Ashton's words with a pleasant smile.

Ashton continues as if Sophia hasn't spoken. "Things happen in the dark. Some good, but mostly bad. So don't wander alone. Newbies get lost out here all the time. You can hear their cries in the dark. Super creepy."

"Are you *trying* to freak her out?" Sophia scolds, blinking at me nervously. "Don't listen to her." Now I can't help but be a *little* freaked out. "The path is paved with luminescent stones, so if you stay on it, you'll find your way."

"It only lights up the path, not the places where you can get lost," Ashton argues. She is seriously confusing.

"The Court's actually really pretty when they decorate it with twinkle lights and lanterns for the balls." Sophia's face brightens at just the mention of it.

"Which only means that they *could* light it up all the time if they wanted. It's proof they're fucking with us!"

"Balls?" I question. "As in Cinderella?"

Sophia beams even brighter at the question. "We have a themed ball each month. Everyone dresses in amazing costumes. Sometimes the Printz-Lee students attend too." She leads us through a line of giant topiaries shaped like animals and teacups that eventually opens into a yard littered with tables shaded by colorful umbrellas.

"It's the school's way of keeping us sane. So we have something to look forward to each month while we're stranded in the middle of fucking nowhere," Ashton explains.

I stare at them with wide eyes, not understanding why a costume party is something to be excited about. It sounds ridiculous to me. "Does everyone have to go?"

"Yes. But trust me, you'll *want* to," Sophia gushes.

Ashton nods in agreement but understands why I asked. "If you don't go, it's because you got busted for something. And the alternative sucks way worse than getting dressed up and dancing for a night. Again, translation, there are ways to make the balls more *fun*." She winks at me and takes another hit from her vape.

Sophia rolls her eyes. "Put that away before someone catches you."

"You need to stop with the innocent act, Sofe," Ashton mocks.

Sophia inhales deeply and straightens her spine, struggling to remain composed. "Anyway, this building is the Great Hall. It's where we dine, gather for assemblies and any big events." Which explains the tables outside. "Hungry?"

"Starving," Ashton answers.

My phone starts beeping, like a microwave going off in my pocket. I pull it out to find the message. *Incoming call from Dr. Kendall.* I look to the girls with an awkward smile.

"Go ahead," Sophia encourages.

When I answer, the Queen Warden beams back at me on the screen. "Hi, Lana. Just checking to make sure you're not lost in the Court."

Sophia pokes her head over my shoulder. "Hi, Dr. Kendall." She waves. "She's still with me."

"Oh, wonderful. I was nervous that Lana might have wandered off," she says, forcing a laugh. I try not to cringe. "You girls enjoy your dinner now."

"Bye, Dr. Kendall," Sophia says sweetly before the screen goes blank.

"You have Dr. Ditz checking in with you?" Ashton asks incredulously. "What the hell did you do to deserve that kind of torture? Not even I've had her check-in on me the entire time I've been here. It's beneath her. You must be really special." Ashton laughs like she's in on a private joke, that apparently only she understands.

"It's probably because it's summer, and not everyone's here," Sophia offers, trying to make me feel better. "I'm sure it has nothing to do with you."

I remain quiet, suspecting it does. And Ashton's mischievous smile lets me know that she does too.

Chapter Four

Although the sorceress warned Thaylina to be wary of anyone who was too kind, too generous and especially, too charming, Thaylina had a trusting soul. She believed that in all hearts, there was good, even if only a small part. And that sliver provided her hope that every person was capable of kindness.

As we pass through each doorway, the device in my pocket vibrates. It's already getting annoying, and it hasn't even been a day.

"Our dorm's monitor is Mrs. Seyer," Sophia tells me as we walk through the trellis of blood-red roses, the entryway to our dorm. The space behind the dorm resembles a stereotypical backyard with hammocks and Adirondack chairs scattered around. "She's away this weekend and will be back on Sunday. She's—"

"The freakiest woman alive," Ashton says abruptly. I laugh at the shock of honesty. Ashton's spastic comments continue to catch me off guard. It's like she *needs* to share her thoughts, because if she doesn't, no one else will see the world the way she does. "Her room is across from the main entrance, and she's always lurking in the halls late at night. Be careful, she can make your life a nightmare. Or give them to you."

Sophia continues the tour as we enter the dorm's grand foyer, with Ashton's added "translations." She takes me into the Quiet Room across from the foyer where we can study. It's also, Sophia says, the only room boys are allowed in. Ashton rolls her eyes and shakes her head behind Sophia's back. There's a dining hall on the other side of the foyer where only breakfast is served during the school year, and sometimes it's used for special occasions, like "ice cream socials." Her words. Ashton's translation, "Where you can find the best munchies in the middle of the night."

With every lavishly decorated room, Sophia lists rules. And every time she does, a heavy weight grows in my stomach. This world that I'm being forced to participate in is overrun with rules. Despite the gourmet meals and beautiful grounds, it's confining. Restrictive. Barred with expectations I have no desire to meet.

Every message I've received today, whether from the judge, or Niall, or the Warden, has demanded something more of me. Something I'm not. Letting me know that who I am is not good enough.

When we reach the common room on the second floor, I'm only half-listening to Sophia gush about how much fun they have on movie nights—but making sure to add what time everyone is expected to be in their rooms.

"I think I'm going to go to my room," I say, heading toward the stairs. "But thanks for showing me around."

"Oh. Okay." Sophia sounds surprised, and even a little disappointed. "You're on the fifth floor. I can show you—"

"That's alright," I insist, desperately needing to be alone right now. "What room number?"

"Eleven."

I turn to say goodbye to Ashton, but she's nowhere to be seen. I can't recall when she disappeared.

"Thanks. Maybe I'll see you tomorrow." I should smile, but I can't fake it. "Is there an elevator?"

"Not for us. It's freight only, unfortunately." She watches as I start up the red carpet with gold scrolling that lines the massive stone stairs. "It was nice to meet you, Lana."

I nod weakly and continue up the stairs. By the time I reach my room, my legs feel like they're about to give out and my heart is pounding in my chest. The weight in my stomach has combusted into a fiery ball.

When I locate room eleven, I scan my phone over the electronic lock and enter. Slumping back against the door, I squeeze my eyes shut. I bite back the lump in my throat, urging me to scream—or maybe cry.

This entire day unravels around me in a whirl. The sentencing in court. Being forced to pack and leave everyone behind. Only to arrive here, a place so foreign, I may as well be in a different country.

It's not that I'd prefer juvie, but it's familiar. I know how to get by. Here, nothing's real. No one is who they truly are. Not the girl who tries too hard to be perfect. Or the one who acts like nothing bothers her. Forget about the Queen of lies who oversees us all. This is not where I belong.

I chose to remain silent to protect my friends. But it was a choice I should never have been forced to make. This is not what I wanted. I'm not supposed to be here. And the only reason I am is because Vic is still out there.

I clench my jaw so tight, my teeth feel like they might crack.

Just thinking about Vic intensifies the inferno in my gut. I inhale deeply, trying to squelch the flames. He'd better hope I never see him again. I breathe in a calming breath and blow him away, then slowly open my eyes.

The room's…white. And I mean, *everything's* white—the walls; the pedestal sink and the ornate oval mirror hung above it; the counter and cabinets next to it; the fur covered beanbag chair on the plush throw rug; the long, narrow desk next to the bookcase; the chiffon scarf draped along the top of the windows; and the ruched duvet covering the full-sized bed in the corner. It's all pure white. Except …

Sitting on a pillow is a zebra. An adorable stuffed zebra with huge sparkly, blue eyes. I find a note tied to its neck when I lift it from the pillow.

Please forgive me.

That's it. Just three words. But I guess that's all he needed to write. When did this get here? With Niall? And why does Joey care if I forgive him? It's not like I'm planning on seeing him again.

I toss the animal in the trash beneath the desk. Yes, the trashcan's white too. Unbelievable.

I flop down on the bed among the sea of throw pillows and stare at the ceiling. Rolling on my side, I can't avoid the huge blue eyes peering up at me from within the trashcan. I groan and shift my gaze to the bookshelf instead. A square glass vase of fresh cut white roses sits next to framed pictures. I sit up so I can get a better look. One of the pictures is of me and my mom. She's resting her head on my shoulder, sitting on a blanket at the park she loves down the street from our house. And there's another of me with Tori and Nina, laughing hysterically with our eyes squeezed shut and mouths open. I've never seen these pictures in print before.

The more I look, the more details I notice.

I push off the bed and examine every surface. Little touches of personalization are everywhere. Tucked in the corner under the desk is a fridge. I open it to discover it's filled with bottled waters and blue raspberry Mt. Dew, which is my favorite. On the desk, next to the white lamp with the feather shade is a small, square-framed picture of me and my grandmother when I was little. I'm sitting on her lap while she's reading me a story. She used to read to me a lot—mostly fairytales. The real, gruesome ones. Not the Disney versions.

But I've never seen this picture before. Ever.

Inside the desk drawer are all of my favorite snacks—gummy bears, Twizzlers, Lindt chocolates, and popcorn chips. Someone went to a lot of trouble to personalize this room. To make it feel welcoming, although it's not exactly my style. I know there's no way Niall decorated it himself. And it wasn't the guys or my mother. But *someone* did. And whoever it is found out a lot about me.

Glassy, heart-crushing eyes peer up at me from within the canister.

"Fine," I huff, picking the zebra up. Before I place him back on the bed, I untie the ribbon and drop the note back in the trash. "I still don't forgive you."

I heft my bags onto the bed and unpack. In the far corner, near the door, is a Narnia-sized armoire. I can barely reach the empty hangers lining a wooden bar. There are already a few items suspended from it, wrapped in white plastic. Must be the uniform I'm expected to wear during the regular school year. I look up at the top shelves that I'll never be able to reach, then stuff everything in the drawers that take up the bottom half of the wardrobe.

When I'm done, I roll up the duffle bags and toss them on the top shelves of the armoire, since I can't use them for anything else. I'm jumping in the air, trying to shove the last one in, when someone knocks on the door. The bag falls on my head. I growl in frustration as the knocker persists. Simultaneously tossing the bag on the shelf and shutting the closet doors, I hope it doesn't fall on me again when I open them back up. They knock *again*. Seriously?

I yank the door. "What?" Still irritated by, well…everything.

No one's there.

I step into the hall and look right. About a dozen rooms line this side, all with their doors closed. I turn around. The hall extends past the common room and grand stairs, to the end of the building. But I don't see anyone, although the lighting is pretty sketchy and every shadow could easily be a person hidden within a doorway or alcove. Remaining perfectly still, I listen. Not a single sound. The silence makes the hairs on my neck stand on end.

I wouldn't be surprised if someone was locked away in a tower. Or a dungeon. If I hear screaming at night, I'll know why.

A beep screeches from within my room. I spin, clutching my chest.

When I walk in, I notice the phone screen is flashing red. That can't be good.

"Shit." I rush to pick it up.

I press the green button to accept the call. Dr. Kendall appears on my screen, her snow-white smile prominent.

"Lana!" she exclaims merrily. "How are you getting along? Have you settled in?"

"Uh, I guess," I reply, disturbed by her exuberance.

"I can see here that you're in your room," her eyes shift to look at something off-screen, "which is good. We'll expect you to stay in for the rest of the night. Usually the curfew is midnight on weekends, but with there being so few of you, we're asking everyone to be in their rooms now."

"Okay." It's not like I had plans or anything.

"Have a good night's rest. You'll be starting your work assignment tomorrow morning."

The screen goes black. I sigh, vaguely remembering Niall saying something about being required to work off my fines and court fees. Apparently, I start tomorrow. Fan-fucking-tastic.

I turn and almost scream.

Ashton is leaning against the doorframe. I guess I didn't close the door when I came back in to answer the phone.

"Holy shit. You scared me." My heart has barely recovered from the phantom knock earlier. This place is going to give me a heart attack before the weekend's over.

Ashton saunters past me without being invited in. In addition to her leather pants, she now has on a flowy long-sleeved blouse and thick heeled boots. Her makeup is freshly done up, and her hair is styled. She looks ready to go out. But where? Especially since we're supposed to be in our rooms for the rest of the night, except...she's not in *her* room.

"Wow, your room is so...white."

"Yeah," I reply with a disgruntled sigh. "It was like this when I got here. It's not really...me."

"You've got to be kidding me." She clicks a switch on a cord suspended along the wall. I cringe when my name appears lit up in white letters above her. How did I miss *that*?

"Holy shit. That's obnoxious," I say, my mouth agape.

Ashton slowly circles the room, trailing a finger over every surface. There's something about the way she's casually invading my space, picking up and examining everything, that reminds me of Nina. I'm either going to hate this girl, or she's about to become one of my best friends.

Ashton flops down on the fur-covered beanbag. "So, what do you really want to know?"

I hesitate. "About what? The school?"

"Anything. I'll tell you. You might as well know what you're getting yourself into since they just abandoned you on the doorstep with a note attached to you."

I shrug because that's pretty much what happened. "And what do you want in return?" Honesty always has a price, and that's assuming she'll tell me the entire truth.

Ashton lets out a small laugh like she thinks I'm funny. "Nothing."

"Really?" I don't believe her. She tilts her head innocently. I decide to ask only what I can afford to offer in return. "Where are you from?"

"New York. Manhattan. You?"

"A shitty town in central Massachusetts." Naming it won't mean anything to her. I choose a question that I doubt she'll answer, just to see if she will. "Why don't you like your parents?"

"You like yours?" she scoffs.

"It's just my mother. And I can't fault *her* for me being who I am."

"That's big of you. I can't say the same. My father's a musician in a rock band, and my mother's a supermodel. I am absolutely who I am because of them." She hesitates, silently contemplating. "You should probably know that almost everyone here is a spawn of a celebrity, politician, musician, well, basically anyone who's anyone. We're their embarrassments. They shipped us off to the middle of nowhere so we don't disgrace them further, even though most of them do that so well on their own."

"That's why everyone keeps talking about security and privacy?" I conclude.

"You won't find any cameras beyond the main gate. Our parents don't want to be concerned about us making headlines at school like we do in the real world.

Which is one of the reasons they chose Blackwood with its military security and high-tech tracking devices. But that doesn't mean they can keep the drugs out of the addicts, the food in the anorexics, or secrets from being exploited."

"So everyone's fucked up?" Now I understand why I was sent here, except that I'm not newsworthy, and neither is my mother. I suppose every private school has to have their token scholarship kids.

"Pretty much. I think it's a requirement for admittance, honestly. And if we get kicked out, our parents financially cut us off. It's in the agreement they make with the school. That way everyone has something to lose. And, trust me, no one here wants to give up their designer handbags or private jets. So, we're forced to actually *succeed.* The rest of the world believes the school's respectable, graduating top collegiate contenders. But it's not like we have a choice."

"I know about that," I mutter.

"What?"

"Not being given a choice."

"So they really didn't tell you *anything?*" This seems to be a point of fascination for her, that I walked through the doors completely blind.

"Nope. Only that I was being sent somewhere *better.* But I don't come from money."

"So what do you have to lose?"

I stop to think about that for a minute. It's either here or juvie, and if they think that juvie is "losing," then they don't know me very well. Granted, I don't want to spend the next six months in a red jumpsuit, going to group sessions where we're taught life skills, anger management or whatever bullshit the counselor reads from a workbook. But it could be worse.

"Nothing."

"Then you're going to be fun to have around," Ashton says with her enigmatic Cheshire smile. She pulls her vape out of her pocket. "Want some?"

I smile back. "Desperately."

Ashton walks over to the windows and slides them open all the way. "They have super sensitive smoke detectors."

"Blackwood goes through all of this trouble to know where we are, how do they not know you left your room? Don't they have sensors or something?"

"They used to have motion detectors in the halls and sensors on the doors and windows. But that was a nightmare because no one stays in their rooms and someone always has a window open. So, they decided to focus on keeping us *in* the buildings with security patrolling the outside. Without our phones, they can't detect where we are, but that's why they have Mrs. *See-er* lurking the halls at all hours. It makes it harder to sneak around after curfew." With a mischievous quirk of her eyebrow, she adds, "But not impossible."

Ashton inhales from the vape before offering it to me. I breathe in the contents and hold it in my lungs for a moment, craving the escape I've needed all day. We each blow out through the screen, our smoke drifting like a cloud into the dark.

"What else do you want to know?" she asks, leaning on her elbows. I take another hit.

"How long have you been here?"

"This is my third year. I'm supposed to graduate in June. Although I have no idea how."

"Not into school?"

"Not into being who I'm not. And I'm an artist. I don't give a shit about any of this."

"I can help you, if you want."

"With school?"

"Yeah. It doesn't bother me, really. It's not like I try, but it's not that hard either. I did my best friend's work for her all the time."

"Thanks," she says sincerely. "But they have tutors, life advisors, and other ways to make sure the work is ours. They're not really grade driven here as much as choice driven."

I shake my head, still trying to understand what the hell that means. "So you can fail a test, but as long as you made the choice not to cheat, you're okay?"

Ashton laughs. "No. Failing is not an option. But they provide you with whatever help you need to pass. It's not a huge school. There's only like three hundred students here during the school year, and barely fifty during the summer. They have a ton of staff, and they get paid a shit-ton to make sure we understand what they teach us. Most of them live on campus during the school year so we have access to them whenever."

"Explain this choice thing they keep preaching about."

Ashton inhales from the vape, her eyes flicker as she tries to put words around her thoughts. "We're here because our parents couldn't be parents, and I guess we failed at being us.

"Blackwood's life advisors customize a plan that forces us to make better choices, whether it's random drug tests, therapy, meditation, or tracking our caloric intake at each meal."

"That's what that screen was for when we ordered dinner?" I ask. When I scanned my phone to order dinner earlier, a screen on the tablet displayed allergies, food restrictions and my macronutrient intake for the day. I didn't think much of it at the time, other than it was weird.

"There's more eating disorders here than anything. You have to remember, we come from a world where image is everything. And that's hard to let go of, no matter how far we are from the spotlight."

Ashton hands me the vape. The edges of the room begin to soften around me as my body eases into the mattress.

"Do you believe in it? What they're doing here?"

I'm still very skeptical. And maybe it's because Dr. Kendall is a living illusion. How can I be convinced that what I see is real when there's a maze within the courtyard that's sole intent is to get us lost?

Ashton hesitates again, tucking her vape back in her pocket. "I don't know. I guess it doesn't matter because I'm stuck here whether I believe or not. But don't trust anyone. That's the best advice I could probably give you. Nothing is what it seems."

"It's kind of my life motto already."

Ashton winks. "Which is another reason it's going to be good to have you here. And don't worry, it only feels like a prison. It's really not. There's always ways to break the rules, if you're willing."

"I have nothing to lose!"

Ashton laughs.

"Meet you downstairs for breakfast? I'm training you at work tomorrow."

"Sounds good." I watch her leave. Just as she closes the door behind her, I realize I didn't ask her where we worked. Guess I'll find out when we get there.

I collapse against the pile of throw pillows and stare at the ceiling, allowing the mellowness to seep into me. It's so quiet. I don't know if I'll ever get used to it. I lift my head, searching for something that plays music. I spot a small, decorative box sitting on the corner of the desk.

I push off the bed to check it out. Inside is an iPod. I didn't even know they made these anymore. It also contains earbuds, a charger, and a portable speaker. I power it on and scroll through the music. It isn't bad. I know a lot of the artists, but a few are new. Someone knows me—a little too well. It might freak me out if I weren't high right now.

I insert the earbuds and select a song. I nod to the beat, strolling around the room. It's twice the size of my room back home. But I already feel locked in. Since no one's monitoring the hallways this weekend, they won't know if I wander around. In truth, I'm craving ice cream and want to find the freezer.

I leave the iPod on the desk and stick a sock in my door, so it doesn't close all the way. I hesitate in the dimly lit hallway for a moment, listening. It's eerily quiet. Which makes me feel like I need to be quiet too. I tiptoe down the hall to the enormous staircase. My bare feet don't make a sound on the carpeted surface. It seems like it takes forever to reach the bottom. Why don't they have a stupid elevator?

I slip through the French doors to the dining room. The moon is shining through the enormous row of windows that look onto the back lawn. The dim light helps me navigate around the tables until I reach the swinging door that leads to the kitchen.

This kitchen is *nothing* like Stella's. Every stainless steel surface is gleaming in the soft over-counter lighting. I swear, even the cool tiled floor looks like it's glowing. Or maybe it's the drugs.

I open cooler door after door until I finally find what I'm looking for. With a huge grin, I select a tub of chocolate ice cream with caramel swirl. It's so huge, I have to wrap my entire arm around it to carry it. I slide a stirring spoon off a hook above one of the counters and walk back through the dining room.

My room is too far away, so I decide to go to the library or great room or whatever the hell the room is called across the foyer. The room that looks like an old guy in a smoking jacket should be seated on one of the wingback chairs, sucking on a pipe, and telling stories for PBS in front of its huge stone fireplace.

Mid-way across the foyer, I hear a creak. And because this place is quieter than a tomb, the sound reverberates throughout the entire entryway. I hold my breath because my altered brain is convinced that'll help me hear better. I slowly turn toward the noise. The door leading to the Court is cracked open. Jostling in the breeze, it releases another squeak. I exhale.

Ignoring the churning in my stomach warning me not to, I creep to the door and peek outside. I don't see anyone. I push the door open farther and step outside. A chill travels up my spine when my feet sink into the thick, cool grass. The warm June air breathes against my face, carrying the perfumed scent of roses. I close my eyes to let it seep in, inhaling deep.

The trellis leading into the Court reminds me of a dark cave. There aren't any lights, but I notice a soft glow emanating from the cobblestone path. I've never seen anything like it. Then again, I've never been to a place anywhere outside of Sherling (not counting juvie).

Adjusting the slippery tub in my arm, I venture toward the black abyss leading into the Court.

"Not a good idea."

I spin around, searching for the male voice that just spoke. It takes a moment for my eyes to distinguish his silhouette, lying on the hammock in the corner near the hedges.

"Um…what are you doing out here?" I inch closer until I'm at the umbrella table nearest him. It's too dark to make out his features, but it looks like he's wearing dress pants and a button-down shirt. Shit. I've been caught by one of the teachers.

"Waiting." That one word is laden with so much arrogance. Definitely not a teacher.

"For who?" I jab back with just as much attitude.

"You, Lana."

My sluggish brain fights to remember if I met him. But I haven't met any guys since I arrived, and the cook doesn't count. "How do you know who I am?"

Although I can't see his face, I can tell his hair is light; it looks almost silver in the moonlight. And the way the shadows play with the angles and curves of his face, it's like he was chiseled from stone. Maybe he's a vampire.

A giggle bursts from my lips.

"What's so funny?"

"You're alive, right?"

"And *you've* been hanging with Ashton tonight."

"How do you know?" I try to sound defensive, but end up sounding impressed that he figured it out.

"Umm…you're holding a giant tub of ice cream, and are about to eat it with a mixing spoon. Can that even fit in your mouth? Wait. I want to see you try."

I look down at the tub that's now dripping with condensation, soaking into my tank top. I rest it on the table, balancing the spoon across the top. "I was hungry."

"Clearly."

Smartass.

"How do you know who I am?" I ask again. My thoughts keep jumping all over the place, but…in slow motion.

He pushes a polished black shoe into the ground, rocking the hammock. He's holding a glass of something in one hand, while the other is slung behind his head like he was out here contemplating the meaning of life.

I sigh dramatically when he doesn't answer. I'm about to lift the ice cream again and go back inside, done putting up with this pompous ass.

"I think the real question is, why are you here?"

I look up, leaving the ice cream on the table. "Where? Out here or at Blackwood?"

"There's no possible way you could afford this school. Someone pulled some major strings to get you in here. Why?"

"I'm here on scholarship," I snap back, providing Niall's explanation.

"They don't grant scholarships at Blackwood."

I'm about to retort with some smartass remark when his answer sinks in. "They don't?"

"No, they don't. Especially not to someone with a criminal record. No one admitted has a record, even if they were arrested, and most were. Their parents are powerful enough to get it expunged."

He's playing with me, and it's starting to annoy the hell out of me. I huff, fed up. "Who are you? And how do you know so much about me?"

"It's why I'm here," he says, his voice almost aloof. "I know too much."

Then it hits me. "What are you, a hacker?"

He chuckles, the moonlight glinting off straight, white teeth. But he doesn't answer.

"Are you going to tell me your name, or do you prefer to annoy the fuck out of me all night?"

"Oh, I like you," he says, still smiling. "You bite."

I roll my eyes. "Really?"

"I'm Brendan."

And now that I know, there isn't a reason to stay out here. I lift the tub of ice cream, the spoon falling to the ground. I bend to pick it up just as deep voices cut through the hedges. I straighten, uncertain what to do.

Brendan rolls to stand—a sudden, silent motion—abandoning his glass beneath the hammock. He's tall and lean, his short hair parted neatly to the side. The mature attire and refined style make him appear much older than a high school student. No wonder I thought he was a teacher.

He nods toward the hedges at the corner of the building closest to us. I eye the door, thinking I can make a run for it before whoever it is, security most likely, comes through the rose trellis. I glance back at Brendan; he shakes his head as if reading my thoughts. He tips his head toward the hedges again just as I hear the voices—they're too close.

I rush toward the corner of the building, Brendan meets me halfway and guides me with a hand on my lower back. I squeak in protest when he pulls the tub of ice cream out of my arms and tosses it in the hedges. I stop and stare after it longingly when it disappears under the shrubbery.

"I'll buy you an entire ice cream truck," he whispers impatiently, tugging my arm. I relent, letting him drag me into the shadows. A beam of light sweeps the yard just as Brendan presses my back against the side of the building, urging me to slide between the stone and the hedge. And just like that, I'm back at the country club, with my heart pounding and green needles stuck in my hair. Except this time, I'm caged in by a hard body that smells of mint and a cool breeze. I press my nose to his shirt and inhale.

"Did you just smell me?" he whispers in my ear.

I quickly lean back against the uneven stone. I can't believe I just did that. I glance up to find him grinning down at me.

"What's the door doing open?" a voice asks. The flashlight searches the corners of the yard. "Do you see anyone?"

"No."

"Radio in and ask if anyone else reported finding windows or doors open."

What feels like an hour later, with Brendan's warm body way too close and his hands on either side of my head, we hear, "There was a window cracked open on the first floor on the other side."

"Are they going to do a security check?" one of the guards asks.

"They did. Everyone's in their rooms." I hear the distinct click of the door being shut "I hate doing the interior patrols. It's fricken creepy as shit." The voice fades as he moves away.

Brendan is so close. I try not to glance up, but I can't help it. He's looking down at me, his face lost in shadow so I still can't tell what he looks like. His lips curve into another arrogant smile. I push against his chest, but he doesn't budge.

"Seriously, you can get off me now," I tell him, my voice edged with warning. He lifts an arm, releasing me. I peek around the corner and then slowly walk back out into the yard. It's empty.

"You're not getting in that way," Brendan says quietly when I reach the doors. I know he's right, but I have to try anyway. They're locked.

"What do I do?" I'm more annoyed that I'm stuck outside than nervous about being caught. I don't necessarily *want* to get caught and have Niall be called back here on my first day. Imagining the disappointment on his face makes my stomach ache for reasons I don't want to explore.

"Back into the hedges." When I hesitate, Brendan beckons, "Come on, Princess, we don't have all night."

My spine stiffens. "Don't call me that," I snap coldly. I follow after him, slipping in between the hedges and the building. A few feet in, he stops in front of a tall wrought iron fence. I look up. There's no way I can climb it.

Instead, he crouches, flips up what looks like a grate, and jumps down. He turns toward me and offers his hand. I ignore him and sit on the edge of the lawn and hop down into the trench. I duck as he lowers the grate back in place. He's forced to walk in an awkward crouch, while I barely have to bend in half. We don't go too far before he stops in front of an arching subterranean window.

After fiddling with it for a few seconds, Brendan eases the window open and disappears inside. When I shuffle to the ledge, he's waiting beneath the window with his arms raised to help me down. I can't see the bottom, so I reluctantly place my hands on his shoulders and allow him to lower me.

Landing within inches of him releases a flush I'm glad he can't see. He doesn't remove his hands from my waist right away. I'm overtaken by his scent again and have to fight the urge to close my eyes and breathe him in.

When I tip my head back, he's wearing that same arrogant grin. "Are you going to smell me again?" If I were sober, I'd probably have punched him at least once already.

"Jackass." I shove him away as he releases a low, rumbling laugh.

Brendan climbs onto something to close the window and takes my hand when he steps back down. My first instinct is to pull away, but there's barely any light filtering through the small window, and I have no idea where we're going.

A small pinpoint of light cuts through the dark, revealing a damp, stone corridor. The light's coming from a phone, and not the school issued one either.

"Where did you get that phone?"

"There's not much I can't get," he replies, his cockiness tempting me to punch him in the face again. "Why? Do you want one?"

"Yes," I answer without hesitation.

"What would you be willing to do to get one?"

I yank my hand free and groan in disgust. "Go. Now. Before I murder you and let the rats eat your carcass."

"Sexy," he says with a chuckle.

I take in a breath, preparing myself before following after him. I stay close behind so I can see each step as we squeeze down the passage that looks like it was hand-dug and re-enforced haphazardly with piles of stones. I try not to think about whether it's stable, or what it would feel like being trapped in here if it caved in around us. Dizziness makes my steps falter as a light coat of sweat breaks out along my skin. By the time we reach a set of steep stone steps, I have to use the wall's support to stay upright.

The stairway is so narrow Brendan slides through sideways. The tight space makes my pulse thrum. My lungs feel like I'm breathing through cotton. I press against the stone, but I swear it's closing in around me...a trickle of sweat rolls down my cheek.

I catch the scream in my throat when a hand comes down on my shoulder. I swipe it away as if it were a spider.

"Touch me again and you bleed," I seethe.

He slides open a door and we enter the Quiet Room on the main floor with its worn leather couches and wingback chairs.

My entire body is shaking when I step through. I collapse against the cool stones of the fireplace, bent over with my hands on my knees, fighting to catch my breath.

Brendan slides the bookcase back into place.

"You gonna be okay?" he asks, his hand hovering above my back.

"Yeah," I breathe out with a shudder.

Once I've pulled myself together, I stand and cross the room toward the shadowy foyer. Brendan follows. I don't expect to find him still behind me when I reach the stairs. I turn to face him from atop the first step.

"Where are you going?" I demand, not even trying to be nice about it.

"Making sure you get to your room okay."

"Thanks for sneaking me in, but I can manage from here," I tell him, crossing my arms over my chest.

"Are you sure? I'd hate for you to get lost on your way to your room."

"I've got it." There is no way in hell he's getting near me or my room…ever. Even if he does smell good.

Brendan steps up next to me.

I can finally see his face. And I think I may hate him.

His hair is naturally platinum blond, not silver. I wasn't wrong about the angles of his face, but he doesn't have the deathly pallor of a vampire. His bronze skin makes him look like he's spent the summer on a yacht. To make things worse, he has big, brown eyes lined with thick lashes and beautiful full lips a guy should never be allowed to possess.

I hate him.

"I'm in room fourteen, on the fifth floor."

When I just stare at him like he's delusional, he adds, "So you can find me when you want me."

"Which will be *never*."

"You don't lie, Lana. Don't start now." He winks.

I glare at him.

He leans down until he's within a breath of kissing me. I defiantly grit my teeth and don't move. "You're going to need something from me eventually."

"Go away."

There's something intrinsically captivating about him. Hypnotic. Like the call of a siren luring a ship into the rocks. Treacherous, yet seductive. I back away, the hairs on my arms standing on end in warning.

"Sweet dreams, Lana."

I watch him exit the door leading into the Court. After a few seconds, I rush over to it and pull to be certain it's really closed.

A thumping sound breaks the silence. I freeze halfway across the foyer and listen. A scraping noise comes from…somewhere. And because I haven't learned a single thing from any of the horror movies I've watched, I follow it.

Another thump can be heard down the hall. Slowly, I continue toward it, hugging the wall. Not sure how this will help protect me, but it's what feels right, so whatever.

I stop in front of a door that's cracked open. I hear a muffled grunt and swearing. Poking my head in, I blink in surprise when I find Ashton staring at me from the other side of the window, trying to force it open. I rush over to unlock the window and slide it open.

"Omigod, I cannot believe you were here. Thank you so much," she gushes as she ducks in and closes it behind her.

"How were you able to reach the window?" I ask, recognizing how far the window is from the ground.

"Step ladder," she explains. "I keep it hidden under the bushes. But I swear I left the window open."

"The security team saw it," I tell her. She opens her mouth to ask how I know this, but I stop her. "Don't ask. It's a long story."

She quirks a brow, intrigued. "Well, thank you for rescuing me." She smells of beer and…something earthy. I can't quite place it.

I must be wearing a similar curious expression, because she silences me with the same response. "I'll tell you later. Right now, I *really* want to go to bed."

"Me too."

I'm exhausted by the time we climb the five flights of stairs to my room, silently cursing every single step, parting with Ashton at the top. This has been the longest day, but not *the* longest. Nothing will ever compare to *that* night.

I enter my room and find "Lana" shining on my wall. I must have forgotten to shut it off. I keep it lit while I change and wash my face. When I click the switch off, the wall beneath my name is…glowing.

"What the…" My heart thumps hard in my chest. I turn on the lights and look around my room, searching for any other sign that someone was, or may still be, in the room. There's nothing except for the words written on my wall that scream at me in the dark.

I KNOW

Chapter Five

The beast watched Thaylina from within his dark cavern as she came and went from the tower, waiting for the day that he would ensnare her, and harness her power for himself. Possessing the ability to prey on others' deepest desires would leave no one invulnerable to his charm.

I was up until *after two* in the morning scrubbing the glowing message off my wall with a round-bristle hairbrush and body wash, so I am *not* happy when my phone starts beeping at eight, demanding a fingerprint. The screen glows with a follow-up message, letting me know I'm scheduled to work from ten 'til four o'clock today. Except, it leaves out *where*.

"Shoot me," I groan, pulling the covers over my head.

Twenty minutes later, I'm awoken again by a knock on my door. "Go away!" Whoever it is, and I'm assuming it's either or both of the girls, knocks again. Bleary-eyed and disoriented, I shuffle across the room to answer it. "I need—"

It's Brendan. Before I can shut the door in his face, his foot jams between the door and the frame. I hope I broke his toe. "Good morning, my fiery little nymph. How'd you sleep?"

"Get out!" I shove at the door, but he opens it without much effort and steps in. He begins looking around in much the same way Ashton did when she entered.

Despite the hype about being big on privacy, evidently there are no personal boundaries at this school. "What do you want?" I demand, crossing my arms over my braless chest, not that it helps much considering I'm standing in the middle of the room in just a tank top and underwear.

Brendan openly ogles me with a grin. "Someone's not a morning person." Unlike myself, Brendan is groomed to perfection and immaculately dressed in a pair of charcoal pants and a pressed black button-down, and of course, the polished black shoes.

I pull on a sweatshirt and yoga pants, before throwing my hair in a messy bun. "How did you know which room I'm in?"

Brendan shakes his head like he pities my ignorance. "I told you, there's not much I don't know."

"I thought that was just your ego talking," I mutter. "Seriously, what do you want?"

"I wanted to walk you to breakfast," he says, focused on the stuffed zebra with a puzzled expression. "But I'd be willing to keep you company in bed if you want to sleep in."

I'm about to tell him just how much *I* know about punching him in the throat, but realize I don't know the way through the Court to the dining hall. I also don't know which room is Ashton's, and there's a good chance she's still passed out. "Can I go like this?"

Brendan shrugs. "Wear whatever you want. I prefer the sleeping attire personally, but this works too."

I roll my eyes. "Are you really this pathetic? Your lines are killing me."

He flashes me his sexiest smile. And that almost *does* kill me. Why does he have to be so fricken hot, while still being a dick?

"Lead the way," I tell him, gesturing to the door. Brendan holds it open for me to exit and then follows. "I thought guys weren't allowed upstairs."

Brendan chuckles. "There's a way around every rule, Lana. *You* should know that."

"Why did you say it like that? You don't know me. You only know what you read when you hacked into the school records."

Brendan stops mid-way down the hall with an eyebrow raised. "You really think I'm a hacker?"

"Aren't you?" I continue past him and down the stairs.

He doesn't answer. I realize after we exit the dorm, that I still haven't seen anyone other than the three people I've met and a couple campus guards. No groundskeepers or teachers. It only heightens the school's unnerving charm. "Doesn't anyone *work* here?"

"Not many. There are only a couple teachers here for the summer session. And you'll rarely see any of the grounds crew or janitorial staff, even during the school year. They make a point to schedule them so they're not seen."

"That's weird," I comment.

"It's an image thing."

"Still weird."

I *try* to pay attention to each path he turns down and the specific gardens and benches we encounter, but it feels like Brendan's taking me a completely different way than Ashton and Sophia did yesterday.

"How was the rest of your night?" he asks, encircling a bright red maple tree on a small rolling hill of lush, green grass. I stop. Brendan turns and takes in my glowering expression with drawn brows. "What?"

"You *know* everything." It's an accusation.

"And?" He says this like I'm slow to catch on. There isn't the tiniest hint of guilt in his voice. I can't read him and it's driving me crazy. Maybe his arrogance is interfering with my ability to detect if he's lying.

"When were you in my room? And why are you fucking with me?" I demand with a bite, losing my patience.

"Umm…you let me in your room, *this morning* after I *knocked*. And I'm not fucking with you, although I would like to—"

"If you say it, I *will* punch you, and not in the face," I seethe. "Stop being an ass. I'm serious. Someone was in my room last night. And you claim to know *everything*. So if it wasn't you, who was it?"

"I wish I could say, Princess, but I have no idea what you're talking about."

"I told you not to call me that," I growl.

"Right. Because it's actually *Fairy* Princess, isn't it?"

Shock cements my feet to the ground. Brendan smirks and continues walking past a small lily pond surrounded by stone benches. My heart rate accelerates. I watch him move with casual-confidence, like he didn't just admit to knowing about Allie. Which means he has access to more than just my school files.

I can't even imagine what he's cursed with, because he doesn't seem to have one redeeming virtue, forget about one that he values above all others.

I storm after him and grab him by the arm. He's stronger than he looks. I might as well be trying to move a tree. Eventually, he relents and glances down at me.

"How much do you know about me?"

"Enough."

"I swear…"

"You're adorable when you're all fierce and threatening. Like a wood sprite gone all *Atomic Blonde*."

I slam my foot down on his instep. He jerks it back, swearing. "What the fuck was that for?!"

"Talk," I demand.

His jaw twitches as anger hardens his eyes. "You don't belong here."

"What?" Of all the things for him to say, I wasn't expecting something so… obvious.

"There are prerequisites to being admitted here and you don't meet any, other than being a fuck up and having a brain. You're not Ivy League material. Your family isn't wealthy or even notable. This school has a reputation, and you don't fit. So, why are you here, Lana? Because of what happened that night? Or because of who you were with?"

I'm speechless for a minute. The dots aren't very hard to connect. But why would Niall arrange to have me sent *here*. How is that protecting Joey and Parker? And how does Brendan know any of this? Because who I was with wasn't in any report.

"How much of what…happened that night do you know?" I'm careful not to admit to anything in case he's just making assumptions.

"What are you really asking, Lana?"

"Do you know the truth?"

This time, he stops walking, a bemused expression on his face. "The truth?" He studies me, a glint in his eyes. "Now I'm intrigued. The truth is the only thing worth knowing. What are you hiding, Lana Peri?"

"I didn't ask the question as a challenge to find out! I just…need to know what *you* know."

"About Allison?"

"Allie," I correct him. "How do you know about her?"

"Sucks what happened to her." The sympathy doesn't reach his eyes. Maybe the reason I can't get a good feel for whether he's lying is because he's a sociopath. He has no emotions to read.

"Is she…" I swallow. "Is she still alive?"

"It's still listed as an assault, not a homicide, if that's what you mean."

I relax, slightly.

"Did you do it? Push her?" he asks so calmly, like he wouldn't be surprised if I answered yes.

My jaw tightens. I burn holes through his skull with my glare.

I storm past him, not sure if I'm walking the right way. But I can't be within three feet of him right now. He's been trying to get inside my head since I met him. And now he is, and I hate him even more for it.

"Go right," he calls out as I near an intersection. When I turn, I notice the animal-shaped topiaries that lead to the Great Hall's umbrella tables.

I *grab a banana, muffin* and an iced coffee, having lost my appetite on the walk over. I seek out the corner table I keep gravitating to at each meal. There isn't anyone else in the dining room. I still haven't seen the fifth student who's supposed to be here with us.

"Hi."

I shake away thoughts that had me staring at nothing and find Ashton sitting next to me, with a cup of coffee and a greasy egg and cheese sandwich—hangover food. "Thank you so much for letting me in last night. This summer would've sucked if I got caught."

"No problem."

"What were you doing downstairs?"

Before I can answer, Brendan sits across from us with a plate of poached eggs, grilled tomato and asparagus. I can't help but make a face. That is *not* breakfast food. At least not for anyone under forty.

"Good morning, Ashton." His eyes drift over every inch of her. "Did you two plan your outfits?"

Ashton's wearing a torn sweatshirt that hangs off her shoulder and a pair of sweatpants. Her hair is barely contained in a low bun, with strands haphazardly sticking out. Even hungover and without a hint of makeup, she's gorgeous.

"Oh," she says like she feels guilty. "You met Brendan."

"Someone had to keep her company."

I make a gagging sound in the back of my throat.

"Were you playing with your toys at the barn last night?" Brendan asks her, unaffected.

A devilish smirk is her only answer before she takes a huge bite of her sandwich.

"I don't know how you do it. Drink piss-warm beer, listen to country music, and sit on bales of hay with people you have absolutely nothing in common with."

"What else is there to do?"

Brendan gives her a pointed gaze, and she fights back a grin.

"What's *the barn?*" I ask.

"It's an abandoned barn about a half mile through the woods," Ashton explains. "Some of us sneak out there in the summer to party with the locals. This town is too small, and until everyone gets back, there isn't much to do. I have to improvise to stay sane or else I can't be held accountable for my crazy. I'll take you with me some night."

"Uh, maybe," I reply, not convinced I need that kind of excitement.

Brendan appears amused by my reaction but doesn't comment. "Are you working today?" he asks Ashton.

"You know I am." Ashton pushes her empty plate away. She checks her watch and asks me, "Want to walk back to the dorm? We should probably get ready. The shuttle's picking us up in an hour."

I flick my eyes to Brendan, who continues watching us curiously, like we're here purely for his entertainment. "Sure."

I take the coffee with me, leaving Brendan alone.

"I'm sorry I forgot to tell you about him," Ashton says as we push through the doors leading into the Court. Maybe *this* time, I'll be able to remember the way back.

"Did you hook up with him last night?" she asks casually.

"What?" I shout. "Gross!"

Ashton side-eyes me like I'm crazy. Maybe my reaction was a little dramatic.

"Relax. I'm not judging. Not many of us have any room to judge."

I stare at her in shock, my mouth open. "You?"

"He knows what he's doing." She shrugs, not bothered. "And he's honest about what it is or isn't. I respect that."

"So he's the school—"

"Don't." She cuts me off before I can label him.

I'm shocked into silence. I didn't think he was someone worth defending.

"He's a friend," she explains. "I get why you might not like him. He has no filter or boundaries, and he should come with a warning label. But, he *is* authentic. Brendan's upfront with who he is, no apologies. And that's why he's one of the only people in this school I trust."

Now I *really* don't know what to say.

"Besides, he can get you just about anything you need."

"For a price," I scoff.

"Doesn't everything in life come with a price?"

I choose to change the subject, unable to wrap my head around the fact that Brendan is trustworthy. "So, where do we work?"

"Oh, you poor girl. Your people are truly cruel to you, aren't they?"

I don't respond, because I didn't think Niall was...until yesterday.

"The Kingston Country Club." Ashton turns down a path lined with tall sea grass. I make a mental note. "I'm not sure where we'll be assigned, but hopefully we'll be on the course today."

"On the golf course?" I'm suddenly afraid they're making me caddy for the summer, lugging golf bags that are as big as I am. "Are you sure?"

She grins. "That's where the fun is."

An *hour and a half later,* we exit the black shuttle that's more like an oversized limousine than a bus. The drive felt like it would never end as we passed endless tree after tree, with a farmhouse and field thrown in to break it up every so often.

I follow Ashton around the side of the Clubhouse to the employee entrance. This country club is set up differently than the one in Oaklawn. The course is sprawled out behind the Clubhouse, with a scenic view of rolling hills and vibrant green trees. I'm convinced there isn't much else to Vermont. The Clubhouse resembles a massive home with yellow shingles. A giant porch wraps around the back to a turreted corner. I only get a glimpse of it before going inside.

"There are two employee entrances," Ashton explains. "This is the Greens entrance, and on the other side of the building is the event entrance. Depends on where you're scheduled to work. The Greens is the casual restaurant where the members who play golf and tennis hangout. Sometimes, families eat in there too, but they usually eat at The Deck by the pool."

We walk down a hall, passing employees dressed in khakis, polo shirts and white sneakers. The sneakers were the only thing I was told to bring. I'm hoping my experience will convince them to schedule me as a waitress, and not with the grounds crew or anything that has to do with golf. I can barely play mini-golf, forget about actual golf.

I follow Ashton into an office with "Club Manager" displayed in gold letters on the door.

A man in a suit sits behind a desk. The office isn't much bigger than the dark wooden desk and the chairs in front of it.

"Hi Cary," Ashton says, gaining his attention.

"Ashton!" Cary greets warmly from behind wire-rimmed glasses and a friendly smile. "This must be Lana." He stands and comes out from behind his desk to shake my hand. "Nice to have you with us."

"Thanks," I say without nearly as much enthusiasm.

"Ashton is going to take you to the uniform closet and have you pick out a uniform for each department."

"Formal too?" Ashton questions in surprise.

"Yes please," Cary confirms. "Lana will be training for fine dining come the winter."

I exhale in relief. I can tell from Ashton's pained face formal dining is far from her favorite thing, but it has to be better than dragging around golf bags—or mowing the grass.

"Once you've changed, give her a quick tour. The two of you will be on the bev cart for the day, so make sure you're out on the course by eleven. Lana, I'll need you to fill out paperwork at the end of the shift."

This brings a shine to Ashton's eyes. "Let's go." She takes a key from Cary and leads me to a door halfway down the hall. "Pick out a uniform from here,

here, here and here." She points to different shelves. "Wear this one today." Indicating the shelves with the khakis and polo shirts. "Depending on your schedule, you may need more than one. But we'll figure that out later. I'm going to take the key back to Cary and then I'll show you where we clock in and change."

I sort through the sizes and hold up the different uniforms, to be sure they'll fit. I meet Ashton in the hall with a stack of clothes. Since I can't clock in without my assigned employee ID, Ashton just points to the computer terminal before taking me to the locker room to change.

The tour is a blur of faces and names that will take me the entire six months to remember, and that's just the employees. Forget about the members Ashton greets by name…mostly old men in some sort of hideous golf attire.

When we leave the Clubhouse, we pass the tennis courts. Ashton mentions them in passing and I don't bother looking since they have nothing to do with my job.

"Lana!"

I almost trip and fall on my ass spinning around at the sound of my name being called from somewhere near the tennis courts.

"Shit," I breathe when I see who it is.

Parker Harrison jogs toward us, wearing white shorts and a fitted navy sports shirt. Following at a distance carrying two tennis rackets is the most beautiful girl I've ever seen. And considering I'm standing next to Ashton, that's saying a lot. I curse the pang of jealousy that jolts through my stomach.

"Parker," I greet him coolly, ignoring the rush I experience at the sight of him. "What are you doing here?"

"I should be asking you that," he says, pulling me into a tight hug. I awkwardly hug him back because keeping my hands by my side would be even more awkward. Over his shoulder, the blonde with the flawless, porcelain skin, crystal blue eyes and raspberry stained, pouty lips smiles brightly at me…like she's happy to see me too. I'm confused by her reaction, because he's not hugging me in a I'm-happy-to-see-you kind of way. His arms wrap around my body possessively, holding me against him as he brushes his lips across my neck. "I've been worried about you."

Parker is reluctant to let me go and I have to slide my arms between us to casually break free.

"Good to see you too. I thought your dad told you what happened."

"No. Not much. I knew you were attending Blackwood, but not when, or that you'd be working here."

"Well…here I am," I declare, stretching my arms wide, painfully aware that the two girls are watching us.

Parker notices when I glance behind him and takes my hand before turning to face her. "Lily, this is Lana. Lana, this is my cousin, Lily."

Cousin? I guess *maybe* I can see it…in the eyes…a little. But I honestly would never have guessed they were related.

"Hi," I reply with a slight nod. "Umm…it was good to see you." I casually try to slide my hand out of his grasp. "But I need to get back to work." I know the polite thing to do would be to introduce Ashton. But I don't want to be polite. Because I don't want to be standing here.

"Hi Ashton," Lily says. "Do you know Parker?" Lily's thoughtfulness makes me feel like an ass.

Ashton smiles at him in the way most girls do. It's like they can't help it. I've seen it so many times before, I'm tempted to roll my eyes at her starry-eyed gaze. I had higher expectations of Ashton. But then again, I'm one of his victims too. "No. We've never met, but I've heard of you."

To my surprise, Parker threads his fingers through mine and offers a polite nod, sheathing the panty-dropping smile that gets him just about everything he wants. "Nice to meet you. Would you mind if I spoke with Lana for a second?"

Ashton glances at her watch. "I guess we don't have to finish the tour right now, but we have to be at the cart station in ten minutes."

"I just need five," Parker says, flashing a hint of his charm at her. She smiles back automatically, bewitched.

"Sure."

Parker wraps his arm around my waist and forcefully leads me away from the girls, combatting my resisting feet.

"What?!" I snap, spinning out of his hold once we're far enough away.

"What do you mean, 'what'?" he asks, confused. "I haven't seen you in almost a month. And the last time I did, was the night—"

"I know what night it was," I interrupt, looking around—afraid of being overheard.

"Lana, I feel responsible in some way."

"Why? You didn't do anything wrong." Then after a second, I add, "Right?" Because I still don't know what happened to Allie after I left her in the stairwell... in the care of Parker and his team.

"No," he assures me. "But I can't help but feel like I should've done something more. To keep you from being," he lowers his voice and whispers, "arrested."

"Well, you convinced your dad to represent me, so there's that. Although, right now I'm not sure if I'm really happy with that decision either."

"Why? What happened?"

"I'm *here*. In the middle of fricken nowhere."

"It's better to be here, trust me."

"I don't belong at that school. This isn't my life, Parker."

"It could be," he says like the possibility appeals to him.

"What?" I stare at him like he's insane.

"I'm just saying, you've been gifted an amazing opportunity. Give it a try. You might find that you belong here more than you realize."

"Why? Is who I am not good enough?"

"That's not what I meant!" He widens his eyes in adamant denial. "But you deserve a chance to do something with your life."

I groan. "I am so sick of people telling me that I need to *be* something. It's such bullshit."

"Lana, we should probably get going," Ashton calls to me.

I start walking around Parker, but he grabs my arm. I eye his hand and then him with a cocked brow. He drops it. "I've been staying at the family's lake house with Lily this week. I need to see you before I go."

As if she could hear us, Lily says, "I'm having people over tonight. You ladies should absolutely come. You know where the house is, right, Ashton?"

"I do. But I don't know if Lana—"

"I'll have my dad sign her out," Parker finishes like he knows what Ashton's about to say.

"Okay," Ashton replies, a smile in her voice. "We'll see you tonight."

I'm annoyed they all decided this for me. So just to be a bitch, I say, "Maybe." And walk away.

"Lana! You'd better show!" Parker shouts.

I grind my teeth and clench my fists as we continue around to the back of the Clubhouse. I catch Ashton's ridiculous grin out of the corner of my eye, like she figured us out and is amused.

I open my mouth to deny whatever she's assuming, but close it and tense my jaw again.

"Not mutual, huh?" she laughs.

"No," I huff. I am so irritated, I can't form words—only grunts and grumbles of frustration. Ashton laughs harder.

"Do you want to go tonight? I'm not sure if you'll be able to since it's only your second night. Newbies have restrictions for the first month or so, but you also didn't mention Niall Harrison's your lawyer."

"You know Niall?"

"Of course. He's one of the best. I should know."

"Really?" I ask, intrigued.

She grins deviously. "We're all at Blackwood for a reason, right?"

I laugh.

"Lily always throws the most amazing parties. It'll be fun. And I'll sacrifice myself, so Parker won't come anywhere near you." She winks, and I roll my eyes.

"I'll go," I say with a resigned sigh.

A golf cart comes into sight, or I should say a bar on wheels. It has two coolers built into the back and shelves stocked with liquor and snacks.

"Hey!" Ashton calls to the guys dumping ice into the coolers.

The blonde straightens. Holy shit, he's tall. Easily over six feet, which means he might as well be a giant. And…I'm staring. Because he's flawless. And I mean in the way sculptors immortalized Greek gods from marble flawless.

The guy with dark hair, who had his back to us when we approached, turns around. "Yes! A hot new girl."

"Shut it, Rhett," Ashton threatens. "Grant, this is Lana. Lana this is Grant…and shithead."

"Hey, that wounds deep, Ash," the dark-haired shithead clutches his chest.

"Hi," Grant says, a genuine smile spreading across his face.

"Hi," I reply dumbly, fighting the urge to smile back, because I know if I do, it'll be one of those doe-eyed girl smiles. And I would hate myself if I looked at anyone that way. So I bite my lip instead, which is also a bad idea, because now I look like I'm trying to give one of those seductive, lip-bite smiles. Please, someone save me from myself.

There's a slight flush to Grant's cheeks, probably from lifting the huge bags of ice. He has the ruddy Scandinavian complexion that tans effortlessly but flushes easily too. He's at the beginning stages of the tan. His blond hair has sun-bleached streaks mixed in with shades of gold and honey.

Heat spreads across my cheeks, and I have to look away because I *never* blush. Fine. He's beautiful. But why the hell am I acting like a star-struck lunatic?

"Tablet's all charged up. There's cash in the box. You're all stocked and ready to serve the course," he tells Ashton. He addresses both of us. "Have fun out there."

"I'll be seeing you at the ninth," the shithead says with an eyebrow waggle that makes me outwardly cringe. Grant laughs at my reaction. I smile at him before looking down again. I swear, a giddy thirteen-year-old has possessed my body.

"Lay off, creeper. You don't want her to file a restraining order on her first day," Ashton throws at Rhett.

Ashton climbs in the front and I sit next to her on the passenger side. When she turns the key, it sounds like a damn lawnmower. I thought it would be much quieter.

The cart beeps when she backs out of the spot and jerks when we move forward. I have to grab onto the sidebar to keep from falling out.

"You'll get used to it," she assures me as we drive along a paved path toward the golf course.

"So…you like the good guys. I never would have guessed," she says with a goofy smile.

"What?" I scoff.

"Grant. I saw."

I roll my eyes dismissively. Only because I can't seem to find the right words to describe what happened. I'm not quite sure myself since I've only been an idiot around one other guy, and that didn't end so well.

"It's okay. I mean, if you were to gush over anyone, Prince Philip is worthy."

"You call him Prince Philip? As in *Sleeping Beauty*?"

"Yes!" she laughs. "Not many get that reference. His last name is Philips. And well, he's a fricken prince, in all the ways that fairytales get it right."

"Are you kidding me?" I snort, disbelieving.

"Not at all. He's a good guy. Again, I would never have guessed you go for that type."

"I don't even know him!" I defend weakly. "Besides, how do you know he's really a good guy?"

The corner of Ashton's lip twitches in a devious smirk. "Because he's not *my* type."

Chapter Six

One day, as Thaylina was gathering herbs and berries in the forest, she heard the most beautiful voice, singing. The enchanting song lured her deep into the woods until she came upon a shadowed figure dressed in an emerald green cloak.

"Why are you alone in the woods?" the deep, smooth voice asked the girl.

"What are you doing alone in the woods?" she asked in return.

"Waiting for you." A tall handsome man came into view. A sly smile on his lips. A shine in his eye. And a sharp point to his teeth. "And now, here you are."

By four o'clock, I've learned that golfers have an easier time parting with their fives and tens after the ninth hole, than most patrons at Stella's have releasing singles. And even though I'll never see a paycheck for all the hours I work, no one can take the cash I make as co-bev cart girl from my pocket. I have no idea what I'll need the money for, but it's nice to know I have it—just in case I need to send some home.

I also learned that, unlike Stella's, the country club is law-abiding regarding its alcohol service. Since I'm under eighteen, I can only dole out waters, sodas and sports drinks, along with any snacks. Ashton turned eighteen two months ago and was recently promoted. Thankfully, *she* doesn't care about the law and topped our Cokes with rum each time we were forced to wait for a golfer to hit the fricken ball.

Which is another lesson from today…golf is *boring*! Because our cart is diesel and loud, we aren't permitted to pass through the course if someone is getting ready to swing or putt. It was torture having to wait for the players to line up their shots. Just swing already!

One of the highlights of the afternoon is when we finally reach the shack at the ninth hole and are able to cool off in the air-conditioned bathroom while the cart is restocked. This is also where I met Stefan, the head bartender. Not in the bathroom, but tending the Ninth Bar. He has this peculiar intellectual, man-of-mystery kind of vibe going on. Ashton says he's a grad student at Columbia and has worked at the club every summer since he was sixteen. He throws parties at his family's summer cabin regularly and doesn't care who attends, meaning all ages welcome. He's all about *good energy*.

"I think he's kissed half the girls on staff, and a few members' wives too," Ashton gossips while we balance with one foot on the toilet, leaning against the counter to allow the cool air from the air conditioner direct access to our underarms. "But he can get away with it. For some reason, he doesn't come across as skeevy. It's like everyone likes him. Everyone. There's this crazy magnetic field around him that attracts people to him, and if some of those people end up kissing him, so be it. It's like it's no big deal."

Even after only meeting him for maybe two minutes, I totally understand what she means.

"See you at Lily's tonight?" he asks us as we're sliding back into the bev cart.

"Wouldn't miss it," Ashton calls to him as she presses on the gas a little too hard, almost rocketing me from my seat. I holler in surprise, which makes her start laughing. I join her. It *was* pretty funny.

"How are we getting to Lily's? Do you have a car on campus?"

"We're not allowed cars on campus, but we'll secure a ride. Don't worry."

Except, I am worried as soon as we step out onto the main steps of the administration building and find Parker waiting for us beside his Land Rover.

"Why are you here?"

"I told you I'd get you signed out." Parker opens the passenger door, waiting. "Did you bring a bathing suit?"

I open the back door and climb in, allowing Ashton to sit in front. Parker's smile falters when I don't do as expected. Whatever.

"They're in here," Ashton tells him, holding up her shiny gold tote bag. "Thank you for driving us. It's sweet of you."

"Of course," he replies as he shuts the door behind him. "I wanted to spend some time with Lana before I left." He adjusts the mirror so can he direct his electric blue eyes right at me.

It's going to be impossible to avoid him, especially without Nina here to distract him. And it's not that I don't like him. Parker is charming, intelligent, and has this irresistible confidence that's incredibly sexy. But for so many reasons, I have to keep my walls up around him, *especially* when I really want to smash them down.

"How big is this party?" I ask as we exit the school's enormous wrought iron gates and pull onto the road that abuts the property. There's nothing but trees on either side. It seriously feels like we're the only ones in this town. It's so weird.

"I'm not sure," Parker answers. "Lily's invited everyone."

"Everyone knows Lily," Ashton interjects. "She's your cousin, right? I thought she said this was her mother's family home that you all share?"

"It is." Parker glances back at me at the mention of his family, probably trying to read my face. Because, yes, I'm silently asking if Joey will be there. He shakes his head ever so slightly. I relax into the seat with relief. I could go all summer, or a lifetime, without having to see him again. "But Lily gets more use out of it than we do, especially during the summer. My mother stays there during the school year to commute to Dartmouth. I almost never come up. It's too quiet for me. I prefer the city."

I fight to suppress a grin, not surprised by his answer. Maybe we are more alike than I want to admit.

Ashton peppers Parker with questions the remainder of the ride, and even though we're supposedly in the same town, it takes us a half hour to get to Lily's because everything is so spread out. And it doesn't help that when we finally turn onto the dirt road leading to the house, Parker is forced to drive like five miles an hour the entire bumpy mile or two.

The enormous luxury cabin is isolated, surrounded by thick woods without a neighbor in sight. I spotted small wooden signs with numbers nailed to trees as we drove in. I assume the dirt drives lead to other homes, but they can't be seen from here. Cars overflow out of the driveway and continue along the tree line. Parker drives past them into the circular driveway and double parks next to an Audi coupe in front of the main doors.

Even though it's still daylight, all of the lights shine through the contemporary wooden cabin with angles of glass and beamed overhangs. I'm having a hard time even calling it a cabin since it's bigger than any house I've ever seen.

As we enter, the music bounces around the open cathedral ceiling and out the open doors to the back. I only get a second to glance around the ultra-modern leather, granite and glass design of the main living space and the shiny stainless and marble kitchen, before we're swept up by the energy outdoors. The party is taking place on a two-level deck that connects to a dock jutting out into the water. People are talking, laughing, swimming, and eating everywhere. It's like a big barbecue, but so much nicer. Everyone is dressed like they just stepped off a yacht, or flew in on a private jet—casual luxury.

I noticed it today at the country club too, or maybe I was more sensitive to it than others because I've never been exposed to this much wealth in my entire life—it was *obvious* who came from money and who didn't. And it wasn't based on if they were working at the club versus a member. Because other privileged students, whether enrolled in private schools or college, work at the country club alongside the local students and residents. And the wealthy weren't more attractive or better dressed. Some had horrible fashion sense, to be honest. But they distinguish themselves in the way they talk, move, and generally hold themselves—the elongated posture, the carefree laugh and the ease in which they do…everything. I think if Ashton were to find herself cut off from her trust fund, she'd still have that extra something about her that screams she grew up with money.

And here at Lily's party, it wreaks of privilege and wealth. I'm choking on it, like walking into a room filled with smokers—the only person who notices the stench is the one who doesn't smoke. The *smoke* doesn't bother me, as long as they don't blow it in my face.

Parker has his hand on my lower back, guiding me through. I silently plead with Ashton to intercept him, and she makes a face that says she's trying. But Parker knows what he's doing, and no matter who approaches, or what obstacle of people we have to maneuver around, he remains tethered to me. And I very much need to break free…before I don't want to.

"You're here!" Lily is in front of us. She's wearing a blush pink string bikini top with a mini white sarong. Her hair is pulled up in a high ponytail, and her skin is glowing. Again, I'm caught off-guard by how effortlessly perfect she appears. "You should put on your suits. Ashton, you know where the changing rooms are downstairs, right?"

"I do," Ashton tells her. "We'll be right back." Ashton takes my hand and snaps me away from Parker before he can react, and I feel like kissing her.

"Thank. You," I exaggerate each word, relieved to have broken free.

"What is the situation with you two?" Ashton walks down a set of steps off the deck that lead to a basement level. She pushes a glass slider open, revealing a cozy sitting room.

"He and one of my best friends hook up regularly. And even though they both say it's nothing, I don't touch anyone my friends have. No exceptions."

Ashton laughs. "Girl, either you won't have many friends at Blackwood, or you won't be hooking up with any guys. It's impossible not to recycle here."

"Recycle?" I cringe, having no problem interpreting the meaning, but disturbed by it all the same. Ashton laughs again. "I don't plan on being here long enough for it to matter."

"He seems like a decent guy, and he's definitely into *you*. I'm not going to throw myself at someone who doesn't want to be with me. Sorry."

"I know. He really isn't a bad guy. I just…I don't trust myself, and I can't face Nina if anything were to happen. I know she's lying when she says she doesn't care about him. And even though they really are toxic for each other, I can't go there. Maybe now that we're away from him, it'll be easier to avoid him."

"I can totally help you avoid."

Ashton hands me my suit when we enter a hall lined with three partially opened plank doors. "Meet me here. We'll walk out together." She disappears into a room. I enter another and find a dressing room with its own shower. And I don't know why *this* is my trigger, but…What the hell am I doing here?

A few minutes later, I emerge in my two-piece, oily-black halter and strappy bottoms. It's a bit of a sporty look, but it keeps everything tucked in place in a way string bikinis don't. Whereas Ashton is all legs in her one-piece that cuts high and plunges low, with a mini sarong loosely draped on her hips. I thank my platform sandals for giving my diminutive stature every inch of added height.

"Drinks upstairs first." Ashton directs us down the hall to a set of stairs that lead up to the main room of the house where we find liquor bottles and mixers lined along the kitchen counter. "Champagne?" she asks, opening a fridge that is stocked exclusively with beer, wine and champagne.

"Sure," I respond, never actually having tasted champagne. I mean, we bought the cheap stuff last New Year's, but we mostly sprayed it all over each other. I've never had *real* champagne. It can't taste worse than piss-warm keg beer.

I take the glass she hands to me and take a sip. The bubbles crawl up my nose, making me want to sneeze. I cringe. I can't keep my nose from scrunching in distaste.

"Don't like it?"

"Just have to get used to it," I explain. Ashton muffles a laugh.

"You can have whatever you want. No sense drinking something you don't like. I'll mix you a drink instead."

I hand it back to her. "That would be better."

Ashton takes the glass of champagne for herself and proceeds to create something made up of a lot of different ingredients. She shakes it and pours it over a glass of ice, topping it with a lime slice. When I take a sip, it has a mint and lime essence, with a touch of something sweet. I can't even taste the alcohol. "So much better. Thank you."

"Of course." She winks at me. "Let me go first so we can *avoid*."

I follow after her. We veer to the left down the stairs and end up at the hot tub.

"Ashton!" a girl in a bright turquoise bikini shouts from the water.

Ashton sits on the edge of the deck next to the girl, only sticking her feet in. I sit next to her, subtly scanning the crowd to see if I recognize anyone from the country club while keeping an eye out for Parker.

"Lana, this is Kacly. She works at the club too."

"I saw you when I was working the counter at The Grille, but we didn't get to meet."

"Oh. We never made it to The Grille today. We got distracted mid-tour," Ashton explains.

I recognize almost instantly that Kaely doesn't radiate the prosperity aura.

"Which school do you go to?" I ask, just to test my theory.

"Kingston High."

"You grew up here?"

"My entire boring life," she says with a heavy sigh. "Until this summer anyway."

In my periphery, a flash of blond catches my attention. I turn to find Grant walking farther down the deck. I take two huge swallows of my drink to keep from doing something idiotic...like call out his name.

Ashton nudges my arm. "I know you see him." I whip around and silently beg her not to do anything stupid. She laughs at my reaction.

"Stop," I plead. "You're making it worse. I'm trying really hard here, and you're not helping."

Ashton snorts. "I've never seen anything like it. It's like you can't function. I noticed earlier today when we were at the ninth."

I close my eyes in mortification at her reference to how I tripped over my own feet when Grant came out of the ninth hole shack with two huge bags of ice hefted onto his shoulders. I nearly fell face first but caught myself last minute. It's not like he was shirtless or anything either. I tried to convince myself it was because I was expecting to see Rhett, and was just surprised when it was him. But that wasn't the truth.

"And again when we were clocking out."

I literally lost my voice when he spoke to me as we were leaving for the day. He said, "Nice to meet you, Lana." That's it. That simple. And I was a fish, gasping for air. What the hell?!

I become this pathetic, swoony puddle of a girl whenever he's within five feet of me, and I'm about to drown myself in the hot tub to make it stop.

"I *swear* to you, I'm *never* like this. I have no idea what's wrong with me."

"What are you talking about?" Kaely asks, looking between us to try to get in on the conversation.

I glare Ashton into silence.

"Lana has a...phobia," Ashton fibs with a huge, taunting smile on her face. "But I think you should face your fear head-on. It's not nearly as scary as you think."

"What's your phobia?" Kaely asks, really wanting to be included.

I'm not trying to exclude her purposely. But I don't really know her, and this, whatever it is, isn't something I want to talk about—with anyone. So I confess the first fear that comes to mind. "Love."

Ashton loses it. Completely. She has to cover her nose to keep the champagne from shooting out of it.

"Stop it," I scorn. "It has nothing to do with him. I really fear falling in love. I was being honest."

"Really?" a male voice asks from the corner of the hot tub, right next to me.

Ashton's eyes become the size of full moons when she sees who overheard me. And now I'm terrified to look.

I feel a knee inadvertently bump mine. I slowly turn and come face-to... shoulder with Grant, sitting on the deck with his feet lowered in the hot tub like ours. I think I *will* drown myself now.

"You've never been in love?"

"No."

"How can you be afraid of something you've never experienced?" He peers intently into my eyes, like he'll find the answers there. I don't blink. My mouth is dry. And breathing takes effort.

"I learn from other people's mistakes. And I've watched as they let themselves fall for the wrong person over and over again." I'm surprised my voice sounds strong despite the wheezing sensation happening in my chest.

"But what if it's the right person?"

"You only *think* it's the right person until they become the wrong one." My voice is even stronger, like it's outside of my floundering body. Even I'm surprised by its conviction.

His mouth twitches in amusement. "You never know unless you try."

"Love isn't a game that you *try* and receive a pat on the back when you fail. It's too big of a risk. Only idiots fall in love. No thank you." I swallow hard. The truth slips out much too freely from my lips. I'm never this transparent.

"Never?"

"Never." I can't feel a single inch of my body, completely lost in his unblinking gaze.

He nods in contemplation, allowing the strength of my conviction to sink in.

I sling back the rest of my drink and heft myself onto my feet. "I need another drink. Ashton?"

Ashton and Kaely are staring at me with big, round, animé expressions. Ashton snaps out of it first. "Yes. I'm dying for another drink. Kaely, c'mon."

As soon as we reach the kitchen, my knees give out and I collapse onto a stool. "Holy shit."

Ashton gawks at me. "The first conversation you have with Prince Philip is to tell him that you'll never fall in love, ever? Omigod, that was...intense."

"You like Grant?" Kaely asks in awe.

"What?" I forcefully shake off the remnants of what just happened. "I don't even know him." I repeat my weak defense because I can't make myself say, "No."

"Heard you broke a thousand hearts out by the hot tub."

I groan as Brendan sits down next to me. "What are you doing here?"

"I was invited. Just like everyone else." He leans in close and lowers his voice. "It's nice to see you too, Princess."

I glower at him.

"Want something to drink, Brendan?" Ashton offers, setting a fresh cocktail in front of me.

"You know what I like," he says with a wink. She cocks her eyebrow flirtatiously. Ashton proceeds to scoop some ice cubes into a glass and pour an amber liquid over the top.

"I know exactly what you like," she says seductively, setting it in front of him. I have to move before I throw up all over both of them. I step in front of the window that overlooks the lake. People are sitting on the dock with their feet in the water. Others are jumping off the end, and a few are floating on inflatable chairs.

I don't remember exactly when I learned how to swim. Sherling has a town pool and we would go when I was little. And I remember my mother taking me to a lake once or twice with a bunch of other families with kids, but the details are hazy. I'm not a strong swimmer. But at some point in my life, I learned how to do it well enough to keep me from sinking. I guess that says a lot about my life in general.

"He's not your type," Brendan says from beside me, looking at the same view. "He has too much...integrity for people like us."

"Like us?" I look up at him in offense. "Don't start comparing me to you."

"Let's put it this way, we're at Blackwood. He's at Printz-Lee."

"So?" I don't know why I'm getting defensive about this. I shouldn't care if I'm Grant's type, or if he's mine.

Brendan grins that mischievous, knowing grin that makes me want to punch him in the throat. "We don't deserve people like him."

And that shuts me up. I don't know how to argue against that.

"I'm going outside," I announce to no one specific, choosing to use the side door out of the kitchen so I don't have to cut through the middle of the crowd.

Brendan's words deflate me, and I hate him for knowing just what to say to make me feel like shit. Dick.

Why do I care what Grant Philips thinks of me? I just met him today. I mean, how much can you actually know about a person after just a few hours? I haven't even spoken with him, other than to declare my vow to not fall in love.

I groan. If I could take back any five minutes of my life…I pause. Yeah, that wouldn't be it. It'd be the time in the convenience store. Definitely.

There's a steady decline of small wooden platforms along this side of the house that eventually dump onto a small private beach. I lower onto a cloth covered lawn chair and watch people jump from the deck and splash into the water. The sun is setting on the far side of the lake, swirling oranges and pinks into the water, like someone dipped in a paintbrush to rinse it off. The surrounding houses are visible from here, nestled around the lake and within the woods.

I release a deep breath when I notice Grant on the dock. He's sitting next to two guys, listening to whatever they're talking about with their animated hand gestures. He's dangling a beer bottle between his knees, nodding along with their passionate conversation, like it's enthralling. As if he can sense me watching him from within this small inlet of the beach encircled by scraggly bushes, he raises his head and peers directly at me.

He smiles softly, and I smile back. I think he's about to stand but then decides against it.

"Avoiding me?" I hear from behind me. I close my eyes and exhale my disappointment. When I look up at him, he says, "Don't answer that."

Parker sits on a lawn chair beside me. "Brought you food." He hands me a plate. It smells amazing.

"Thanks." I take the plate filled with beef skewers, grilled vegetables and potato salad. He holds out a fork. "And you know why I'm avoiding you."

"She's not here, Lana. And why would she have to know?"

I ignore him and stab a potato.

"Not like Sherling parties, huh?" he notes, not following up the insinuation that just because Nina's not here, it's okay for something to happen between us.

I let out a short laugh. "Nothing like Sherling parties. I shouldn't even be here."

We eat in silence for a minute.

"No, you shouldn't." His voice is quiet with a hint of apology. "I mean, you should never have been arrested."

I place my plate on the glass table next to the chair. "What happened after I left that night?"

Parker sets down his plate and sidles next to me on my chair, facing me with his hand resting on my hip. His eyes lock me in, the brilliant blue delving deep. "I didn't know how badly she was injured, I swear. They wouldn't tell us anything when we dropped her off, and we couldn't stick around in case they called the police. But I promise you, she was conscious when we left her."

"She was?" My heart skips in my chest. "Did she say anything?"

Parker's brows scrunch in thought, trying to remember. "Something about having to help her. Don't let him hurt her." He looks up, his face lighting with realization. "She meant you, didn't she? She was talking about you."

I swallow.

"Remember that one truth you promised me—"

"Don't," I beg. "Please don't use it now."

Parker gently rests his hand on my cheek. "You can trust me, Lana."

I open my mouth, unsure what's about to come out, a protest or a confession. But nothing does.

"Please," he urges. "Maybe if I knew, I could help. I won't let anyone hurt you."

"I didn't push her." The easiest truth to confess.

"I know," he says, surprising me.

"You do?"

"Of course." He looks at me in confusion. "You thought I'd actually think you'd be capable of that? I've seen you in some crazy fights, Lana, but you're not cruel."

Except, I can be. "But you told me to keep my mouth shut."

"Yeah, because I wanted to take care of everything. To protect you."

"And yourself."

Parker tilts his head, not denying it. "I didn't know what exactly happened, but I knew you were involved. And you weren't dealing with it very well, so I needed to get you out of there. Tell me what happened?"

I hesitate, searching his eyes. Can I trust him? And even if I did, what could he do?

I open my mouth. The truth's about to slip from my tongue when I hear footsteps clicking along the wooden planks. Parker closes his eyes in frustration.

"There you are," Lily sings, coming up beside us. "Sorry. Did I interrupt something?"

"No, it's fine," Parker replies, standing. "What's going on?"

"Nothing. I just haven't had a minute to speak with Lana yet." She drags a chair to the other side of me as Parker sits back in his seat, picking up his plate. "I wanted to ask how you liked your room?"

"What?" I look from Lily to Parker. He shrugs, not knowing what she's talking about.

"At Blackwood? I wasn't sure what colors you liked. The guys weren't any help. So I decided to keep it clean and simple. But I really hope you like it."

"You decorated my room?"

"Yes." She beams, her smile is vibrant and kind. I instantly feel guilty for not liking it. I mean, it's not *that* bad.

"That was really nice of you," I say, sincerely. "Where'd you get the pictures?"

"From Olivia." She adds, "Parker's mother," when I look confused. I nod, like that makes sense. Except it doesn't. How did Parker's mother get pictures of me?

"I know Kingston isn't where you want to be, but I promise we'll have the most unforgettable summer!"

"Maybe I should stay," Parker interjects.

"You know you can't," Lily tells him, pouting slightly. And somehow it looks sincere and adorable on her.

"I know." Parker sighs.

"When do you go back?" I ask him, suddenly not wanting him to leave either. I want so much to trust him, so I don't have to be alone with the truth. But is he capable of helping me if I do?

"Tomorrow."

"Oh." I slouch in the chair, unable to hide my disappointment.

"I'll be back though," he assures me. "We'll figure this out."

"What are you talking about?" Lily asks, looking between us. Then her eyes widen like she suddenly understands. "Oh!"

But now I'm confused. I turn to Parker for an answer. Then I hear someone shouting my name.

I cock my head, listening. "Is that…"

"Ashton," Lily confirms.

"I should find her." I stand and reach for my plate.

"I'll get it," Parker tells me, getting to his feet. Before I can walk away, he grabs my hand, pulling me toward him. My heart does this flippy-skipping thing in my chest. I'm trying to decide if it's excited or afraid when he wraps his arms around me and murmurs low in my ear, "You really can trust me. Even if it's only as friends." He meets my eyes, letting me know he's serious. "You know I want more than that, but if it's all I can get, I'll take it." He leans down and brushes his lips against my cheek.

"Lana!" Ashton hollers, much closer.

"I have to go," I say softly, reluctantly easing out of his arms. Just as I turn around, Ashton appears, her eyes frantic.

"There you are! We have to go, right now! I totally forgot about the early curfew-thing this weekend!" She grabs my arm and pulls me after her.

"I can drive you," Parker calls after us.

"Lance is already waiting for us in your car," she tells him over her shoulder, still yanking me behind her. She pushes her way through the crowd; swears trail after us as drinks spill and jostle.

Parker is still in pursuit. "Lance has the Rover?"

"He said to get it from the school tomorrow when your father comes to visit." There's a crowd congregating right in front of the entrance to the house. "Move!" Surprisingly, they do.

I'm half tripping, half being dragged through the house, wanting to pull away from her talon grip. But I'm too busy trying not to fall on my face.

"I'll see you tomorrow!" I hear Parker say from somewhere in the distance.

"Bye!" I call back, not sure where he is or if he can hear me.

"Hurry!" Ashton orders the driver, sliding in the passenger seat. I pop in the back.

We fly out of the driveway almost as soon as my door closes. This guy isn't nearly as careful on the dirt road as Parker was. I'm jostled and bounced on the seat.

The headlights reflect off a sleek black GT at the end of the driveway. The vintage car stands out among the newer luxury vehicles. Before we turn away, the beams reflect off a shaved head in the driver's seat. I stop breathing for a second. Straining in the seat, I twist around as we pass the car, trying to get a better view. But it's too dark.

"Hey, I'm Lance." I settle back on the leather to face him. The driver has shaggy, dirty blond hair. His reflection flashes a friendly smile through the rearview mirror.

When I look into his eyes, I want to die. Another fricken Harrison!

Chapter Seven

"I heard you singing. Will you sing for me?"

"And what will you give to me?" he asked, cunning in his eyes.

"I don't have anything to offer."

The man smiled, his fanged teeth gleaming. "Oh, but you do."

The handsome man stepped behind a tree. Thaylina followed, but he was gone. She couldn't stop thinking of the mysterious man. Even long after she returned to the tower.

So, you're Lana," Lance continues when I don't say a word. "My brothers are barely talking to each other because of you."

Ashton rotates in her seat to face me. "Ooh, scandal!"

"I didn't know there were three of you," I say, trying to change the subject. "Are there any more Harrison siblings I should be warned about?"

Lance laughs. "Nope. Just the three of us. And I don't need a warning. I'm nothing like my brothers."

"That's why he attends Blackwood with us," Ashton announces proudly.

I scoff. "Because you're so innocent."

"No. I just don't hide my faults."

"That's noble of you," I say, sarcastically. "Is your father also your lawyer?" I don't expect him to answer.

"No, Dwight is," he says with a grin, letting me know he's not bothered by my prying.

"Dwight? As in my court-appointed lawyer?"

"Uh, no. Dwight, as in an associate at my dad's firm. But yeah, same guy."

What? He's been representing me for two years. Why did he lie to me?

"You have *two* lawyers?" Ashton's eyes widen like she's in awe of me. "I'm officially obsessed with you."

"You didn't know, did you?" Lance darts a glance at me through the mirror again. I shake my head.

"It doesn't make sense," I say out loud. I probably shouldn't, but maybe Lance knows something. "I've never paid for a lawyer. Why would your dad do this?"

Lance shrugs, either because he doesn't know or refuses to answer.

It takes us half the time to get back to Blackwood with Lance driving. And thankfully, there aren't any cops on the road. Per usual, there's *no one* on the road.

Lance parks in a lot off to the side of the guard booth, next to about a half-dozen other cars. As soon as he turns off the car, Ashton hits the ground running.

"Move!" she yells over her shoulder. "Eight minutes 'til curfew!"

Lance takes off after her, and with a sigh, I chase them both down. Why do I always have to run to keep from getting caught?

I struggle to remove my platforms. Our feet slap the marble as we race through the foyer of the administration building. We continue through the Court, the branches and flowers reaching for us as we pass. The luminescent cobblestones are disorienting under my feet. I sprint to keep up, knowing if I fall behind I'll be lost.

"See you in a few," Ashton yells to Lance as he veers right toward the guys' dorm and we continue left.

I can smell the roses before I see them.

My phone beeps.

"Shit," I mutter.

"They're checking in?"

"Yes."

"Faster."

We race through the doors and take the stairs two at a time. Ashton could easily take three if she wanted, but my legs are struggling to reach two. My thighs are on fire, and my lungs are gasping for each breath.

My phone beeps again.

"How many more beeps before I'm screwed?"

"One." We reach the fifth floor. "Come to my room after."

I'm hurling my body toward my room. My hand is shaking as I hold it under my door monitor. I lift it to my face to accept the video call as I'm walking across the threshold.

A man appears on the other side. His head looks like it was haphazardly chiseled from rocks. Undeniably ex-military. He doesn't look happy. Or maybe he always looks like this. "That was too close. I wouldn't advise doing it again." Then he hangs up.

I collapse on my back onto the bed with my arms splayed. Holy shit. My heart is pounding, and I'm actually sweating. Just so I wouldn't be caught out of my room after curfew. This is so stupid.

At this moment, I realize, I'm still in my bathing suit. I can't even imagine that video feed if they had surveillance.

I change into a pair of fitted sweatpants and a cropped hoodie before leaving my phone on the desk to go to Ashton's. I stick a flip-flop in the door, so I don't lock myself out and walk down the hall. Except, I don't know which room is hers.

Then again, it's not too hard to figure out. All I have to do is follow the music. I stop in front of room twenty and knock just as the door opens. Ashton jumps back in surprise, looking like she was about to leave.

"You found me!" She opens the door wider for me to enter. "I'm going downstairs to drag Sophia up here. I'll be right back."

Before I can react, she slips past me and is gone. I turn to find Lance and Brendan lounging on a light grey couch that's pushed against the wall under a loft that holds up Ashton's bed. Her room is so…Ashton. She is scattered all over, from the framed abstract and cityscape photographs on the wall to the plush furniture that looks like you could sink in and get lost. Not to mention the graffiti mural taking up the entire wall behind the bed and couch. It's sexy but has an attitude at the same time, like a supermodel flipping off a camera.

I remove a lacy bra from a chair and flop down, still feeling the ache in my body from the sprint to the room.

"Want some?" Lance holds up a bottle of champagne.

"Sure," I sigh, willing to give it another try. Not that I can be picky.

"Here, top it with this," Brendan offers, reading my less than enthusiastic response and reaching into Ashton's fridge to pull out a bottle of fresh squeezed lemonade. He pours some in the champagne flute and hands it to me. I tentatively take a sip and nod in appreciation.

"Thanks." I look to Lance who's sipping his champagne. Everything about him screams "guy." The slouchy khakis, the half tucked t-shirt and the disheveled mop of hair on his head that flips out around his ears and nearly covers his eyes. But he's so at ease tipping the elegant glass to his lips, holding it by its stem. The contradiction is sending me on another trip to Wonderland.

"You're the fifth student?"

"Until tomorrow."

"Where have you been?"

"Spent last night at the lake house."

"What year are you?"

"Sophomore? You?"

"Soph…" I stumble, realizing we're moving into a new school year. "Junior."

"Are you sure?"

"I forgot for a second. Spending the last few weeks of school in juvie messed me up."

"You went to juvie?" they ask in unison.

"You've never been? Neither of you?"

They shake their heads.

"My dad picked me up at the station the night I was arrested. I was barely in the holding cell."

"Never been arrested," Brendan says.

Lance and I stare at him, calling him out on his lie. Except, unlike everyone else, I can never tell when he's lying.

"Swear." Brendan rests a hand on his heart. "My principal couldn't exactly press charges for sleeping with his wife. Maybe for accessing his hidden account and helping her take all of his money, but they never proved it was me."

I blink.

Lance starts laughing. "That's the best!"

"What were you arrested for?" Brendan asks Lance.

"Dealing," Lance says. "Charges didn't stick."

"Were you?" Brendan pushes.

"It's complicated." He looks to me briefly, like I might understand. Although I can very much understand *complicated*, I can't imagine how it applies to him. Then I do.

Parker.

"You covered for him?"

Lance shrugs a shoulder, not admitting or denying. I roll my eyes. Just when I'm about to trust Parker and believe he cares, he reveals another conniving, self-serving side of himself that forces me to see the truth. He doesn't care about me. He just wants to be sure nothing that happened that night will come back to get him.

"And you?" Brendan looks to me. "What horrible thing could you have done to be sent to a juvenile detention center?"

"You went to juvie?" Ashton bursts out from the other side of the room, with Sophia behind her. Sophia stares at me with her mouth open—and maybe just a little fear in her eyes.

I groan. "I'm not like you guys. I don't have parents who have a criminal lawyer on retainer."

"Or a publicist to spin a story about having the flu when their daughter is found passed out in a bathroom at an L.A. club." Ashton sits on the bench against the window.

"Or a doctor who'll write script after script of whatever drug you ask for to keep the envelopes of money coming in." Sophia smooths her skirt under her and slides onto the bench next to Ashton.

We all stare at Sophia. "What? I know we never talk about why we're here, but it happened whether we say it out loud or not."

Ashton explodes with laughter, swinging her arm around Sophia affectionately. "I need a drink. Sofe? Wait. Are you supposed to drink on your meds?"

"If I did what I was supposed to do, I wouldn't be here."

Ashton presses a sloppy kiss to her cheek.

While Lance pours the girls a glass of champagne from another bottle that appears out of nowhere, Ashton opens the windows behind them as far as they will go.

She pulls open a drawer in her black lacquer desk and removes the books, pops the false bottom and pulls out a box. I grin. She is totally my favorite person right now. Ashton reveals a mini bong and a bag of weed.

"You get me," Lance says, holding out his fist for her to bump.

As Ashton's preparing the bong, Brendan pursues the lingering question. "You never told us what you got sent to juvie for." I glare at him because *he* knows. He grins his obnoxious taunting grin. I wonder if my hands will fit around his neck.

"Yeah, what were you busted for?" Lance asks, watching Ashton hungrily.

"Which time?"

All of their heads turn in unison to stare at me...again.

"Omigod, stop! I told you, I don't come from money!"

"How are you here?" Sophia asks, puzzled.

"Exactly," Brendan adds emphatically, like he's making a point.

"Your father," I say to Lance. "He got me in. I have no idea how, but I'm here. It's part of my plea agreement."

"For what?" Lance asks before tilting the flute to his lips.

"Armed robbery."

Lance chokes on his champagne.

"I mean, aiding and abetting an armed robbery and obstruction after the fact."

"So you know who did it and wouldn't give them up?" Lance translates, understanding legal-speak.

"Exactly."

They all nod in appreciation. I may have just earned a little respect.

"Who did it?" Brendan asks. I know what he's doing, asking these questions in front of everyone so I'll feel pressured to share the details he doesn't know. I seriously want to strangle him.

"If I refused to tell the police to clear my name, why the hell would I tell *you*?"

"Because it doesn't matter anymore. You're already serving your time." Then he studies me, intently. "Oh. That's why."

"Why?" Sophia and Lance ask at the same time.

"Whoever it is has something on her."

"Not exactly," I admit. "It's complicated."

"The lies are always complicated. The truth never is."

"Wow, that's so deep," Lance says, tilting his head in reflection.

"Shut up, Brendan," I snap.

"Who's up first?" Ashton asks.

"Give it to me," Sophia demands, taking us all by surprise.

Ashton tells us she had the bench they're seated on custom built so she can sit and blow the smoke out the window. Genius.

"Your room is amazing," I admire, continuing to notice details that capture her personality.

"They did a good job," Ashton agrees.

"You had someone design this? It looks like you've been here for years."

"Friday," she corrects.

"Where were you last year?"

"The junior floor downstairs."

"Then why am I up here? I'm not a senior."

"You are an enigma, aren't you, Lana?" Brendan points out as if he's enthralled with the idea of me. "Nothing about you makes sense."

I bare my teeth at him.

"Be careful," he informs everyone, "she may look like a sweet and adorable pixie, but she bites."

"I think pixies really do bite," Sophia says thoughtfully, handing the bong to Ashton.

"So you're saying Lana's an angry pixie?" Ashton studies me like she can't quite see it.

All of a sudden a detail clicks into place that should have been obvious hours ago. Maybe my mind was purposely avoiding the truth. "Your brother goes to school here, doesn't he?"

Lance nods. "Printz-Lee."

"Of course," I groan.

But that's an entirely different school, somewhere else in the forest of this town. I shouldn't have to ever see him. I *try* to find comfort in that.

"Parker told me what happened between you and him, but what—"

"Don't," I implore with a slight growl.

"Are you attracted to trouble, Lana?" Brendan teases, taking his turn at the window.

"No, she likes the good guys," Ashton blurts unfiltered. I roll my eyes when both Brendan and Lance laugh.

"There's no such thing," Sophia sighs solemnly. "They're like unicorns. Only a few left."

This makes me laugh, because she looks so sad at the thought of it. "You're right, Sophia. They *are* unicorns."

"Is that why you've vowed to never fall in love?" Brendan asks. "Because you're waiting for a unicorn?"

"I'm not waiting for anything."

"She didn't *vow* not to fall in love," Ashton corrects, taking the bong back for another turn without progressing to Lance or me. "She said she was *afraid* to fall in love."

Oh, Ashton and her drug-induced betrayal.

Sophia nods, like she totally gets it. "I'm afraid of wrinkles."

"Growing old?" Lance clarifies.

"No. Wrinkles. On my clothes. I spend hours ironing and starching. I practice sitting just right and tucking in my shirts perfectly, so they don't rumple. It completely stresses me out."

"Here, this'll help," Ashton says, handing the bong back.

"Hey!" Lance protests, launching up onto the bench with his hand extended. "Complete the circle."

"Oh, yeah, sorry." Ashton passes it to him. Instead, she pats Sophia on her head. "I'd totally hug you, but I don't want you to be afraid of me."

I'm not high. Not yet, but this moment is the funniest thing I've ever seen, and I can't hold back the laughter. Which ricochets across the room, igniting an uncontrollable roll of laughter from everyone.

At that inopportune moment, clarity sobers me in an instant. "Shit."

Brendan and Lance seem to be the only ones who hear me. I stand and start pacing. "Shit."

"What's wrong?" Lance asks. "Come up here, this will mellow you out."

I stare at him and his offering of the bong, but what he says doesn't reach me. I'm too lost in my own head. Trying to figure out what the hell I should do.

"Lana?" Ashton's voice is soft and soothing. "You're looking like the angry pixie."

Brendan's beside me, carefully ushering me away. "What did you just realize?"

I peer up at him, but I can't focus. I'm completely freaking out. My head is spinning, filtering through a thousand different possibilities. My hands are sweaty, and my mouth is dry.

"C'mon," he urges, gently setting a hand on my back to guide me out of the room.

"Where are they going?" I hear Sophia ask as the door closes behind us.

"Lean back against the wall and put your head down. Take slow, deep breaths through your nose." I can hear him speaking, somewhere.

I feel the solidity of the wall to my back and a hand pressing me forward.

"Focus on your breathing. In and out."

I grip my knees as I breathe in and release each breath. The chaotic swirls dissipate. My pulse calms. And then I feel like collapsing. I slide down the wall until I'm seated on the floor.

"He goes to school here," I mutter.

Brendan lowers himself next to me. It takes him only a minute to realize. "The guy you're covering for?"

"Yeah," I breathe out.

It wasn't panic exactly that overtook me. It was a combination of everything—anger, frustration, annoyance and okay, maybe a little panic. It felt like I was filled with every explosive emotion that could fit inside of me. Because I have no idea what to do. And I don't do helpless well.

I continue to stare at the wall for what feels like ten minutes, trying to formulate some sort of plan.

"Is this about the convenience store or Allie?" Brendan asks from beside me. I forgot he was here.

"Allie," I answer numbly.

"Is it the same guy from the convenience store?"

I turn my head to stare at Brendan. My stony expression answers for me.

"Did that girl who called in see anything?"

I shake my head. It unnerves me how much he knows about the case.

"So it's your word against his?"

I nod.

"Why would they believe him over you?"

"I'm the one with the record," I answer. "And history of fighting."

"He doesn't?"

I shrug. "He's not a nice guy. But I doubt there's a record of it."

"Right, because he goes to school here."

"Not here. Printz-Lee."

"Even worse." Brendan is quiet for a second. "What if it remains unsolved?"

"Why should he get away with it?" Anger ignites my words.

Brendan studies me for a second, like he's seeing something he hadn't noticed before. "Is justice that important to you?"

"She didn't deserve what happened. And if she doesn't make it..." My jaw flexes as the rage overtakes the other emotions. "Justice won't be enough."

"I take it you're not afraid of him?"

"Hell no. He's an asshat. But he's also unpredictable. He won't care who he has to hurt to protect himself. And I can't let that happen." I realize I've shared too much, with a guy I'm still not convinced I can trust, and stop myself from revealing more. I need to get away from him. I rise from the floor. "I'm going back to my room."

"Want some company?" Brendan winks.

I groan in exasperation. "Get over yourself." I begin to walk away, but then I spin back around. I didn't want to have to do this, but I can't think of a way to avoid it. "Can you ask Lance to come to my room?"

Brendan laughs in disbelief. "Are you serious?"

I glower back.

"Fine," he answers before pushing open the door to Ashton's room.

A few minutes later, there's a knock, and when I open it, Lance is leaning against the doorframe wearing a dopey grin. "You wanted me?"

I roll my eyes. "Get in here." He comes in and shuts the door behind him. "I need your help."

"With what?" he asks, plopping down on the beanbag.

"I need to talk to your brother."

Chapter Eight

Concealed by the cloak, he remained hidden from the sorceress's view. For if she had known of the beast within the cavernous shadows she would never have left her most precious Thaylina alone the evening she went into town. Once the sorceress was out of sight, the wolf emerged. Licking his sharp teeth, he looked up at the girl standing before the tower's window.

*I*t only takes me forty-five minutes to find my way to the Great Hall for breakfast. Everyone else chose to sleep in. On my way back, my phone beeps.

When I accept the call, I'm startled by an older woman with narrowed eyes and dark hair pulled back in a severe bun. I move the phone away, not wanting her to be that close to me even if she's only on a screen.

"Lana Peri, I'm Mrs. Seyer, your dorm monitor." Before I can say anything in return, she continues, "You have a guest in the administration building. Don't keep him waiting."

Then she's gone.

Guest? Must be Niall.

I stop myself from spinning around and getting completely disoriented. I'm facing the girls' dorm. The administration building is directly behind me. So I carefully pivot to face it. Now…to get there from here. I weave in and out of corridors of hedges and several gardens, 'round a pond and through the birch forest, finally reaching the wisteria tunnel. I'm pretty fricken proud of myself by the time I enter.

And run right into Brendan exiting a door next to the entrance.

"Hi," I gasp, his hands holding my upper arms to stabilize me.

"Can't resist, can you?" He grins lazily, his cockiness emanating like pheromones.

"Lana?" I look over his shoulder to find Niall standing within the same doorway. Brendan releases me. "You know each other?"

"Unfortunately," I say as Brendan says, "Definitely."

Niall looks between us. "Watch out for each other. Okay?"

"My pleasure," Brendan replies, then winks at me before disappearing into the Court.

"Brendan's your client too? Is there anyone here you don't represent?"

Niall ignores my comment. "Parker wanted to see you before he left, but I thought it'd be best to meet privately. How are you adjusting?"

I look around the foyer. But Parker's already gone.

"It's only been two days." I enter the room to find it filled with brightly colored Baroque furniture and a crystal chandelier centered above a high-gloss violet coffee table. A window overlooks the Court, filling the room with natural light.

"Yes, but you and I both know that a lot can happen in one day, so how were your two?"

If I didn't know better, I would think he was messing with me. But when I turn to him, there isn't a hint of playfulness on his face or in his eyes. Perhaps he honestly thinks the world can burn down around me in twenty-four hours. Sadly, it can.

"They were fine." I sit in the chartreuse chaise by the window.

"You begin classes tomorrow, correct?"

"So I was told, although I don't know what classes I'm taking. But I'm used to not being told things until they're actually happening."

He picks up on my jab. "There was no reason to inform you where you were going before we arrived because it wouldn't have mattered. I could have given you a name of any school in any surrounding state, and you'd still be attending regardless if you knew the name and location or not."

"You're such a lawyer," I shoot at him like an insult.

"So I've been told."

"But this isn't just *any* school, is it, Niall?" I ask fervently. "There are so many more expectations here than any state program I could have attended. They demand effort, and not just any effort, but exceptional results. So what happens if I can't live up to what all of you want me to be? Do I go back to juvie? What do I lose if I don't become my *best* fucking self? Huh?"

"Two years." His voice is stone.

"What?" I'm stilled by his words, my body rigid with shock.

"You'll lose two years if you fail out of this school. It was the judge's condition to your enrollment."

"I thought it was a six-month sentence in juvie that you requested to be served here?"

"No, we go back in six months with a progress report. And if you aren't engaging, then you'll go to the juvenile detention center or a state-run reformatory until you're eighteen."

If I weren't sitting, I would have collapsed.

"Armed robbery is a serious crime, and they want you to cooperate with them. In absence of your cooperation, the judge made a decision he believed to be in your best interest. And this was the result. We're fortunate to have this opportunity, trust me. So please take it seriously."

I close my eyes to gather myself. "Trust me. I am."

"I brought your personal possessions that were taken from you after your arrest." Niall places a large, white plastic bag on the coffee table. "And I have a gift from your mother." He sets a pink box the size of a grapefruit on the table. It's wrapped in a thick sheer raspberry ribbon, tied in a perfect bow.

"Thank you," I say, barely audible. I feel like I've been punched in the gut, unable to draw in enough air to find my voice.

Two years.

There isn't a trust fund to threaten me with, so they chose the only thing they could…my freedom.

"Do I have any chance of going home?" I'm still worried about my mother, no matter what she says. She's a masterful liar. She guards her pain in her heart, until her body betrays her. So the only way I'll know how she really is, is to see her for myself.

"For visits, yes. But not for a while. I've offered to bring your mother with me when I come up."

"Can I see my friends, or even talk to them?"

"That'll be determined by the school. I'm not going to interfere with their program. You're here for a reason."

I whip around. "And why's that? Because I covered for someone who could destroy my friends' lives?"

Niall's face doesn't betray his emotion, but his eyes do. Sympathy reflects in them, which only angers me. I don't want his sympathy. I want him to clear me, to get me home.

"Do you want to tell me who he is?"

I grind my teeth together. Rage boils up inside of me, filling my eyes with tears. I fight the urge to punch something, not knowing how else to release it.

My silence is my answer. And his is mine.

"I spoke with Dr. Kendall, and she's agreed to lift your probationary period this summer. Typically, new students aren't allowed to leave campus unsupervised for the first sixty days. But she's agreed to allow you off-campus access, as long as you keep up with your school assignments, don't miss curfew, and are accompanied by one of my sons."

"Why do I have to be with one of your sons?"

"Because both the school and I trust them. And I thought you did as well.

Was I wrong to assume that?"

"Why did you tell Brendan and me to watch out for each other?" I ask to avoid answering, because I don't fully trust anyone, forget about the Harrison brothers.

"I only meant that since you obviously know each other, and have both been through a lot, it might be good knowing someone is looking out for you." Niall studies me, a worried line creasing his forehead. "Am I reading all of this incorrectly? I'm trying to do what's best for you, Lana, so if there's something I'm missing, let me know."

I can't argue with him. He knows more than I do about Brendan, his sons, and why he requested that I be sent to this specific school. Maybe it's as simple as the fact that Niall already visits regularly to see his sons, and other clients, so this is his default school for all the dysfunctional teens in his life. Or…it's for a reason I don't understand yet.

"You have no idea what's best for me."

"Maybe someday, you'll see it differently," he replies solemnly. "I have to go, but call me if you need anything. You should hear from your mother tomorrow."

I don't look at him when he leaves, focused out the window, watching a butterfly flutter around the blossoming tunnel.

When I finally turn around, Brendan is seated on one of the wingback chairs, watching me.

"You realize that your creep factor only escalates the longer I know you, right?"

"I like going unnoticed, until I want the attention."

I shake my head at his confusing statement. "Whatever." I swing my legs over to sit up. "What do you want, Brendan?"

"I believe we can help each other." He steeples his fingers with his elbows balanced on the arms of the chair, like a devious mastermind. When I don't respond, he continues, "I may be able to help you clear your name and get you out of here, if that's what you really want."

"In exchange for?" I ask, knowing there's more.

"Information."

"What kind of information?"

"Any that I ask for."

"Yeah, right," I scoff, standing to walk out of the room.

"You'll need me if Allie dies."

My heart misses a beat at just the thought. "They don't have a suspect." I start toward the door.

"They're going to find the witness."

I spin around before I reach for the doorknob. "The girl?"

"Yes. They're getting a lot of pressure from Allie's parents."

"What do they know?" I ask, panic settling in my gut.

Brendan raises an eyebrow, taunting me.

"I won't betray anyone."

The corner of his mouth quirks. "You continue to surprise me."

"Why?"

"At first I thought it was defiance that kept you from cooperating. Self-preservation. But then you say it was to protect your friends. And I didn't expect that. But I get it. Now, you'd rather be convicted of *another* crime you didn't commit, for what? Because you don't want to betray someone you hardly know?"

How can he possibly know that what happened to Allie could affect Parker? I want to ask, but he may mean something else entirely. He has a tendency to speak in riddles, a trait he shares with Ashton. No wonder they're friends.

"How can I possibly have information you want?"

"What I'm really asking for, Lana, is for you to answer the questions I ask, without avoiding them. There's something I've been trying to figure out for a long time, and now that I know more about you, I have a feeling you may have some of the answers I need."

"You're so confusing!" I exclaim in frustration. "You want straight answers out of me, but nothing you say makes any sense! At least with Ashton, I can blame the drugs, but with you...what are you talking about?"

Brendan shakes his head as if in warning, holding his school phone in his hand. I shoot him a questioning look.

A knock on the door turns our heads. The older woman from my phone pushes the door open without waiting for a response. She's taller than I expected. I thought she'd be a petite, frail woman, but she's tall and intimidating in her simple gray dress and severe bun. Not someone I'd be dumb enough to accept apples from, that's for sure.

"The shuttle is here to take you to work," she announces. I check my phone, surprised by the time. Luckily I don't need to get anything from my dorm room. I pick up the bag Niall left on the coffee table, and drop the gift inside.

"Thanks," I say to her, but she's already gone. Brendan stands and we walk out of the room together. But then he continues across the foyer alongside me. "Where are you going?"

"To work," he tells me like I should know this.

The thought of Brendan working is confounding. He's too pristine and manicured—I doubt he's performed a day of physical labor in his life.

I'm surprised to see people waiting in the administration office when we pass it. Then I remember the rest of the summer students arrive today.

The gravel drive that encircles the buildings is busy with moving vans and dark sedans dropping off the summer students. The country club shuttle idles in front of the main entrance. Brendan and I are the only ones on it.

"What did you want to tell me?" I ask him as soon as we drive past the gates. Brendan holds up his finger, taking his phone out of his pocket. He gestures for me to hand mine to him as well. I surrender it, baffled by his paranoia. He sets them on the front seat of the shuttle and then walks to the back to sit in the last row. I follow.

"Explain," I demand.

In a hushed tone, Brendan says, "It's their phone. Their service. With their tracking device. You don't think they can turn on the microphone or camera whenever they want?"

"They can do that?" I ask in shock.

"I have."

I gawk at him.

"Have you learned nothing in the two days you've known me?"

I close my eyes and shake my head, disturbed by every new thing Brendan reveals. But what's even more messed up is how open he is about it. And, as he said, it's only been *two days*! Maybe he's not afraid of being honest because he knows I won't say anything. Bastard.

"Explain how Niall's your lawyer," Brendan asks.

"I know his sons." I reluctantly concede to the questioning, but only until he asks too much.

"How?"

"Parker goes out to some of the same places my friends and I do back home. And I just met Joey…that night. Why am I telling you this?"

"Did you ask who's paying for you to go to Blackwood?"

"No. It didn't come up." Honestly, it wasn't a priority when I spoke with Niall. I was more concerned about *why* I was sent here at all.

"You need to ask him," he insists, obviously frustrated by my lack of knowledge or concern. But Brendan's not exactly clarifying why I should care either. "How else do you know Niall?"

"What are you talking about? I don't…" But then I realize my mother knew him before I did.

"Tell me."

"No. Not until you explain why you're asking so many questions. What do you think I can help you figure out?"

"Who killed my mother."

I stare at him. His dark eyes don't waiver. His lips don't quirk. There's a gravity to his tone. He's serious.

"I'm sorry," I whisper. "You think Niall had something to do with her death?"

"He knows who did."

Chapter Nine

Thaylina saw the man in the dark green cloak peering up at her from the bottom of the tower, and her heart leapt at the sight of him.

"Are you going to let me up?" he called to her.

The girl raced down the steps to unlock the door, disregarding the sorceress's instruction to not let anyone in.

"I knew you would," the man said, following her to the top of the tower.

The shuttle comes to a stop. I tear my eyes away from Brendan's and look out the window. We're already here. The ride felt way too short today.

"We'll talk later." Brendan stands and moves swiftly down the aisle, picking up his phone before exiting the shuttle.

It takes me a minute to force my legs under me. I practically fall as I stumble down the steps. I'm being suffocated by secrets. And most aren't even mine.

"Lana, you'll be training with Kaely today at The Grille," Cary tells me when I clock in at the computer. "You know the correct uniform for The Grille, right?"

"Yes," I reply absently, walking in a daze to the locker room. I am so lost in the haze of half-truths, I don't register there's a body standing in front of me until I bump right into it. "Sorry."

My eyes connect with Grant's sky blue ones. He's holding my elbow to balance me, a look of concern on his face. "Lana? You alright?"

"Oh, yeah. Sorry. Just...thinking."

"And that makes walking difficult?" he teases.

I shake out of my daze and offer a weak smile. "Evidently."

"Where are you working today?"

"The Grille."

"That's too bad. I'm at the Ninth Bar with Stefan. Save me a seat at staff meal?"

"Uh, sure," I reply, my brain slowly deciphering what he said.

Grant continues past me, glancing back once as I stand like an idiot, staring after him. My brain seriously can't handle any of this today.

I need a minute to process everything. Everything other than Grant. I can't seem to function around him at all, so I'm not going to waste my thoughts on what the hell that all meant. I need to figure out why Niall's so evasive about how he knows my mother. Why he's been representing me for years *for free* without me realizing it. And who's paying for my tuition to Blackwood, since Brendan is obviously hung up on that one.

Which brings me to Brendan, who is also represented by Niall. And he's fixated on these details more than I am. Why does he care so much? And truthfully, why should I? The answers to these questions won't clear my name and make sure Vic gets what's coming to him—without involving my friends. *That* should be my priority. The rest of this is just an unnecessary distraction.

Except...I can't stop thinking about the bomb Brendan dropped on me on the shuttle—someone killed his mother. And Niall may know who.

Maybe I should talk to him, just once.

"Did you forget your combination?"

I startle.

"Oh no. I'm just out of it this morning." I've been standing in front of my locker, staring, not realizing Kaely's been standing beside me.

"Ashton?" she asks, as if that's the only explanation needed. Guess everyone knows about her recreational habits.

"Actually, no." Kaely's already dressed in her uniform. "Sorry, I'll be fast. Meet you down there?"

"Sure." She smiles and walks out of the locker room, her thick, wavy auburn ponytail swaying behind her.

When I grab my Grille uniform out of the locker, a piece of paper flutters to the floor. The side that lands up is blank. I bend to pick it up and find written in red capital letters:

STAY AWAY FROM HIM

The lines are neat and precise as if they were drawn with a ruler. I don't know why my first instinct is to look around the locker room, but I do. Like the person who wrote it might be lurking in some corner, watching. But it's empty, until three girls enter, laughing and chatting. They separate to go to their lockers to change for this shift.

"You okay?" one asks from the locker a few down from mine.

"Yeah," I reply, shutting my locker. Before she can say anything else, I take my uniform into the dressing area to change.

First the message on the wall, now this. It has to be the same person. Someone who knows what happened? That's the only thing that makes sense. But then, who's *him*? I groan in frustration. Whoever's fucking with me is doing a shitty job with their threats because I don't know what the hell they mean! Be specific, Crazy!

I *see Brendan walking* toward the golf carts ahead of me and jog to catch up.

"Are you doing this?" I shove the note at him.

He takes it from me and reads it. "My, you move fast, don't you, Lana."

"What?"

"Looks like a jealous girl warning you off of her man."

"That's stupid. I just got here and have barely spoken with anyone besides you. Do you have any psycho exes I should know about?"

Brendan scoffs. "I don't do girlfriends, exactly for this reason." He hands back the note. "Watch yourself. Whoever she is, she doesn't like you."

"She? You're the only one who knows anything about me—*illegally*, but still."

"I don't play mind games."

"Liar." He's a master at mind games; that was obvious on day one.

"Not like this." He nods toward the note in my hand. "I'm open to sharing what I know when you agree to do the same. Ambiguous threats aren't my style."

He walks away, approaching a man with a hideous checkered hat and a bulging stomach. They shake hands and Brendan gets in the driver's seat of the golf cart. I now notice he's dressed in pressed khakis and a navy polo shirt with *KCC* embroidered on the left side of his chest. He pulls on a white baseball hat before pulling away.

He's a caddie. His job is to help members play golf. Bullshitting all day. How appropriate.

I don't know which door is the service entrance to get into The Grille, so I approach the counter where Kaely is handing an ice cream to a dripping wet boy in a bathing suit.

"Hi!" she greets me cheerily. "The staff entrance is on the right side under the stairs." She gestures to the side of the building.

I find the door where she indicated it would be and enter a storage room. Wire shelves are stocked with non-perishable food and drinks. I hear voices coming from the front and follow them. There's a small kitchen and service area where a tall, lanky guy stands at a grill, flipping burgers.

He notices me and gives me a goofy grin. "Hey!" His reddish-brown hair hangs in his eyes under his backward Kingston Country Club baseball hat, and the scruff on his chin looks like the only hair that'll grow on his body.

"Hi," I say, continuing to the counter where Kaely and another girl are taking orders from more kids in bathing suits.

"Order's up," he calls from the back, tapping a bell.

When Kaely turns around to pick it up, she smiles at me. "Hi! Help me with the order?"

I follow her back to the service counter where she introduces us. "Lana, this is Squirrel. Squirrel, this is Lana."

I've heard a lot of nicknames, but never this one. And I can't even begin to understand how someone can earn the name. He doesn't *look* like a squirrel. I feel my eyes squinting as I stare at him, trying to figure it out.

"Welcome to KCC, not to be confused with KFC." He tosses a burger into the air so it flips a couple times before landing with a sizzle back on the grill.

Kaely laughs. "Can you grab the hot dog and fries?" She holds out a tray with two burgers wrapped in foil.

We spend the afternoon serving hot dogs, burgers, fries, ice cream and a million other concession stand items to kids and parents who came to spend the day at the pool. I'm told that upstairs is a seated restaurant called The Deck, with a more extensive casual menu and a deck that looks out onto the course. Everyone has to start at The Grille first. Squirrel calls it a rite of passage, like we're in some tribe together.

I don't earn any tips working The Grille, which sucks. But it's easy. Except for the screaming toddlers who drop their ice cream on the pavement and the kids who squirt ketchup all over the counter instead of their fries. It still doesn't compare to the drunken customers at Stella's who spill more than they consume, try to grab my ass, and end up in fights.

Kaely is patient, a necessity when dealing with the chaos of orders that come at us all afternoon. I don't talk to the other girl too much—of course, I can't remember her name. And Squirrel is…entertaining. I'm pretty sure the guy was born stoned. His high functioning ability to keep up with orders while singing to whatever song is playing and offering unsolicited philosophical insight is rather impressive.

"It was cool to meet you. You have a totally stellar aura," Squirrel says to me at the end of my shift as he scrapes off the grill. "See you tomorrow at Stefan's?"

"Uh, maybe," I say, not sure what he means—about my aura or meeting up at Stefan's.

"Oh, you have to come!" Kaely exclaims, carrying her cash drawer with her as the new girl takes over her position at the register.

I think about the stipulations Niall put into place, that I'll have to go with one of his sons—meaning Lance since Parker is leaving today and I'm not ready to see Joey, even if he was here.

"If I can," I tell her.

We walk to the fenced-in area behind The Grille. "I have to bring my drawer up to Cary. I'll meet you back here after."

Ashton didn't bring me to the staff meal yesterday, wanting to return to Blackwood to get ready for Lily's party as soon as our shift was over. She also said the food was way better at school and she almost never eats at the club. But Grant is waiting for me—I hope. And the shuttle won't be here for another twenty minutes, so I might as well check it out.

Four picnic tables with umbrellas are concealed within a tall, white fence. Chafing dishes are laid out on a banquet table in the corner. I explore the options and find chicken fingers, fries, pasta and a garden salad. Now I understand why Ashton doesn't eat here. But I'm not picky, so I scoop some chicken fingers and fries onto my plate and pour a glass of water from the big orange thermos at the end of the table, before searching for a seat. Two of the tables are filled with adult and college-age employees. I opt to sit at the empty table near the entrance.

Grant slips through the opening behind me and sits to my right.

"Saved a whole table," he notes. "Nice."

I bite my lip to keep the smile from blossoming. "I'm not great with small talk. And I've already forgotten everyone's names. Sitting alone was safer."

"Do you remember mine?" he teases.

"I do."

He waits for me to say it.

"Grant," I say with a roll of my eyes. "Are you eating?"

"No. I just wanted to see you before you left."

"Why?" My pulse is racing, making my hands sweat.

"To invite you to Stefan's tomorrow. I'm staying with him for the summer. And every Monday, when the club is closed, he invites people over. I wanted to make sure you knew about it."

"What time?"

"People come and go throughout the day and night, so whenever. Bring a suit. Or sleeping bag. Whatever. It's pretty laid back."

"Umm, I'll try."

"Not sure I like that answer, but it's better than no."

The smile has yet to leave my face. My cheeks are going to start aching soon if I don't calm down. "If it were up to me, I'd definitely be there. But…it's not."

"Oh." He looks confused. "Are you…seeing someone? Parker?"

"No!" It comes out so loud a few heads turn at the table next to us. I cringe. Grant laughs.

"I guess you don't like him much."

"It's not that, it's just…no. I'm not seeing anyone. That's not the reason. I'm new at Blackwood, so there are rules about leaving campus. Basically, I need a chaperone."

"That could make dating difficult."

"I don't date." I can't stop the honesty from spilling out, revealing the most horrifying truths. It's like he amplifies my curse.

He hesitates. "You don't date. You're afraid to fall in love. You're killing me." He grins this beautiful, heart-stopping grin. "Are you opposed to guys as friends?"

"Yes." I want to smash my head on the table as soon as I say it. "I mean, I'm *not* opposed to being friends with guys."

"Have you ever?"

"No. But I don't like many people, so it doesn't mean anything. I only have a couple friends back home."

Grant continues to laugh at the unabated honesty, like it's adorable and not projectile humiliation. Meanwhile, I want to crawl under a rock. "Maybe I can be the first," Grant says, pushing off the table to stand. "Hopefully, I'll see you tomorrow."

I close my eyes as the gate closes behind me. What just happened? And why is my heart beating like crazy right now? Omigod, please make me stop already.

I stand and toss my untouched food in the trash. Kaely enters the gate as I'm about to walk out.

"Sorry, I have to change before the shuttle gets here. I'll see you later."

"Okay," she says with a smile. I think she's always smiling. Can a person genuinely be that nice? And happy? "Hope you can make it to Stefan's tomorrow." Before I can walk away, she leans in and says, "Oh, and I just saw Grant leave. He was smiling. I think he likes you." Her eyes shine like she's excited by the idea of it.

"Umm...what?" I say, trying to shake off the remnants of him still floating around me, making my head buzzy and my heart crazy.

"He does. I can tell. So you *have to* come to Stefan's tomorrow!" Her megawatt smile is on the verge of forcing me to smile in return. I walk away before it does.

When I exit the employee entrance after changing, I find Parker waiting for me by his Land Rover.

"Have dinner with me before I drive back to New York?" When I hesitate, he adds, "I already cleared it with Blackwood. And we still need to talk."

I consider what Brendan said earlier about giving information to get it, and maybe Parker *can* help me. If I locate the girl before the police do, I can explain and keep her from implicating me. I don't know how Parker can help me with Vic. I'm still not convinced he should know what happened in the stairwell. Because that would mean telling him *everything* about that night. I've learned the hard way that it only takes one person to talk before everyone knows. And I don't trust him.

He holds the passenger door open for me. "Thanks."

"Have you spoken to Nina or Tori since you've been here?" he asks when we pull out of the parking lot.

"They're not *approved*."

"That sucks. Sorry."

"Whatever."

"Do you want to call them now?" He offers me his phone.

I think about it but decide against it. "Calling Nina from your phone probably isn't a good idea. I doubt she'd even answer."

Parker chuckles cockily. "She'd answer." When he notices my glare, he fumbles. "I mean, she and I still get along." He mutters, "Shit," under his breath.

"Maybe dinner isn't a good idea."

"Lana," he pleads, "I'm sorry. I shouldn't have said it like that."

"Take me back to the school," I tell him, crossing my arms.

"What is it?" His grip tightens on the steering wheel. "Are you jealous? Is that why you're being like this?"

"Are you kidding me, Parker? You don't care about me. You're only worried about how everything affects you. *That*'s why I'm being like this."

Parker pulls off into a scenic overlook where one other car is parked above a valley of rolling hills.

He stares out the windshield, a muscle ticking in his jaw. When he finally speaks, his voice is low and controlled. "I can be a jackass sometimes, I know. And say really pompous things." He turns to face me and takes my hand. "But I *do* care about you, Lana. And I want to help."

"Me or yourself?"

"Why do you say that?"

I try to ignore the hint of hurt in his voice. "I know that you're one of the organizers, and what happened in the stairwell can come back on you if anyone finds out. You need me to keep my mouth shut so you don't get busted."

"But you wouldn't tell anyone, I know that. I trust you."

"Maybe I *should* say something."

Parker doesn't respond. Instead, he pulls his hand away and adjusts in his seat to face the windshield again.

"A girl is lying in the hospital in a coma. Don't you think that's more important than your illegal business?"

Parker turns his head toward me. "Of course. But neither you or I put her there. And letting the police know about the party won't make a difference. That's not what's going to help her."

"But saying who pushed her, will." It's the obvious conclusion, if only it were that simple.

"Then tell them."

His encouragement takes me by surprise.

"What?"

"Tell them who did it. Don't continue to protect whoever it is."

I fall back against the seat, defeated. "I'm not protecting him."

"What? Is it the other girl? Are you worried about her saying something to the police? She was wasted. She could barely tell me what she saw when I asked her *that night*, forget about now."

"She saw me. Only me."

"But she didn't see what happened. She came in after."

"Right. But I was the only one there. She can identify me. Then I'll either be forced to tell or…" It'll be the convenience store all over again. "I don't have any proof."

"Who—"

"Don't ask me. I won't tell you."

"Why? Because you don't trust me?"

"Because it won't make a difference if you know," I say, using his words against him. "I'll figure something out. I just want Allie to be okay." I blink back the tears that have invaded my vision. "She didn't deserve what happened to her.

She was trying to help me…"

"Hey," Parker soothes, unbuckling his seatbelt and mine so he can pull me against his chest. I don't resist. "I want *you* to be okay. Please let me help you. I really do want to, and not for selfish reasons, I swear."

"You can't," I murmur, my face pressed against his shoulder.

"Tell me this and we can drop it, for now." Parker tilts my head up to look into his delving blue eyes. "I heard what Allie said at the hospital. Whoever he is, are you afraid he's going to hurt you?"

The concern in his eyes is authentic, and I feel like a bitch for believing he was that selfish. His question is too complicated for a simple truth. Because honestly, Vic might try to hurt me. He's capable of anything, I'm aware of that.

My eyes are unwavering; I want him to see my conviction. "I'm not afraid."

Chapter Ten

"I've decided to sing for you," he told Thaylina once they entered her home.

Thaylina squealed delightedly, wishing for nothing more.

"But first, you must do something for me." He unfastened his satin cloak and wrapped it around her shoulders. It was heavy on her delicate frame.

"What is it you want?" Thaylina asked, more curious than frightened.

*I*t's strange walking into the Great Hall and finding people sitting at the tables for dinner. I'd somehow gotten used to the stillness on campus the past couple of days. Although I can't say the same for its eeriness.

I find Lance seated with Ashton and Brendan at the table in the corner that I always gravitate to.

"How was The Grille?" Ashton asks when I sit.

"Messy," I answer, making her laugh. "What did you do today?"

"Went shopping…online. I was granted internet privileges so I could try to find something to wear for the Ever After Ball."

"Right. The Ball," I say with a pained expression. "It feels weird saying that. Can't I just call it a dance?"

"If you want. But you might offend the social committee."

"I really don't care. So, when's this *dance*?"

"August nineteenth." Ashton scoops up a mound of chocolate mousse and then turns the spoon upside down to stick in her mouth, savoring it like a lollipop.

"Are you going as a princess?" Brendan taunts, leaning back in his chair with an ankle propped on his knee. He looks so smug; I want to kick the chair out from under him just to watch him fall on his ass. I return his smartass remark with a flip of my finger. He shouldn't be surprised by my hostility every time he calls me that. He only does it to piss me off. And it does.

"Maybe you should go as the angry pixie," Lance chuckles. "You kinda already have that down."

"You might want to start searching soon," Ashton adds.

"We have two months," I gape, not comprehending the importance of finding the right costume for a stupid dance.

"It'll be here before you know it."

"Not eating?" Brendan asks with a smirk. I never know what he knows, or what he pretends not to know. It drives me crazy. He's determined to press every single button I have until eventually I'm forced to murder him.

"I already ate."

"Please don't tell me you had the staff meal?" Ashton remarks with a horrified expression.

"No. I went out to eat."

Lance's attention flashes to me. He knows. Before either Ashton or Brendan can ask who I went out with—I see the question dancing in Ashton's eyes—Lance asks, "Did you open the present from your mother?"

"Uh," I eye him suspiciously. "Not yet. But I will when I get back to my room."

Ashton and Brendan glance between us, picking up on the not-so-subtle private message Lance is trying to convey about the gift I received from Niall this morning. Now I'm pretty sure we *all* know it isn't from my mother.

"So," I say loudly, to redirect the conversation. "What's everyone doing tomorrow? Are you going to Stefan's?"

"That's right!" Ashton exclaims, her eyes lighting. "It's the first party of the summer! His parties are always so amazing." Then she flops back in the chair, deflating just as quickly. "But I don't know how we'll get there. I usually secure a ride from someone at the club."

"I can ask Lily," Lance offers. I bite my cheek to keep from smiling like an idiot, knowing I'll get to see Grant tomorrow. Seriously, what is happening to me?

"Let us know what time," Brendan chimes in, my excitement evaporates a little with the realization he'll be coming too.

"Lance, can I talk to you?" I ask.

"Sure," Lance replies, a hint of curiosity in his voice. He stands, and I follow him outside. "What's up?"

"You know about my off-campus conditions, right? That I have to be with you or one of your brothers?"

"Yeah. My dad told me."

"I hope that doesn't make things awkward for you. But I see you the most, and right now, you're the only brother I can tolerate for any length of time."

Lance laughs. "No. It's fine. Seems like we're going to the same places most of the time anyway. I'm sure we can work it out if something comes up. My dad trusts me, but I *am* at Blackwood for a reason."

"Because you covered for your brother."

"Exactly. So if you ever need me to cover for you, just ask."

I grin. "That's not why I wanted to talk to you. It's just that we don't have a way of communicating without phones. You and I don't have classes together, and you don't work at the country club, so…how can we make plans to go off-campus?"

"Uh, right." Lance quietly contemplates this for a moment.

"You can always hide notes," Ashton suggests from the other side of the top hat topiary.

"Ashton, what about *be quiet and listen* did you not understand?" Brendan scolds. The two of them emerge from behind the shrubbery. I cross my arms and glower at Brendan.

"What?" Ashton defends. "It's not like she's telling him something we didn't already know. And I can help. It's actually something I've been wanting to do since I started coming here, but everyone I mention it to thinks it's stupid. They prefer to pass notes, which is so 1990."

"And hiding them pushes us back another century," Brendan says with an exhausted sigh.

"But this way, we can all see it," Ashton sneers playfully at Brendan. "Like a group text. Especially since most of the time, we'll be going together anyway. Like tomorrow, Lance can leave a note letting us know when Lily's picking us up…if she can."

Lance looks to me for approval. I shrug. "It's better than the *no* idea I had."

"Where?" Lance asks Ashton. Her Cheshire smile emerges, and I know she already has a hiding spot in mind.

We follow her to the birch forest. I can't say I'm surprised by this. Nor am I surprised when she pulls out a vape sealed in box within the hollow of a birch tree. The hole is small, barely large enough for Lance to fit his hand inside. And because it's so small, it blends in with the rest of the black marks on the trunk. But it's also deep, hiding whatever's inside below the line of sight.

"How do you possibly remember which tree it is?" Lance asks, looking around at the trunks that all blend together in their scattered white and black pattern.

"I remember the number five," Ashton explains simply.

When we all stare at her in bemusement, she continues. "Three over from the edge of the swing and two forward."

"I…guess," Lance says like he can't quite see the pattern. But I have to smile because only Ashton would remember it this way. And because it is so arbitrary, we'll probably never forget.

"I have an old jewelry box that will fit in there perfectly. We can leave the notes inside."

Ashton and I sit on the swing, sharing her vape, while we work out the mechanics of secret note passing in a tree. I had no idea the complexities that would go into signaling that a note is hidden, and indicating who sent it and read it. But we eventually work it all out, and it's hopefully easy to remember. And the fact that we're resorting to hiding notes in trees to pass along messages is sad in its own right. But it's better than throwing hollowed acorns in each other's windows.

When we return to the main path, I pause at the entrance of the rose trellis, watching Brendan and Lance continue toward their dorm. Ashton already left us to go to the library. Brendan must sense me lingering because he looks over his shoulder just before they disappear. A few seconds later, he re-emerges, without Lance.

"I'll answer five of your questions if you answer five of mine." Maybe it's the mellowing effect of the THC that's making me so accommodating, because originally I was only going to answer three.

He grins. "Why five?"

"I was inspired by Ashton," I reply with an inadvertent giggle.

"These questions cannot be left inside the birch tree," he stresses. "It's in-person only."

"Of course," I say like he's crazy for even having to say it. "I would never want the others to know, or have it in writing."

"Good," he says in relief. "I'll figure out where and when and let you know."

"Okay."

"Why'd you change your mind?"

"Because I have a thing for knowing the truth."

"It's the only thing worth knowing." He winks before disappearing around the corner.

The first thing I do when I reach my room is dump out my personal possessions onto the bed, hoping Niall overlooked my phone and it's still inside. He didn't. The most valuable thing in it is my leather jacket, which I'm thrilled to have back. I'm shocked to find the tip money in a sealed plastic baggie. I lift the wedding band from the small pile of rings and bracelets I was wearing that night.

"Fucker." I wonder how Nick explained its absence to his wife. Which then makes me think of my mom.

And even though—or maybe because—I'm high, the worry that swarms inside of me feels as heavy as storm clouds. My mother isn't inept, but she's not responsible either. We looked out for each other. She calms me when I can't see beyond my own rage, which is usually incited by someone who hurt her. And I do everything I can to keep her from being hurt.

Now she's hurting, and I'm stuck *here*, unable to help her. She can't hear me telling her she's so much better than half the people in her life. That they don't deserve her kindness or forgiveness. That I wish she didn't believe so easily. And she in return would say that she wishes I would trust more. That I should allow more people in so they can experience how caring and loving I truly am. I would then shrug off her words, allowing the anger to grow until it billows out and I end up in a fight with someone who says the wrong thing, or takes advantage of space that doesn't belong to them, or touches a part of me no one has a right to touch.

My mother would be waiting for me with an ice pack and a sorrowful expression. But never a lecture about how disappointed she is. She doesn't need to. Her eyes tell me more than that. They tell me she blames herself for who I've become. It only makes me angrier. Because I'm not her fault.

I wish I were home with her, because right now, I need her as much as she needs me.

The heaviness of the storm swirling inside me turns volatile quickly. I let out a growling scream of frustration and tear the mountain of decorative pillows from the bed and fling them across the room.

"I don't belong here!"

I collapse on the bed and scream into a pillow at the top of my lungs. I keep screaming until there isn't any air left and the sound chokes out of me.

A knock draws my attention. "Lana?" Ashton calls from the other side. "Can I come in?"

I swipe the tears from my cheeks and let out a long breath to collect myself.

There's a woeful look on Ashton's face when she enters, and before I know what's happening, she's bending over and wrapping her arms around me. She practically suffocates me within her fierce hug, my face pressed into the sharp angles of her shoulder. I'm too shocked to do anything but stand there with my arms dangling limply by my sides. When it's obvious she doesn't plan on letting go, I hug her back.

"My heart needed that," Ashton tells me with a warm smile when she eventually releases me. "Thank you."

How does a person respond to that? Then again, who says things like that?

"Uh, sure. No problem."

"And if you ever need to scream again, and I mean *really* scream, I have the perfect place. So just let me know, okay?"

I blink. "You have a screaming spot?"

"Everyone should have a screaming spot."

I smile. "Thanks. I may need it… a lot."

"Then let's go now." Before I can react, she's pulling me out the door and down the hall.

Ashton doesn't ask what's wrong, or if I want to talk. I think she's so used to hiding her truth from the world, that she feels she doesn't have a right to ask another person theirs. And for someone who is so careful with the truth, it makes me sad for her, to be so lost in a contrived life. She's learning, in her own quirky ways, to interact honestly. It explains her riddling comments and bouts of candor; she's trying to let the world see her, underneath all of the glamour and beauty. And that's when it occurs to me, her curse is *Authenticity*. And maybe that's why I instantly felt connected with her, even if she is strange. We both seek the same thing, to be honest with who we are. I just hope I'm not forced to witness her destruction when her curse comes for her.

When we reach the foyer, we go through the doors of the main entry—that I have yet to use. We descend the stone steps and cross the gravel drive that encircles the ring of buildings.

A large field stretches out before us until it suddenly falls away. All I can see beyond that is water.

"It's Blackwood Lake. The same lake Lily's and Stefan's houses are on. Except they're farther north," she tells me. "In Kingston, everyone either lives on the lake side or the mountain side, with downtown in the middle. We are, obviously, on the lake side."

"I always thought we were surrounded by woods. But I guess I never really explored the campus beyond the Court."

"This is one of my favorite places because no one comes out here. It's like they forget there's anything outside of the buildings once they enter."

The field is bigger than I originally thought, and it takes us a while to reach the edge, and that's exactly what it feels like—a preschooler took scissors to the edge of the grass, cutting it off in a jagged line, leaving behind a steep and drastic drop to a rocky shoreline.

"Holy shit," I breathe out, experiencing a slight heart-palpitating sense of vertigo. There isn't a fence or any sort of protective barrier. If someone were to keep walking, they would plummet and land on the jagged earth below. I look down at the lake water softly lapping at the sharp angles.

"This way," Ashton beckons, walking toward the woods. Oddly, the wrought iron fence extends all the way to the end of the property, determined to keep us separated us from the other side.

Ashton unexpectedly takes a step off the edge and my heart skips a beat. It looked like she walked off the lawn onto nothing. But considering I can still see her, cut off at the knee, there must be *something* there. I have to walk all the way to the end of the grass to view the flat slabs of rock jutting out haphazardly. Each rocky shelf protrudes from the sheer cliff-face and looks like they might snap if jumped upon. They form a torturous path all the way to the water's surface.

Ashton walks along the ledge until she reaches the farthest point that hangs over the lake. Watching her stand so close to the edge quickens my pulse.

When I haven't moved from the safety of the grass, she laughs. "C'mon. It's not as scary as it looks."

I carefully lower onto the slab, focused on my feet, fearing the slightest misstep will cause me to fall to my death. I glance up to find Ashton. There's a slight breeze off the water, causing wisps of her hair to float around her head.

"This is Screaming Point."

"That's what it's called?"

"It is now. As of today. Because it's what we need it to be." She takes my hand. "Ready?"

I look out at the dwindling light dancing on the dark surface like the lake is capturing every last bit of the sun before it disappears. I close my eyes and find that place inside that is always angry. That hates my curse. That needs Allie to live. And Vic to burn. That wants to hurt every man who has ever broken my mother's heart. Or touched what wasn't theirs. And every person who has ever lied when they claimed to love. I don't have to search for long, because it's always there, waiting to explode.

I open my eyes to look into Ashton's sapphire blue ones, and nod.

We face the water and inhale deeply, giving our anger, frustration and sadness a breath of life before we unleash it onto the world in the most powerful scream that's ever been launched from this cliff. And it's freeing. More than I ever thought possible. I allow my heartache to take flight, releasing it into the setting sun to be dragged down beneath the horizon.

And what's left when there aren't any more screams to give is a radiant smile. Ashton and I face each other, our hands still clasped, and we start laughing. It's a true, bonding laughter because we just shared something sacred. If anyone were to witness it, they would think we're insane. And maybe it's that crazy within each of us that makes the laughter louder and deeper until I have to wipe away the tears creeping out the corners of my eyes.

"Thank you, Ashton," I tell her as we start back across the field. "My soul needed that."

She smiles at me brighter than the sun, and I smile back. And without a doubt, I know, she is the best kind of friend. The kind who will always create places to scream, and reasons to hug, to make the pain easier.

When I get to my door, there's a Post-it waiting for me.

Open the box!

"Crap," I mutter, realizing that I forgot to open the gift, too caught up in my screaming breakdown.

So, that's the first thing I do when I enter. And inside, is a phone. I smile. "Thank you, Lance," I say out loud, picking up the note that's tucked beside it.

Don't turn this on while on campus. They will find it.
As soon as you can, CALL ME. - Joey

Chapter Eleven

"Look into my eyes, tell me what you see," the handsome man requested. "What is it that my heart desires most? What is my intention?"

Thaylina struggled to move within the wrap of the silken fabric. But she still did not fear him. Not until she peered into his eyes and saw the truth.

I **barely roll out of bed** in time to make my life advisor appointment. After a quick brush of my teeth, I throw on a pair of cut-offs and a tank top and rush out the door. Thankfully, I'm faster at crossing the Court, otherwise I'd really be late.

When I reach the second floor of the administration building, I find a woman sitting at a desk at the top of the stairs, where the common room is located in the dorms. The rest of the room is filled with club chairs where a couple other students are waiting. From the petrified looks on their faces, they're either in trouble or they're new.

"Hi, I'm Lana Peri. I have an appointment."

"Take a seat."

I hesitate a second to make sure she's actually human, considering how detached and flat her voice sounded. Her eyes never even left her computer screen. Someone hates her job. Or people.

I haven't even reached a seat when I hear, "Lana?" I freeze. I know that voice...too well. I slowly turn with a ginormous smile plastered on my face. Queen Warden would be proud.

"Mr. Garner. Wow. Are you stalking me?"

He flounders, "Wha-What? No." He lets out a forced laugh, his eyes glancing nervously to the woman behind the desk. Her attention torn from the screen, she studies him suspiciously. "You're funny. Um, why don't you follow me."

I whisper as I pass her desk, "Totally stalking." Her suspicion darts to me, and I practically jump back from the assaultive glare.

"Lana," Mr. Garner scolds from down the hall.

I follow him into an office the size of a dorm room. They really weren't original with their building designs, were they?

There's absolutely nothing on the beige walls and there's barely any furniture in the room either, other than a desk and a few chairs.

"Minimalist. Who knew," I say, spinning around.

"I haven't had a chance to do anything yet. I arrived late last night. It'll look different next time we meet."

"Why are you here, *Isaac*?"

Mr. Garner's face remains expressionless, but his eyes harden just enough to let me know I pissed him off. Then he shakes his head and rubs the bridge of his nose under his glasses, like I've already given him a headache. "Can we please not start off this way?"

"What do you mean? We go way back."

"You know exactly what I mean. Why don't you have a seat."

"Not until you tell me why you're here. I don't believe in coincidences." Then it occurs to me. "Niall Harrison got you hired here, to watch over me, didn't he?"

"He may have let me know about an open position and provided a letter of recommendation. It's a great opportunity, so I accepted the offer."

"How do you know Niall?"

"I told you, I grew up in Oaklawn. It's impossible to live there and *not* know the Harrisons in some way. His wife was actually one of my professors at Dartmouth. They're a very—"

"Powerful?"

"I was going to say influential family, but even that sounds wrong. They're… invested."

"In what? Me?"

"I suppose you're a type of investment. They want you to succeed."

"What is up with that word? Succeed! And who's going to determine when I've *succeeded*? When I have a college diploma? A six-figure salary? It's such bullshit!"

"You don't want to go to college?"

"I don't know what I want. But I'm sick of everyone wanting it more than I do." I'm so worked up by this point, I'm pacing the room.

"That's fair," he says calmly.

His answer stills me.

"No one can make you want something you don't. They can't force you to study. Or be invested in your academics. They can hope you find something you're passionate about and explore it. The only one who has to want it is you."

"I'm impressed, Mr. Garner," I say, finally coming around to sit across from him. "Did you learn that in one of Professor Harrison's classes?"

He laughs. "I'm actually supposed to go by this script" —he places his hand on a three-inch binder— "as a Blackwood life advisor. I've been trying to memorize it the last couple weeks, and between you and me, I can't. Right now, you're my only student. I'm going off script. So don't get sent to my office every other class period or else they're going to start questioning my methods."

"I keep telling you, I *try* to stay away."

"Maybe here the teachers will be more equipped to handle your…honesty."

"We can only hope."

"I want to review your plan and provide you with your summer course schedule." He flips open another three-ring binder that's nearly as thick as the "best self" script. Colorful tabs stick out between sectioned off stacks of papers. I lean over to read a couple: Academics, Health, Legal…I lean back when Mr. Garner finds the page he's searching for and returns his attention to me.

"Because this latest arrest was for possession, you'll be subjected to random drug tests. If you fail them…"

"I'll fail for at least the next thirty days."

He closes his eyes and sighs. "Thank you for admitting you used, but that's not helping us, Lana."

"I'm just saying, no sense giving me one since it's not going to be clean for a while. Just trying to be helpful."

He presses his lips together to keep from smiling. "I don't schedule them. But I will see what I can do. That doesn't mean you have a free pass over the next thirty days. They may have you take one anyway as a baseline, and just anticipate the positive THC level, since I assume that's what needs thirty-days to cleanse from your system."

"You would know," I say, the insinuation notable.

He doesn't react. "Since you've had multiple infractions involving fighting over the last three years, you'll be assigned to group therapy focused on healthy emotive expression, beginning this fall."

"You can seriously say that with a straight face? Why can't they call it anger management like the rest of the world?"

Mr. Garner bites his lower lip to keep the smile from forming. I know he thinks this is just as ridiculous as I do. "It's been advised that you partake in," he swallows before reading, "an exhaustive physical activity or calming meditative practice."

"They want me to have sex?"

Mr. Garner's head whips up, his neck and cheeks emblazoned in a deep red flush. "Join some sort of sport or club. Something to use as an outlet to help keep you calm that doesn't involve drugs, fighting…or sex."

"So you're saying I *can't* have sex?"

He removes his glasses and closes his eyes, rubbing them with his fingertips. "I cannot and will not advise you to have sex. But I will ask you to be safe and use some form of protection if you choose to."

"Aren't you so glad you accepted this position, Mr. Garner? Think of all the life advising you'll be offering me."

"Honestly, I think you could probably advise me."

I laugh. "So *you're* not having sex, Mr. Garner?"

"Lana." It's the stern voice again. The one I know all too well. It comes out as a warning, like I'm about to cross a line. But we both know it really means, I already have.

After breathing in and out slowly through his nose, he closes my binder and directs his attention to me. "I've read a lot about you. I know why you're here. But I don't feel like I really *know* you. You hide behind sarcasm and shocking candor. But I am here…for *you*. Whenever you need me. Whatever you say to me is between us. Unless, of course, it puts you or someone else in danger. You can let me see you, Lana."

I don't respond. I know he's sincere about every word he just said. But I don't know if I'm ready to be *that* honest.

A *half hour later,* with my course schedule in hand, I leave Mr. Garner in need of Prozac and a shot of whiskey. I'm only taking three classes, but considering it's summer, it sucks. Predictably, they're the classes I did the worst in at Sherling High: chemistry, American government and French.

The first hidden message is waiting for me as I pass the birch forest and spot the red ribbon tied to the swing. And because no one else has made their mark on the back of the note, I know I'm the first to see it.

L is picking us up at 1:00. If anyone needs more time, leave a note.

Lance leaves his ↕ mark as a signature. The strategy behind the symbols is that if the box is ever discovered, we don't want anyone to know who it belongs to, so we each mark the note with our symbol upon sending and receiving it. I take out the marker and draw ∞ on the back, indicating I've read it.

After showering and dressing for class, I grab a Mountain Dew and a bag of popcorn chips as my breakfast substitute, since I didn't have time to get to the Great Hall. Then I'm off to chemistry, the class I'm scheduled to attend on Mondays and Wednesdays. I have to use Sophia's buildings map to figure out where it's located, and end up running into a few dead-ends on my journey through the Court. One of them being a strange garden filled with marble statues. I come to an abrupt stop, feeling like I've stepped onto a stage and am standing in the spotlight. Except my audience is a bunch of creepy statues in various stages of fracturing, arranged in curved rows. I back away and turn at the last minute, feeling like one of them might start walking after me. I practically run back to the path I was on before I made the wrong turn. I'm *never* going to get used to this place.

Eventually, I find the entrance to the science building—two Greek-style marble pillars that are at least ten feet tall, with tangles of ivy crawling up them.

The interior is similar to every other building I've been in, except the stairs are covered in a navy-blue rug and the walls are decorated with abstract geometric art. From what I can see at a glance, the Quiet Room on the first floor is reminiscent of a study room in a library with rows of tables lined with small lamps. On the other side of the foyer, where our dining hall is, are closed doors with nameplates on them.

There are only three students in this class when I arrive. And that's all there is, just the four of us. We're given tablets during class that recognizes us with our thumbprint. And for the next hour and a half, I try not to fall asleep face first onto my desk.

When we're finally excused, I'm overcome with a burst of energy, like it's been dormant and just waiting to be set free. And my mouth and cheeks battle to let that stupid smile emerge in anticipation of seeing Grant.

I stop by the Great Hall and grab a lunch to-go so I can get ready for the party.

While I sort through my clothes, I try to talk myself out of this absurd excitement. Whatever's overtaking my entire being at just the thought of him needs to go away. I want control back, especially of my own emotions.

Lily's waiting in a silver Lexus SUV in the drive after we check out to leave for the day. Her hair is a silken sheet of blond held back by a thick coral headband, making her look even more sophisticated than she does naturally. It's a style I've never been able to pull off because my hair refuses to be tamed no matter what products or straightening irons I use. I have mine twisted into a low side bun to keep it contained.

When we arrive, people are spread out everywhere. Stefan's cabin has the more traditional feel of logs and beams with a giant stone fireplace and a wrap-around upper level with bedroom doors off of it. It's big and open and easy to navigate, mostly because it's one giant room with the exception of the kitchen and dining area, but even the entries leading to them are wide and expansive.

Just about everyone is outside, for good reason. This house is on a hill overlooking the lake with a huge backyard and a set of wooden stairs between it and a private beach. There are people playing corn hole, lawn darts, football and bocce spread out all over the grass, and sand volleyball on the beach. It's kind of a ridiculous setup, especially when I notice the trampoline floating on the lake with people jumping on it or bouncing off into the water.

The scent of barbecue fills the air as a guy attends to the food on two huge black grills. Music is blasting through speakers on the wrap-around porch. It's so much different from Lily's party. It's playful and filled with laughter and shouts of sportsmanship. There's nothing pretentious here.

"Let's get a drink," Lily suggests, leading the way back into the kitchen before I can linger too long, scanning faces. I think I'm doing okay not thinking about him until I finally admit that I've never really stopped. I don't like what's going on inside of me, but I have to believe that eventually I'll get over it.

"Lemonade?" Lily offers, holding up a glass pitcher. "Do you want me to add vodka to it?"

"Sure," I reply. She hands it to me after she dumps in a shot. "Thanks." I take a sip and nearly spit it back out.

"What's wrong?"

"I think it already had vodka mixed in," I say with a body-shuddering cringe.

"Oh my gosh. I'm so sorry," Lily says, biting her lower lip. "Do you want to dump it?"

"No, it's okay. I'll add ice. Maybe it'll water it down a little." I scoop some ice out of a bucket in the freezer and drop it in my cup. I try to stomach a couple more sips until the initial shuddering reaction goes away. It doesn't take long before there's an intense swirling in my head.

Brendan and Lance disappeared pretty much as soon as we arrived, so Lily, Ashton and I stand on the porch and take in the mayhem of lawn games before us. And that's when I see him, playing football with a bunch of guys and girls, most running around shirtless or in bikini tops and bare feet. He's one of the few with a shirt still on, thankfully. I watch as the ball is passed to him and he dodges hands as he runs toward the goal, tagged last minute by a girl who chooses to wrap her arms around him versus tap him.

A tearing pain flashes through my chest. "Fuck."

"What's wrong?" Ashton asks, trying to look at what I am, but I turn around and lean my butt against the railing instead.

"I'm just hating my body right now."

"Why?" Lily says like she's offended for me. "You have one of the best bodies I've ever seen. Seriously."

"Oh, that's not what I mean exactly. But thank you." I've actually never been body conscious. I'm short, and maybe a little too top heavy for my height, but the rest of me fits into the clothes I like, so that's all I really care about. I don't work out other than rushing around at the diner. Well, and the boxing gym, but that wasn't a regular thing. It was something Tori's oldest brother, Javier, took me to every once in a while. He said if I was going to be fighting anyway, I might as well have proper form. I actually enjoyed going, to be honest.

"Then what?" Ashton asks.

"Forget it," I tell her, but refuse to turn around. I need to get this under control; it's driving me insane.

"Hi!" I hear from the stairs. We turn to find Stefan walking up to greet us. "So happy you're all here. Help yourself to anything. Play with whatever or whoever you want," he says with a flirty crooked smile, "and just…be happy." He offers each of us a hug and brief kiss on the cheek. If anyone else were to say or do this, I would think they were a creep. But there's a genuineness to Stefan that keeps it from crossing the awkward line.

"Thank you," Lily says sweetly. "We promise to behave."

"Mostly," Ashton adds with a smirk.

Stefan laughs before finding more faces to greet and bodies to hug.

"Want to go float on the lake?" Ashton offers.

"Yes," Lily responds enthusiastically.

"Um, I'll meet you down there," I say, not ready to get wet just yet.

The girls disappear down the sloping grass toward the water. I take a couple more gulps from my cup, barely tasting the vodka any longer, which isn't the best sign. But maybe it'll help me calm the hell down and act like a normal human being. That thought lasts as long as it takes Grant to cross the lawn and hop up the steps to greet me. "You made it!"

Damn him and his stunning smile.

"Yup," I say, my mouth winning the war with my cheeks and smiling just as big.

"Where's your chaperone?"

"I actually have no idea," I say, looking around for Lance.

"Does that mean you can get in trouble?"

"Is that an offer?" The corner of my mouth raises flirtatiously.

He laughs.

"We were about to start a game of whiffle ball. Wanna play?"

I make a face of dread.

"Have you ever played?"

I shake my head.

"We won't judge. C'mon." He offers his hand and I take it, my chest tightening at his touch. "Do you know the general rules? They're pretty much the same as baseball."

"I think so."

"Then you'll be fine." We walk to the other end of the yard where a guy is laying down rubber bases and a large group of players wait to begin. Grant introduces me by name but leaves the individual introductions up to everyone to do themselves.

Thankfully, I'm on his team, and we're up to bat first. I watch the batters and plays, Grant providing a bit of insight. I've been forced to play softball in gym for what feels like my entire life, so I know the general concept of how to swing the bat, although I find this plastic one extremely light, and the unpredictability of the pitches impossible to hit. I get on base a couple times, earning a trumpet of cheers from my teammates. And I even make it home once when a huge guy on our team slams the ball—it's declared a home run when it makes it past the azalea bush. The rest of our team awaits with high fives as we run across home plate, and Grant wraps his hand around mine when I slap his hand.

"Not bad," he says, pulling me toward him.

"It might be the vodka," I tell him. "Makes me better, just like playing pool. I improve with a buzz."

"Oh," he says in surprise, and maybe a little disappointment. "I didn't realize you were drinking."

"Are you?" I ask, his answer strikes me as odd. I know he does. I saw him with a beer at Lily's.

"I wasn't, but sure, I'll get a beer. Want another drink?"

My cup is tipped over on the grass. There wasn't much left in it anyway. "Please."

We walk back to the house, trying to stay out of the way of the other games being played.

"This is fun," I say, looking around.

"You say that like you're surprised."

"I've never been to a party like this before. I come from a kind of small city. Most people don't have backyards."

"And I come from a small town where there are yards. And gossip. And status. I've always admired the anonymity of a city actually, even a small one."

"Feeling judged?" I ask light-heartedly.

"Feeling the weight of expectation," he says seriously, opening a cooler on the porch to pull out a bottle of beer.

We continue into the kitchen and I look at him from across the island, pouring the vodka-lemonade from the pitcher, minus the extra shot. "Do you feel pressured to be perfect? You kind of have a reputation for being a good guy."

He chuckles and his cheeks flush slightly. "You say that like it's a bad reputation to have. I actually hope that I *am* a good guy, but I'm far from perfect. What about you? I know you must feel the pressures of expectation, being a student at Blackwood. It's not an easy school to get into."

I want to laugh, and bite my tongue to keep from saying, *easier than you think—all you have to do is majorly screw up, or in my and Lance's cases, cover for someone who has.* "Yeah, I guess. But fuck their expectations. I'm going to do whatever I want."

Grant smiles wide. "Not sure I completely understand, but I like it."

Somewhere between Grant going to the basement for more ice and me having to use the bathroom, we lose each other for a while. I meet up with the girls, who are floating in chairs on the water, and choose to sit on the dock with my feet hanging off instead of going in. Up until Lance sneaks up from behind, scoops me up and jumps off the end.

I peel off my tank top and cut-offs and let them dry on the dock while I join the girls in a floaty chair. We kick water at Lance and a few other guys who playfully try to tip us over. Eventually, we make it back up to the house to grab some food when the late afternoon drifts into the evening. The kiss of the sun can be felt in the tightness of my skin, and I'm hoping it doesn't turn into a burn despite the multiple applications of sunblock. Thankfully my jean shorts are dry from baking on the deck, and I pull them over the hot pink bikini bottoms, choosing not to cover up the strappy bikini top.

"Receive any more love notes?" Brendan asks, sitting next to me on the blanket we laid out, while the others are loading their plates with food.

I thought I could spend one day without having to worry about who's out to ruin me. Leave it to Brendan to remind me of my reality. "Not unless you've hidden one that I haven't found yet."

"I'm telling you, it wasn't from me," he says, holding his hands up in innocence. "Doesn't it concern you a little?"

"Maybe if I knew what the hell it was about." Which reminds me…"I'll be right back." Leaving my plate of food on the blanket, I walk through the house in search of my bag that I tucked under the front porch before we entered.

I pull the phone out of my bag and turn it on. Joey's is the only contact listed. I think about texting, but know we really need to talk.

He picks up on the second ring and answers like he's been expecting me. "Hi, Lana."

"Hi," I say quietly.

"I'm glad you called," he says, the low tone of his voice shoots right through me with a shiver. "I've been worried about you."

I close my eyes, fighting the urge to hang up because just hearing him speak is affecting me, and I hate it. "Where's Vic?"

"He's in Europe for the summer. He left last weekend."

"Will he be returning to Printz-Lee?"

"I don't know. Are you worried?"

"Only about Allie," I tell him.

"I know," he says quietly. "Me too. She's still in a coma."

"How do you know?"

"Because I check every day. Lana, after you told me the truth about what happened that night, I searched the hospitals to find her. I've been struggling with what to do. I hate not being able to do anything to help her."

"Me too. But I don't know what other choice we have until she wakes up."

"Let me tell my father about the convenience store."

"No," I say adamantly. "Besides, that doesn't matter now. And it won't prove that Vic hurt Allie."

"But if he's arrested for the armed robbery, he'll be off the streets."

"Will he? Really?"

"I don't know." I can hear the defeat in his voice.

I sigh. "Let's not do this, okay? I'd rather focus on Allie. She's the one who needs us."

"What do we do?"

I rub my forehead. "I don't know. But there has to be a way to prove he did it, even if she doesn't wake up." The thought of her not recovering makes me nauseous.

There's silence on the other end.

"He won't hurt anyone else. I won't let him, no matter what happens."

"You don't know what he's capable of," I tell him, remembering the look in Vic's eyes before he shoved Allie down the stairs. It was ruthless. He grinned at me, like he enjoyed it. "I can't do this right now." I hang up without letting him respond and shut off the phone.

I pace the width of the driveway for a while, trying to be rid of the trembling in my hands. When I go back inside, I pour another drink—hoping it'll help. I shouldn't have called Joey. Except, I needed to know that Vic wasn't here.

The shadows stretch across the grass as the sun begins its descent on the other side of the lake.

"There you are!" Ashton exclaims, throwing an arm around my shoulder when I step onto the porch. She's drunk.

"How did this happen?" I ask Brendan, who's standing beside her.

"Someone kept forgetting the lemonade already had vodka in it." Brendan slides an arm around Ashton's waist to shift her weight onto him. "We're going back to campus."

"Oh," I say, the sudden inebriation now making sense. "Do you have a ride?"

"Yeah. Another Blackwood guy." Before he guides Ashton inside, he says to me, "Don't lose your way, Lana." And then he leans over and sucks on Ashton's neck, making her giggle. "Or you could always join us."

I groan in disgust.

I leave them and walk onto the grass. A guy is setting logs onto a fire that's just started to burn in the fire pit, and a few other people are sitting around it with guitars. More gravitate toward the scene. I find a chair and pull it closer to sit and listen.

I'm soon lost in harmonious voices singing acoustic folksy rock music, mesmerized by the flickering flames. My mind is a blur of thoughts I wish I didn't have to think about.

"Want to go for a swim?"

I turn to find Grant crouched beside me. It's nearly dark. I have no idea when *that* happened.

"Sure," I say with a bright smile.

He takes my hand and pulls me up from the chair, not letting go as we walk down the steps to the beach. The air is still warm, but without the sun, the water feels cooler than it did this afternoon. I shiver when we wade in.

Grant's strides are much longer than mine and within a few steps, he's up to his waist and plunging under the water. He emerges, and his glistening, sleek body stops my progress. It actually stops everything. My breath. My heart. My thoughts. I stand there staring.

"Are you coming in?" he calls, pushing off and gliding backward, his arms swinging casually over his head in smooth, long strokes. He looks like he belongs in the water, moving within it effortlessly.

I continue to walk out until the water is covering my chest. We're the only ones in the water, and the voices and guitars from the party fade the farther out we go.

"Want to float on our backs and look at the stars?"

"I've never tried floating before."

"Come here," he says, offering me his hand. My feet lift off the sand when I reach for it, letting him pull me in deeper until I know I'm in over my head. "Lay back. I've got you."

I flip and lean back until I'm facing the sky. My feet poke out, but my butt keeps sinking. Grant has a hand on my lower back and another on my upper thighs. "Relax. Push up a little with your hips." I adjust. "Breathe and let go." He slowly takes his hands away, and somehow I stay afloat. "You've got it."

I can barely hear him with my ears filled with water. I close my eyes and turn everything off. My thoughts. My fears. My guilt and shame. And just drift. My lips stretch into a smile when I feel his fingertips reaching for my hand, gently pulling me closer until his fingers slide between mine. I open my eyes, but I don't look over, afraid that I'll disturb my balance and sink. The sky is sparkling. I've never seen so many stars in my life.

I feel the water slosh against me. Grant's other hand slides along my stomach to my waist. I tip up, realizing he's standing beside me. I rest my hands on his shoulders to stay afloat since we've drifted farther out. He grips my waist to keep me anchored to him. There's still distance between us, like we're slow dancing in middle school.

His eyes search mine, and I try to move closer, wanting there to be no distance at all. But his arms stiffen, resisting. "I really want to kiss you right now, but I can't."

I know he sees the hurt cross my face. I've never been very good at hiding my emotions. I remove my hands and try to kick away, but he doesn't let go.

"I have this…promise, to myself, that I won't do anything with a girl if either of us have been drinking. Even if it's only a drink. Not even a kiss."

"Oh," I breathe out. "That's why you looked disappointed earlier when I mentioned the vodka."

"Yeah," he smiles. "I didn't want to make any assumptions about what might or might not happen between us today, so I couldn't exactly ask you not to drink, just in case. I mean, I knew what *I* wanted to happen, but I didn't know if you felt the same. We haven't really spoken much before today."

"True. But yeah, I'm pretty sure I wanted the same thing you did. Damn lemonade."

He laughs, the water rippling around his chest.

"So it doesn't matter if I *feel* sober?"

He shakes his head. "There shouldn't be a gray line when it comes to consent. I never want to be a regret."

"Wow. You really are cursed with *Integrity*."

Grant chuckles lightly. "Integrity's a curse? I never really thought of it as a bad thing."

"We're all cursed," I tell him, wrapping my hands around his forearms. "*Integrity* just happens to be yours."

"What's yours?" I can feel the tension in his arms relax, allowing me to float a little closer.

"*Honesty.*"

"I can see that." His smile reflects in the low light. "That's not a bad thing either."

"It's a curse for a reason," I argue weakly, not really wanting to go into the full explanation.

"Well, at least I'll always know you're telling the truth."

"Even when you don't *want* to know," I add as if to warn him, but it only makes him laugh.

"I'd still want to know."

This moment alone with Grant, floating in the water and revealing our truths under the stars is probably the best moment of my entire day. It would make my entire year…if he'd kiss me. And it's at this inopportune second that my brain decides to kick in. It's dark. It's been dark for a while. "Omigod, what time is it?" Panic floods my core.

"What?"

"I'm going to be late." If I'm not already. I push away and kick toward the shoreline. "You don't know where Lance is, do you?"

"No," Grant says following after me. "Why? What time are you supposed to be back?"

"Ten-thirty."

"Oh shit," he mutters as I scoop up my clothes and rush up the steps. I can't remember where my jeweled flip-flops are, but at this point, barefoot it is.

I run across the lawn, Grant right behind me. "Do you need a ride?"

"Uh, Lily's supposed to drive us."

"She left."

"What?!" I'm full out panicking now. I stop in front of a girl I saw speaking with Lance earlier. "Do you know where Lance is?"

"He went inside with Stefan."

I continue into the house.

"I'll get you a ride," Grant hollers to me from the porch as I start calling out for Lance.

I climb the stairs to the second level of the cabin and begin opening doors. "Lance!" The third door down, I find him…with Stefan…on a bed. I close the door quickly. Never saw that one coming. "Shit." I hope they didn't notice. They looked a little too pre-occupied to realize I was there for that second. Thankfully, they were still clothed, well, mostly.

I rush back down the stairs and out to the front of the house, searching for my bag under the porch.

"Lana?" I hear Grant call from above.

"Yeah?" I answer, my hand touching the fabric.

"Uh, are you under the porch?"

"Getting my bag." There's something glowing red inside of it. "Fuck." I pull out the phone and hold my breath when I answer. Mr. Garner's face fills the screen.

"Where are you?"

"On my way back. I'm so sorry. I'm with Lance, and…"

"Lance has an overnight pass. You don't." Now that makes sense. Wish I knew that…oh, a couple hours ago when Brendan and Ashton left.

"Sorry. I didn't know, and lost track of time."

"I can cover for you for the next half hour. When I call back, it's your official curfew check-in. Be in your room."

"Thanks, Mr. Garner." I stuff the phone in my bag. Above me, Grant is standing next to a girl in a cute blue sundress.

"This is Talia. She was about to leave and can take you back to Blackwood. I'd come with you, but she's going home."

"It's okay." I'm really hating that I'm literally running away from him right now. I look to her. "Ready?" She already has her keys out, recognizing the frantic look in my eyes.

"Let's go," she says, striding down the driveway to the Honda Accord parked a few cars down. "Trust me, I know all about missing curfews."

"Bye, Lana!" I hear Grant call after me in the distance, but I don't look back.

I duck into the passenger seat and collapse against it as she zips the car out of the spot and races down the road, like she's trying to get me back before the last chime of midnight. Which isn't far from the truth.

I hate having a curfew. And running. I *really* hate running.

Chapter Twelve

The man's heart was filled with cunning and deceit. Savagery and death. Thaylina saw that he was not a man at all. Beneath the charming mask hid a cruel and heartless monster. And he intended to take away her power, so she could no longer see the goodness in any heart, forever cursed to only see their lies and betrayal.

"Go away," I groan, reaching blindly for my beeping phone.

I roll onto my back to hold the screen above my face, even though my eyes are still closed, and scan my thumbprint.

"Meet me in the foyer in fifteen minutes," Mr. Garner's voice comes through too loudly.

I pry open one eye. "Why are you torturing me at seven-thirty in the morning?"

"You owe me for last night. I'm collecting. Get up. Put on some sort of workout clothes, and meet me downstairs. Otherwise, I'll send Mrs. Seyer up to retrieve you."

"You're not my favorite person right now," I mutter, hanging up.

I kick the sheets and comforter off and stretch out with a yawn. To make this day even worse, I have two classes, and I'm not working at the country club—which means I don't get to see Grant. I hate today.

Mr. Garner is waiting for me in a pair of baggy, navy basketball shorts and a gray t-shirt that looks like it's been washed fifty too many times.

"Um, are you forgetting something?"

I'm not in the mood for guessing. "What?"

"The rest of your outfit." His neck is flushed and he's having a hard time making eye contact.

I look down at my spandex booty shorts and sports bra. I don't have true workout clothes, because I don't work out. And it's not like I have cleavage hanging out or anything. This sports bra is practically a cropped tank top. "Stop being a prude, Mr. Garner. You demanded I be awake right now. Get over it."

"Let's go," he says with a heavy sigh.

"Where exactly are we going?" I ask when he turns right at the rose trellis—that has a red ribbon tied to it. It's almost indistinguishable among the blooms of the same color.

"We're going to tour the rec center. Figure out a way to keep you from punching people you don't like."

"But how else will they know I don't like them?"

He turns his head and gives me a menacing stare, obviously not appreciating my sarcastic honesty.

We weave through the Court until we reach the building after the guys' dorm. "You know your way around pretty well," I note, considering he's only been here a little over a day.

"After we met, I explored the Court all afternoon. Spent most of it lost, but I eventually figured it out...sort of."

The rec center's entrance is a stone archway with a small pond on one side and a waterfall on the other—oddly tranquil for a gym. But this isn't just any gym, and that's evident as soon as we enter. This building's interior is distinctly different than every other. But I guess it has to be. It houses the same wrap around staircase, but it's made of what looks like glass, instead of stone. And each floor above is lined with a similarly clear glass railing. It's ultra-modern, despite the stone walls.

I'm struck by a clean, almost floral scent and the sound of trickling water as soon as we enter. The entire stone wall next to the Court entrance is slick with water sliding along its surface and dripping into a narrow fountain.

Mr. Garner waits for me to take it all in for a minute before beckoning. "We have someone scheduled to give us a tour."

Behind the French doors that seem to be in *every* building, is a counter with a couple of women behind it wearing uniforms that reminds me of a hospital or clinic. On the other side of them are closed doors labeled: Massage Room 1, Massage Room 2, Chiropractic, and Reiki. Everything is in soothing colors of white and turquoise.

"Good morning," the woman with almond-shaped eyes and striking cheekbones greets us when we walk in. She has a glow about her, like she was just polished, her tan skin flawless and her smile luminescent. "You must be Lana and Mr. Garner."

"Yes," Mr. Garner replies. "Good morning."

"Your tour guide will be right out to show you around. If you'd like to wait in the recovery room, you're welcome to. It's across the hall."

"Thank you." We exit and cross the hall where we find a room filled with couches and ethereal music that will put me back to sleep if we stay too long. I eye the containers of water with fresh fruit and berries floating in them. What is this place?

Mr. Garner must read my confused expression, which is the most obvious of the influx of emotions rushing through my head as I try to make sense of this. It's so completely different than anything I've experienced on campus. Too different. "You have to remember that most of these students are very pampered in their regular lives. Their parents expect some semblance of that to be available to them at school."

"Right, because what else would they be paying for?" I reply with a broken laugh.

A minute later, a man walks in wearing a fitted sleeveless sports shirt and shorts that are a little *too* snug. He resembles stacks of square blocks made up of body parts with his arms jutting out from his shoulders. It doesn't help that he has a flat-top and square jawline.

"Hi. I'm Mack."

"Seriously?" I laugh. I can't help myself. He couldn't be any more of a muscle-head stereotype if he tried, name included.

"Excuse me?"

"Ignore her," Mr. Garner says, stepping forward and offering his hand.

Mack proceeds to give us a tour, starting downstairs where the pool, locker rooms, and sauna are located. We wind our way up the stairs, level after level. We're shown the basketball and racquetball courts, the group fitness and spin rooms, the weight and cardio centers, until we reach the top floor where a track is suspended above all of it. The inside of the track is lined with a wall of glass, allowing us to look down upon the open stairwell and the cardio and weight areas below.

From here, I spot a separate boxing center partitioned off from the weight room that he didn't bother showing us when we were down there. I can only imagine he thought it would be wasted on us since Mr. Garner is lean, although athletic. But he looks more like a marathoner than a fighter. And, I'm a girl. I guess karma decided to throw my stereotyping back in my face.

Mr. Garner notices the boxing area too. "Do you offer lessons?"

"You're interested in boxing?" Mack asks, not hiding the surprise in his voice.

"No, I am." I stare at him, daring him to make a comment about my size. Or my gender.

But all he says is, "Cool."

"You can sign up for lessons or class slots on the tablet outside each room," he explains, leading us back to the lobby. "Do you want to start today? I don't have anything booked this morning with the campus being fairly empty right now."

"Sure," I reply, while Mr. Garner says, "I think I'll stick with the treadmill."

Mack doesn't let me pound the shit out of the heavy bag. He forces me to *work*, which only makes me want to pound the shit out of *him*. He has me do a million crunches, toss a medicine ball, jump rope, and do these crazy footwork drills. He said we'd get into hitting next time. That's if I survive *this* time.

"I hate that I don't hate you," I tell Mr. Garner when we leave, my body dripping with sweat.

"Still need to work on your positive emotive expressions," Mr. Garner teases. "But at least you're too tired to punch someone, which is kinda the point."

"I'm done listening," I say, walking away. My legs feel like they're made of rubber. Just the thought of crossing the Court to read the note waiting in the tree makes me want to fall over. But I force myself to go, only to find an antagonizing message addressed just to me from Brendan.

∞ *Get in trouble?* ♂

How did he know? How does he know anything?

I rip up the note and leave it in the box, removing the ribbon from the swing and sticking it in there as well so Lance and Ashton don't think they have a note waiting for them too.

After showering, I go to Ashton's room to see how she's feeling.

When she answers the door, it's obvious she feels terrible, with her hair a sad mess on top of her head and the long t-shirt hanging limply off her shoulder. Her liner is smeared around her eyes and she's pale, despite spending the day in the sun.

"Are you alive?" I ask cautiously, following her into the room. She crawls under a blanket on her couch.

"No," she mutters. "I can't believe I drank like that."

"I didn't realize you were until you couldn't stand on your own anymore."

"What happened to you? How'd you get back? I told Brendan that you needed a ride, but he said something crude about riding Grant." She pokes her head out so just her eyes are showing. "What happened with Grant?"

268

I scrunch my nose. "Nothing. He wouldn't even kiss me."

"Why the hell not? I would have." This makes her laugh. "I mean I was probably drunk enough that I would have, to be honest." I laugh with her.

"He won't do anything with a girl if either of them has been drinking."

"Holy fuck. Forget about Prince Philip, he's a fricken saint!"

"Speaking of, please tell me you and Brendan didn't…"

"No," Ashton assures me. "He's definitely *not* saintly, but he would never take advantage. That doesn't mean we haven't hooked up while drunk, but not when I was *that* bad."

"Good," I say, but it still doesn't feel right. It's not like I haven't had my share of drunk-sex with Jensen. Hell, we almost never had sober sex. But just thinking about what Grant said about there being a gray line of consent, especially when alcohol is involved, makes me look back at it differently, wondering if I would have had sex with him all of those times if we, or even I, were sober. The sourness in my stomach intensifies when the voice in my head answers, probably not.

And that's just taking *sex* into account, forget about kissing. I don't think I have enough fingers to count the number of drunk make-out sessions I had at parties or in the dark corners of bars.

"Maybe he's too good for me," I say with a sigh. "I'm more demon than saint."

"I prefer angry pixie," Ashton giggles. "Besides, what guy doesn't like a girl who bites a little."

"Are you still drunk?" I ask, laughing at her.

"Probably."

"Want me to bring you back something to eat?"

"No thanks. I have stuff. I think I'll go back to sleep until my class this afternoon."

Before I leave, I say to her, "We should make a pact to watch out for each other."

Ashton folds the blanket back from her face. "What do you mean?"

"When we go to parties, or anywhere, really…that we make sure the other is safe or doesn't drink too much. I wouldn't want someone hurting you, or you know, you doing something you didn't want to because you're high or drunk."

Ashton smiles softly. "You'd do that? Promise to protect me?"

"Of course. And I never break my promises, ever."

She smiles bigger, her eyes shimmering. "I promise to protect you too."

"I'd totally hug you right now, but you stink," I say, making her laugh.

When I shut the door, I have to swallow hard against the lump in my throat. But it doesn't keep the tear from escaping. I know I'm not being emotional just because I recognize how much I care for Ashton. It's also guilt for not being able to protect Allie from Vic. And sadness that we need protecting at all.

I *have two classes* on Tuesdays and Thursdays. American government in the morning and French right before dinner. This means I'm not scheduled at the country club on Tuesdays and Thursdays. I've never been so disappointed about not being able to work.

When I do return on Wednesday, Ashton and I are assigned the bev cart again. I can't stop smiling. I'm not even trying to fight it.

Kaely is in the locker room when we walk in.

"Where were you Monday?" I ask, realizing she wasn't at Stefan's even though she was so excited to go when I last saw her.

"Had to help my mom with something," she says with a huff. But her signature sweet smile is quick to return. "But I'll see you on Friday for—"

"Work," Ashton interjects. "Yeah, we know. We're all working at The Deck together." Ashton flashes her a tight smile with enlarged eyes.

"Oh, right," Kaely says, her cheeks pink. "I forgot that you knew that."

They're acting weird.

"What was that about?" I ask Ashton after Kaely leaves us at the golf carts to go to The Grille.

"Nothing," Ashton says dismissively. She's lying. She knows that I know she's lying. But it doesn't matter right now because Grant just came out the door carrying bags of ice. Rhett too, but I don't care about him.

Grant smiles when he sees me, or us, but I convince myself the smile is just for me. I am so ridiculous right now.

"I didn't know you gave swimming lessons," Ashton says, making my eyes widen.

"What?" Grant asks, glancing between us.

"Oh, I must have heard wrong," she replies with a knowing smile. Grant looks to me and I can only shrug awkwardly. I'm going to push her off the moving golf cart.

"See you at the ninth," he says as I take a seat. I wave.

When we're far enough away, Ashton starts laughing hysterically as I hide my face in my hands. "You just waved goodbye. You didn't say a single word to him the entire time. You just waved."

"I may never tell you anything again," I sulk. "I can't believe you said that."

"It was funny." She's still laughing when we get to our first set of golfers. I can't fake being upset. I mean, it was funny. And I *was* pathetic.

I *waved* at him.

By the time we get to the ninth hole shack, my shirt is pasted to me and loose strands of hair are stuck to my cheeks. It is so disgustingly hot out, I think my knees are even sweating.

"I'm going to have Stefan make us frozen drinks," Ashton tells me when she shuts off the cart.

"I'll be drying boob sweat in the bathroom."

She laughs as she walks away.

I don't see Grant or Rhett when I enter the shack. Good, because I need a few minutes to cool off and fix my hair. It's completely out of control from the humidity and Ashton's maniacal driving. She has two speeds—dead-stop and foot pressed all the way to the metal. I may need the chiropractor at the rec center before the end of the summer.

I'm balancing with a foot on the toilet and the other on the bathroom counter with my shirt pulled up to allow the cool air direct access to my cleavage when the door pushes open.

"This feels incredible," I tell Ashton. But when I turn my head, it isn't Ashton standing there, it's Grant.

He looks at me in fascination, like he never thought to stand on the toilet with his shirt pulled up to cool himself off. "Uh…"

My mouth opens. Nothing comes out.

"Sorry." Grant turns to leave.

He's about to walk through the door when my mouth decides to say the most asinine thing ever. "I'm sober."

He stops. Before he faces me again, I quickly pull my shirt down to cover myself. When he turns to look at me, his mouth is quirked like he can't quite believe I said that. Neither can I.

"And you're also standing on a toilet, in the shack bathroom."

"Yeah, right," I say, stepping down. "I was just saying…that…I'm sober…in case you wanted to know."

He chuckles. Then takes a step toward me. I hold my breath, hoping. "I *am* going to kiss you, Lana. But not here."

"Good. I think." I bite my lip to keep another bout of unfiltered honesty from escaping.

Grant laughs again, forever amused by my absurdity.

"I have mango and pineapple or strawberry and kiwi," Ashton announces in the distance, her voice growing louder. "I told him to keep them virgin in case Grant…oh, hi Grant."

I close my eyes and swallow.

"I'm not a virgin," he tells her, teasing.

"Good to know," she says with a cock of an eyebrow. "Are you, Lana?"

"What? Omigod stop!"

Grant and Ashton burst out laughing. I am the funniest person on the planet today, apparently.

"I'll take the mango." Grant passes it to me after taking it from Ashton, since he's blocking the doorway.

"Ashton, would you mind helping Stefan at the bar for the rest of the afternoon?" he asks her without taking his eyes off me.

"Yes! I finally get some action. I mean, behind the bar. You know, pouring drinks."

"We get it," I say to shut her up, because obviously neither of us can stop our mouths from being stupid right now.

Grant and I drive off in the bev cart, leaving Ashton with Stefan at the Ninth Bar.

"Let's get the obvious questions out of the way," he says, pretty much as soon as we're moving. "I'm eighteen. Senior at Printz-Lee. One sister, Faith, who's fourteen, and one brother, Garrett, who's eleven. We have a golden retriever named Max. My father's a principal at one of the local elementary schools, and my mother's a cardiac surgeon. We live in a small town you've never heard of in Connecticut. I have no idea what I want to do with my life other than travel and see as many places as I can before I am forced to grow up. I'm on the crew team and play lacrosse. And well, that should cover the general biography."

I blink. He peers over at me in expectation. "Your turn."

"I'm Lana. Nothing else really to know beyond that."

"C'mon," he coaxes. "No brothers? Sisters?" I shake my head. "What year are you?"

"Junior." Then reluctantly add when he nods in encouragement, "I live with my mother in a small city you've never heard of in Massachusetts. No dogs, although this stray cat likes to pee under our front steps and it smells horrible." He lets out a laugh. "I've never been outside Sherling until I arrived here last Friday." His brows rise. "My mother does whatever she has to do to take care of us, as do I. And I'm not really a team player, so no sports."

This amuses him as well.

"Why are you here for the summer?" I ask him just before we reach the next group of golfers.

"My father thought it would be good to have some experience, working," he tells me uncomfortably. "I know, it sounds terrible because it's not that I didn't *want* to work, but they won't let me during the school year. And every other year, we've traveled somewhere during the summer."

"Huh, I've been working since I was thirteen."

The golf cart stops a little harder than I'm sure he intended. He's looking at me with a bewildered expression as the golfers approach the cart.

When we take off again, I decide to say, "I'm not a private school kid. I wouldn't be here if someone else weren't paying for it. I don't come from money. And I have no idea what I want to do with my life, and I'm not worried about it."

His mouth turns up. "I like everything about you."

"Even my honesty?"

"Especially your honesty." We stop to wait for a guy to putt and when we're waved on, he says, "And as much as I try not to lie, I do. But I won't ever lie to you. I think it's only fair."

"That's your curse talking," I tease.

"You and your curses," he says with a chuckle. "You'll have to explain them to me another time."

We come to a stop next to a group of guys, younger than most of the golfers by at least four decades. I'd guess they're in their late twenties. But they're acting like they're still in high school with the way they talk shit and jostle each other.

"I'll have Johnny Walker Black on the rocks"—one of the more pompous players orders from Grant— "and a bottle of water." He then proceeds to slide his hand along the back of my shorts to cup my ass.

I freeze.

Grant must sense my tension because he stops mid-scoop to look across the cart at me. His eyes tighten, registering something's wrong, even though he can't see exactly what from his position.

And then the guy squeezes.

Fury licks up my spine. It must be transparent on my face from the shock I see in Grant's eyes. But before he can react, I reach behind me and take hold of the guy's thumb and twist it around like I'm trying to flip him onto his back using only his digit. His entire body contorts, trying to gain some relief from the wrenching. He hollers out in pain.

"See this body?" I growl into his ear between clenched teeth.

He squeals when I tug a little more.

"It's not yours to touch."

"What the hell?" one of his friends calls out when he realizes what's happening.

I release him. He shakes his hand vigorously. "Bitch." I smirk, malice still simmering in my glare.

Grant hasn't moved in the few seconds the entire thing went down. I glance over at him suddenly realizing how this must have looked. Shit. I give him a tentative half-smile, knowing my uncontrollable anger can be a lot for anyone to witness. Guess I'll need more boxing lessons.

"Uh, you guys are cut off for the rest of the day," Grant says, his voice authoritative, not allowing any room for them to argue. "If you have a problem with that, you can talk to the manager. But I'm not serving you. C'mon, Lana."

"Are you serious?" a bigger, oafish guy bellows in disbelief.

We drive off before they can make a scene. Or more of one.

"I'm—"

"Are you okay?" he asks, interrupting my apology. I wish he hadn't seen that side of me. But I'm not sorry for almost ripping the guy's thumb off.

"Oh yeah," I say dismissively. "I used to work at a dive bar. That was nothing, trust me."

"Nothing? I don't know if I'd say that. But you may have ruined his golf game, which is the least he deserves." He looks over at me with a crooked smile and admiration in his eyes. "You are unlike any girl I've ever met."

"I guess I should've included, 'I'm mean,' as part of my bio."

Grant laughs loudly, earning an annoyed scowl from golfers within earshot. Golf really is the dumbest sport.

"Please don't ever change," he says, gaining control over his laughter as we roll to a stop. Then he leans over just before we exit to serve the approaching golfers, his breath tickling my neck. "And I really can't wait to kiss you."

"I'm still sober," I tell him, my cheeks blossoming from the huge smile on my face.

We spend the rest of the afternoon asking each other a thousand questions about our likes, dislikes, favorite books, movies we loved, foods we hate, even wishes made blowing out birthday candles. It was like we were on a first date…at work…if I dated. But he never does kiss me, no matter how many times he could have, and I wanted him to.

After I'm done changing in the locker room, Cary asks me to join him in his office. "I heard about what happened at the twelfth hole."

"Omigod, I'm so, so sorry," I say in a rush before he can continue. Panic overtakes me, and apparently my mouth too. "Is he okay? Did I break his thumb? I know I shouldn't have assaulted a member, and I'm really sorry. I promise it'll never happen again."

"Lana," Cary says calmly. I press my lips together to keep from saying more. "I'm sorry this happened to you and I wanted to be sure you're okay."

"What?" I ask in confusion. "Me?"

"Yes. We take what happened very seriously. No one, I don't care if he's a member or the President of the United States, has any right to lay his hands on you. I want you to feel safe working here. That member has had his privileges revoked temporarily, so that he understands that his behavior will not be tolerated on our premises."

My mouth drops open. I finally utter, somewhat coherently, "You're worried about *me*?"

He smiles warmly. "You're part of the KCC family. Of course I am."

"Thank you," I say. "I'm fine."

"Good. I'll see you on Friday then."

I'm still in shock when I walk out of his office and almost walk into Grant who is standing by the staff entrance.

"Thinking again?" he teases.

"Huh?" I ask, redirecting my attention. "Did you tell Cary about what happened?"

"Yeah. He needed to know. What happened wasn't okay, even if you did dislocate the guy's thumb. Which was pretty impressive, by the way. Besides, I wanted to be sure none of the other bartenders served those guys while they were here."

I've never had anyone stand up for me before, other than Tori and Nina. But they'd be right there with me, punching and clawing, not defending my honor.

I throw my arms around Grant's chest, because I'm too short to wrap them around his neck, and hug him, totally taking him by surprise. After the initial shock of my reaction wears off, he hugs me back, tight. "Thank you," I say, my voice muffled within his arms.

He squeezes me again before we both let go.

"Um, how was your day?" Ashton asks from beside us.

I grin insanely. "I kicked ass and served the thirsty. You?"

"I made out with Stefan and got a buzz."

Grant and I laugh in surprise. "On that over-share," Grant declares, "I guess I'll see you…" He hesitates. "Um, Monday, if you can make it to Stefan's." He frowns, and I mirror the expression. "I can't believe it's going to be that long."

"What about Friday?"

"My dad is coming into town. He wanted to spend the weekend together."

"Oh," I say, not hiding my disappointment. "Then I'll see you Monday." It's like my entire body deflates as I watch him walk toward the employee parking lot.

"Aw, he didn't kiss you, did he?" Ashton slings her arm around my shoulders as she directs us toward the shuttle. I reluctantly tear my eyes away from watching Grant walk away.

"Nope. He didn't kiss me."

Chapter Thirteen

The beast laughed as the girl fought to be free of his cloak. But it was a magic cloak, hexed to trap anyone within its bind who was not the man meant to wear it. She fought for her breath, choking as it grew tighter and tighter. And as promised, the beast sang.

I *should be careful what I wish for.*

At seven-thirty, Mr. Garner wakes me and drags me to the rec center again, where Mack is waiting to torture me. At least today, he lets me punch stuff.

"Is this our thing?" I ask Mr. Garner when we're walking through the Court afterward, sweaty and sore.

"I want to make sure you have a safe outlet for your anger."

"Or…you're making sure I know how to hit harder when I do get into fights."

And I wish I never said that, because when Mr. Garner wakes me on Friday morning, he introduces me to Jasmine's meditation and yoga class. And I thought Mack was bad? Jasmine and her soothing words of inner peace and letting go, all while twisting and balancing my body in the most inhuman positions, is so much worse. My mind is far from calm. I want to tip Mr. Garner over, watching him flow through the positions like he's water. I'm on the verge of screaming when she finally strikes the gong to end our session.

"I really hate that I don't hate you," I mutter again when we leave. "I've decided that's our mantra."

"We'll work on that," he says with a smirk, looking relaxed and all zenned-out.

Later that morning, before meeting Ashton and Sophia for breakfast, I finally connect with my mother. We missed each other's calls the entire week. It's brief, both of us avoiding honestly answering how we're doing. I miss her. And today of all days is harder than any other.

I don't expect her to say it. She never has in the past.

"I love you. You were *my* choice." This is what she tells me every year.

"I love you too," I say before hanging up. There are so many questions I want to ask her, about how she's feeling, if she's keeping up with the bills, but mostly about how she knows Niall. I couldn't ask any of them, not today.

I wander into the Court, not ready to see the girls at breakfast. My heart aches and my throat constricts to fight back sobs. I weave through an intricate labyrinth of hedges until I come upon a heart-shaped rose garden at its center. I am lost in my grief when I feel his arms wrap around me from behind.

"Happy Birthday, Princess." Brendan kisses the top of my head. I shove him away. "What? No birthday love?"

"Not as long as you keep calling me that," I seethe, facing away to wipe the tears from my cheeks.

"Honestly, it's what comes out naturally when I see you. I swear it's not to remind you of that night. I'm a bastard, but I'm not *that* twisted." After a moment of hesitation, he says, "I'm sorry. I'll try to refrain from saying it. But I make no promises." I can feel him studying me, trying to circle around to get a better view of my face. I continue to evade him, turning my head to hide my emotions.

"Why are you crying?"

"How did you find me?" I ask, deflecting.

"Followed your GPS," he answers honestly. "Now, tell me what happened? Why are you upset, today of all days?"

"Because it *is* today." I sit within an egg-shaped swing set at the edge of the garden. Brendan pushes his way inside and sits next to me. It's tight because it's not meant to be shared, so I'm practically on his lap. "What the hell?"

"Relax, I'm not coming on to you." He pulls my legs across his lap and I adjust so I'm sitting at an angle on the cushion. "Talk to me. I won't leave you alone 'til you do."

"Why do you care?"

"Lana, cut the shit."

I close my eyes to fight back the tears that start to form at just the thought of saying it out loud. "I miss my grandmother." I swallow hard.

"When did she die?" he asks, his voice careful as if just asking might hurt me.

"Almost three years ago. But it's harder today, because…I guess, it was our day," I explain in a rasp. "My mother has always had a hard time celebrating my birthday. I think it has to do with my father, since he left her seventeen, pregnant and heartbroken. I have a feeling he was the love of her life, and she never got over it. And I'm the reminder of that heartache, even sixteen years later."

I have Brendan's rapt attention. His deep brown eyes take in every word, his hand gently gripping my knee as if to console me.

"Why am I telling you this?"

"Because I'm a good listener," he answers with a small smile. "You were about to tell me about your grandmother."

I can't look at him when I start talking, so I pluck at a loose thread on the cushion. "She would take me out every year. I think it was more to keep me away from my depressed mother, but we always did something crazy. For my tenth birthday, we went to all the ice cream places in town on a mission to try ten different flavors. I thought I was going to be sick. At one point, I was obsessed with *Thumbelina* and wanted to live in a flower. So for my eighth birthday, we plucked them from people's front yards or window boxes and created a huge bouquet. Just ridiculous things. The last year, for my thirteenth birthday, we sprawled out on a blanket and had a picnic in front of a memorial statue in the center of the city while cars honked at us. We looked up at the clouds and made up stories. She was always telling me stories, but mostly twisted fairytales." I let out a broken sigh. "I wish she was here." *She'd know what to do*, I choose not to say out loud.

"I'm close with my grandmother too," he says quietly. "My mother was only a couple years older than yours when I was born."

I shift my eyes to examine his face, surprised by the vulnerability in his voice.

"How old were you when…?" I can't quite bring myself to say, murdered.

"Four. I found her."

"What?" My voice shaking from shock.

"She overdosed."

"I thought you said…" I begin, so confused.

"Another time," he says patting my knee. "Suicide isn't the best birthday talk." His tone transitions into something lighter, his eyes blinking back to the present. "I'm sorry your grandmother isn't here with you and you're stuck with all of us. But, you'll remember this one. I promise." He grins like he's keeping a secret.

"Does everyone know?" I ask, cringing.

"You're spending your birthday with a bunch of delinquents. Of course they know! We need any excuse we can to party."

I let out a short laugh.

Brendan ducks out of the egg swing and offers me his hand. "Lily's hosting tonight after work, so wear your sluttiest dress. Or just come in your birthday suit. Either way, I can't wait to spank you."

"And… you just ruined it." I make a sound of disgust in the back of my throat as I push myself out of the swing.

*K*aely, *Ashton and I* spend the afternoon serving at The Deck. It doesn't take me long to catch on because I've done this most of my teen years, except this place is much slower paced than I'm used to, and not nearly as loud. Even though I know he's not here, I still find myself looking out the window or over the edge of the deck every time I hear a golf cart go by, wishing it were Grant.

The girls are upset that Brendan told me about the party. They were hoping to keep it a surprise until we arrived, which makes me glad Brendan told me—I hate surprises.

I let Ashton curl my hair, which I reluctantly agree to leave down after she begged me the entire day. And miraculously she figures out how to tame it and keep it from frizzing out around my head. The waves she's spun into it give it a life I'll never be able to duplicate. Nina never understood why I had hair the length of my back, but refused to wear it down. Maybe if I had someone to style it every day, I would.

"Can I pay you in gummy bears to do my hair for me whenever I want?"

"I'd prefer THC gummies, but I'll take whatever you have."

I do wear a dress, but it's far from slutty. It's a powder blue baby doll dress with delicate t-back straps. It's a bit short, falling to my mid-thigh, but anything longer would look like a nightgown on me. It has several layers of flowing chiffon over a fitted slip, and with my wavy hair resting down my back, I'm feeling pretty amazing. I slide on the thick-soled wedge sandals that wrap around my calves and apply a coat of gloss to go with the rose gold hues Ashton and I decided I should wear.

"Let's go celebrate my fricken birthday," I say to our reflections as Ashton and I admire ourselves one last time in the mirror. She's wearing a pair of black and white striped high-waisted pants that hug her tight to the knee before flaring out dramatically. They make her already long legs look endless. She's paired them with a black sequined bandeau. I don't think she has any shoes on, but I can't see her feet under the bell bottoms. She looks like a rock goddess with her naturally wavy dark hair draped over one shoulder, and her jewel tone blue eyes darkly lined.

We couldn't look more opposite if we tried. Light and Dark.

I hesitate before leaving the room, making sure I have Joey's phone. I'm planning to call Nina and Tori tonight, even though I don't have their cell numbers memorized. I may be able to figure out where they are by calling places where they might be. It's been over a month since I've been out with them. Granted, it was the worst night of my life, but I still miss them. I miss talking and laughing at the most ridiculous things together. The trouble we'd start, or finish—depending if it was me or Nina. Flirting. Dancing. Manipulating our way into places we didn't belong but acted like we did. We didn't waste our time sharing dreams we knew would never come true. We lived every second like it was the last memory we might make together. I hope that night isn't it. We deserve so many more.

And I hate that they don't know where I am.

Before I can leave the room, my Blackwood phone beeps in my purse. I click on the incoming message.

You've been granted an overnight pass. Have fun. Be safe. Happy Birthday, Lana. –Niall

"What is it?" Ashton asks when she sees the smile emerge on my face.

"I'm sleeping over. Are you?"

"I am now." She smiles back.

We each throw together an overnight bag before rushing to the front of the administration building where Kaely's been waiting to pick us up.

"Where are the guys?" I ask Ashton when I don't see them waiting.

"They said they'd meet us there."

The house is a beacon of light in the dark woods with the light glowing through the angles of glass. The driveway is already filling with cars. All of these people are *not* here to celebrate my birthday. Everyone I know could fit inside this car, forget about the ten or so that have already arrived and those that continue to show up in the short time it took us to park and walk to the house.

"Happy birthday!" Lily exclaims, waiting for us within the open door. She hugs me tight. "I'm so happy you're here." My heart warms at the sincerity of her tone. She got the "hair down" memo evidently, but hers is sleek and straight, parted in the middle. And she's wearing a white empire dress with a silver sparkling belt beneath her bust-line. I'm kind of obsessed with her style and can't wait to be closer friends so I can start borrowing her clothes. That and she's probably the sweetest person I've ever met.

"Come in! What can I get you to drink? I heard you don't like champagne," she leads us through the open living space where a small cluster of people linger with champagne glasses in hand. It looks like she stocked up on champagne more than anything else in the beverage cooler.

"I can make you a champagne drink you'll probably like," Ashton offers, making herself at home behind the island that is currently substituting as the bar.

"That's an interesting ring," Lily notes when I rest my hand on the counter. She lifts it to examine Nick's wedding band on my thumb.

"I told her it looks like a guy's wedding ring," Ashton says, having noticed it while we were getting dressed.

"It's a reminder," I tell them. "To never fall in love."

Lily's mouth rounds and her eyes dip. "That makes me so sad." Then she hugs me…again. "Please don't be afraid to fall in love. The right guy is out there for you somewhere."

I laugh at her endearing attempt to console me. Even if I don't need it.

"Don't tell her that," Ashton says, laughing as well.

"It's her phobia," Kaely chimes in, like this explains everything.

"Oh! I should take your bags upstairs for you," Lily exclaims suddenly when she notices them on the floor, like she's being the worst host. "I'll be right back."

We hand our bags to her and she disappears up the stairs.

"Is she really this nice?" I ask, still getting used to Lily's infinite thoughtfulness. It makes me wonder if that might be her curse.

"As far as I know," Ashton replies.

"She reminds me of you Kaely," I say.

"Really? I don't think we look anything alike." She takes a sip from her champagne flute.

Ashton and I exchange a glance and try not to laugh.

"You're adorable," Ashton tells her, making Kaely unveil her blinding smile.

Champagne flutes in hand, mine tasting lemony, but not as sweet as lemonade, we walk out onto the top deck where the party is apparently taking place. And I nearly drop my glass as my step falters. Ashton grabs my elbow to keep my ankle from twisting.

"Whoa, can't start falling now. We have a long night ahead of us. Save the falling for later, preferably with a guy beneath you."

Kaely giggles. "You sound like Brendan."

"He may be a bad influence," Ashton says playfully.

I don't respond to any of this because I'm staring at the gorgeous face of Joey Harrison, who hasn't taken his piercing blue eyes off of me since I stepped out of the house. He offers a small smile, his dimple creasing slightly. He's even more breathtaking than I remember in a white button-down under a sports jacket and fitted dark jeans.

"Please don't come over here. Please don't come over here," I chant under my breath. But he's already moving.

Ashton mutters, "Oh shit. Not another one."

"Happy birthday, Lana," Joey says, leaning over to brush his lips against my cheek, igniting a spark that shoots through my entire body. He must feel it too because I hear him inhale quickly before moving away. "You look incredible."

"Thanks," I utter, willing my feet to take a step back to break the magnetic pull between us.

"Hi," Kaely says cheerily, snapping me out of it. "I'm Kaely."

"I'm Wil." He offers her his hand to shake.

"Wil?" I ask in confusion.

"It's what they call me at school."

"Oh, right," I say, faintly recalling how everyone refers to him by something different since his full name is made up of three first names. "I'm not calling you Wil."

He chuckles. "I don't want you to." And we're staring at each other again. The only reason I know this is because Ashton clears her throat, reminding me the world exists outside of his attention.

"We're going to look for our friends now," Ashton announces, escorting me away by my upper arm. "Nice to see you, Wil."

"Yeah. I'll talk to you later, Lana."

"What the hell is it with you and these Harrison boys? Thankfully you don't react this way around Lance."

"I don't think Lance likes girls," I tell her as we weave through a few groups to create some distance between me and Joey.

"Lance likes whoever he likes. Stefan just happened to be who he liked that day."

"Wait," I say, shifting to face her. "Have you and…"

"No," she quickly assures me.

"I have," Kaely admits casually. "He was my first actually. And only."

We both stare at her in shock.

"We've been hanging out when he stays here, since school ended. And it… happened," she explains. "He was really sweet. And hot."

Nothing should surprise me anymore. But this does.

"Do you have feelings for him?" Ashton asks.

"I like him," Kaely admits, dipping her head coyly. "But, it's summer, and I kind of don't want to ruin it. It's easy right now. So whatever."

Her words sound rehearsed, like she's trying to convince herself as well as us. That paired with her avoiding gaze makes it obvious she's not being completely honest, even with herself. Maybe she feels lying will keep her from getting hurt. I know all the signs, having lived with a *Believer* for a mother. Someone who's always convinced a guy is right for her until he makes it very clear he's not.

"Don't settle for *fun* if that's not what you want. You are not a toy," I tell her, my words probably more chastising than they're meant to be. "You deserve to be worshipped. And if he or any other guy doesn't see that, then fuck them." I choose to add, "Not literally," just to make sure she understands, because as much as I adore her, she is a bit clueless.

"Yeah, fuck 'em!" Ashton holds out her glass for each of us to tap.

"Happy birthday, Pixie," Lance says from behind me, reaching in to tap his glass with the rest of us.

"We were just talking about you!" Ashton declares. Kaely's mouth rounds.

"You just said, *fuck 'em*, so," his eyes dart between us, "it's either going to be a really interesting night, or you know about me and Kaely."

"Sorry," Kaely says, with a cringing smile.

"I'm fine if they know," he says. "But are you okay? Did I do something wrong?"

"Uh, we're going to get another drink," I announce, pulling Ashton after me to let them talk without an audience.

"Hey, I wanted to hear that," Ashton sulks.

"Sometimes you say things that maybe should stay on the inside," I tell her, before taking a large swallow from my drink so we can get another.

"Maybe," she admits reluctantly. "Sometimes *you* should say the things you're really feeling on the inside."

I laugh. "Maybe."

We find Lily inside, pouring champagne for new arrivals.

"Allow me," Stefan says, appearing from somewhere. "Shot for the birthday girl?"

"Yes!" Ashton and Lily holler in unison. I laugh.

He makes us a round of shots that taste like fresh watermelon and mint. And gives me a second immediately after.

"Come help pick out music," Lily beckons, taking me by the hand. "We need to get people dancing."

She leads me to a tablet where I scroll through songs and create a playlist.

"Should I have warned you about Joey being here?" she asks, leaning against the arm of the leather chair I'm sitting on.

"You call him Joey? Not Wil?"

She giggles like I'm being funny. "I grew up with him, just like you. I call him by the name we did as kids."

"I didn't really grow up with him," I tell her, not wanting her to think I'm more familiar with Joey than I am.

"Well, you know what I mean," she says, shrugging it off. "But I know how he feels about you, and I'm guessing you don't feel the same?"

"Uh." I shift uncomfortably. "I don't know if *I* know how he feels about me. It was just one night, and it was the craziest night, so maybe he thinks he felt something that was only heightened by adrenaline or something."

"I don't think so."

I look at her curiously, and she offers a small sad smile. "But if you don't feel the same, then you can't force it, can you? Anyway, I should've told you he was coming. I'm sorry."

I nod, because I can't say anything in an attempt to make her feel better that would be honest. Yeah, I would have liked the heads up. No, it's not really okay that he's here. And what the hell is she even talking about with the whole feelings thing?! We *just* met. It was *one* night.

I focus on creating the playlist for a few more minutes before Lily takes it back from me and switches the music over, allowing the electronic beats to blast through the speakers. She presses a few buttons on the tablet and the lights dim and begin flashing and pulsing—outside as well. People holler in response and soon bodies are moving to the beat.

Lily takes my hand and we snag Ashton away from Brendan to drag her outside with us. Kaely is sitting on Lance's lap, so we completely destroy that moment when we tug her away. We dance until our bodies are slick and my curls are a mess. Stefan continues to deliver shots that make getting lost in the music that much easier. The entire time, I feel Joey watching, his eyes shooting electrified shivers along my skin. But he stays away. And I'm thankful he does because if he were to come up behind me, I know I'd let him put his hands on my hips and his mouth on my neck.

"Which room are we staying in?" I ask Lily, needing to use the bathroom and get a bottle, or two, of water.

"Second door in from the stairs," she says, taking my hand and spinning herself beneath it. "Hurry back."

I squeeze through the crowd, not cognizant of when this many people arrived.

I find our bags on the ends of two queen beds in a huge bedroom that overlooks the decks and the lake. Thankfully, there's a bathroom connected to it. After rinsing the sweat off my face and dabbing it from my cleavage, I reapply makeup and return to the bedroom, where Joey is looking out the window, watching the people dancing below.

"What are you doing in here?" I ask. He spins around.

Joey has a flat, square box in his hand wrapped in the same raspberry ribbon that was used for the phone box. "Wanted to give you this. But I didn't think I should in front of everyone."

"You bought me a present?" I approach him slowly, careful not to get too close. I try so hard not to look into his eyes, but when I reach for it, his hand brushes against mine and a spark of heat courses through me, all the way to my spine. I glance up, and he's as still as I am.

"You felt that," he says so low I can barely hear him. "I know you did."

I swallow and take the box from him before moving away. Inside is my headband. The one that resembles a tiara with its intricate weave of crystals. The same one my grandmother gave to my mother, who then handed it down to me. My eyes water at the sight of it. I was convinced I'd lost it. It shimmers as it catches the light.

"I found it in the grass," he explains. "It was broken, so I had someone fix it. I had a feeling it meant something to you."

I swallow the emotion caught in my throat, remembering how I wore it every birthday since I was ten, paired with some ridiculous tulle skirt. "Thank you."

I take it out and tuck the box inside my bag, before sliding the headband on my head. I approach the mirror hung above the dresser and adjust my hair around it. Joey steps up behind me and I shift my gaze to his reflection. He smiles at me. My heartbeat picks up. He inches closer. I can't breathe. His hand skates along my shoulder, down my arm to my hand. I close my eyes. His lips dance along my skin. I lean back and dip my head to the side, allowing him access. He grips my hip and spins me to face him. I'm practically panting, my entire body pounding. I reach up just as he bends toward me. His mouth is urgent as his fingers dig into my hips, pulling me against him. I moan into his mouth, sliding my fingers into his hair.

I'm lost in his touch. This kiss. The pressure of his body against mine as he clutches me tighter. We trip toward the bed. He's just about to pull me down with him when something breaks. Or shatters, like it was trapped and fought to be released.

It's a thought. Three words.

It's a lie.

I push him away. And the veil of lust lifts. I can breathe fully as soon as he releases me. I blink as if roused from a dream. A very vivid and hot dream. But still, it's not real.

"Did I do something wrong?" His expression is mixed with fear and concern. "Lana?"

"I can't do this." My words are slow and methodical, like I'm coming to this realization as I'm saying it. My heartbeat slows and returns to normal. "It doesn't feel right."

"Uh," he says, unable to respond because he knows it felt amazing. But that's not what I mean. It didn't *feel* right, emotionally. I wasn't connected. And I'm not saying I need to have feelings to kiss him. But considering how much passion there was behind it, I should feel *something*.

"I'm sorry," I tell him, my eyes flickering between his, trying to find words to explain. To erase the pain that causes his eyes to flinch. But how do I tell him that what we have between us is an illusion. The draw. The attraction. The need. It's just lust. And the part of me that fought to break free from the enchantment of his touch, knows it's not what I want. "I wish it was more."

"Do you? Really?" He sits on the bed and runs a hand through his hair. "Because if you do, then let it be more. I have feelings for you, Lana. It's not just physical for me."

"It's just physical for me," I say in a whisper. He closes his eyes as if absorbing a blow. Damn my curse. "That's what I mean. I wish it was more than that. But it's not. And that's why I'm sorry."

He nods slowly.

"And Joey, how can you possibly have feelings for me? We only had one night–"

"You don't remember," he says with a humorless laugh. "I've met you before, Lana."

I narrow my eyes, searching my memory. "I would have remembered."

"Guess not," he says with a defeated shake of his head. "I was at a house party in Sherling with Lincoln the summer before freshman year. You were there with the girls. We talked for a while. I wanted to ask for your number, but you disappeared."

"Was…Parker there too?" I ask, fearing the truth. That was the summer Parker kissed me. I talked to him at a party for a long time, or at least, I thought it was him.

"I think so."

Please don't tell me I confused them in the near-dark basement apartment. When I came back from the bathroom, I searched for the guy I'd been talking to, but couldn't find him. So I leaned against a corner to observe everyone, like I usually do. That's where the guy I was looking for found me, or so I thought since they look so much alike. But it was *Parker* who kissed me.

Holy shit. I kissed the wrong guy.

I try to process this as Joey continues.

"I'd see you out sometimes when I was with my brother. We didn't speak again, not until last month. I wanted to talk to you so many times. But...you're intimidating."

"Seriously?" I laugh, suddenly wondering if it would be different between us if he had been the one I kissed that summer, and not Parker. Maybe I'd feel a connection beyond the physical, like he feels for me, if we had more moments together, getting to know each other.

"It was hard crushing on you from afar," he admits with a crooked grin, his dimple creasing. He is gorgeous, there's no denying that. And for a minute, I'm tempted to ignore the voice in my head and jump on him. But I know he wants more than that, and then *I'd* be lying to *him*. He deserves better.

"You used to come over to our house when we were kids," he says, catching me off guard. "We were young, like really little. Did you know that?"

I shake my head. Surprised, but not.

"I don't really remember it either. But I found some pictures and videos stored away while I was in the attic last week."

"How does my mother know your family?" I ask, having never come across a single picture of her with the Harrisons.

"I don't know. They wouldn't tell me much when I asked about the people in the pictures, only that they all lost touch. But I knew the girl in some of them was you. You're easy to recognize, even when you were barely old enough to walk."

"Don't you think it's strange that we knew each other when we were little? And now neither of our families will admit it? Especially since your dad's helping me." This leads me to ask, "Do you know if he's paying for me to attend Blackwood?"

"I don't know," he answers, surprised by the question. "The whole thing *is* strange. I didn't know he already knew your mother when I asked him to represent you." He pauses for a moment, contemplating. "I've been working for him in his office this summer. I can look into it, if you want. If it's important to you. Maybe he represented her or something?"

"I'd like to know," I say, grateful. "I don't like secrets. They're almost as bad as lies."

"But don't you have your own secrets?"

"I don't have many. And you know one of them."

"You can trust me." His brilliant blue eyes pierce mine, and a rush of sparking current flows down my limbs.

"I know." And I really do. I'm convinced Joey's honorable and will do what is right to protect the people he cares about—*Honor* is most likely his curse. This could explain his struggle to *keep* my secret, because he wants to do what's right for Allie as well.

"I wish you could trust me with you too."

I can only offer a weak smile in apology.

He stands, smoothing out his clothes. "Friends?"

"Don't you hate that word?" I tease.

"Right now, more than any other. But I don't want to lose you...again."

"You won't." I walk over to him. As soon as I embrace him, I can feel the electric surge begin to take over, and I quickly break the connection.

"Maybe we shouldn't..." he says, his chest rising.

"Touch?" I want to laugh. "It's intense, isn't it?"

Joey shrugs, his cheeks reddening. I bite my lip in regret, realizing it was even more for him than it was for me.

He walks to the door and waits for me. "C'mon. Let's celebrate you."

A few eyes follow us when we walk down the stairs together. But I honestly don't care. Let them think what they want.

"Birthday girl!" Ashton hollers from the bar. I smile. "Come have another drink with me!"

I turn to ask Joey to join us, but he's already outside. I understand the need to escape me. But the distance hurts. I can feel the chill of his absence. I also feel free of something that was trying to take over. I never want to be controlled, not even by my own impulses.

I accept the champagne flute from Ashton and clink with her glass.

She leans close to me and whispers conspiratorially, "I'm going back to the school with Brendan."

"Are you sure?"

She nods with a wicked smile.

"He doesn't have an overnight pass?"

"I don't think anyone at Blackwood would ever trust Brendan with an overnight pass," she shares with a chuckle.

"Then no more drinks for you." I take hers out of her hand and swallow it down way too fast. I think I'm about to sputter bubbles out of my nose. "That was horrible." I shiver.

Ashton laughs at me and picks up a bottle of water instead.

"I guess someone should have sex on my birthday." I sigh, toasting to her water bottle. "Just please don't ever share details about the two of you." I wince at just the thought of Brendan—I can't even finish the thought.

We walk back out to the deck where Lily and Kaely lure us onto the dance floor. There are still a crazy number of people here and, for the first time, I wonder what time it is. But then quickly decide that it doesn't matter—I don't have a curfew tonight!

At some point during the next dozen or so songs, my shoes come off, and I lose Ashton to Brendan.

Before he leaves, he kisses me on the top of the head, and whispers in my ear, "You really do look like a princess." Then quickly adds, "Don't hurt me for saying it." Ashton drags him away before he can see my stunned reaction at hearing the same words Allie said to me. Kaely takes my hand and spins me around, shaking me from my stupor. Lily hands me another shot.

What feels like hours later, the music transitions to something quiet and soulful. People start collapsing on furniture—talking, kissing, or passing out. I fumble my way to the end of the dock and sit to dip my sore feet in the water. Oddly the water feels warmer than the air. I hadn't realized how cool it had become outside until I stopped moving.

I shiver.

A suit jacket is draped around me. I tuck my nose into its collar without searching for its owner. It smells of ocean and sunshine. I don't know where I come up with those scents, but that's what it reminds me of. Grant appears next to me, his dark dress pants rolled up and his shoes off. He dips his feet into the water.

"Happy birthday, Lana."

My eyes tear up. I have no idea where this sudden burst of emotion comes from. I blame the case of champagne I consumed tonight. Or…maybe…it's him. Because seeing his beautiful face next to me right now makes my heart ache in the best way. "You're here," I choke out.

"Hey," he says soothingly, pulling me against him so I'm nuzzled under his arm with my head on his chest. "I'm sorry it took me so long. I actually didn't know about tonight until…well, it doesn't matter. I'm here."

"And I'm so n-n-not sober." I hiccup between my emotions, wiping a fat tear from my cheek.

Grant laughs. "Didn't expect you to be." He runs a hand down my hair. "You look beautiful."

I tilt my head up lazily. "I looked so much better earlier."

"Then I'm glad I wasn't here. I may have broken my own promise." He smiles warmly. He's wearing a white button-down, unbuttoned enough to make my eyes wander, wishing I could see more. His body was made for a suit, making him appear refined and…well, princely.

"You look beautiful too," I tell him, because he does.

His mouth quirks as he brushes a hair from my cheek and tucks it behind my ear. "How was your birthday?"

"Fun," I tell him. "We danced…a lot."

"You like to dance?"

"Love it."

He eases away. I gasp in despair at the separation. He towers above me. "Then dance with me." He offers me his hand. I grin and take it, getting up unsteadily onto my feet and letting his jacket fall from my shoulders. And that's when it becomes apparent, that I am a miniature human next to his broad, gigantic frame. But he doesn't tease me or make a comment about how tiny I am, like he easily could. Instead, he takes one of my hands and twirls me, my dress becomes floating petals. I laugh giddily as he settles me against him, my hand still cupped in his, pressed over his heart. He wraps his other arm protectively around me, not letting me falter, and it's like the foot difference doesn't matter. We fit perfectly.

I don't hear music playing, but we find our own rhythm within the water rippling against the dock. The deck lights are all off except for a singular sconce outside the door. We sway beneath a sky of dazzling starlight.

"Thank you for coming," I tell him, my head pressed to his chest, my eyelids heavy.

"Wouldn't have missed it."

After getting lost in him for an imaginary song or two, he asks, "Want to go inside?"

"Sure." When we turn toward the house, I catch sight of a silhouette standing before a window on the upper floor just before it disappears. "I wouldn't have let you kiss me tonight, even if I were sober."

Grant stops. I fumble to sit in a chair in front of the dwindling fire pit. He lowers in a chair next to me.

I cover my face with my hands and confess. "I kissed someone tonight." I peek between my spread fingers, braced for his reaction. He remains quiet, waiting for more. There's always more. My curse amplified by Grant, mixed with champagne, makes everything project from my mouth in a whirl of words. "I knew it felt wrong as soon as we kissed. But it was someone I've been with, and it happened. But it won't ever happen again. And I just had to tell you. I don't know why."

"Wil?"

I nod, not wanting to know how he knew. "Are you friends with him?"

He nods. "We play lacrosse together."

"Does that mean you don't want anything to do with me now? I have my own rule that I won't ever touch a guy my friends have been with…"

"I don't have that rule," he says with a small smile. "It doesn't feel good to hear it. But that's part of your curse, right? The honesty?"

"I didn't have to tell you," I say collapsing dramatically against the chair, regretting that I did.

"But you wanted to," Grant takes my hand, "which means…something, even in your current state of questionable sobriety." He grins, teasing. "You *want* to be honest with me. Even when it sucks. I don't hate that. And I know we're still…new. And you don't date. So, we'll figure this out."

"Whatever this is," I say, knowing it isn't anything I've experienced before. I can't hold back with Grant. And as much as it should scare me to be this honest, this open, this exposed with him—even when I'm drunk—I'm not. I feel safe to be exactly who I am, my cursed *Honest* self.

Chapter Fourteen

The song released from the beast's mouth was not of love. It did not bring joy to Thaylina as it had in the woods. It broke her heart. She cried for him to stop. She begged to be released. Her pleas went unanswered. He hissed in her ear, "You wanted this."

I **walk down the stairs** the next morning with one eye cracked open and a piercing headache.

"Why are there so many windows?" I mutter, unable to escape the sunlight that makes everything hurt so much worse.

"Good morning," Lily chimes, sipping from a champagne glass with orange juice in it. "Mimosa?"

"Champagne hates me," I grumble, sitting on the stool and rubbing my temples.

"Or we have leftover birthday cake?"

I smile, or try to, because even that slight facial movement cracks my skull. "Yes, please.

I expected more people sprawled out or grumbling with hangovers alongside me. "Where is everyone?"

"Just you and me. Joey left with Grant last night. I'm not sure where Lance went. And everyone else crawled out of here when they were sober enough to drive earlier this morning."

I stopped listening to everything after "Joey left with Grant." I'm trying to decide if the two of them leaving together should be freaking me out as much as it is. Freak-out aside, I had wanted to talk to Joey this morning about getting in touch with Nina and Tori.

Using the maps app, the *only* app on the phone, I looked up the numbers to the strip club where Nina works and a couple of the bars we go to in Sherling. But the people answering the phones were uncooperative and unwilling to ask around for them. Douches.

I also discovered while exploring the phone that it doesn't have texting or camera capability, and everything beyond the volume and contacts page is passcode protected. And I don't have the passcode. So basically, its only purpose is to receive and place calls to Joey. I'd call him now, except...he's with Grant.

Lily sets down a huge slice of chocolate cake in front of me.

"Thank you so much for last night," I tell her, digging the fork into the frosting. "It was a really amazing birthday."

"My pleasure," she says with a genuine smile. "What were your three wishes?"

Ashton declared that I get three wishes, because that's how it should always be. To which, Brendan snidely remarked, "Be careful what you wish for. You may not be able to handle three of me." He received an elbow in the ribs from both me and Ashton.

My first wish was for Allie. That she fully recover and be avenged.

The second was for my mother. That her heart and body be healthy, and that she find peace. (I blame Jasmine for the last part.)

And the third wish was for me. I paused before making it, looking around the room at the people surrounding me, smiling and laughing. Then I proceeded to blow out every lit candle, wishing that I always know who my true friends are.

"If I tell you, they won't come true." I stuff a mound of cake into my mouth.

Lily releases a small tinkling laugh. "Do you believe that?"

"Do you believe they'll come true at all, whether I say them out loud or not?"

"I think we always receive what we deserve, and belief has very little to do with it. It has more to do with our character and how that balances out on the scales of good and evil. Can't have one without the other, right?"

I study her curiously. "But isn't good always supposed to win in the end?" I can barely function, forget about contemplate karmic balance. And we're going down a strange and windy path right now. Because I *know* good doesn't always win.

"I think so," she answers, her lips smiling around the glass as she tips it back. "At least I hope it will."

L*ily drops me off* at the country club for my afternoon shift. Being on the bev cart with Ashton for the afternoon is both a blessing and a curse. It's easy. But her erratic driving makes my head splinter in half and my stomach churn, so I'm pretty miserable most of the shift. When we get back to campus, I skip dinner to take a nap. I set an alarm since I still have to go to the library to pick out a book for the American government report.

When I wake, I'm feeling better, but not great. The last thing I want to do is go to the library. I dump out my overnight bag on the bed, in search of my Blackwood phone. An envelope slips out from within the box Joey used for my headband.

Inside is a black and white photo of a group of people sitting on a sloping lawn. Behind them, I can make out a fraction of a wrap-around porch attached to a large white house that's too big to fit in the frame. The group appears to be having a picnic; platters of food and glasses are spread out on several blankets. And as much as it initially appears to be a posed group photo, there's a sense of movement, like the picture was taken before anyone was ready. Two younger women, maybe teenagers, are sitting close, laughing with open mouths. Another woman is facing away; her face obscured by dark hair. A smiling man is bent down, scooping up a small laughing boy, and a visibly pregnant woman is watching them adoringly. Another woman is smiling for the camera, but appears distracted, looking sidelong at a man who seems to be the only one ready, posing with a tight-lipped smile. I absorb the entire scene at once. My attention narrows in on the blonde with the ponytail who's laughing beside the girl with an Audrey Hepburn inspired pixie. She looks just like me.

"Omigod," I breathe out. It's my mother.

I flip the photo over to find the familiar red ink and the linear lettering.

HOW MANY MORE LIVES WILL SHE DESTROY WITH HER LIES?

What the hell? I hate these cryptic messages! Just tell me what you want already! Whoever it is must be getting some sadistic thrill out of pissing me off. What does this have to do with Allie, or me, or my mother and the Harrisons?

Maybe it's time to get answers to the questions I've avoided asking. I have to talk to my mother…in person. That's the only way I'll know if she's telling the truth.

I examine each face again. I only recognize one other. Niall Harrison. He's the man picking up the boy, who has to be…Parker. The woman behind Niall and Parker, must be Mrs. Harrison, pregnant with Joey.

On the bottom right corner, "Nantucket, Labor Day Weekend" is scrawled in black ink. I do a quick calculation. This is right around the time my mother found out she was pregnant with me. I know this because my grandmother told me how my mother was afraid she would go into labor on graduation weekend, when she was due. But instead, there are pictures of her in a cap and gown, that looks like a tent because of her protruding stomach. I arrived two weeks later.

Did she meet my father on Nantucket? And what is she doing with the Harrisons? Who are the rest of these people? Especially the girl sitting next to her—they look like they're friends.

Endless questions rush through my head the more I study the image. I know it's useless. I can pose all the questions I want to myself. The only way I'll get answers is to ask the right questions to the right people.

I flip the photo over and read the message again. For the first time I consider maybe it's not a threat, but a warning.

Stay away from him. It could easily be a warning as much a threat.

I know. That was a stupid message, probably just to get my attention, because it could mean anything.

This is so frustrating!

I have to talk to Joey about the pictures he found in the attic. Maybe he'll recognize this one too. In the meantime, I'm going to have to talk to the person who unnervingly knows more secrets than he should, and hope that he's not the guy I'm being warned to stay away from.

I tie a red ribbon on the post of the small wooden bridge that passes over the koi pond leading to the guys' dorm. Then I leave a note in the tree, telling Brendan to meet me in the library.

I wait at the library long after I find my stupid book for American government. And I keep waiting, not knowing if Brendan saw the ribbon or checked the tree. I miss the instant gratification of texting. Even when someone didn't text back right away, at least I knew they received the message. The librarian eventually kicks me out a half hour before curfew.

When I exit, the Court is dark.

"Shit," I groan, never having walked through the Court at night by myself. Everything is shadows and sharp silhouettes. I know there isn't a flashlight feature on the Blackwood phone, having searched for it when a lipstick rolled under my bed.

The cobblestone path emits a spooky, radioactive glow, but as Ashton translated during our tour, it won't show me which way to go. I scan the rooftops across the Court, trying to find the peak of the girls' dorm, but it's impossible to distinguish among the identical possibilities. So I start in the general direction that

I *think* it's in. I can't even keep the presumed building in view because I'm too busy watching my footsteps to stay on the path, occasionally getting swatted in the face with a branch.

I'm going to be late for curfew. I know it. But maybe they'll see I'm in the Court when they track my phone and come get me. At least I hope they will.

I hear a rustling somewhere close by and freeze mid-step, listening for voices.

"Hello?" I say loudly, wanting it to be anyone, even Dr. Kendall or the rock-head security guard.

No one responds. But the distinct sound of a branch breaking sets my hairs on end.

I rush down the path that starts veering away from the direction I want to go until I'm about to walk into water. I stop abruptly, teetering on one leg. I notice a glowing spot sticking out of the water a couple feet in on the left. Then another to the right. I wonder if this section's been flooded. But as my eyes adjust to the moonless night, I can see that there are swings dangling above the water, and logs immersed, intended to be sat on. Large reeds and water lilies blossom out of the water along with round balls of what looks like moss. This is a garden strategically designed to be navigated and explored by stepping and balancing atop the water.

Fricken fantastic. I never want to meet the geniuses who are responsible for this place.

Although each garden I've discovered within the Court is fairly small, it still surprises me every time I discover a new one. Regardless of how vast the space, it's curious that they all fit. I'm beginning to suspect that they change the Court a little every day, whoever *they* are. Because just yesterday, when I thought I was about to enter the garden with the mermaid fountain, I found myself in a small field of plastic pink flamingos and pinwheels, a vivid display of color and sound. It was peculiar and awe-inspiring at the same time.

But if they're always working on the garden, changing it, *when* are they doing it? I've never come across a single gardener, although the hedges are perfectly trimmed and the grass is mowed. Then again, I've only been here a week, and I work off-campus. I suppose there's time for them to maintain it without being seen. But a reconstruction seems almost impossible to conceal.

"Lana, who cares!" I say out loud, knowing this isn't the time to contemplate the mystery of the Court's construction. I take a breath and step onto the glowing footpath, balancing on one foot, then the other as I search for the next stone.

The water splashes.

I almost fall over. It sounded small, like someone tossed a stone in the water. "Hello?" I call out again, balanced in the middle of the pond. I wait. Silence. My heart is pounding. When no one responds, I hop to the next stone, wanting to rush across. I'm even tempted to walk through the water, but I can't tell how deep it is and fear what may be on the bottom.

When I finally reach the dry path, I search for the rooftops again and try to figure out which building I thought was the dorm. At this point, it doesn't matter. I'm past curfew. *Any* building will do.

Wait.

I pull out my phone from my messenger bag. Frustrated with myself for waiting this long to use it to call for security. But when I press the button to light up the screen, nothing happens. The battery's dead. I swear I charged it at Lily's last night. Unless…in my drunkenness, I plugged in the wrong phone. And Joey's phone is somewhere on my bed right now.

"Dammit!" I cry out, tempted to throw the useless phone in the water. I shove it back in my bag and continue to follow the glowing cobblestones. When I come to an intersection, I choose the path that looks like it'll lead to the closest building.

Until the path starts curling away again. No wonder students have breakdowns and start crying when they lose their way in the dark. I'm on the verge of being one of them. This place is maddening!

Someone coughs behind me. I whirl around. Or at least, that's what I thought it sounded like. This time I don't call out. I'm either being paranoid and hearing things, or someone's following me. I'm wishing for my pink switchblade right about now. Out of habit, I reach for it in the small tear in the bottom seam I made to hide it when I'm at school. It's empty.

I continue to walk, but with each step, I'm shrinking, or everything's growing. The hedges on either side appear to be getting taller and taller until I'm swallowed by the dark. Even the glow of the cobblestones becomes so faint I can barely see where I'm walking. Which explains why I collide with a wall of branches, walking into a dead end.

"You've got to be kidding me!" I holler, sputtering out needles.

On the other side of the hedge, I hear the pounding of footsteps. Someone's running, coming closer and closer. I back into the corner of the hedge, seeking safety within its solidity, and listen as they approach. It's like they're running right beside me—if I reached out, I could touch them. And just as quickly, they're gone, the pounding rhythm gradually fading.

I'm not alone.

When it's silent again, I feel for an opening, some passage to allow me to slip through the hedge without backtracking. That's when I discover what I thought was a wall is actually two overlapping lines of hedges with a narrow corridor between. Whoever was running, really was right next to me.

As much as I don't like the idea of following in the same direction as the runner, this path brings me in the direction of the closest buildings. And maybe, the runner is lost too and not trying to torment me. But that doesn't explain why they didn't respond when I called out.

Whatever. I can speculate all I want. It's only going to drive me crazy because I'll never know unless I find whoever it is. Or they find me. And honestly, I'd prefer neither of those things to happen.

I run my hand along the hedges, feeling for another faux wall, when a stinging pain forces me to pull back. Thorn bushes are woven into the wall, making the narrow passage even more treacherous to navigate. This school really is twisted. How is any of this making me into a better person? If anything, it's making me angrier.

When I'm finally free of the thorny corridor, I find myself in an open garden. Beds of flowers are planted around a massive tree with a twisting trunk and thick boughs that splay wildly from the center, forming an expansive canopy of leaves. I follow a path of thick grass that parts the flowers and encircles the tree. I feel insignificant beside it. The tree must be a hundred years old. It has that majestic feel to it, like it's been on this earth longer than any of us and has seen and heard many secrets in its lifetime. Secrets that are now confined within the rings of its smooth, whirling skin. I rest my hand upon it, wondering if it'll whisper them back to me.

The breeze picks up, and I hear an indistinguishable voice rustle through the branches. My legs tangle and I trip clumsily, circling and searching. A light gust sweeps through again, and I swear I hear it. A low whisper, like a buzz of bees. I can't quite decipher the message being carried to me in the wind. I wait for it to speak again. My pulse races in anticipation.

The rustling of leaves reaches me first, then within the cool breath of air on my cheeks, I hear it, drawn out until the one syllable sounds like an entire song.

"Ruuuuuuuun."

I spin around. The wind grows stronger, loose strands of hair whip against my face. It feels like an approaching storm, but when I look up, there isn't a cloud in the sky, only sparkling stars. The branches creak and the leaves clap frantically until my ears are filled with the violent rage of the wind ripping at the tree.

So…I run.

The path steers me through a curtain of dangling branches of a willow tree. I sweep them aside and find brief shelter beneath their canopy. I continue to sprint through to the other side, thrusting an arm out to toss the branches aside. When I emerge, I'm instantly struck by the silence. Everything is perfectly still.

My foot catches on a raised stone, and I sprawl on a set of wide steps, my knees and elbows absorbing the shock of the fall. These cobblestones are covered in moss—the impact bruises, but doesn't cut my skin.

I remain on my hands and knees a moment, catching my breath. Raising my head, I take in my new surroundings. The path curves and winds through a Japanese garden. Pushing myself off the ground, I survey the serene setting, or as much as I can in the dark. The small bonsai trees are easily identifiable, and I hear water trickling from somewhere. I find a stone bench under a miniature pagoda and sit to calm myself.

Hours must have passed since I left the library. What if I never find my way out? I know I'm being irrational. The Court isn't infinite, although right now if feels like it is. I'll reach one of the buildings…eventually. Maybe I should stay here. Let them find me. Don't they say to stay in one place when you're lost to make it easier to be found? But I guess it depends on who's looking for me. I still don't understand why I haven't heard a single guard.

I stay in the garden long enough to grow frustrated. I'm getting out of this fricken place, even if it takes me all night. Within my renewed conviction, my rational thoughts have convinced me that it was my hysteria that turned the wind into voices and footsteps. I imagined it. Because why would anyone follow me? What's the point? Besides, how would they know their way around in the dark any better than me? These thoughts don't really explain anything, but they make me feel brave enough to stand back up and keep going.

I walk for what feels like days, okay…hours. The distinct sound of the seagrass rattling in the breeze reach my ears, and I rush toward it. Finally, a garden I recognize. I select the path that I'm certain will bring me to the dorm.

I gasp with relief when I smell the roses. And when I reach the trellis, I release a broken sob, heavy with exhaustion.

A ribbon is tied to it with a piece of paper flapping in the gentle breeze. I untie it.

DO YOU KNOW WHO YOUR FRIENDS ARE?
WHERE ARE THEY NOW?

I crumple the note in my fist. "Fuck you," I seethe.

Whoever's sending me these notes, whether threats or warnings, has to go to school at Blackwood. And since there aren't many students enrolled for the summer, how hard can it be to figure out? Whoever it is, knows me—or at least, they think they do.

Do I know *them*? And that's when my grandmother's voice echoes loudly in my head.

Trust no one.

Chapter Fifteen

Thaylina closed her eyes to the blackness in his heart. She struggled against the green cloak, but she was not strong enough. His hot breath stroked her neck. Thaylina cried out when his fangs pressed against her tender skin.

Lana?"

I sit up.

And tip over, landing on my stomach with a grunt. The empty hammock rocks above me.

"Are you okay?" Mr. Garner's voice carries from somewhere, also above me.

I shake off the weariness that clings to me like a scratchy blanket and push myself off the ground. "Maybe."

"What happened to you? I've been up half the night wondering where you've been."

"I got locked out," I explain, stretching my eyes open, fighting exhaustion. I didn't sleep much, even after I found the dorm. And despite what everyone says about Mrs. Seyer being everywhere, she must have awful hearing because I pounded and screamed at the door until I felt like my wrist was about to break. I opted to sleep on a hammock but startled at every sound, my rational voice silenced by paranoia. It was the best night ever, and I say that with sincere sarcasm.

"My phone died."

Mr. Garner sighs heavily. "Well, I'm glad you're okay. Looks like you had a rough night."

I can only imagine what I look like, and I have no desire to find out.

"What time is it?" I ask, recognizing that I can now see what was once shadows and silhouettes.

"Five-thirty. I came out to look for you as soon as the sun rose. Security did a sweep around the perimeter, but they don't check the Court when the dorm monitors are in residence, at least that's what I was told. Their priority is keeping people out and you in. When your phone didn't come online, they checked your last location and knew you were on campus, and that's all they cared about. I argued with them for an hour, but they said you were in *violation*. And it was up to the school to hand out sanctions once you came back online. Guess it happens all the time. Regardless, they should have searched for you in the Court."

"Thank you," I say, appreciative that someone realized I was missing. "But I don't know if they would have found me. It's impossible to see anything in there at night, forget about finding someone who keeps moving. That's probably why they *don't* check the Court."

"It still isn't okay. C'mon, I'll let you inside. Try to get some sleep. And as much as it sucks, you're expected to attend class this morning."

I collapse on my bed without removing a single item of clothing or cleaning off the clutter from when I dumped my overnight bag. I regret that decision when I'm woken by my phone beeping what feels like minutes later—making sure to charge it was the only thing I accomplished before falling on my face. My neck hurts, my knees ache and I have something sticking into my side. I reach down and pull out a brush and drop it on the floor.

I lift the phone to find a message from Mr. Garner.

Thought you'd need an alarm to wake you in time for class. This is it.

Why do I have to be his *only* job?

I force myself out of bed, regretting that skipping isn't an option. Blackwood has zero tolerance for absences. I could lose off-campus privileges for the summer, which includes working at the country club. If I was confined to this campus for the next two months, I would seriously go insane.

Dirt, leaves and needles swirl around the drain when I shower. My body aches from falling, and I have a dark bruise forming on my left knee. My arms are marred with superficial scratches, and my head aches, like I bumped it—although I don't remember doing that. The mysterious head injury could also explain why I thought I heard things. It feels like a strange dream now that I'm looking back, like none of it was real.

The Court has returned to its whimsical semblance when I enter, taking the well-traversed path to the Great Hall for breakfast. Until I can't. Where I usually veer right around a fountain is now a straight path that leads to a sculpture garden of abstract art made of twisted metal.

I'm about to scream in frustration when I hear, "Good morning."

Brendan.

"Where were you last night?" I yell.

He raises a brow, taken off guard by my hostility. "Uh, bad night?"

"The worst," I growl, clenching my teeth to contain my emotions. "I left you a note to meet me at the library. I tied a ribbon on the bridge."

"It's not there. I never saw the note. Why, what happened?"

I shake my head, wanting to put it all behind me. "Forget it."

"What did the note say?" he persists.

I hesitate. Instead of reaching in my messenger bag for the photo that I planned to share with him last night, I cross my arms over my chest. "Convince me I can trust you."

"What?" he chuckles in befuddlement like I just asked him to stand on his head and tie his shoe.

"Convince me I can trust you," I repeat slowly, enunciating every word so clearly, he can read my lips too.

"I can't," Brendan answers simply, not even making an effort. "There's nothing I can say or do that will convince you to trust me. You and I aren't the trusting types. But that doesn't mean we can't use each other to get what we want."

"And you still want information?"

"Among other things." He winks.

I punch his arm.

"Ow, okay, okay. I was only playing," he moans, rubbing the tender spot. "What do you want, Lana?"

"The truth."

He laughs again. I glower, done with amusing him. "Whose version?"

"The *actual* truth," I say impatiently. "Someone's playing games with me, and I don't know why. I thought it had to do with what happened to Allie, but I don't think it does anymore."

"Lana, the actual truth doesn't exist. You should know that better than anyone. It's always tainted by someone's lies. I can try to help you decipher between the two. But first, you have to tell me what's going on."

My phone starts buzzing. It's Mr. Garner. I look to Brendan, who nods for me to answer it.

Mr. Garner appears on the screen. "Hi. Just making sure you're moving."

"About to grab something quick to eat on my way to class," I tell him. Brendan begins walking with me. I allow him to take the lead through the new garden since he apparently knows where he's going. He must have some sort of Marauder's map that changes when the Court does, because there's no way anyone can adapt this quickly.

"Okay. So, you're restricted to campus today. Sorry, there was nothing I could do even after I explained what happened. Apparently, they hold you responsible for making sure your phone is charged."

"Whatever," I say in resignation. Stefan's is the only place I'd go today, but I'm not in the mood to be around anyone, not even Grant.

"If you need to punch something, let me know," Mr. Garner offers with a sympathetic smile.

"Bye." I click off the screen.

"Why is your life advisor offering to let you punch him?"

I roll my eyes. "I'm taking boxing lessons as part of my anger management treatment, or whatever ridiculous name they call it."

"It's not working," he scowls, rubbing his arm. "What class do you have now?"

"Chemistry." I pull open the door to enter the Great Hall.

"I'll meet you in the foyer after your class."

Brendan doesn't enter the dining hall with me. Instead, he disappears down the hall, which leads to…I have no idea where, because this is the only place I've been inside this building.

I grab an iced coffee and breakfast burrito to-go before continuing to class, hoping another new garden doesn't pop up and throw me off course. I'm barely going to make it on time as it is.

N*early two hours later,* I've learned nothing. My lab partner probably wants to murder me. And we have our first test on Friday. How do we already have a test?

"Blackwood offers peer tutoring," the chemistry teacher, no I don't remember his name, says to me after class while he reviews my class assignment. "You could probably use the extra help. We bring on Printz-Lee honor students during the summer months. I can arrange for the chemistry tutor to meet with you tomorrow if you'd like."

"Sure," I answer automatically, too exhausted to care that I'm already in need of tutoring.

"What time?"

"Um." I hate that he's forcing me to think right now. "I have to work in the morning and then I have two classes. Could they meet in the evening?"

"I'll check. If I can arrange something, I'll message you."

"*What took you so long?*" Brendan asks when I finally walk into the foyer.

"I suck at chemistry," I tell him plainly. "Already need a tutor."

"Oh, Lana. You don't need a tutor. Maybe you should try staying awake in class." He is so patronizing. I'm tempted to throttle him.

I sneer. "Stop being a freak. Do I seriously need to put tape over my phone's camera and mic when I'm not using it to keep you from invading my life?"

"I do," he answers honestly.

Of course he does.

"Where are we going?"

"My room."

When we reach the bridge leading to the guys' dorm, I expect him to sneak me in some secret entrance, but Brendan continues to the main doors and holds one open for me to enter.

"What about your monitor?"

"He sleeps during the day," he explains. "Doesn't think we're capable of getting into trouble when the sun's up. Foolish man."

I follow Brendan all the way to the fifth floor. "You're not a senior."

"I was assigned this room when I arrived last year," he explains. "Now, I refuse to change rooms. You'll see why."

Brendan's room is as orderly as he is with a broken-in leather couch, a recliner and an impressive floor-to-ceiling bookcase. His bed is a built-in loft, like Ashton's, to allow room for the massive furniture. The space is predictably masculine, but it gives off a regal vibe I wasn't expecting. Then again, he does eat and dress like a forty-year-old man. Apparently he lives like one too.

"Take a seat," he offers, sliding open the cabinet next to the sink. He pushes the shelf so that the bottles of Evian swirl around and disappear, replaced by a row of liquor bottles hidden behind a secret compartment. "Drink?"

I shake my head.

Brendan pulls out a bottle of scotch and pours a small amount in a tumbler.

"You are not who you appear to be, are you?" I release a humorless laugh.

He smirks. "That obvious?"

"Maybe you're a changeling," I contemplate out loud. "You look sixteen, but nothing else about you is..."

"Except my stamina." He winks.

"And your maturity. But then again, fae are just as egotistical and flirtatious. Maybe you should go back to living under your hill. The Unseelie Court must be missing you by now."

"Are you about to tell me one of your fairytales, prince—" Brendan stops himself, grimacing apologetically.

Time to change the subject.

"Here's how this is going to—" I don't finish my sentence; a framed picture halts my words.

"Lana?"

I stand and cross the room to his espresso stained, floor-to-ceiling bookcase that lines the entire wall. There's a roll-top desk built into it, and, as much as it surprises me, it's filled with books. Along with personal touches—pictures, golfing trophies, decorative art pieces.

I pick up the picture of the two teenagers, maybe a little older than we are now, and stare at it. They're sitting on the bow of a sailboat, their faces concealed by oversized sunglasses, but the smiles on their faces shine as bright as the sun.

"Who's in this picture?"

"The girl on the right is my mother when she was eighteen. I don't know who she's with. But I like the picture because she looks so happy."

"The girl on the left," I start, but have to pause to take a breath, "is my mother."

"Really?" Brendan lets out an amused chuckle. "No way."

But when I turn to him, his smile falls. He knows.

"Our mothers were friends?" I demand when I realize he's *not* surprised by this.

"Apparently." Brendan swallows down the rest of the scotch.

Still holding the picture, I sit down on his couch. Brendan remains standing, leaning against the counter next to the sink.

"I've received three messages while I've been here. The first night, the message *I know* was written on my wall in glow-in-the-dark paint. The second message was in my work locker the day I started. You saw that. And last night I received another one. It was in my overnight bag when I came back from Lily's." I reach inside my messenger bag and hand it to Brendan. "At first, I thought they were threats, about the night Allie was hurt, because that seemed like the obvious secret—even though the messages didn't really make sense. But now..."

Brendan stares at the picture. "You think it has to do with our mothers?"

"Maybe. But I still don't know what any of the messages mean," I say. "Have you received any?" He shakes his head, turning the photo over to read it. "So whoever it is, is targeting me. And last night, after I received that picture, I started to wonder if maybe they were warnings and not threats. Except..."

Brendan looks up when I don't continue.

"I was locked out of the dorm last night because my phone was dead. I ended up spending half the night lost in the Court. I swear someone was in there with me, although I'm second guessing that now. It might've been in my head. But whoever's leaving these notes knew I was out there, because they left this." I hand Brendan the crumpled note.

"*This* is why you needed to know if I'm trustworthy?"

"It's someone who goes to the school. Who knows who I am. And they had access to my bag at Lily's. There aren't a lot of people to choose from. Every one of them is someone who is supposed to be a friend."

"The friend's comment was just to keep you quiet, I'm sure of it."

"Probably."

"It doesn't mean it's one of us. All this person needs is access to your room, which means they have campus clearance. That could include teachers, administration, or—"

"Life advisors," I mutter. Mr. Garner was essentially hired to look after me, and he has connections with the Harrisons. Maybe he's trying to warn me. But I quickly dismiss the thought, he's not the dramatic type…I think. "So it could be anyone."

"I think we should focus on why, instead of who anyway." He meets my eye. "So don't tell anyone else."

"I think Joey may know where the picture came from. He told me that he found others of us together as kids, before we were old enough to remember. He may know who else is in this picture, or at least where it was taken."

"Don't tell him about the messages. I'll make a copy of the photo, so he doesn't see the back. I think we need to keep that between us."

"Why?"

"Instinct," he says like that's a valid reason.

"You always listen to your gut?" I taunt.

"Pretty much," he admits without a hint of sarcasm. "I'm very perceptive, and it usually keeps me out of trouble. It's my vices that bring me down."

"What? Hacking, stalking and sleeping around?"

He laughs half-heartedly. "The third one is close enough to the truth. My perception is skewed when it comes to women I care about. I have a hard time cuing in on her intent until it's too late. It's like I'm blind to her faults until she's out to ruin me. So now, I don't do relationships. Keep it purely sexual, no emotions. That way I don't get screwed over, pun intended." He smirks flirtatiously.

I roll my eyes. "Explains the trust issues."

"Told you we're a lot alike. And it turns out, we have more in common than I originally thought." He pours himself another drink. "I'm going to tell you something that no one else knows. And not because I'm ashamed, but because it's none of anyone's fucking business, and I've been able to keep it to myself while at Blackwood because no one asks."

He takes a long draw from his glass. "I grew up on Nantucket. My family owned a small bookstore. We weren't wealthy, not like the people who came in on their yachts every summer. Or like the students at Blackwood. Niall arranged for my admittance at the beginning of last school year, just like he did for you. He won't tell me who's funding it, claiming it's a scholarship program. Something he's arranged with the school. When he presents candidates with potential, they accept them under certain conditions. It's good PR for them to boast how they help students from all backgrounds to become top scholars, and Niall gets to change lives. But I know it's bullshit. They're receiving money for tuition. I've seen their financial records."

"But you don't know from where? Do you think it's Niall?"

"Blackwood tuition for three of us, then Printz-Lee and NYU on top of that? I doubt it. I considered that maybe his firm orchestrated some sort of fund, because we're definitely on their pro-bono client list. But I haven't found anything in their records."

"I never would have guessed that you didn't come from money. You act like you belong here, among the privileged."

"I do," he says with a smirk. "They're not any better or worse than us. In fact, I guarantee I have a better relationship with my grandmother than most of them do with their parents. Money has nothing to do with how I present myself. I grew up middle-class, exposed to the upper echelon. I caddied on the island. Overheard a lot. Learned more. Manipulated and seduced the right people to get what I wanted, until I got caught. And it wasn't even a billionaire's daughter. It was with the damn principal's trophy wife. So naive."

"You had feelings for her?"

He shrugs. "Lesson learned. But always the hard way."

I grin, familiar with the sentiment. "That's the only way to learn apparently."

Brendan smiles before focusing on the picture again. "So our mothers were friends. But how did they know the Harrisons?"

"I don't know why my mother was even on Nantucket," I say, overwhelmed by how much I don't know about my own mother. "There's no way she could've afforded it."

"Would she tell you if you asked her?"

"I can try. But if I want her to tell me the truth, it'll have to be in person. She can be really...sensitive when I bring up anything to do with my father. And I think she was pregnant, or soon would be, when this was taken."

"My mother was pregnant with me by about three months or so in this picture." His eyes widen. "Holy shit. Every woman in this picture is pregnant except for one, unless she is and just isn't showing."

"What?" I ask, taking it back to examine it. He's right. The woman with the dark hair, whose face is obscured is visibly pregnant. The black and white photo makes it more difficult to see the bump since she's wearing a dark dress. "Do you recognize anyone else?"

"The blonde who isn't pregnant looks familiar, but I can't place her. I don't know who the other man is, and the dark-haired pregnant woman is impossible to identify. You also have to remember, someone's taking the picture."

"And someone is cut off," I say quietly, squinting at the blur of a figure on the left side. Brendan sits down next to me. "Do you see him, his arm and legs, like he's running to get in the picture?"

"This photographer sucks," Brendan notes. "I wonder if there's another one with everyone in it, where we can clearly see their faces."

"Whoever's doing this is twisted. I don't understand what they want. None of it makes sense." I shift to face Brendan and ask the question I only asked once about my own, "Do you...know who your father is?"

He shakes his head. "My grandmother says he was a summer tourist. There for the season and never seen again. My mother didn't even know how to contact him to let him know she was pregnant. My grandmother thinks he may have been married."

"How old was your mother when she had you?"

"Twenty."

"So she was nineteen here. And you said she was eighteen in your other picture with my mother. That means they knew each other for at least a year."

"This weekend wasn't the first time your mother came to the island then, because my mother never left it. Not once."

"Seriously?"

"That's what I've been told."

I flop back against the couch. "This has something to do with the Harrisons. I know it." My eyes flip up to meet Brendan's dark gaze. "You said Niall knows who killed your mother. What did you mean by that? I thought it was suicide?"

"I don't think I'm ready to share that yet." His voice is quiet but with a note of anger, deep and menacing. I nod in understanding. "We start with finding out how your mother knew mine and what their connection was to the Harrisons."

He stands and sets down his empty glass on the sleek onyx coffee table. "C'mon. I want to show you something."

"What?"

"The reason this is my room."

Brendan approaches his bookshelf and pushes against a section of it, and it pops open, swinging away from the wall.

"How many secret passages are in this school?"

"A lot," he says over his shoulder as he disappears into the wall.

"And how many of them are you responsible for?" I'm thinking the room didn't come with the bookshelves already in it.

He clicks on a string of lights and illuminates his signature cocky grin, then disappears up a ladder. It's tight. I swallow before following after him, reminding myself to keep breathing as I climb. Thankfully we don't have to go up very far before we end up in a room. Or more like a crevice of an attic. Brendan has to bend over to keep from bumping his head on the slanted beams. He hits another switch and the space fills with the hum of electronics coming to life.

"So this is where the creeping happens," I say, taking it all in.

An old desk and banquet table along with several two-drawer file cabinets outline the perimeter, every surface is covered by a keyboard, monitor or hard drive. A three-shelf bookcase is filled with tiny monitors. When I examine the ones that are on, I recognize the feed. It's Blackwood's outer perimeter.

"I thought you said you didn't come from money?" I question, accusation heavy in my voice. Not that I know anything about what I'm looking at, but the equipment appears new and expensive.

"I didn't say I don't make it," he quips.

"You are scary."

"Oh, you have no idea," he replies, still wearing the arrogant grin that causes shivers to erupt down my spine.

I *try to convince myself* that confiding in Brendan was my only choice if I want to get any answers. But I'm not convinced he's trustworthy. *Perception* is his curse. He's not at all who he appears to be but can somehow see right through everyone else. He's so forthcoming with the truth, it almost makes *me* uncomfortable. Then again, like he said, the truth can be manipulated…by perception. Everyone has their own version.

Now I'm freaking myself out and am seriously regretting getting him involved.

Brendan could very easily be behind all of this. Maybe he blames my mother for his mother's death. It's hard to believe he didn't see my resemblance to her in the picture he has on his bookshelf. I look just like my mother when she was a teenager, even with her oversized sunglasses on. He wasn't surprised when I told him who she was—he already knew. Brendan sought me out and has been messing with my head from day one, asking questions he already knows most of the answers to.

I can't trust him.

Chapter Sixteen

The door to the tower flew open and the sorceress appeared before them. She cast a spell to release Thaylina from the confines of the cloak. The girl tumbled to the floor, scraping her knees and elbows. She lay on the cool stone, awaiting the return of her breath.

I can't believe I agreed to this extra shift at the country club. Mr. Garner neglected to mention when he relayed Cary's request, and admittedly I didn't ask, that I'd be working from seven 'til ten so that I'm back in time for my eleven o'clock class. The golf course is barely functioning this early in the morning. Only the diehard golfers are out on the course. I come across some of them prepping their carts when I shuffle down to The Deck.

I definitely don't expect to find a guy doing laps in the pool. I don't think it officially opens until like nine or something. I stay close to the side of the building to get a better look. Whoever it is, he's taking it seriously, wearing a swim cap, goggles and long fitted swim shorts, like they do in the Olympics—the only time I've ever watched swimmers compete. I admire the lines of muscle rippling along his back with each stroke. I can only imagine what his chest looks like.

I duck back when he finishes at this end of the pool, sweeping the goggles and cap off in a fluid motion as he dunks his head under the water.

"Lana?" Cary beckons before I can see the swimmer's face.

I spin around and crash into a stack of chairs stored against the building. I reach to steady them just as they topple over and make the loudest noise ever.

"Sorry," I cringe. Cary watches this entire disaster curiously. I can't bring myself to turn around to see if the guy in the pool witnessed this, but he'd have to be deaf not to have heard it.

"You okay?" Cary asks, helping me stack the chairs.

"Yeah, just humiliated," I admit, because I have the most horrifying curse in the world. Cary chuckles lightly.

"Well, I have the keys you'll need for the storage rooms and cages. Don't worry about inventorying the liquor. The bartenders take care of that weekly. Just the paper and dry storage. The charts list everything so you know what to look for. Start here, then go out to the ninth hole storage, and finish inside the Clubhouse. You'll find several storage closets in the main building. One for paper products, like napkins and towels, and another for dry storage, like sodas and non-perishables. That's it, pretty simple."

He hands me a tablet and shows me how it's broken down by tab. Thankfully, it's something I can do half-awake, because that's as much of my brain that's functioning this morning.

"Thank you for coming in to do this on your day off," he says.

"No problem," I answer and watch him walk away before rounding the building to the employee entrance.

I slip the key in and open the door. I scan the storage room, deciding where to start. I've just begun counting bundles of hand towels when someone appears in the entrance leading to the service area.

I yelp and he hollers at the same time.

With my hand to my chest, I stare at Grant standing in the doorway holding a sports drink, wearing the same swimsuit as the guy in the pool. His bronzed skin is flushed from exertion, and he's still glistening wet. My heart doesn't calm at the sight of him. If anything, the crazed wet hair and smooth sculpted definition of his broad, muscular chest makes it beat faster.

"Lana? What are you doing here?"

I can't speak. I open my mouth and my erratic pulse cuts off every word I try to form. Heat creeps up my face and fills my cheeks. I think I need to sit down. This is way too much to handle this early in the morning.

"Are you okay?" he moves toward me. I hold up my palm to stop him. "What?"

"I can't," I say, shaking my head, forced to close my eyes to gather my stupidity.

"Are you having an asthma attack?" His voice is filled with concern. "Do you have an inhaler?"

I shake my head. He sets his hand on my shoulder. "What is it?"

I exhale and shake off his touch. "I wasn't prepared to see you half naked."

He laughs. "Are you serious?"

"Sorry. I know that sounds very sexist, but I really can't function with you standing here looking like that."

"Wow. I guess I'll go then." His tone heavy with amusement. "You're hilarious."

"Or something," I say, completely mortified and still unable to look at him.

He leans in close and murmurs in my ear. "Now you know how I feel every time I see you. And it has nothing to do with how much skin you're showing."

I bite my lip to keep from smiling. I turn just as he disappears out the door.

Somehow, I'm able to compose myself and remember how to count, then spend the next three hours doing exactly that.

Apparently, on Tuesdays, Grant lifeguards at the pool. And according to Kaely, who is working the bev cart with a forgettable guy, it's the most popular day. He doesn't sit upon the lifeguard chair shirtless, thankfully, or else there would be a hell of a lot of teen girls and mothers pretending to drown just to be saved. But him—in the red shorts and the white tank top with a pair of black sunglasses—is still enough to attract the members who appreciate the artistry that is Grant Philips. He seriously belongs in a museum for people everywhere to admire. Okay, I know I'm being ridiculous.

Before changing out of my uniform, I leave a voicemail for Joey, asking when he's coming back to Kingston. I tell him that I found something I need to show him. And of course he has to call back while I'm changing and the phone is in my locker. I curse when I see his missed call and voicemail.

"Hey Lana, I'm leaving for Nantucket with my family on Thursday for the Fourth. We're going to be there for a little over a week. I'll come up when we get back. I found something I need to show you too. Hopefully you can make sense of it, because everything I'm thinking is a bit crazy. Can't wait to see you."

At this point, it *all* seems crazy. I hate that I have to wait two weeks, but it's not like I'm going anywhere. Maybe we could figure this out if the weirdo were more direct and didn't leave abstract messages and photos of parents' past. And hearing that Joey's going to Nantucket is disturbing, considering the photo was taken there. But it would make sense if the house in the picture is theirs.

I arrive back on campus in time for American government and take a nap before French. I probably should've used that time to shower and put some effort into looking like a human being, but the day is lost on me. It's not worth the effort.

I refasten the hair tie around my nest of a topknot, rub some deodorant under my arms and walk down to dinner in a pair of cut off sweatpants and a cropped tank top. I'm tempted to take one from Ashton's dress code and go barefoot but settle on a pair of flip-flops.

I receive a message from my chemistry teacher before I make it out of the dorm.

Tutor is meeting you in the library at 7:00 in study room A.

Oh, crap. I turn back around and climb up the flight of stairs to get my messenger bag out of my room. I won't have time to come back after dinner.

I *smile when I see Lily sitting* at our table. "Hi. Come for a visit?" I didn't know we were allowed visitors outside of lawyers and parents. But maybe if she's on Lance's approved list.

"Yes and no," she replies. "I'm tutoring this summer."

My day may have just improved. "Please tell me you're my chemistry tutor."

She grimaces in apology. "I'm not a science girl, sorry. I'm a writer."

"When are you meeting your tutor?" Ashton asks.

"After dinner." I sigh dramatically. "I hate chemistry."

"Then you're not doing it right," Brendan says just to be annoying. Ashton yelps in surprise when he does something to her under the table.

"Gross," I grumble.

"The Fourth of July carnival's this weekend," Lily announces. "We should all go together."

I look to Lance since I can't go without him. Because some dumbass deemed him more responsible than me. It's a good thing I like him.

"Sounds good," Lance replies for us both.

I leave them in the Court to meet my tutor in the library. I have to ask the librarian where the study rooms are located, and she leads me down a narrow spiral staircase to the basement level where study cages house desks and empty bookshelves. Interspersed between them are wooden doors marked with gold letters, beginning with A and ending with study room D.

"Your tutor must not be here yet," the librarian says, flipping on the switch outside the door before unlocking it for me. "I'll bring them down when they arrive."

"Thank you," I say, entering.

The room isn't much bigger than the chemistry closet I used to hide away in at Sherling High. Yes, I'm aware of the irony now that I'm meeting a chemistry tutor…in a closet. There's a round wooden table with a half dozen chairs. And that's it. Guess they don't want students getting distracted while studying.

But they weren't counting on my tutor either, because he is going to be one hell of a distraction.

"No way," he says from within the doorframe.

I laugh at the cosmic joke. Because of course it's him. Especially after my bumbling humiliation this morning. Add that combined with the fact that I haven't showered or even brushed my hair today. Someone somewhere in the cosmos is laughing hard. Guess Grant won't be dumbfounded by my blinding beauty now.

"You know what? I'm not surprised," I tell him when he sits down on the other side of the table. Good thing he's distanced himself because I'm afraid I don't smell all that great right now. "Fate and I are feuding, and you're my punishment."

He grins in amusement. "You believe in fate?"

"I don't know if I believe in *fate* exactly. But I don't believe in coincidence either. Anyway, I'm not failing philosophy, so who cares what I believe."

"Another time, because I do," Grant says sincerely. "Are you really failing chemistry?"

"Not yet," I reply, slumping back in my chair. "We have our first test on Friday and I will be if you don't help me pass it."

"What are you having difficulty with exactly?"

"Staying awake."

He laughs. "That could be a problem. Why don't you show me what you're working on."

I may have to continue saying dumb things this entire tutoring session just to keep him laughing. The sound is deep and throaty and comes from a real place. His laughter makes me smile, whether I realize I'm doing it or not. And I must be staring and smiling dopily at him right now because he has to clear his throat to get my attention.

"Did I lose you already?"

"Uh, no," I say, pulling the tablet out of my bag. "I'm here, sort of. I haven't had much sleep the past couple of nights. Sorry if I'm out of it."

"I'll try my best to keep you awake," he says, moving to the chair next to mine so we can review the information on the tablet together.

Oh, I'm definitely awake now.

An hour later, I emerge from our closet, without being kissed. I know that's not what we were in there for, but closets have a reputation for a reason. Grant remained the ultimate professional, even when our knees inadvertently touched or his arm rubbed against mine. He was all about making sure I understood chemistry. Which I did…and felt. And now, I hate Brendan for his stupid comment at dinner.

Grant is brilliant. And patient—very, very, patient. He's kinda scary-perfect.

"Do you have any flaws?" I ask him when we reach the main level of the library.

"Of course I do," he scoffs. "I could list them for you. Or let you find out for yourself."

"I like a challenge," I reply with a teasing smirk. "Thank you for helping me."

"Let me know how you do on the test?"

"I will. I'll tell you when I see you at the club on Friday."

"Oh, um, I wanted to ask if you wanted to go to the carnival on Saturday."

"We're going," I say with an enthusiastic smile, now that I know he'll be there too. When he presses his lips together, I realize that's not what he meant. "Oh. You were asking me on a date, weren't you?"

"I wasn't going to call it that because you said you don't date, and your *chaperone* would need to be there, but…yeah. I was hoping you would go with me. But a group thing sounds good too." He doesn't say the last part with much fervor.

"I'll win you a prize," I tell him, trying to make up for disappointing him.

He smiles weakly. "See you Friday, Lana."

That wasn't the reaction I was going for. I watch him walk out the main entrance, before heading back to the dorm.

I wish I'd known he was asking me on a date before I told him about the group. But … would it have mattered? I shouldn't date. Right?

I have to remember that school's starting up in two months and he won't be working at the country club any longer. He attends a different school. I don't have a car. We'll never see each other. I know this is weak reasoning. But then I look at the ring on my thumb, and it's the only reason I need.

T_he carnival is held_ at the ski resort on the mountain side of Kingston. I get a glimpse of downtown as we drive through, and it's cute, in a small New England town sort of way, with all of the storefronts lining one main road—which is predictably called Main Street. There's not much to it, but it screams quaint and charming.

"We'll have to take you on the ten-minute tour of downtown Kingston sometime," Ashton says from beside me.

"I think I just saw it in the thirty seconds it took to drive through."

"They have this old movie theatre that only shows two movies. You can tell they tried to update the seating, but like twenty years ago." She leans in closer so only I can hear, "Is Grant meeting us there?"

My smile is my answer.

And it makes its encore appearance when we find him waiting for us at the ticket booth with Squirrel and Stefan.

"I hope you don't mind that I bought your tickets," he says, handing me a strand of paper tickets while everyone else gets in line to purchase their own.

"Thank you," I say, taking them from him and folding them up to slip into the front pocket of my cut-offs. "I'll be sure to win you the biggest stuffed something I can find."

He reaches for my hand just as Kaely squeals, running straight toward me from across the carnival, and attacks me with a mauling hug.

"Um, I just saw you two hours ago at the club," I say, smothered by her thick bushel of hair.

"This is going to be so fun!" she exclaims.

Grant and I don't get a moment alone together the entire time we're at the carnival. Which ends up being completely okay because it probably would've been awkward to separate from the group. It was meant to be all of us, together. And I wouldn't have wanted it any other way. I've never laughed so hard in my entire life—watching Squirrel and Kaely squirt water into clowns' mouths like they were Olympic competitors; hearing Lance scream like he might pee his pants on the twisting ride that turns upside down; or trying to make a chain, holding each other's hands on the swing ride, and failing.

"I think I'm going to throw up," Kaely says after we trip off the Tilt-a-Whirl.

"I warned you not to eat that fried dough before we got on," Ashton says, holding Kaely by the arm to help her balance.

Lily giggles. "Your nose still has powdered sugar on it."

Kaely sticks out her tongue to try to lick it off.

I make a fist and rub it, which makes her sneeze…all over my hand.

"Omigod, that was so gross!" I shake my hand that's now sprayed with saliva.

"Sorry," she says, crinkling her nose. Ashton, of course, thinks it's hilarious. It's disgusting.

"There's hand sanitizer outside the porta-potties," Lily informs me sympathetically. We walk over together so I can kill all of Kaely's germs covering my skin.

"Where are the guys?" Ashton asks.

"They were supposed to be at the cage, spinny ride thing," Kaely says. And as odd as her description is, I know exactly which one she's talking about. We start in that direction and I can see Grant standing next to Stefan, waiting for the other guys to unload. He's kind of hard to miss. The giggling trio of girls standing about five feet away from him think so too.

I nudge Ashton and she leans down to listen. "Please don't tell me I act like that around Grant."

She inspects the girls and makes a pained expression. "Oh no. You're awkward but not PG-awkward."

"Uh, thanks…I think."

"PG, as in parental guidance. We call them that because they have parents who give them curfews, and chores, and check-in to make sure they're alive after ten o'clock at night. They're sheltered. They have no idea how to act around hot guys. They wouldn't even know what to do with themselves at a club."

"I've never been to a club," I admit.

"But you have a fake ID and get into bars," Ashton argues.

"True."

"They're so easy to spot too. Usually found giggling and whispering with their hands over their mouths."

"Are you talking about the PG-girls?" Lily asks.

"Then what are you?" I ask Ashton.

"We," Ashton corrects. "You're not like them. You're one of us. And we're…unrated."

Lily laughs.

"We don't have restrictions. Or rules. Or curfews. Or parents who actually know where we go on a random Tuesday night, forget about a Friday."

As much as I love my mother, Ashton is describing my life pretty accurately. Although I'm not bitter about the lax parenting like Ashton appears to be.

"What am I?" Kaely asks, concern flashing in her big hazel eyes.

"You're PG, sweetie," Lily says, wrapping an arm around her shoulders. "Don't worry. It's a good thing. It means someone cares about you. I used to be PG."

"What happened?" I ask before I can stop myself. "You don't have to—"

"It's okay," she says with a nonchalant shrug. "My dad moved out. My mother started drinking. And then didn't stop. So they both kind of forgot they had a daughter. Now…I'm unrated. Before this summer, they never would have let me spend it alone at the lake house for a weekend, forget about two months. It's sad really. Not for me. For them. I hate watching them completely fall apart, knowing there's nothing I can do to stop it."

"I know that feeling," I say quietly. She gives me an understanding smile.

"Who knew self-destructive parents could be so bonding!" Ashton cries out, encircling us with her arms and crushing us against her.

Kaely looks on sadly. "Get in here, PG," Ashton calls to her. Kaely smiles and bounces into our crazy hugfest. I've never been around such touchy-feely girls before. Nina, Tori and I would hug, but these girls bring the mush up a level.

"I can't breathe," I choke out from the middle. They laugh and separate to free me.

"What the hell are you looking at?"

The hostile voice sets off alarms, having heard the precursor to a fight one too many times in Stella's. My head swivels in search of the guy about to punch someone. The girls don't seem to notice.

He's not hard to locate, wearing a backward baseball hat and a loose-fitting tank top with exaggerated armholes to show off muscles that he needed a shot in the ass to get. He's standing with two other morons who are nodding along with whatever he says, because they don't have minds of their own. I notice the previously giggling girls standing off to the side, eyes darting around nervously.

And then...I see who Roid-Rage is talking to.

Except Grant doesn't know he's being challenged, not yet anyway. He's standing alone, focused on the guys, who are standing in line for more tickets. He turns his head, sees us, and smiles. He takes a step our way when the guy hollers at him again.

"Hey, man! I'm talking to you! What the hell's your problem?"

Grant hears him this time and swivels to face him. "Uh, excuse me? I don't have a problem. Sorry, there must be a misunderstanding or something. Have a good night."

I groan. He's such a fricken nice guy. It's about to get him killed.

"Oh, no," Ashton says, having picked up the douche-baggery unfolding across from us.

I slowly walk in Grant's direction, my attention solely on Roider. His hands keep clenching into fists.

Grant spots me and continues in my direction. I don't make eye contact because I know what's coming, and I need to be ready for it.

"Oh shit," I say under my breath.

"Hey, piece of shit! Don't walk away from me!"

I start running.

"Lana!" Ashton shouts in alarm.

Just as the guy comes up behind Grant, ready to blindside him with a crushing blow, I bend forward and plow into him with my shoulder, throwing him off balance. His elbow comes around and collides with my jaw just as we topple to the ground, my knee strategically landing between his legs.

"What the fuck?!" he chokes out when he realizes I'm on top of him, my left hand holding him down, digging into the soft flesh under his jaw.

And because he has a tiny dick and couldn't feel the impact of my knee (that should have incapacitated him), he grabs one of my braided pigtails and tugs. He's about to slug me, but I swing first, my fist coming down hard across his jaw.

"Stay down," I seethe in his ear. I pull back to land another punch, but before I can, arms wrap around my waist and pull me off of him. I kick and elbow the solid body that has me hoisted in the air.

"Lana, stop. It's me," Grant says, continuing to back away from the guys.

"Fucking pussy!" one of the morons yells. "Have to have a girl fight for you."

Grant calls out over his shoulder, "She hits better than I do."

As soon as he sets me down, I prepare for their retaliation. But nothing happens. Instead, Limp-Dick walks away with his friends, the girls trailing a good five feet behind them, like they're embarrassed they came together. I can hear him bitching about being sucker punched and that he wasn't about to hit a girl. Whatever.

When I turn around, our entire group is staring at me. Kaely looks traumatized. Brendan appears impressed, as does Stefan. Squirrel…he may have missed it, too focused on the bag of flavored popcorn he's digging around in. Lily is covering her mouth with her hands like she's trying not to scream. And Ashton has an eyebrow raised in a *what the fuck was that* kind of way.

"What the hell, Lana?" Lance pushes his way from within the middle of everyone. His face is red, like he's about to have a heart attack. "Are you *trying* to get arrested again?" He clutches the top of his head, his bright blue eyes huge. "Because you know if you do, you're so screwed. And there's nothing my dad will be able to do to help you."

I gape at him in shock, surprised by his anger. Even more surprised that he cares and *that* is why he's angry. Lance realizes what he said a little too late and looks around at the eyes that are even more shocked then they were a second ago—because there were only two other people in our group who knew about my arrest record. And Lance just broke a pretty sacred vow by exposing me like he did.

I glance up at Grant for the first time. He doesn't seem shocked exactly. His expression is more contemplative, like he's putting pieces of me together that he didn't know were missing.

Ashton is the first to break from the group. "Are you okay?" She hugs me.

"You're bleeding," Lily notices, standing on the other side of me. "I'll get some ice."

"I'm fine," I try to assure her, swiping at the small trickle of blood on the corner of my lip. I must've bitten my cheek when he elbowed me. But Lily's already gone.

"That was the craziest thing I've ever seen in my entire life," Kaely babbles, still in shock.

"Welcome to *my* life," I tell her with a small smirk. Brendan lets out a laugh but cuts it short when Lance glares at him.

"Would you mind if I drive Lana back to the school?" I'm not really sure who Grant's asking, but Lance shrugs in approval. Then Grant asks me, "Is that okay?" I nod.

I shoot Ashton a worried glance, afraid this car ride will be the end of whatever Grant and I are.

"I'll see you at school," she tells me, sharing my concern. "Come find me when you get back."

I give them a weak wave and walk off with Grant. After a few steps, he slides his hand in mine and squeezes. I relax…just a little. Hoping there's still a chance he won't give up on me just yet. We continue the rest of the way to his car in silence.

Grant's car is straight out of a black and white, classic Hollywood movie. It's some sort of navy-blue vintage convertible coupe with a white racing stripe down the middle. I don't think I could've designed a better car for Grant if I tried. He opens the passenger door for me to get in.

Before he starts the car, he faces me. I hold my breath, waiting for him to tell me how reckless and stupid I was. Instead, he runs a hand along my jaw. I wince.

He leans over and brushes a feather-light kiss against it. I close my eyes and hold my breath, wishing he'll follow it up with one on my lips. But he shifts away and starts the car.

Even when I start breathing again, it still doesn't feel like I'm getting enough air.

"What time's your curfew?" he asks as we wind through country roads, the sun shooting rays of orange and gold through the trees as it nestles into the horizon.

"Midnight," I tell him, trying not to smile. Because that's hours from now, and I doubt he's preparing to spend the next three hours telling me why he never wants to see me again. I was so scared that after he witnessed the worst of my truths, he wouldn't be interested anymore. And the fact that it scared me, scares me even more.

I glance over at him, his golden hair ruffling in the wind. He shoots me a crooked grin before taking my hand and kissing the back of it. "I'll have you back in time. I promise."

"I'm not worried," I tell him. *Not anymore*—I don't say out loud.

The sun is completely gone and the darkness has settled in around us when he turns down a narrow paved road, which is surprising because I was convinced every side road in this town was dirt. A dense forest encroaches on either side of the road, without a property in sight. Grant pulls the car onto a dirt patch at a break in the trees. The headlights illuminate a clearing.

He gets out of the car and pops the trunk. I open the passenger door and get out, looking around to try to understand why we're here. Grant appears beside me with a blanket and a cooler. "C'mon." He offers me his hand and I let him guide me into the field, the overgrown grass tickling my bare legs. I wonder if this was meant for our date.

Grant sets down the cooler and spreads out the blanket. He sits and I settle down next to him. He reaches into the cooler and pulls out an ice pack, handing it to me.

"I'm really okay," I assure him, because I know I'm fine.

"I'm not, so please ice it for me. It'll make me feel better."

Stunned by his genuine concern, I take the ice pack from him and rest it gently on my jaw, that only seems to hurt when touched.

"You came prepared," I note with a small smile.

"I came hopeful," he clarifies. "So you've been arrested…for fighting." It isn't a question, more of a summation of the facts.

"Yeah," I answer barely audible.

"When you get into these fights, do you start them, or is it like tonight?"

"Well…I technically started the fight tonight, considering I hit him first."

The side of his mouth tilts up in amusement. "You were defending me. That guy was about to take me out, for whatever reason, and I never saw it coming. Essentially, you saved me."

"I guess I kinda did, huh?" I reply, unable to hide my cocky grin. He laughs. "So to answer your question, yes, it's usually like tonight. I don't go looking for fights, but if someone threatens me or someone I care about, then I have to protect them."

Grant cocks an eyebrow. "But does it always have to resort to violence?"

"I don't know," I answer honestly. "It's my first reaction." I cringe at the admission. "That's bad, isn't it?"

Grant reveals a small smile. "I wish I could say it isn't."

"I'm working on it," I say, my lips twisted in a guilty furl. "Have you ever been in a fight?"

"No," he answers without hesitation. "I've never felt compelled to punch anyone. It can get physical in some of the rivalry lacrosse games, but it's mostly shoving. And even when friends of mine get into fights, I'm usually breaking them up and talking everyone down. So, I was being honest earlier—you really do punch better than me."

I let out a breathy laugh.

"Are you serious about working on it? Your anger, or whatever it is that compels you to punch first?"

"Yeah, I am. I claim I fight in defense, but I guess it's fueled by anger. I've never really thought about it before, I just…react."

"Do you know what triggers it? I mean, beyond being protective of you and your friends?"

My heart is pounding and my palms are sweaty. I've never been this honest before, not even with myself, and it's making me anxious, like I'm on the verge of having a panic attack. I experience those when I'm in enclosed spaces for too long. So I'm familiar enough with the cues to sense one is about to take over. If I don't get control over it now, soon, I won't have control at all.

I close my eyes and focus on breathing, deep and slow.

"Lana? Hey, it's okay." His hand caresses my back in an attempt to soothe me. I nearly jump at his touch. "You don't have to tell me. I didn't mean to upset you."

"It's how I make sure I'm heard," I tell him in a whisper, my eyes still closed. "As a girl, especially my size, guys think they have a right to me. To touch. To degrade. To dismiss me. So I fight because that's my voice. That's how I say no. That's how I tell them to fuck off. That's how I make it clear that I'm *not* theirs. It's how I know they hear me." I open my eyes and stare directly into his.

"Is that why you don't date?"

I consider it a second. "Maybe." He intertwines his fingers with mine. "I don't want to belong to anyone. I'm not a possession. I'm not *his*. I've seen it so many times, becoming lost to another person. No longer identified as an individual, only as an *us*. Until one of them decides *us* isn't enough and leaves, because they always do. I *won't* lose myself to anyone. That way, they can't take me with them when they leave me."

Grant is silent. And I want to disappear. I just admitted something so honest and vulnerable, something I didn't know was true until I said it out loud. His presence in my life is dangerous to my curse. I have no way of protecting my honesty; my deepest hidden truths slip out so easily when I'm with him.

I'm fumbling for something to say to lighten the seriousness that's enveloped us when he leans forward. I barely have time to react before his mouth touches mine.

Soft, full lips find me. I lean into him, into the kiss as my mouth slides over his. And everything is quiet inside me, so very still. Even my heart stops beating. In its place, a burst of light radiates from the center of my chest. The warmth of it expands until it is all of me. And within the calm that has settled over me, I can feel everything all at once. The small gasp of air he breathes into me, the fine stubble along his chin, the give of his lips and tickle of his fingers dancing along my neck. It is sensual and intense. Gentle and passionate. His kiss awakens something inside of me, and when I open my eyes, nothing looks the same.

Grant is looking at me like he's never seen me before, yet he's been searching for me for forever. Or maybe that's how I'm looking at him. And behind him, tiny stars are dancing across the field.

Wait. Maybe I got hit in the head harder than I thought.

I swivel to admire what's surrounding us. Small, flashing lights hover and swirl around the tall blades of grass.

"Fireflies," I acknowledge in awe. "I've never seen them in real life before."

"This is why I brought you here."

"Not to kiss me?" I tease.

His smile is so wide, it causes me to smile too.

"That was what I wished would happen, but the fireflies are why we're here."

I lean my head against his shoulder. Grant shuffles closer to wrap his arm around me and rest his chin on my head. It is...magical, watching what seems like hundreds, maybe a thousand, tiny orbs flicker and flutter around us in a haphazard rhythm.

"Can you promise me something?"

I don't respond.

"When you feel that anger building again, if it's possible, will you call me instead of letting it take over? Maybe I can talk you down, or at least try. I didn't like seeing you get hurt, or watching you hurt someone else, even if you have an impressive swing."

I remain quiet for another second. "I can't."

"Oh, right," he recalls. "Blackwood's strict technology policies. I'm officially your tutor, so I'm on your approved call list. You can add me directly into your contacts. I may already be there actually."

I pull back to face him. "Really?"

He nods. "So, will you...call me?"

I frown. "I can't make that promise. I'm sorry." I don't want to have to depend on someone else to help me gain control over my emotions, even my anger. I should be able to do it on my own. They're my emotions after all.

"I get it. It's okay. You haven't known me that long. I have to earn your trust still, I understand." He gives me a quick kiss. "But I like a challenge too."

I smile, recognizing my words from the other night at the library.

"I still haven't found any flaws, other than you don't know how to throw a punch."

"That's a flaw?"

I smile wide. "Even if you never hit someone, you should know how to punch. I'll teach you."

He laughs. "Great."

"So how did you find this place?" I ask, scooting close so his chest is pressed to my back. He encircles me in his arms and my body relaxes into him.

"I drive when I need to think," he says, his voice low and soothing. "And this town has plenty of windy roads to get lost on. One night, I was convinced I really was lost and pulled over to check the map on my phone. That's when I noticed this clearing. It seemed so strange to come across several acres of overgrown grass and wildflowers in the middle of the woods. But there's something about this spot that's...magical." Warmth flows through me when he uses the same word to describe it. "I kept coming back to it, hoping I'd be able to share it with someone." Grant kisses the top of my shoulder, eliciting a wave of tingles down my arm. "I knew it was you that night we floated on the lake."

Chapter Seventeen

The beast growled in anger and lunged for the sorceress. Thaylina was still too weak to aid the sorceress as she fought the beast. She could only hear the thunderous crashes of their battle. Until there was only silence.

H i, Sophia?" I say slowly, but it sounds more like a question than a real greeting.

"Hi!" she chirps happily, sitting across from me on the shuttle—smoothing her skirt beneath her so it doesn't wrinkle.

"I didn't know you worked at the club."

"I don't," she says, holding up her tote bag. When I still look confused, she explains. "I'm a member. I mean, my parents are members. Well, just about everyone's parents are members." I want to shake her to make her get to the point, but I continue to smile stiffly instead. "I'm going to the pool." She leans in like she's about to share a secret. "I usually go on Tuesdays but I found out Grant is lifeguarding today."

I nod slowly, stiff smile still in place, not recognizing this chatty version of Sophia. It's like she's hopped up on something…then again. "How do you know that?"

"I have someone who works there make a copy of his schedule for me. I know, it sounds so sketch. But have you *seen* him? I mean, he is the most gorgeous guy I've ever seen. And he's so nice. Seriously, the nicest person ever. You know him, right?"

Stiff smile. Nod.

She sits up straight in her seat, posture pin straight, smiling like a lunatic. I need some of those happy pills.

"I keep wanting to ask him out. But I can't even *talk* in front of him. Do you think he'd go to the Ever After Ball with me? I would die. Like, truly and completely, die."

"Who are we talking about?" Ashton bounces down in the seat in front of me.

Sophia shifts her eyes from Ashton to me, almost like she's asking my permission to reveal her crush.

She bites her lip and whispers, "Grant."

"Oh, right! How was that? I'm still pissed you didn't come to my room last night. Home by the stroke of midnight, my little Cinderella." Ashton pats me on the head.

"Are you high already?" Sophia asks Ashton in a paranoid whisper, shifting her eyes around to make sure no one's listening.

"Sophia wants to ask Grant to the Ever After Ball," I intercept. Ashton's eyes grow wide in understanding.

"Do you think I should?" Sophia asks Ashton, looking all nervous and adorable.

"Um, I don't know. What do *you* think, Lana? I mean, you talk to him more than I do." She gives me her *what the fuck* look with a quick shake of her head. Sophia focuses on me, hope gleaming in her blown-pupil Bambi eyes.

"You never know," I say. "You may be perfect for him."

Ashton smacks me on the back of the head. "Sorry. You had a mosquito. Was going to suck out your brains and make you an idiot."

Ow, I mouth, glaring at Ashton.

"Do you think so?" Sophia squeals at my comment, ignoring Ashton's assault on me.

"Excuse us a sec, Sofe," Ashton says, pulling Sophia from her seat and shoving her up the aisle.

"Ashton!" I scold. She pushes her way into my seat and sticks her face right up in mine. "What the fuck—"

"—is wrong with you?!" she finishes in a hiss. "I adore that little pumpkin perfect, but she is *not* meant for Grant."

I roll my eyes. "It's not for me to decide."

"Did something happen? Was he pissed that you punched out some guy to protect him? Because I thought that was pretty hot. And I didn't think he had an ego that would get all pissy about a girl—"

"No, he wasn't mad. I mean, he didn't love seeing me get into a fight. But…" I sigh. "Listening to Sophia go on about him made me question what the hell I'm doing. I am absolutely serious when I say I don't date. And if he wants that, it can't be with me. So, he needs to know he has options. I'm not an option."

"What are you then?"

"I'm…me. No title. No commitment. No expectations. No emotional involvement."

"I thought you didn't lie," she snaps angrily and gets up, leaving me dumbfounded, my mouth hanging open. What just happened?

Ashton is assigned the bev cart with Rhett. I almost feel bad for him when she floors the cart and drives away in a fury, bottles clanging on the shelves.

I get sentenced to toddler-hell with Kaely at The Grille concession stand because every mother with a child is at the pool today to gawk at Prince Philip atop his throne. It's kind of disgusting the amount of drool happening, and I don't mean the toddlers.

"Do you have it?"

The boy nods wrapping his chubby hands around the base of the ice cream cone. "Are you sure?"

He nods again. I let go. And ten seconds later, it's on the ground. His bottom lip juts out and his eyes fill with tears.

"Please don't scream, kid," I mutter. Then louder with a sing-songy voice, "No worries. I'll make you a special one."

I pour soft-serve ice cream in a cup, stick a cone upside down on top of it, and throw gummy bears around it from my personal stash I store under the counter. Not Ashton's *special* gummies, though those might chill these sugar-hopped kids the hell out. Where are their parents? Why do I feel like half my job is babysitting when I'm stationed here? And today is especially chaotic.

"I never want to work the stand ever again when Grant is on lifeguard duty," I grumble to Kaely.

"It's usually not this bad on Tuesdays," she says. "It must be because of the holiday weekend. And, well…him. So are you two—"

"Nothing," I cut her off. "We're nothing."

"Order's up!" Squirrel calls out. I walk away from her and her wide, shocked eyes.

Squirrel is singing to a song that isn't playing anywhere but in his head, flipping burgers, turning dogs, and frying fries like he's on a ride at Disneyland. *He* is the happiest place on earth.

"How do you function?" I ask, loading up a tray with the order.

"Huh?" he asks, turning in my direction. His next words come out broken, like he's listening to them in his head before repeating them out loud. "Oh, um, I just…exist. And like, express gratitude for being alive. You know?"

"No," I say, and leave him to his gratifying existence.

"Are you okay?" Kaely asks, wiping chocolate off the cheeks of a small child who couldn't find the spoons so decided to eat the hot fudge sundae with his face.

"I'm…" But I can't say it. I'm not fine. But I don't really know what's gotten into me, other than Sophia's comment on the shuttle.

I search for her in her vintage polka dot bikini and cat-eye sunglasses. She's applying sunscreen and glancing up at Grant from beneath her dark lenses to see if he's watching. But he's not. He's watching the mayhem in the pool. He blows his whistle at some boys who are wrestling to push each other in. The ultimate professional. "He's so fricken nice, isn't he?"

"He is," Kaely responds like it's an indisputable fact. "We all deserve a nice guy, Lana."

"But he's not *mine*."

"Then step aside girl," the third cashier says, walking by with popcorn and cotton candy. I almost forgot she was here. "Let someone else have a shot. There are plenty of us who would claim that man in a second."

"Right. I should, step aside," I say feebly.

Kaely opens her mouth so wide she looks like a blow-up doll. "You can't let your phobia claim you, Lana." She says this with such conviction, I half expect her to thrust her fist in the air. "You have to face it head on, and be stronger than your biggest fear."

"What the hell you talkin' 'bout?" the girl asks from the other side of Kaely. "There ain't nothin' to be afraid of with that man, except keepin' other women from stealin' him."

"Grant wouldn't let anyone steal him," Kaely says like she's appalled by the idea and feels compelled to defend his honor.

"Because it should be his choice," I say quietly.

Kaely nods, like the argument is settled. But that's not what just happened. He needs to know what his choices are, or are not, before he can make that decision. I need to remind him.

A*t the end of the shift,* I feel sticky, sweaty and have ice cream smeared in places that it shouldn't be. I never want to be a mother. After today, I'm contemplating getting my ovaries removed. Right now, I want nothing more than to shower and lie in a hammock with a book for the rest of the night.

Ashton parks the bev cart as we pass. Rhett looks like he's about to kiss the ground and thank the Universe that he's still alive. She doesn't look at me. I can't believe she's this upset with me for doing the right thing. But I guess I don't really know her that well.

As Kaely and I continue up the small hill to the main building, I spot Lily walking off the tennis court with Lance. She waves when she sees us. We walk by Brendan leaning against a golf cart talking with an older gentleman. Their conversation looks serious and intense—Brendan's probably offering him insider trading tips.

"Lana!" I pause when I hear Grant's voice. Kaely does as well. I wish she'd keep walking. He runs up to us, still in his lifeguard gear. "Hi," he says with a bright smile.

"Hi." Why do I feel like everyone stopped what they were doing to binge watch us like we're Netflix?

"Are you guys still coming over tomorrow?"

"I think so," I reply, glancing around. They really are staring. All of them. What the hell?

"Can you come by early, like around noon?"

"I can ask." This is so awkward. Go back to whatever you were doing, people! We're just talk—

This thought is interrupted by Grant's lips. It's not a long kiss. But it's long enough for me to lean into him, forgetting we're not alone. Until I remember… we're not alone. Grant pulls back and smiles. "I'll see you tomorrow."

I can't move.

Kaely is covering her mouth like a PG-girl. And everyone else dramatically goes back to whatever they were doing like they weren't watching, but it's so obvious they were.

Ashton struts up to me and leans down so we're eye level. "He just *claimed* you in front of ev-er-ee-one. What are you going to do about that, huh? Because it's not nothing. Not to him." I think she's a second away from poking a finger into my chest, and that wouldn't go over too well. Instead she laughs like a villain and storms off.

I try to shrug it off, like it really was nothing. Whatever.

But I can't.

"Shit," I groan.

Just to rub it in, Brendan appears and drapes an arm around me. "Didn't I warn you that he's too good for people like us?" He chuckles. "You really do have to learn everything the hard way, don't you, my feisty little pixie?"

I shove his arm off and outpace everyone to the locker room. I don't bother looking over at Lance and Lily. Maybe they know that it won't last. That it's just a summer thing and means nothing. *Someone* needs to know this…especially me.

By the time Lance, Brendan, Ashton and I arrive at Stefan's the next day, I've convinced myself that I just have to be me, not the stupid, giddy version who loses herself every time I'm in Grant's presence. That way we can just be…nothing. We can be two people who like to hang out and kiss, and maybe other things if he'll let me. But absolutely not *us*-like.

Stefan, Squirrel, Grant and a couple other guys are putting out lawn games when we emerge from the house into the backyard.

"We're *really* early," Ashton observes from beside me, finally acting normal again. Or at least, I hope she is. "Want to lay out for a while?"

"Sure," I reply, walking toward the beach.

When she doesn't walk with me, I turn around. She gives me a questioning look.

"What?"

"Aren't you going to at least say hi?"

"They're busy," I tell her and keep walking.

"Hey!" Grant calls to me. I stop and close my eyes, silently reminding myself to do what I always do when I'm around guys I hook up with. Just be me.

I turn. "Hey." I fight the smile that wants to hijack my face. My heart is pounding. I silently curse my body which has completely abandoned the plan.

He walks over to me and bends like he's about to either hug or kiss me. I do the worst thing I possibly could...I take a step back. He straightens, completely confused. My pulse spikes.

"We were going down to the beach," I say, trying to sound light and casual. "Unless you guys need help?"

"No, that's fine." His voice is cautious, like he's trying to read me. I give him a tight-lipped smile. "I just wanted to say hi." Then he walks away. And my heart seriously twists in my chest.

"So, this is *you?*" Ashton scowls in disapproval. "You're kind of a bitch." Then *she* walks off, leaving me alone with the truth.

Yes, I am.

I hide on the beach for the next hour while they finish setting up the backyard.

I have no idea what I'm doing. I thought I was helping him by letting him see me. I wanted to remind him that I'm not *his* to kiss in front of everyone. To be claimed. I thought I made that clear. But *this*...sucks. Because I *like* kissing him. And talking to him. Fuck! I like *him*. What the hell am I supposed to do with that?

Because I'm also afraid of him. Or more accurately, of being destroyed by him.

When a few more people arrive, they all come down to the beach and Stefan recruits me to play beach volleyball, claiming they're short a player—although Ashton is sitting on a chair, watching. And she's tall and plays volleyball for Blackwood. I've seen pictures.

"I'm officiating," she tells me with a shrug, like it can't be helped.

Of every sport there is, this is the one I truly and completely suck at more than any other. It's not a small person's sport—I can't spike or block; I get pummeled by my teammates because they don't see me under them when we both go for the ball, and I can't serve to save my life. I can dig. It's the only thing I'm decent at because I'm already that much closer to the ground.

Predictably, Grant is on my team. And just to torture me, he's shirtless.

I stand in front of the net, staring down my nemesis. "You're going to spend the game eating the ball from all the spikes someone else is going to shove down your throat."

"You're adorable," Brendan says with a wink, totally killing my shit-talk. "Can you even reach the top of the net?"

I flip him off and hear someone laugh. No, correction. I know exactly who's laughing.

Grant.

It's four-on-four, or three and a half, because I really am only half a player.

"Do you know how to set up the ball for a spike?" Grant asks me when we're positioned next to each other in front of the net. I have my hands resting on my knees, like I know what I'm doing. But really, I'm just imitating everyone else.

"No," I tell him.

He takes the ball and demonstrates, tapping it straight up in the air with his fingertips. Then he tosses it over the net for Squirrel to serve.

"If you do that, as high as I did, this far in front of me," he indicates with his hand, "I'll take care of the rest."

"Okay," I reply, trying to sound like I understood. I didn't really.

My team basically plays around me, hitting the ball before it's even remotely low enough for me to reach it, spiking it and throwing themselves on the sand like they're desperate to return a grenade before it hits the ground and explodes. I just try to stay out of their way.

"Nicely done, Lana!" Ashton claps when I fall on my butt, barely avoiding being trampled by Lance.

"Sorry," he says, offering his hand to help me up. "Didn't see you there."

Our potential victory has come down to this game point. Grant and I are on the line again. "This is it, Lana. You're going to set me up." He doesn't look over at me, anticipating where the serve will go, but he offers that crooked grin that I'm fall—nope, not *that*…that I like, *a lot*.

The ball goes back and forth over the net. I tilt my head and watch it. As if Grant beckoned it, the ball starts floating down to me. I have a second to realize no one is coming to knock me out of the way. This is all mine. So…I tip it back into the air with my fingertips. It doesn't rebound quite as high as Grant's did, but it's still high enough for him to jump up and slam it down, making a deep indent in the sand on the other side.

Our team hollers in triumph. Grant turns to…I think he's about to hug me, but I slap his hand. Yup. I just gave him a high-five.

"Good job!" I say, like he's a six-year-old. Grant's brows furrow. Stefan pats him on the back. Lance rushes in from behind to pick me up and spin me around.

"Lana, I'm so proud of you. That was so good, my little pixie!"

I laugh and almost topple over when he sets me back down.

The group has gotten bigger by now, but it's still maybe only about twenty people.

I sit on a chair next to Ashton, and Grant settles on the sand in front of us.

"How did you do on the chemistry test?" he asks.

"Right! I forgot to tell you," I say, almost too enthusiastically, trying to ease the awkwardness—but failing. "I got a ninety-one. So thank you."

"You knew it," he says, looking proud. "You just needed to learn it with your eyes open."

I laugh.

"How was the bev cart with Rhett?" I ask Ashton.

"That boy doesn't have an off-switch," she says with a roll of her eyes. "I'm half tempted to set him up with Sophia."

"You know Sophia, right Grant?" I ask, watching for a reaction. Not sure which one I'm hoping for though.

"Yeah, uh, I tutored her last fall in biology. Nice girl. But yeah, she does have a tendency to talk a lot when she's nervous." No reaction, at all.

"She's really sweet, though a bit neurotic," I say. "But she's pretty. And she has the coolest colored eyes."

Grant looks at me, questioning.

I hear Ashton groan and say under her breath, "Please stop."

"I think she likes you. Maybe you—"

"Foods up!" Stefan calls from the backyard.

"I'm starving!" Ashton exclaims, pulling me off the chair. I look over my shoulder. Grant is still seated, watching me leave with a confounded expression. He may even look a little...hurt.

What did I just do? That's not how that was supposed to go. I was supposed to be reminding him of his options. Let him know that other girls are interested in him. But instead, it sounded like I was trying to set him up.

"I think I get it," Ashton says, loading her plate with...everything.

"Are you high?" I ask, thinking maybe she has the munchies.

"Not yet. I just like food." She licks the smudge of potato salad from her thumb. She does a quick scan to make sure no one's within earshot before leaning in to whisper. "You like him."

Then she struts off. I close my eyes and groan before following after her.

"Try to deny it," she challenges when I sit next to her on the porch swing—that's on the porch and not in the middle of a weird birch tree forest.

I stab the fruit salad like I'm trying to kill it before stuffing it in my mouth. I'm really regretting telling her about my curse right now.

"You can't," she taunts. "Because you do. I *see* you, Lana. It's what *I* do, and I know what you're trying to do. But you're not actually being *you*. You're being a cold, bitchy girl who I'd like to smack upside the head. There are way too many cold and bitchy girls at Blackwood during the school year, you'll see. I don't need my closest friend to be one of them."

I do what I do best and remain silent. I want to react, but she just said a lot, and I can't defend or verbally acknowledge most of it. And some of it, I'm not sure I even understand.

"It's okay to like him, Lana. He's a nice guy. And although you're *not* the nicest person all of the time, he still likes you."

I whip my head toward her in offense. But end up sighing, because she's right. I know this better than anyone because…well, I'm me.

"And just because you like him, it doesn't mean you're going to fall in love with him. *That's* what you're afraid of, for whatever twisted reason—that probably has to do with your mother. So just have fun. Be not with him…but with him." She hesitates and tilts her head like she just confused herself. I know I'm confused.

"I'm your closest friend?"

She laughs. "You're a skilled deflector, huh?" She sets down her plate and hugs me. "Fine. No more *like*-talk. And yes, you are my closest friend. I can trust you because you are who you are when you're not possessed by a demon."

I laugh. "Thanks, I think. And I know I've been off. I'm too in my head. So, thanks for not smacking me…again."

I stand to throw my plate away. Grant intercepts me on my way back to Ashton. "Do you have a second?"

"Squirt gun fight!" Squirrel hollers, carrying a bucket filled with long, white and orange plastic guns.

"Let's go! You're on my team," Ashton says, appearing out of nowhere and taking my hand to pull me toward the bucket.

"We seem to have even numbers to make it guys versus girls," Stefan proposes. "It'll be easier to know who's on your team."

No one objects. Ten girls versus ten boys. I'm not sure if I should be impressed or horrified that the guys own this many squirt guns. And these aren't the tiny, cheap ones that need to be filled up after five squirts. These water guns have full pump-action, drenching capabilities.

Ashton and I strip down to our bikini tops. I keep my shorts on with my metallic peach halter top. While Ashton bares all the way down to her cherry-red string bikini. I think I hear a few gulps as she kicks off her sandals. I'm starting to wonder if her mother is Gisele, but she's not married to a rock star, or old enough. Whoever the supermodel is, Ashton definitely has her body.

I don't know why I'm compelled to search for Brendan. But when I find him, he's sweet-talking one of the other females. She's curvy and about to bust out of her bikini top if she walks too fast, forget about runs. I glance over at Ashton, but she's not paying any attention to him. She's scanning our opponents with laser beam focus, like she's trying to decide who to take down first. I think if she had black liner, she'd draw marks under her eyes.

"This is the plan," she says to me, propping her squirt gun against her shoulder like it's a military weapon. "We're going to let them take out the easy targets first. That'll distract them long enough to allow us to slip around behind the shed. I'll get on top and ambush them from an aerial position. You flank them from the other side."

"You're going to do what?!"

"Go!" someone yells, and Ashton takes off. I scramble after her.

"Ashton, I don't think climbing on top of the shed is a good idea."

"Maybe you're right," she hollers over her shoulder. "Get down!" She dives behind a hydrangea bush. I crouch next to her. She uses the bush as a shield and shoots at a couple guys approaching from the other side. "Behind us!"

I roll onto my back and unload on someone, just as I'm being pelted in the face.

"Are you okay?" Lance calls, laughing. "I didn't mean to get you in the face."

"Jerk!" I yell, trying to get him in the face too, but hitting the back of Stefan's head. "Sorry!"

Ashton and I take off running, pursued by Lance and Stefan. They get distracted by bouncing cleavage, so we run down to the beach.

"This was a bad plan," Ashton says, peeking over the stone wall. "We've pinned ourselves in."

"What are we doing exactly?" I ask. This isn't paintball and we don't have a flag to capture. I don't understand the point of strategizing.

"Taking them down," she says in a menacing voice. Brendan's back is to us. Ashton shoots him in the butt, although I have a feeling she was aiming between his legs. Not even I'm that cruel.

We duck when he spins around. With our backs to the wall, we tip our heads up with our guns at the ready. His head pokes out over the edge and I shoot him in the forehead. He hollers as he rolls away.

And then, we're ambushed. Stefan and Lance jump over our heads and roll on the ground, rebounding to their feet and shooting at us like they're in some action movie. Grant and Squirrel are on the stairs, and Brendan is soaking us from above.

I'm trying to shoot at them while protecting myself at the same time. It's useless.

"Retreat!" Ashton yells. We take off for the dock, abandoning our guns on the beach. When we reach the end, we jump off. I make some attempt at a dive, while Ashton does a cannonball. We emerge laughing. I may have started laughing before I reached the surface, and I'm coughing between bouts of laughter.

To our surprise, the guys jump in after us, hollering in the air before they splash in the water.

Stefan grabs ahold of my ankle and pulls me under. I yelp just before I swallow a mouthful of lake water. From under the water, a hand grabs my wrist and pulls me up.

I re-emerge hacking, and come face-to-face with Grant.

"Are you okay?" he asks, concerned.

I cough, still swallowing more water than air. "Yeah. I keep forgetting I can't breathe underwater."

He grins.

I look around for something to hold onto, because I never mastered treading water very well. I kick off toward the trampoline. It's far enough away from the water-war—that now involves everyone—to keep me from being dunked again. Why use squirt guns when we have an entire lake?

Grant follows at a distance, probably to be sure I make it to the trampoline safely, being the responsible lifeguard that he is.

I reach for a rope on the side of the trampoline. I think he'll swim off and join back in with everyone else, but he continues to tread water near me, remaining a good five feet away like he's afraid to come closer.

"I'm not the best swimmer," I tell him. "Never took lessons."

"I kind of figured that when you didn't know how to float on your back. It's one of the first things they teach you after blowing bubbles."

"I can blow bubbles," I say and dip my mouth in to demonstrate. He laughs.

"You're halfway to being a tadpole swimmer."

"I'm a quick learner," I say with a smile, and he smiles back.

Then his expression becomes serious. "I'm sorry about yesterday."

I press my lips together, not sure what to say, because I'm pretty sure he's talking about the kiss.

"I shouldn't have kissed you like that in front of everyone. It took me a while to figure out why you were avoiding me today. Then it all made sense when someone asked where you were, like I'd know. Like we're together."

"Like we're an *us*," I say quietly. Grant nods, silently apologizing. He continues treading water but has come in a little closer.

"Do you want to…hold on? I mean, I'm sure you had to tread water with a hundred-pound weight strapped to you in SEAL training, but you can hold on to the trampoline with me if you'd prefer."

"It was a two-hundred-pound weight," he says, revealing his gorgeous smile again. "But yeah, I think holding on would be easier."

He swims in and reaches for the rope next to me. Now he's much, much closer, and I've forgotten how to breathe.

"I heard everything you said the other night about why you don't date. And I'd never want you to lose yourself to me. But I'm not interested in Sophia, or anyone else. I like you, Lana. And I'm not really sure what to do about that while still respecting your no-dating rule."

I swallow, thankfully not water this time.

"I like you too," I say, wishing I could've remained silent. "But I can't date you."

He nods regretfully, his eyes downcast. I think he's about to push off and swim back to the group, but he redirects his sky-blue gaze at me. "What if we make up our own rules? No titles. No...ownership, but exclusive. I couldn't handle seeing you with another guy, and not because I want you to be *mine* but because I think I'd be devoured by jealousy."

"I can't imagine you jealous, or even angry. I'm not convinced you have any flaws."

"I have them, trust me. Yesterday proves it. I was so wrapped up in wanting to kiss you, that I didn't even think, or care, that other people were around. I didn't take into consideration if it would upset you. I was selfish. And as much as I'm sorry I did it without asking, I'm not sorry for kissing you. It's all I've thought about since the firefly field."

I'm staring at his lips. "Yeah, me too," I say in a rasp. Now it's all *I* can think about, not that I haven't played that kiss on repeat in my head since it happened. But I freaked out, thinking he wanted more than I'm willing to give him. And that fear turned me into a *demon*, as Ashton so fondly called me.

"So what do we do? What do *you* want to do?"

"Kiss you," I murmur. He laughs.

"We'll get to that," he says, floating around so he's in front of me. He reaches above my head and holds onto the rope with both hands, caging me in. "Want to give this non-dating thing a try?" His gaze lowers to my mouth. "You be you. I'll be me. And we'll just hang out, and talk, and be really good friends, who kiss, and—"

"Yes," I utter, capturing the words that never leave his mouth.

I wrap my legs around his waist. One arm pins me to him while his other keeps him attached to the trampoline. This kiss is frantic, filled with wanting. I gasp as his tongue dances with mine. A groan rumbles deep in his throat. I let go of the rope and slide my arms around his neck. His one-handed grip of the trampoline is the only thing keeping us from floating away or sinking.

Grant kisses along my jaw and down my neck, teasing with his tongue. I tilt my head, tangling my fingers in his hair. The entire world has disappeared. We are in our own fantastical realm filled with light and warmth. I'm almost convinced that if he let go, the water would form a bubble around us just so we could stay joined together.

He returns to my mouth, and his hand slides up my side, a thumb just under my bikini line. I swear I'm a second away from untying it myself when I hear, "Whoa! Sorry."

"That's where you went," Ashton says, her head tipped over the edge of the trampoline a couple feet above us.

Lance is at the ladder, climbing up. He jumps on the trampoline, and must tackle Ashton because I hear her yell, "Hey! I was watching!"

I expect Grant to let go and separate, but he leans in and asks, "What's the PDA rule?"

I open my mouth in surprise.

"Because if you say we can't touch in public, I may need a ten-foot radius and a shock collar to remind me."

I laugh. "So *I'm* your flaw?"

Grant smiles. "Far from it." He kisses my cheek. "My impulse to kiss you, perhaps."

"Can I think about it?" I ask, still half in this world and half in the realm our kiss created. "I'm still a little…"

"Lost? Like you're not sure it was real or you were dreaming?" he finishes, completely in sync with what I experienced.

"Exactly," I answer, in awe.

"It was real," he assures me but releases me at the same time. The cool water instantly makes me very aware that this is not a dream as it fills in all the spaces his warm body was pressed against mine.

He floats on his back, kicking his legs to distance himself. I watch, questioning my hesitancy to be with him for everyone to see, even if we're *not* dating. The black diamonds on my thumb flash in the sunlight as a reminder.

I won't fall in love with him.

He smiles and his eyes twinkle with playful but seductive mischief.

I can't fall in love with him.

He dips his chin in the water and blows bubbles. I laugh.

I shouldn't fall in love with him.

"Stop looking at me like that," he says. "Or I'm going to make up the rules for you." My heart skips a beat at just the thought.

Please stop me from falling in love with him.

Chapter Eighteen

Thaylina rose to her feet, in search of the sorceress, only to find her lifeless body at the bottom of the tower. The entire kingdom shook with the scream the girl released. Thaylina knew that she would forever be cursed with heartache from that day forth.

rownies!" Ashton exclaims** when Squirrel is about to bite into it. She snatches it from his hand and shoves it into her mouth, tearing off a huge piece. She moans. "They're my favorite," she declares with her mouth full.

"You don't say?" he chuckles, reaching for another from within a plastic bag. "Want one, Lana?"

I take it, and just as I'm chewing my first bite, he adds, "They're magic brownies." I try to stop swallowing, but I can't make it come back up.

Ashton looks at me and laughs. "Oh, no more kisses for you tonight!"

I stare at the evil brownie. "I wish you had told me that, like, ten seconds ago."

"Oh, sorry. I thought Ashton said you were cool with herbs," Squirrel says apologetically.

"I am. I just…well, screw it." I continue eating it. "It'll make the fireworks that much prettier."

"That's exactly what I was thinking!" Squirrel exclaims like his mind is blown that we shared the same thought.

I glare at Ashton who is still laughing at me. "If I don't get kissed, then neither do you."

"Maybe I'll kiss you then," she snaps back.

We stop. She scrunches her eyes like she's not quite sure she meant to say that.

"Umm... I won't hold you to it."

Squirrel nibbles on his brownie, watching us intently like we're the most fascinating creatures he's ever come across.

Grant and Stefan had to run to the country club to help them deal with an emergency or something. The club is hosting a cookout at one of the member's houses, and a bartender was running late...I really don't know the details. But they said they'd be back in a couple hours. And when he does come back, I hope he doesn't take my being high as his answer to the PDA question.

An *hour later,* we're lying under a tree, our sundresses splayed on the grass around us. Ashton is using Squirrel's stomach as a pillow, and my head is on her stomach, so we create a zig-zag pattern.

Ashton sweeps her fingers across my forehead, brushing my overgrown bangs to the side and tucking them behind my ear. The tickle of her fingers on my skin is sedating. A rustle of leaves has captivated my attention. It's like they're waving at me.

"Why do they call you Squirrel?" I ask.

"Because, when I was little, I used to hide food in my closet. When my parents asked me why, I told them it was for hibernation."

Ashton and I laugh. "That is the best story!" she exclaims. "I love it. Except...love is so confusing." Her stomach flexes beneath me as she talks, jostling my head.

"I don't believe in love," is my response.

Squirrel starts laughing so hard that Ashton is forced to sit up, which makes me sit as well. When he realizes we aren't laughing with him, he slowly calms. "I didn't know you were serious."

I nod.

"Love exists, whether you believe in it or not. Just like magic."

I look to Ashton, who is seriously contemplating this as valid. "Yeah, you're right."

"Um…what?"

Ashton lays on her side, her head propped on her elbow, to face Squirrel. I turn toward him and sit cross-legged, tucking my skirt beneath me, preparing to absorb whatever wisdom Squirrel is about to unleash.

"Love isn't something you can hold onto, or will into being. It already is, because we are it. Love is us, at our essence."

"Then how come it hurts? Breaks hearts? Destroys lives?"

"That's not love. That's fear. Fear rules our minds. Every time we overthink and try to talk ourselves out of our feelings, that's fear talking. And when it's threatened, when love starts to take over, it speaks louder, trying to make us believe we're not worthy of being loved, or it's only going to hurt us. But love never hurts. Not ever."

I just stare at him. His words are like butterflies flitting around his head, and I try to hold on to them, but they're all jumbled up and I'm not sure which butterfly spoke first.

"What was in the brownies?" I ask.

"I don't really remember, but it's organic," Squirrel says, twirling a strand of Ashton's hair around his finger.

"What happens when we fall in love?" Ashton asks, lining the palm of my hand with hers and examining the way our fingers press together.

"You don't get to choose who you love. You are love. So when you share that love, you're sharing you. You never really fall in love exactly. It's a connection. A bond. Our souls recognize that connection long before we do. Love can't be given or taken away, it can only be experienced in a beautiful symbiotic way that fills up your entire being."

"Like light," a voice inside me says.

Squirrel is quiet for a moment. "Yeah. Like light." I guess he heard that voice too.

"What are you doing over here?" Kaely asks, sitting down next to me.

"Being light," Ashton replies, running a finger along my arm that sends a cascade of shivers through my body.

"Oh," Kaely says, thinking about this. "I don't understand."

"That's because your fear is talking," I tell her. I think I got that right.

"Are we sharing our biggest fear?" Kaely asks, getting excited. "I'm so afraid of falling down a hole and getting stuck, and then calling out and nobody hearing me. Then I'll be stuck in the ground by myself forever."

"That's terrible!" Ashton exclaims, like she can feel her fear. "You have to step over those holes so they never get you."

"I will," Kaely promises.

"I think your real fear is being forgotten," Squirrel says, his green eyes kind and thoughtful.

"Yeah, maybe," Kaely replies, seriously considering this. We all stare at him like he's the wisest person we've ever seen.

There's a small voice in my head that is shouting in the distance, "What the fuck is going on?" But I just tell it to be quiet and maybe take a nap.

Lance and Lily find us. "Lily!" Ashton exclaims.

"What did I miss?" Lily asks, standing above us like a glowing goddess.

We're quiet, because it's so much. I have no idea how to even try to tell her everything she missed.

"Brownies," Ashton explains. And I nod, because that's really it.

Lance starts laughing. We smile back.

"What's so funny?" Kaely asks, smiling too.

"Dude, you shared your brownies with the girls, but wouldn't share with me?"

"Ashton stole it from my mouth," Squirrel explains.

"I did," Ashton confirms, with a solemn nod. "I have a brownie addiction."

"And you?" Lance asks me.

"I didn't know they were magical."

"I didn't get any brownies," Kaely sulks.

"C'mon Kaely," Lily says, offering her hand. "We'll find the alcohol instead."

"You won't get kissed!" I call to them as they start to walk away. Lily shoots me a curious glance but then keeps going.

"No, *you* aren't getting kissed," Ashton clarifies.

"I thought you said you were kissing me?" I am so confused.

"Wait. What's happening? They're going to make-out?" Brendan appears over Lance's shoulder.

I frown. "I don't like your voice."

When I look down, Ashton is kissing Squirrel.

"Uh, no, that's not happening." Brendan pulls her off the ground and over his shoulder like she weighs nothing. He is seriously strong. I wonder where he hides his muscles.

"Hey!" Ashton hollers. "Put me down. You said no relationship. You said no monogamy. You told me no. I can do what I want!" She's flailing her arms and legs. Brendan ignores her and everyone staring after them, his hand resting on her butt to keep her skirt from riding up.

"Omigod, I'm Brendan," I gasp.

"Uh, I hope not."

I look up and Grant is standing next to Lance. He glances from my stunned face to Lance. "What's going on?"

"Squirrel shared his brownies with Lana and Ashton."

Grant chuckles. "You really must not like kissing me, huh?"

"I love kissing you!" I protest passionately. "I didn't know they were magic! I didn't believe in magic. But now I do. And I'm so sorry. I tried to make them come back up, but they got stuck."

Lance laughs again, thoroughly entertained. Grant smiles. Squirrel nods his head like he completely supports everything I just said.

"Stefan's starting the boat to take people out on the lake to watch the fireworks, if you want to go," Grant says, but he's looking at Lance, not me.

"Sounds good. You're going to stay here with her?" Lance gestures to me and releases another quick laugh. I didn't realize I was so funny.

Squirrel is on his feet, walking toward the lake. "I'm all about fireworks, man." He appears way more whole than I feel.

"Don't miss the fireworks," I tell Grant, feeling sad.

"I won't," he promises. "Can you stand?" He offers me his hand.

"Are you coming?" Kaely asks as she and Lily approach with big thermal cups.

"We're going to stay here," Grant tells them, helping me onto my feet. The grass feels squishy between my toes. I stand there curling them into the cool, soft blades. When I look back up, it's just Grant.

"Where'd everybody go?"

"To the boat. Well, not everyone. Want to watch the fireworks with me?"

I let out a depressed sigh.

"What's wrong?"

"I think I'm broken."

"You're not broken," Grant says with a chuckle, wrapping his arm around me and guiding me down to the beach. "You're just chemically imbalanced."

"Oh," I reply. That earns another amused laugh. I'm having a hard time keeping up with what's so funny.

When we reach the beach, I stop. "This feels so weird." I sink my toes farther into the sand. Then I kneel down to bury my fingers too. "This is amazing; you should feel it."

"I'm going to strangle Squirrel," I hear Grant mutter, bending down to coax me back to my feet.

"Don't do that," I plead urgently. "He's a wizard."

Grant smiles and leans down to press his lips to my forehead. "I won't really,

I promise."

We continue onto the dock and when we sit on the end to slip our feet into the water, I sigh audibly. I lean against Grant, my head over his heart. He has an arm bracing me so I don't topple into the water.

"Your love is very loud." It pounds against my ear. "What does it feel like?"

I gaze up into his cloudless eyes, and he offers me the sweetest smile. "You don't know?"

I shake my head. "I've only seen it hurt."

He nods in understanding. "Love doesn't hurt. Ever."

"Squirrel said that."

"He is a wizard," Grant confirms, like that explains it. I nod.

"But you've...been with someone before, right?" Then he quickly says, "I shouldn't have asked you that. Forget it."

"I'm not a virgin," I confirm. "But Jensen wasn't love. He was...sex."

"That's sad."

"I guess," I admit, trying to remember Jensen's face.

"How'd you meet?"

I take in a breath, wanting to be sure the words form properly. "At a bar. I was lying about my age. He was lying about his. Found out he was only a few years older than me, not twenty-three. And he never found out that I wasn't twenty-two."

"A relationship based on lies, that's never good."

"We weren't in a relationship," I correct quickly. "We were just bodies for each other. No feelings. No talking, not really anyway. No love."

Grant's quiet.

"I don't want that," he finally says.

"You're not that," I admit, tipping my head to focus on him. I decide to lay on my back and rest my head on his lap to get a better view. "You know more about me than anyone in my entire life."

His head tilts down so I can see all of him. "Really?"

366

"Yeah. You ask me, and I always tell you the truth. I can't stop my mouth from being honest."

"I thought that was your curse?"

"My curse doesn't make me talk. Only makes what I say true. But I can't hide in silence from you. And that scares me."

"Why?"

"Because you'll eventually learn a truth that'll make you not like who I am."

I watch his throat move as he swallows.

"I can always forgive the truth, Lana. But it's much harder to forgive a lie. So I'd rather know than for it to be kept a secret."

"What does love feel like?" I ask again.

Grant runs his hand along my cheek. "Find out for yourself."

The sky crackles and sizzles before it explodes. I sit up and search for it across the water in time to see a colorful burst of fire in the sky. "It's beautiful."

Grant encases me in his arms, easing me against him. "Very." I wrap my arms around his, keeping him close.

I watch in awe as the spectacular display of colors dance across the sky, sparkling and swirling. I'm mesmerized and can't take my eyes off of them the entire time. Even when Grant leans down and presses his cheek against mine. I smile, but don't look away from the explosion of lights.

When it's over, my heart is beating so hard.

"How are you feeling?"

"Incredible," I tell him. He laughs, his breath tickling.

We wait on the dock until the boat returns. Ashton jumps from it and yells, "Let's dance!"

She spins and leaps, her dress fluttering around her like she's an exotic bird. I giggle and push up to stand. Grant remains seated on the dock. "C'mon, let's dance." I run after her, and someone turns on the music. She grabs my hand to twirl me around and around.

"**A**re you sure you have them both?" Grant asks Brendan for the third time. "I don't mind driving them."

"I've got them. I promise," Brendan assures him...again.

"I'm trusting you," Grant says, sounding very serious.

Ashton and I are huddled together at the door, mesmerized by their conversation.

"I know. I got it. I won't let anything happen to your girl."

Grant's eyes connect with mine in concern. I smile to make his worry go away. "We're good." He leans down and kisses my forehead. "I'll see you tomorrow."

"Tomorrow?"

"Tutoring session," he reminds me.

"Study room A," I say. "I'll be there."

"I love you guys," Ashton announces, hugging everyone within wingspan.

"Let's go, love," Brendan says, taking her hand, and because I'm still captured in her embrace, I stumble after her. I look behind me from beneath her arm in search of Grant. I want to say I love you too. But I'm not sure who will hear me.

"**W**alk in straight lines," Brendan directs as we cross the parking lot and onto the gravel driveway.

"There aren't any lines," Ashton says, looking at the ground. I look too.

"Nope, no lines."

"Then just follow me," he says patiently. So we do.

He checks us in with the security guard at the main entrance, and we walk through the foyer of the administration building. Brendan leaves us at the doors to the girls' dorm. "I'll be right up."

"Where's he going?" I ask Ashton. She shrugs. So we go inside and climb the stairs. As we reach the third floor, I let out a short scream. A woman is standing on the landing with her arms crossed, glaring at us.

"Mrs. See-er!" Ashton cries out, pointing. "I told you she's everywhere!!"

We run up the stairs the rest of the way. Ashton follows me to my room. When I open the door and turn on the light, everything is upside down.

"What happened to your room?" she gawks.

"It got dissected," I say in awe.

"Someone really doesn't like you, Princess," Brendan declares from behind us. We both spin around in surprise. "What did you do?"

My entire room is stripped and shredded and broken. I bend down and pick up the head of the zebra. "Oh no."

On the wall, in bright red paint is:

BITCH!

"Yup," I tell the wall. "I know."

I *sleep in Ashton's room.* So does Brendan, which wasn't weird until I wake up, sober. Thankfully, Ashton's in the middle. We both have an arm around her that is also holding the other's. I pull my arm back like his is on fire as soon as I take this all in. Then I proceed to knock my head on the ceiling in attempt to flee.

"What are you doing?" Ashton groans.

"I have to meet my life advisor," I tell her, crawling over her to reach the ladder.

"I'll call my designer today. We'll fix your room," she tells me as I reach the door.

I don't have much time to take in the destruction when I enter my room in search of workout clothes. My phone's blowing up with messages from Mr. Garner demanding I hurry up.

At breakfast, after the most miserable session with Mack to date, Ashton has color swatches ready for me to pick out and storyboards to choose from. When I ask her who's paying for it, she responds, "Parental guilt." So I let her black Amex pay for whatever she wants.

"So, who did it?" she asks hesitantly. I know she's not one to pry when information isn't volunteered, but the concern on her face wins over her inner struggle not to inquire.

"I don't know," I reply.

"How long's this been going on?" Lance sets his breakfast plate down next to me. I know he wasn't here when Ashton and I were looking over her ideas, so he learned about it from...

"I had to tell him about the room," Brendan defends just as my thoughts point to him. "I need his help cleaning it up after class." I glower at him.

"I should know about these things anyway." Lance sounds offended that he's been excluded.

"Me too!" Ashton pipes in as a second thought.

"Why?" I ask.

They look at each other, then at Brendan, who shrugs.

"Why does Brendan get to know?" Lance demands. "I'm the one who's supposed to be protecting you."

"Wow, someone's taking their chaperoning duties a little too seriously," Brendan grumbles, crossing his arms and leaning back in his chair.

"Because Brendan seems to be around every time it happens. Maybe because he's the one doing it. I haven't decided yet."

Ashton and Lance stare at Brendan. He laughs like I'm joking.

"How many times has this happened?" Lance questions again. "And who has it out for you?"

I roll my eyes and choose my words carefully. "If I knew, my room wouldn't look like someone took an ax to it."

"But how did they gain access without your phone?" Ashton asks. "There aren't many girls in the dorm right now."

"It's not hard," Brendan chimes in, earning him another round of suspicious glares. He holds up his hands in defense. "I'm just trying to help."

"Or throw suspicion off yourself!" Lance accuses emphatically, his raised voice gaining a few curious glances from surrounding tables. He leans in and asks quieter, "Did you sell access to anyone?"

"What does that mean?" I stare Brendan down.

"Who do you think I got your phone from?" Lance informs me, nodding toward Brendan.

"No wonder I can't access anything," I complain.

"Except the map app. Didn't want you getting lost." He winks. Then thinks better of it. "But you did anyway."

"What?" Ashton asks, looking between us. "What's been going on between you two?"

"Ew!" I cringe in disgust. "Not anything you should be worried about." I violently shiver.

"No need for the dramatics," Brendan scolds. "I've been trying to help her figure out who's been leaving her messages…on her wall. That's all."

It's a good thing he doesn't have an issue lying because I'm having a hard time staying close to the truth without revealing too much.

"I have to get to class," I announce, standing up.

Ashton looks at her phone. "Yeah, we all do." No one remarks on the fact that Brendan doesn't have a class right now.

When we split up in the courtyard, Brendan walks with me.

"Hey! Where are you going?" Lance demands when he notices.

"Walking Lana to class," he tells him with a cocky smile. "Someone has to *protect* her." Lance glares and flips him off. I elbow him in the ribs. "Ow!"

"Knock it off," I sneer. "Antagonizing him is only going to make him more suspicious, or make him want to punch you in the face. Come to think of it, *I* want to punch you in the face! You were *not* helpful in there!"

"I've been thinking that maybe we should let them in on some of it," he offers quietly. "More sets of eyes may be better. Ashton's room is right down the hall from you. If she's paying attention, she may notice someone who doesn't belong, because I'm not convinced it's a student, or at least not one at Blackwood."

"How do you know?"

"Because I know who has my tech. This person doesn't."

"So, there's another one of you?"

"Darling, there's no one like me." He flashes a seductive grin. "But it's someone who unquestionably has skills, especially if they're gaining access to the campus undetected. I may make it sound easy to avoid detection, but it's really not. Their security is on point, and their technology is custom designed. It's not a joke. I just happen to be better."

I hold back the eye roll. "I don't want to tell them *everything*."

"They only need to know about the messages on the wall. The rest we keep between us, especially if it has anything to do with Lance's family."

"But maybe he can tell us more about the picture."

"We have his brother for that," Brendan reminds me. Except Joey won't be here for another week.

"Fine," I concede with a heavy breath. "They know about the room. But I don't want them knowing anything more; not the picture or the other notes. Nothing about our mothers or Niall either. And absolutely *nothing* about Allie."

"Agreed. Have you had a chance to look over your room, to see if the person left anything behind?"

"Other than my namesake on the wall?"

He laughs.

"No. I haven't looked for more warnings or pictures. Maybe it's not the same person. The messages in my room seem different, angrier."

"Perhaps." Brendan nods like it hadn't occurred to him before. "But to have two people out to get you is a little excessive, even for you."

"Three, if you include…" I shut my mouth.

"The guy who hurt Allie? Do you think he'll come after you if she wakes up?"

I shrug, not wanting to think about Vic on top of everything else. He's still in Europe, I hope. I'll deal with him when Allie opens her eyes.

"Make sure you have my phone on you at all times. It doesn't have to be on for me to locate you."

"You're not a very good stalker if you let the person know you're stalking them," I jeer.

"Just keep it with you." There's a heavy note of seriousness in his tone, so I don't argue. If I didn't know better, I'd think he was worried about me.

By now, we've reached the history building and Brendan waits for me to enter. "What do you do when you're not in class?"

"I do what I do best," he waggles his brow. "I watch."

"You're so creepy!" I call after him as he disappears into the Court. I'm seriously questioning whose side he's on. But that's obvious—Brendan is only out for Brendan. I hope he doesn't ruin too many lives in pursuit of his answers.

Chapter Nineteen

In the years that passed, Thaylina grew strong and fast. She no longer resembled the kind and beautiful girl she once was. She had become a huntress, willing to defend any who were deceived by charm and promises of a song.

hen I return to the dorm, my door is open. I creep along the wall, wondering if I'm finally going to catch the crazed psycho in action.

But I deflate when I find Mr. Garner assessing the damage with his hands on his hips.

"Mr. Garner?"

He turns to face me. I can't tell if he's angry, worried, or both. "What is going on, Lana?!" When I don't answer right away, he continues, "I received a message from Mrs. Seyer that she was concerned you and Ashton were partying in your room late last night. And I come up to find this." With open palms he presents the cataclysm that used to be my room, his eyes are wide in confused shock. "Either you girls take partying to a whole other level, or you're being harassed."

I pause with a tilt of my head, not sure how to answer, because Ashton and I were definitely on a different plane last night.

"And what are *you* doing here?" Mr. Garner demands, focused behind me.

Brendan is standing in the doorway. "Helping clean up." He holds up a box of garbage bags.

"I've got it!" Ashton proclaims, still in the hall. "This is the perfect bed for your..." Her excitement deflates when she stumbles in to find Mr. Garner. "I have permission!" she declares, holding up the tablet with a furniture site on the screen.

Mr. Garner sighs. "Why does everyone know but me? Lana, I'm supposed to be the person you go to when things like this happen."

"I knew you'd be worried," I tell him. "And look, you are. So I was right!"

He sighs. "Let's go." He directs me out of the room. "I also came to escort you to your first drug test."

Brendan laughs. He seriously laughs. I really am going to punch him in the face. At least Ashton is kind enough to look horrified on my behalf, which probably isn't helpful either.

I'm really hoping I get a free pass and they use it as my baseline test, as Mr. Garner thought they might when we first met in his office. I honestly have no idea what they're going to find, especially after last night. Mr. Garner silently walks me into the nurse's clinic inside the administration building. He's been internally battling with whatever it is he wants to say the entire walk over.

Blackwood doesn't mess around when it comes to their drug testing. That's apparent as soon as I see the test tube next to the rubber tourniquet. It's basically impossible to hide drug use in a blood test.

"Meet me in my office when you're done," Mr. Garner requests and disappears out the door, leaving me with the pissy nurse.

Issuing only short directives, she doesn't even warn me when she's about to insert the needle. And for the benefit of thoroughness, she administers a saliva test as well. I've only ever provided urine tests in juvie, and those can easily be switched. So this is intense. Guess I'm going to be sober for the next five months.

I automatically think of Grant, and suddenly sobriety doesn't look so bad. Not at all.

The nurse must think I'm high. I'm still sitting, all dreamy-eyed with a stupid smile on my face when she's done.

"Leave," she tells me with a scrutinizing squint of her eyes.

Mr. *Garner's office looks* nothing like the cavernous space I first entered a few weeks ago. It almost resembles a guy's dorm room with its comfortable furniture, a basketball hoop hung on the back of the door, and photographs covering the wall—shots of Mr. Garner and random people on mountain tops, in a kayak in what looks like the jungle, and other exotic locations. Except he has a desk in place of a bed.

"Well, hello, Mr. Garner," I say, admiring the space. "Who knew you were an actual human being."

"Shut the door, Lana," he instructs, sitting down behind his desk. I comply. "You've had quite a few mishaps in the short time you've been here. What's going on?"

"What are you talking about exactly?" I'm suddenly nervous about how much the security cameras may have caught.

He starts counting them off on his fingers. "You almost miss curfew on your second night. You get locked out of the building because your phone wasn't charged properly a week later. And now, your room is completely vandalized by someone who you've obviously upset. What else am I missing? Oh! Right, the drugs that you claim that we'll find in your system after being here for only a weekend. I won't make you tell me where you got them, but c'mon, Lana! Any fights you want to confess to while we're at it?"

I look down.

"Really?" he exclaims in exasperation. "I am obviously sucking at my job."

"This has nothing to do with you," I protest. "You're doing great! Dragging me out of my bed first thing in the morning to make me hit stuff, or seek inner peace. It's really helping, I swear. I don't want you to lose your job over me."

Mr. Garner closes his eyes with a shake of his head. "That's not what I'm worried about. Being here is supposed to be your opportunity to experience something better. Not to bring all of your chaos with you."

"Maybe I *am* my chaos," I offer with a shrug. "It comes with me wherever I go."

He rubs a hand over his face. "You exhaust me."

I bite back a smile. "I could say the same. I will only get out of bed at the crack of dawn for you, Mr. Garner."

"Do you know who's targeting you?" he asks with a sigh, ignoring my snarky retort.

I shake my head.

"I need to hear you say it."

"No," I state clearly…for the record…in case his office is bugged and that's why he insisted I say it out loud.

"I'm going to speak to security, again, about their interior patrols. Maybe they'll post someone outside each entrance of the dorms on the Court side."

"Good luck," I tell him, standing because I presume we're done.

"Call me if anything strange happens, or you find yourself in a predicament that won't look good on your record. No matter what time. No matter where you are. I'll come get you. And if I can, I'll keep it between us." He stands to walk me out. "I really am here to help you, Lana. You're my entire job."

"Sad, isn't it?" I say with a smirk.

"Get out," he says with a chuckle. "Don't do anything stupid."

My *phone beeps on my* way back to the dorm with a message from my chemistry teacher.

Chemistry tutor rescheduled for 7pm on Thursday.

This day just keeps sucking. But I guess rescheduling makes sense. We haven't had class since our test so there isn't any new material to cover. I was just really looking forward to seeing Grant, and maybe kissing him…if he'd let me. Then again, he takes his responsibilities so seriously, he probably wouldn't. But his integrity and dedication are part of what make me…I hesitate. How exactly was I about to finish that sentence?

Respect him. Yup. That's it. I groan and want to smack my own head. Where's Ashton when I need her?

Come to my room.

A sticky note is stuck to my door. I assume it's from Ashton and not Brendan. When I enter her room, I'm shocked to find Lance and Brendan too.

"Did Mrs. Seyer let you up?" I ask.

"We're part of the devastation crew," Lance explains with a cunning grin. He's lounging on the couch playing a handheld video game with his feet propped up on a hot pink leather ottoman.

"The what? You know what, forget it."

"Let's go," Ashton announces. "We're going to pick up your mess and move your things in here for when Serge arrives tomorrow."

"Who?"

"My designer. His team is coming to transform your room tomorrow."

Sometimes I forget that Ashton is super wealthy. Granted, she has that air of prestige emanating from her. Now that I consider it, it's more of a glamorous vibe, like wind should be blowing in her hair as flashbulbs go off every time she enters a room. Underneath all of that, she's pretty chill. She's not bitchy or snooty. Nor is she pretentious or superior. So when she talks about her designer and his team, it's like being splashed in the face with ice water—a not-so-subtle reminder that we come from completely different backgrounds, even if we currently find ourselves in the same place.

We spend the afternoon cleaning up my room. I would mourn the loss, except it never really felt like mine. It does piss me off that the psycho tore the head off of the adorable zebra Joey gave me and ripped up the pictures of my friends and family. It seems so…senseless. What could I possibly have done to make someone hate me? Because that's what it feels like.

I haven't been here long enough to bring on this level of disdain. So it had to have followed me from home. Everyone I know at Blackwood, except for Ashton and Sophia, has some tie to my life; some even before I was born. And this includes Brendan and Mr. Garner. I can't believe I even have to consider Mr. Garner as a suspect. I can't believe I'm using the word *suspect*.

And if it isn't someone from Blackwood, as Brendan believes, then I am completely at a loss. I never met the others until I arrived. And unless I did something without knowing it to gain an enemy…Well, that is a possibility. My candor isn't always appreciated. But when I factor in all the messages, and now the picture…I'm back to being utterly confused.

"I hate the mind games," I growl in frustration. "Just fricken tell me what you want!"

Everyone stops.

"But the melodrama is the best part," Brendan quips.

I chuck a throw pillow at him that has its guts hanging out.

"Want one?" Ashton asks, gummies in her hand. "Will make this more fun."

Lance takes one. Brendan shakes his head.

"I can't," I tell her regretfully. "I'm the official sobriety poster child."

"He must be an amazing kisser," Ashton muses like she envies me.

"Are you talking about Grant?" Lance asks. "What's going on with you two? Is it serious? Are you going to ditch me every time we go off campus now? Because I'm responsible for knowing where you are. And nights like the carnival can't happen all the time."

"Why don't the two of you have to take drug tests?" I ask, deflecting what was starting to sound like an overprotective interrogation. Lance really *is* taking his chaperoning role way too seriously. "You were both busted for drugs."

"My parents won't allow it," Ashton explains. "They don't want it on record in case it gets leaked to the press."

"My dad won't allow it either," Lance repeats. "Doesn't want it potentially used against me."

"But I have to?" It's not that I need the drugs, but I hate my every move being monitored…by Lance and the school. I don't need anyone dictating what's best for me, or questioning where I go, or with whom.

"Yours is court ordered," Brendan says.

"Why do you know that?" Lance scowls at him. "I'm seriously starting to wonder if we should be trusting you."

"Don't," I interject automatically.

Brendan scoffs. "It's an obvious conclusion to make. She's the only one who has a record among the three of you, so I'm sure there were conditions to her sentencing."

"I think we're done," Ashton announces, assessing the room and trying to deflate the growing tension.

"Thanks for helping me," I tell them. The guys don't say anything; they just nod awkwardly. Ashton chooses to hug me and give me a sloppy kiss on the cheek.

Ashton and I carry the only two bags of clothes that survived the attack, while the guys leave with trash bags filled with the remains.

When *I'm lying on Ashton's* couch that night, she asks, "Tell me about everyone's curses again. What's Brendan's?"

"*Perception*. He sees everything."

"Except how I feel about him."

"That's part of his curse too. He *can't* see what's most important to him, that's why it'll eventually ruin him."

"Yeah." She yawns. "What about Lance?"

"Lance is cursed with *Nobility*. He's a good guy, but may not always stand up for the right people."

"I like Lance," she mumbles. "Tell me more."

I list everyone and their curses until we're too tired to open our mouths.

Mr. *Garner wakes me* for a yoga and meditation class first thing the next morning, followed by a detox session (his words) in the sauna. Ashton decides to join us, and I hate them both for their ability to stand on one foot, with their eyes closed, in a still tree pose. I look more like sea grass blowing in the wind than a tree. Peace and I did not find each other once again. But the hot steam of the sauna did help leach the toxins from my body. I haven't felt this clear-headed in forever.

Grant isn't working when we arrive at the country club. I should probably ask Sophia for a copy of his schedule. Or maybe I could just ask him. But that would be weird.

No. I'll ask Sophia. Also weird, but not as bad.

I finish my shift at The Deck and find Grant clocking in on my way to the locker room.

"Hi," he says. I smile like I just inhaled helium. "What happened to you yesterday?"

I frown. "What?"

"Our tutor session? You didn't show."

A flash of panic shoots through me. Did I read that message wrong? "I got a message from my teacher that it was changed to tomorrow."

"You did?"

I nod. "Why didn't you call me?"

"I don't have your number. At least not until you call me first."

"I'm sorry." Now I need to find a reason to call him. I can't really remember the last time I called a guy to talk. Maybe because that was *never*.

"Weird I didn't receive a message," he says, looking concerned.

"But I'll see you tomorrow, right?" I ask, hoping he doesn't already have a commitment.

"Uh, yeah. Tomorrow." He still looks bothered by the mess up in scheduling.

"Are you okay?"

"I was…a little worried…that you were distancing yourself again. Monday was…Well, a lot was said."

"I remember," I say, offering a gentle smile.

"All of it?"

"Yup," I tell him. "Even the parts when I was in Wonderland. It feels like I'm looking at those memories from a thousand feet in the air, watching myself. But I remember."

His face becomes thoughtful, almost pained actually—like he's struggling to find the words to ask a question he's afraid to know the answer to. So I stretch up on my toes and kiss him, hoping that gives him the answer. His mouth eases into a smile even before my lips leave his.

A throat clears.

We turn to find Cary standing behind me. "Uh, as much as I'm a fan of young love, I will have to kindly ask you to refrain from expressing it while you're working."

I bite my lip, my cheeks blossoming with color.

"We're not," Grant chokes out, his eyes flashing to me nervously. "It's not…"

"Relax, Grant. I'm not scolding you like I'm your father. You're not in trouble." Before he walks away, he adds, "I'm actually happy for you both."

Grant closes his eyes and grimaces. "I'm sorry. I didn't know how to fix that, to keep him from thinking…"

"It's okay. We can't control what anyone else thinks. As long you and I know what we are, or what we're not."

Grant relaxes a little, but the worry lingers in his eyes. I'm not sure if it's because we were caught by Cary, or if it's what I said. "Okay. Then I'll see you tomorrow?"

I nod and watch him walk away. I guess it is a little complicated, to be together but not. Except that's the whole point; it's not something that fits in a box. The more we think about it, or what everyone else will think about it, the more complicated it will be. And it's *not* complicated…or it's not supposed to be. And now…I'm confused again.

I'*m not allowed to see* my room until Serge has completed its transformation. He and Ashton spend most of Thursday together. They asked me to join them, but after ten minutes of his exaggerated hand gestures and words flying out of his mouth so fast, he sounds like he's speaking in a foreign tongue, I told them I needed to go to the library to work on my American government paper.

Before I reach the library, I receive a message.

You have a guest at the administration building.

When I enter, I find Parker waiting for me. He smiles as soon as he sets his brilliant blue eyes upon me. I sigh, hating that he still captivates me.

"Hi," I greet him, surprised to find him in Kingston. "I thought you'd be in Nantucket with your family."

His brows scrunch. "How do you know my family's in Nantucket?"

Crap.

"Your brother," I say, trying to play it off. I'm not sure what his deal is with Joey, and I really don't want to be the reason they continue with their stupid squabble. So it's probably best if Parker doesn't know we've been in contact.

He nods in understanding. "Right, Lance couldn't come this year because of classes." Then he says, "I came back early. I found out something that I wanted to share with you."

"You didn't have to end your family trip for me," I say, overwhelmed that he felt he needed to come here and tell me in person.

"I did," he says almost excitedly. "We found her." He looks around the foyer. "Is there somewhere private we can talk?"

I lead him to the room where I met with Niall when I first arrived.

"Found who?" I ask as soon as the door closes.

"Mara, the girl from the stairwell."

My mouth has a hard time forming words for a moment. "H-h-how?" I stutter.

"One of my partners is a tech guy. Brilliant. He designed our entry app, and vets the list. He was able to track her down. Something about triangulating and crosschecking…I don't remember, to be honest. But he obviously knows what he's doing, because he found her."

"Does he know why you were looking for her?" I'm suddenly concerned that one more person knows about my presence in the stairwell.

"I was vague. Obviously he knew about the girl who fell."

"Allie," I remind him, insistent that he call her by her name.

"Allie," he repeats. "Sorry."

"So how do I talk to her?" I ask eagerly.

"You?" Parker scoffs. "You're not talking to her."

"But I need to explain what happened. I don't want her thinking I hurt her friend."

"She's not going to say anything."

"How do you know?" I don't like where this is going. He's being evasive.

"Because I talked to her. She understands what's at stake."

"And what is that exactly?"

"Don't worry about it."

My heart skips a beat at his non-response. "You better not have threatened her, Parker!"

He laughs off my reaction. "I told you I was going to help you. So I did. It's done." He looks down at his watch. "I'm driving back to New York, so I have to get going."

"You drove all the way up here just to tell me this?" I ask, suspicious, because he's being really…strange.

"No. Not exactly."

I wait for him to explain, but he doesn't. I want to scream at him to tell me what the hell is going on.

"Walk me out?" He nods toward the door.

"You realize how weird all of this is, right?"

"No," he answers sincerely. "I care about what happens to you. Friends or whatever, I'll always take care of you."

I try not to make a face and call him out on his bullshit, because my gut is telling me something's off. I consider myself an expert at detecting untruths, and he's *not* being completely truthful.

I walk him out to the front steps of the administration building.

"Come here," he beckons, opening his arms. I lean into his hug, resting my head on his chest.

"This still doesn't feel right, Parker. I know you're not telling me everything."

He kisses the top of my head and assures me again, "You don't have anything to worry about."

When I ease out of his arms, I catch a glimpse of Grant and Lily walking along the circular drive toward the library. I'll need to explain to Grant what he might've just witnessed between Parker and me. But...should I have to? Because we're not really *together*. The parameters of non-dating are so...fuzzy.

"So what, your rule doesn't apply to *him*?" Parker nods toward Grant just as he disappears.

"What do you mean? And how do you know about Grant?"

"You go to school with my brother. You're friends with my cousin. And they used to date."

"Lance and Lily?" I question in abhorrence. "How close is your family?!"

"Lily and Grant!" Parker stresses impatiently. "They dated for like a year. It was serious. Nothing casual like what Nina and I had. And you won't even go on a date with me. But you can be in a relationship with him? Why bother with the bullshit excuse about not touching guys your friends have been with? You just had to tell me you weren't interested."

I'm not going to argue with him about semantics because I *did* tell him I wasn't interested. I may have wrapped that message within my friendship rule. But...what the fuck?! "They dated? For a year?"

"Yes." He drives the point in emphatically. "They broke up last winter. But I was always under the impression it wasn't permanent. Like they planned to get back together."

"Who said that?"

"Lily. She asked for some time apart," he informs me.

"Not Grant?" I clarify.

He shakes his head.

"Oh," I breathe, my head reeling. My heart is fluttering in full-blown freak-out mode. "I gotta go."

I don't hear anything else Parker says as I walk away, following the same path to the library that Lily and Grant took. My phone beeps and I absently remove it from my messenger bag.

Tutor session changed to study room D.

I talk myself down from totally freaking out. Because…well, what do I have to be freaked about? He's not mine, I shouldn't care. Except my pounding heart doesn't give a shit. It *does* care and needs answers. Now.

When I walk into the library, I search for either Grant or Lily. I find them *together* in an aisle toward the back of the library. When I come upon them, they appear to be engaged in a serious conversation. So I do what Brendan would do (he's obviously a horrible influence) and I move along the aisle next to them to listen. I know, I'm going to hell. But at least Brendan…yeah, that doesn't help.

"I didn't know it was serious," Lily says quietly.

"It's…complicated," Grant explains, his eyes lower in apology. "But I'd like it to be."

"Oh," she breathes. "I just thought you were having fun. I didn't realize…"

"I thought this was what you wanted?" he asks, concern drawing his brows together.

She smiles warmly. "It is." Her smile transitions into her vibrant one. "I'm happy for you. I was just surprised when I saw you together on Monday."

"That's why I wanted to tell you…to be honest with you about how I feel about her." His eyes flicker, waiting for her reaction.

"Well, thank you, I appreciate that. And I really am happy for you." Her expression is heartfelt, her smile never wavering. But I can't see her eyes from my vantage, peering through the small space above the books.

Grant studies her for a second, like maybe he sees something that makes him hesitant to believe her. But then he smiles softly. "We're good? You and I? I will always care about you, Lily. Always. I'm here for you whenever you need me."

"So good," she says lightly, still smiling affectionately. Grant pulls her to him and gives her a hug. I get a glimpse of her face as she blinks back the shimmer in her eyes. She is *not* good. But damn, she's an amazing liar.

I feel like the slimiest scum of the earth after witnessing that. I really am a vile creature right now.

I slink off to the study room early to collect myself and figure out what the hell I'm going to do about all of this. Why didn't he tell me about him and Lily? The more I think about it, the more frustrated I become. By the time I reach the basement, I'm preparing my "what the hell" speech.

Distracted, I realize too late that I'll need the librarian to unlock the door. But when I reach the end of the aisle, I find the door to study room D isn't closed all the way. I turn on the light and enter to wait inside. I leave the door open, watching for Grant.

I can't sit, so I pace. And think…way too much.

Lily obviously still has feelings for him. And she's been nothing but kind to me. She is the sweetest person on the planet. What the hell is he doing with me? I mean, not *with* me, but…whatever. He has *feelings* for me? Like serious enough feelings that he has to tell his ex-girlfriend?

I cup the back of my head with both hands and groan in frustration. What am I doing? Besides falling in love with him.

"Holy shit," I say out loud and then cover my mouth in shock. *Holy shit. Holy shit. Holy shit.* —continues repeating in my head.

"I'm falling in love with him," I gasp.

"You weren't supposed to do this!" I yell at my heart, or soul, or whatever part of me that decided to connect with Grant against my will. Squirrel's love explanation is a little hazy right now.

The door slams shut. I turn around expecting Grant. But no one's there.

"What the hell?" I mutter, walking to the door to crack it open again. But it's locked.

The light shuts off.

"Hey!" I yell, slamming my fist against the door. "Someone's in here!" I wait. No response. "Hello! Open the door!" I slap against the wood, jostling the door handle. Nothing.

I can't see a thing. It's so black it's like I've been locked in a tomb.

My heartbeat picks up and I draw air into my lungs faster and faster.

I shake the doorknob and pound. "Let me out!" I scream at the top of my lungs. "Please! Let me out!" The last word breaks into a panicked sob. "Please!"

I'm light-headed and feel like I'm going to fall over. I slide my hand along the door to the wall. Pressing my back against it, I bend over like Brendan showed me, breathing in slow and deep. But I can't fill my lungs. My pulse is racing. I can't breathe. Oh, no. I can't breathe.

I slink to the floor, fighting for air.

"Stop it!" I holler, but the laugh gives away that I don't really mean it.

He reaches over me, his chest brushing against mine as I hold the remote out of his reach. But it's not really. He could easily get it from me if he wanted. His mouth is so close to mine. I swallow hard.

I squirm farther down the couch, squealing when his hand grabs my waist and tickles me. I've had a crush on him for so long. I'm hoping so hard that he might finally kiss me. I know he's older. But I'm finally looking like a teenager, and not the little kid he watches when my mother works late, and my grandmother has to cover the night shift at the pharmacy. I've only ever been the little kid upstairs to him. I want him to see I'm not anymore.

I slide down to the floor. "We are not watching your stupid show." I attempt to crawl out of his reach, still laughing, not realizing my skirt has slid up and my underwear is peeking out.

"Since when do you wear lace underwear?"

I whip around and pull the skirt down, my face flaming red.

"You're wearing a bra now too, huh?" His eyes slide over my curves. I have the biggest boobs in my grade. It's so embarrassing. I try to hide them with baggy shirts. But today I'm wearing a tank top. It's hard not to notice that I'm not a flat-chested, pig-tail wearing little girl anymore. I wanted him to notice. But now that he has, my stomach feels sick.

He crawls over me. Something's different. My heart isn't beating with excitement anymore. It's pounding with fear.

He leans in to kiss me, but I turn my head. "Don't."

"What? You don't want me to?"

"I do," I fumble. But I don't really mean it anymore. His breath feels hot on my cheek. His body is balanced above me like he's doing a push-up. "I don't know."

"You know you do." He lowers himself. And I flip over before he's on top of me, trying to scramble out from under him. He presses me into the carpet, my hands are pinned under my shoulders. I squirm. "Yeah, you know you do."

"Get off," I choke. "I can't breathe."

His body is heavy. I try to push up, to knock him off, but I'm not strong enough. He presses harder against me. My lungs can't suck in air. "I can't breathe. Stop."

A hand slides along my thigh and cups my butt cheek. He squeezes.

I whimper. "Get off me!" I struggle to move, but he's so much bigger than I am. So much stronger. He's crushing me. I need to get out. "Get off me!"

His jeans rub against me; I can feel him. His hand grips the edge of my underwear. He pulls at it. I whimper again.

"You wanted this."

"No. No. No," I sob. My breath is caught. There's no air left.

"What the hell do you think you're doing?!" my grandmother shouts.

He scrambles off of me. The pressure on my chest releases but I'm still gasping for air.

"Get the fuck out of my house!" She follows him out of the apartment to the stairs. "You little piece of shit! I trusted you!"

I hear muffled words behind the closed door. Followed by a thumping so loud it's like he's jumping down the stairs to escape. Then there's silence. I remain balled up on the carpet that has burned my knees and my elbows. I cry until all the air is gone.

My grandmother doesn't return. I only know she's dead at the bottom of the stairs when I hear my mother scream hours later. I still haven't moved.

"Lana?"

I open my eyes. The light is on. I'm on the floor with my knees pulled up into me, my arms holding them tight.

Grant is crouched in front of me. My eyes flit around wildly. His face. The open door.

He gently sets a hand on my shoulder.

"Don't touch me!" I scream and push him back. He stumbles to his feet. "Don't fucking touch me!"

Brendan is standing within the doorframe. His face hard and unreadable.

I stand. "Just don't touch me," I cry again. Grant holds his hands up, giving me space.

I bolt toward the door. Brendan backs away to allow me room to pass him.

Lance is in the hall. He flattens against the wall as I race by him.

"Lana!" Ashton hollers from farther down the corridor. I run up the stairs just as I hear her say, "Let me do this."

My feet can't move fast enough. Sobs fight to crawl out of my throat. I feel like I'm going to explode. I weave through the Court, branches scraping my arms. My feet stumble over uneven cobblestones. I don't stop, even when I'm released on the other side of the girls' dorm, continuing to sprint across the field.

I jump down to the cliff and fall to my knees on the rough surface. I slam my fist into it over and over again. I can't feel the pain, even when my skin splits and blood paints the stone. I choke on the cries that finally claw their way out from within my chest.

I lift my head and scream. The scream comes from somewhere so deep, so buried, I feel it in the darkest hollows of my soul. It extends across the water until it reaches the setting sun, where every last horrific shriek is captured and dragged down with it. And then it's gone. My demons are swept away with the wind.

I collapse.

My head falls upon a lap. Strong arms comfort me in my weakness. I'm enveloped by the warmth of her body protecting me. She rocks me, consoling. Absorbing my pain and making it her own.

"I'm sorry for what happened to you," she says in my ear. "For what he did to you." Because she knows. "I scream out his name too sometimes."

The name she screams may be different than mine. But he's still the same person. The one who didn't hear us say no. Who made me start punching first. The one who took away my beliefs. And then cast my curse upon me.

"I trusted you." My grandmother's final words. And that trust killed her.

Chapter Twenty

One day, Thaylina caught sight of the green cloak fluttering in the breeze as it darted between the trees. She followed it into the forest, her dagger strapped to her thigh. The huntress crept up upon the beast disguised as a man as he lulled a woman with a sultry song.

Ashton walks me back to the dorm. She won't let go of my hand, even though I keep promising her that I'm better. And I do feel better. Everyone really does need a screaming spot.

I hug Ashton and leave her outside my door, still wearing a worried expression. I try to smile to reassure her…but it's not very reassuring.

I'm too exhausted to do anything but shower and dress in a tank and shorts before crawling into bed. My brand-new bed. The room is spectacular, and I want to appreciate it more, but I can't even focus enough to take in all of the magnificence that Serge and Ashton put into the space.

I do know the bed is huge and feels like a cloud. I knock off the pile of pillows (an abundance of throw pillows must be a designer thing) and slip under the silky pale grey sheets. The duvet is silvery blue and is the softest thing ever. Above me, sheer curtains encase the bed, hung from poles attached to the ceiling. I leave the sheers open and lay on my side.

Small lights dance across the wall in a random pattern. They remind me of…

fireflies. I smile. I guess I'm glad that I do tell Ashton everything. Or everything pertaining to Grant anyway.

A plush navy-blue couch is pushed up against the wall with an oval, shiny-white coffee table in front of it, set upon a silvery-blue rug that matches the duvet.

A new desk replaces the old one in the same spot. This one is metallic silver, and it has an ornate bookcase attached to it, teetering toward the ceiling so high that it's tempting gravity.

Words are scattered in black upon the white walls in the most elegant calligraphy I've ever seen.

Honesty
Belief
Trust
Kindness
Boldness
Authenticity
Thoughtfulness
Honor
Loyalty
Respect
Confidence
Perception
Nobility
Perfection
Compassion

The curses. All of the ones I've revealed to Ashton, including who belonged to them. In the middle of all of our ruin are Squirrel's wise words. The same ones Grant repeated.

Love never hurts. Ever.

I laugh. She's not subtle, is she?

A knock jostles me from near sleep. "I swear I'm alright," I yell, knowing it's Ashton.

"Open up!" she demands.

I groan, crawling out of the comfort of the huge bed and turn on the light.

When I open the door, I blink. Standing behind Ashton are Brendan, Lance and…Grant.

"How—"

Before I can finish that sentence, Ashton pushes her way in. "We're having a sleepover. I call big spoon."

The guys slip by me with a nod hello. Grant stops in front of me and searches my eyes. When I smile weakly, he pulls me into him and hugs me tight. I feel like crying again, but don't have any more tears left. I bury my face in his chest and hug him back.

"I'm—"

"Don't say it," he tells me before I can apologize. His voice is firm like there's no room for argument. So I squeeze him tighter.

"Um, you might want to close the door before we get busted," Lance says, jumping up and landing in a sprawled position on the couch.

Grant closes the door.

"How did you guys get up here?" I ask, then look to Grant. "Especially you?"

"I just never left," he explains. "Lily drove us, so I told her to go without me. And…" He hesitates.

"We're sworn to secrecy," Lance explains.

I search for Brendan and he winks.

"Another one of your secret passages?"

"Wait. You know about them?" Lance asks, sounding insulted once again that he was left out.

"Long story," I say. "But you guys don't have to—"

"Shut it," Brendan growls. "We're here. We're staying. Get in bed so we can all cuddle."

"Wait. Uh." Grant leans in and whispers. "Is there somewhere private we can talk a second?"

I motion toward the door to the bathroom that I share with the room next to mine. Which is currently empty.

"We don't want to hear you having sex!" Ashton hollers.

Grant's eyes widen.

"He doesn't find toilets seductive," I reply with a cheeky grin. "I already tried that."

Grant laughs, recalling the day he walked in on me drying off boob sweat in the ninth hole shack's bathroom.

The guys don't get it, so they just eye me like I'm crazy. Ashton laughs because of course she knows. Except now that I re-examine their faces, Brendan's looking at *Grant* like he's crazy. I shake my head at him and follow Grant into the bathroom.

The first thing he does is turn on the light.

"Is this okay?" he asks, scanning the small bathroom that houses a shower and toilet.

"Yeah," I assure him with an appreciative smile. "Just keep the light on."

"I'm deathly afraid of spiders, just so you know. Your claustrophobia has nothing on my reaction to finding one of those *things* on me."

He evokes a laugh, which I know is what he was trying to do. To help me feel better about my panic attack in the library.

I love this guy. Dammit. Stupid Squirrel and his magical brownies.

Grant's eyes narrow, looking down at my hand. Then they widen in alarm. He gently cradles my right hand and examines it. It's red, swollen, and scraped raw. "Can you bend your fingers?"

"Not right now. It's throbbing and feels like it's on fire, but I don't think it's broken." I don't tell him that I've fractured my hand before…and my wrist—which forced me to learn how to throw a punch properly.

"Have you iced it?"

I shake my head.

Grant sticks his head out of the bathroom. "Ashton, do you have ice or ice packs?"

I don't hear Ashton's answer before Grant closes the door again. "Guess it was too much anger for a phone call, huh?"

"Yeah." My answer is hushed. "Way too much."

"I'd hate to see whatever took the brunt of it." He smiles softly.

"It didn't move, so I kind of lost this fight."

"But did you?" he asks, his blue eyes peering right into me. "I mean, do you feel…any better?"

"I do." And there's more honesty in those two words than I can possibly relay. But I know he sees it in my eyes.

"Good." He shifts uncomfortably before continuing. "This could probably wait, but part of me doesn't feel like it should."

I'm silent.

"Lily and I used to date."

I lean back against the wall, needing to brace myself.

"I didn't tell you because of your rule. When you first told me about it, I wasn't sure what to do because we were still just flirting. And I really didn't know if you and Lily were friends. I mean, I knew you weren't before you came to Blackwood because I would have heard about you. So, I wasn't positive if it still applied. Because you *weren't* friends with her when we dated." He's nervously over-explaining. It's so fricken endearing and cute. I decide to put him out of his misery, shutting his mouth with my lips.

Grant wraps his arms around me and holds me close, like he's thanking me with a hug. I pull away before the kiss can progress. "I know. Parker told me today."

He leans back a bit. "I'm *trying* not to be the crazed jealous guy, but can you please explain you and the Harrison brothers? I spoke to Wil—"

"You what?" I interrupt.

"Yeah, the night of your birthday. He asked if he could crash at Stefan's. Said something about…" He closes his eyes in realization. I raise my brows to encourage him to continue. He sighs. "He said it was probably *safer*. Just realized what that meant." I bite my lip, knowing exactly what that meant too. "Anyway, I told him I was interested in you, and that I knew the two of you had history. And I wanted to be sure it was okay, that it wouldn't affect our friendship or make it strained between him and you."

"You did that?" I ask in shock.

"Yeah, of course. I thought it was the right thing to do. And that's why I told Lily about you today. I needed her to know that…well, how I felt. She and I dated for a long time, and I still care about her, so I needed to be honest with her."

"Your curse…" I shake my head in disbelief. "And could Lily and I be any more opposite? Are you sure you're not rebounding?"

Grant laughs. "Really?" I nod. He becomes serious. "No. I'm not. We broke it off last December. And the *reason* we decided to end things is because she wasn't being honest with me. She was shutting me out, and I didn't know why."

"You *both* decided to end things, not just her?"

"We talked about it and decided together after I told her I felt disconnected. She wouldn't explain what was happening with her. I knew it had to do with her family. But it was impossible to be there for her, to be a part of her life, if she refused to confide in me. And I need that. Honesty is really important to me."

"You'd prefer full, unabridged, blatant, sometimes cruel, and always sarcastic honesty?"

"Completely," Grant says flashing me his gorgeous smile.

"You may be an idiot," I tell him, chuckling.

He laughs, hard. A deep, rumbling laughter. "I'm an idiot? So does that mean, you are too?"

I crinkle my eyes in confusion.

"The first time we spoke, you said you'd have to be an idiot to fall—"

"Oh!" I stop him. "Oh!" My lungs just collapsed. "Uh…" I take a deep breath.

"Um."

He laughs at my inability to say a single coherent word. "Lana, I'm confessing. I *am* an idiot."

"O-kay." My breathing is labored—my heart is constricting airflow because it's beating so fast…in my throat. "Anyway,"—the worst segue ever after he just confessed to being in love with me—"Parker and I are close, but we're just friends. The Harrisons, the whole family, have this weird protective gene, and they look out for me, for reasons unknown. I'm kind of stuck with them."

Allowing my awkward change of subject to slide, Grant asks, "That's why Lance is your chaperone?"

"Yeah. His father—"

I'm interrupted by a loud bang on the door. "Get dressed! I need to use the bathroom," Brendan bellows from the other side.

"Hold it for one more minute!" I yell back.

"What's his story?" Grant asks, nodding toward the door.

"He's a necessary evil."

Grant chuckles. Then he leans down and kisses me gently. "Let's ice your hand."

When we emerge, Ashton and Brendan look disappointed that we aren't flushed and disheveled. Lance just eyes Grant warily, like he's trying to decide if his intentions are honorable. Seriously, the overprotective brother vibe is getting worse. I think he's forgotten that he's a year *younger* than me.

I crawl on the bed next to Ashton and she places the ice pack on my hand with a pained expression, securing it with an Ace bandage. She has me take a couple ibuprofen too. "If it doesn't look better in the morning, we should go to the clinic for x-rays."

"They have an x-ray machine on campus?" I ask in surprise.

"Of course," Ashton answers. "They want to keep all medical information sealed, or as much as possible. The press loves that stuff."

"And I thought Printz-Lee was big on privacy."

"Oh, you have no idea," Lance tells him, his head propped on a throw pillow with a blanket that I've never seen before covering him. "I claim the couch, by the way. No way I want to be anywhere near that bed with the four of you in it."

"Lance!" I scold. "We're not—"

"Speak for yourself," Brendan says, washing his hands at the pedestal sink.

"Keep your pants on," I tell him, my tone threatening.

"C'mon," Ashton beckons, pulling the blanket back. "I already called big spoon, so get in here, Lana."

Grant takes off his shoes and socks and crawls across to the far side against the wall in shorts and a t-shirt. Brendan turns off the lights and I slide in next to Grant, facing him, while Ashton takes her big spoon position behind me. And I don't want to think about Brendan on the other side of her. We all fit...barely.

"Your room is pretty amazing." Grant is focused on the ceiling. I tilt my head up to see tiny lights blinking like shining stars above the bed.

"Ashton did it for me," I tell him. She squeezes me with her arm draped around my waist.

"Do you like it?" she asks, almost sounding nervous, which is so not like her. A swarm of guilt overtakes me. I should have said something to her a long time ago.

"I love it. Thank you. I still haven't seen everything, but it's incredible."

Grant sits up as he notices the far wall. "Are those?" He doesn't finish. He sees the fireflies. Or I *think* that's what he's looking at. There's a lot to take in, but there's not much light to see anything else.

Ashton giggles.

"You know?" Grant asks, settling down beside me.

"I know everything. So get used to it."

Grant laughs.

"Everything?" Brendan asks anxiously, and I want to throttle him. At the same time, Lance demands, "Know what?"

"I hope so," Ashton sounds alarmed. "What don't I know?"

"What don't *I* know?" Lance echoes. "What the hell?"

I can't open my mouth. My silence is Brendan's assurance that I haven't told Ashton anything he and I agreed not to, so he answers, "You both know everything you're supposed to."

I hear Lance grumble, dissatisfied with that response.

"Why did Ashton redecorate your room?" Grant asks.

Now we're all silent.

"Why, what happened?" He leans up on his elbow, searching for someone to answer him.

"I'll tell you tomorrow," I assure him, setting my hand on his shoulder to coax him back down.

"There's a lot I don't know, isn't there? You four have a thing between you, like some sort of bond that connects you?" Grant questions, recognizing something I hadn't. But he's right. We are bonded by something inexplicable. Maybe fate brought us together…but that would mean I'd have to believe in it.

"I thought *I* was cursed with *Perception*," Brendan says.

"How do you—" but I stop myself from asking him how he knows about the curses—Ashton told him.

"Is this what girls do when they have sleepovers?" Lance asks from the couch. "Say they're going to sleep, but then talk all night?"

"Are we keeping you up past your bedtime?" Brendan mocks.

"You're still on my suspect list," Lance calls to him.

"Suspect list?" Grant asks.

We all say together, "Tomorrow." And then laugh.

Grant shifts so he's facing me and takes ahold of my uninjured hand. His eyes focus on mine, and they shine in the twinkling light. I want to lean over and kiss him, but prefer not to open that door with Ashton and Brendan behind me. So we just lay there, speaking silently with subtle twitches of our lips, a quirk of a brow, and gleam in our eyes. Until one of us, I don't know who does it first, closes their eyes and drifts to sleep.

Within the protection of the big spoon, with Brendan and Lance breathing heavily in the background, and Grant's hand firmly gripping mine, I whisper, "I'm an idiot too."

I crack an eye open to see Grant's lips curve into a brilliant smile.

With the sun faintly shimmering through the windows, I squint to find Ashton staring at me. Grant has taken over the big spoon position behind me, and Brendan is a sloppy spoon with an arm thrown around Ashton and his face planted in the pillow behind her.

She smiles brightly when I blink awake, a little freaked that she's been watching us sleep.

"Sorry if I have morning breath," she whispers.

"I can't smell it, but you may want to stay where you are just in case."

As quietly as she can, she half-mouths and half-whispers, "I love this." She nods toward me and Grant cuddled together. "I'm trying really hard not to use the word *together*. But seriously, get over it."

I try to contain my laughter so I don't wake Grant.

I look over at her and Brendan. I adore her. Him, not so much. So I don't understand his appeal. "Pretend they're not here and answer honestly. What do you like about Brendan? Because I don't get it."

"He can be the sweetest, most thoughtful person when he's not being an egotistical asshole. But nice guys aren't my thing, remember?" Ashton makes a scrunched up face when he squeezes her waist, fighting to hold in her squeal. When she opens her eyes again, she asks, "What do you like about Grant?"

"That he's not capable of being an egotistical asshole."

I can feel his breathy laugh as his chest shakes behind me.

"What do you like about me?!" Lance shouts. Apparently everyone's awake and listening.

"Pretend you didn't hear him," Ashton whispers loudly. I smile. She raises her voice. "So Lana, what do you like about Lance?"

I speak so Lance can overhear every word. "Um... I guess that he doesn't screw over his friends, and the friend he does screw, he's super sweet to and would never do anything to hurt. Because he's noble and will protect her from getting hurt."

Lance groans. "Kaely knows how I feel. So butt out."

Ashton and I laugh.

"You *are* protective of your friends, aren't you?" Grant whispers.

"Ssshh," Ashton hisses. "You're not here."

The room fills with groggy laughter.

"We should go," Brendan announces, rolling off the bed. Ashton protests when he moves away. He leans down and kisses her cheek. "We need to be out of here before the rest of campus wakes." Then he randomly adds, "And why the hell is Lance's curse *Nobility* and Grant's is *Integrity*, while I'm stuck with *Perception?*" He sounds seriously upset by this.

"I don't make them up," I tell him. "You are the professional stalker after all."

"What?" Grant pokes his head around my shoulder to glare at Brendan.

"She's kidding," Brendan says in attempt to put Grant at ease.

"Not really," Lance chimes in.

"I'll explain later." I kiss Grant's hand. "But you guys really should go. I'm already in trouble."

"Why?" Grant questions with concern.

"Wow, you really don't tell him anything, do you?" Brendan accuses. I shoot him a threatening look, and he reveals his arrogant smirk.

Grant kisses my forehead and crawls out of the bed. His hair is rumpled, as is his shirt. I think he may look even more amazing first thing in the morning, all mussed up. Even more than he did in his suit. Well, maybe not.

"Are you undressing him with your mind?" Ashton asks. I reach up to cover her mouth with my hand. But because it's my left hand, I end up swatting her in the forehead.

"Ow!" she exclaims. "What was that for?"

Grant chuckles. "You guys are…I don't even know. I'm glad I got to see it though." He directs his attention to me. "Are you working at the club this afternoon or at the event tonight?"

"Tonight," I answer, hopeful he says the same.

"Me too!" Ashton exclaims.

"I think we all are," Brendan says, but then looks to Lance. "Except pretty boy over here. How did you get out of work—" Then he shuts up, realizing we have a new person in the room who doesn't know we all have court fees or fines to work off. Blackwood's privacy policies keep the rest of the world from knowing the truth about the requirements for being accepted here. I don't think Grant knows either.

Grant realizes that Brendan has stopped talking because of him. "Is this another thing you're going to explain later?" he asks me.

I look around at everyone, asking for permission.

"Only if you're a keeper," Lance stipulates.

My eyes widen. "What?"

"He doesn't get to know unless you two are serious. If he wants in on the group, and our secrets, he can't be a fling."

Everyone stares at me for the answer, including Grant.

"I'll talk to you tonight, okay?" I confirm, not agreeing to anything. He nods.

After the guys leave, I face Ashton, biting at my lip nervously. "What do I tell him?

She shrugs like it's a simple answer. "The truth."

Chapter Twenty-One

The beast did not see the girl creeping within the shadows, too enthralled with the milky white skin before him. Just as the beast bared his fanged teeth to taste the woman's flesh, Thaylina struck. Her blade sunk deep, penetrating his blackened heart. The beast's eyes widened in surprise.

The event at the country club is a wedding. I didn't even know they held wedding receptions here, but I've never been on the event side of the Clubhouse either.

It's the first wedding I've ever been to, and it's…a lot for a cynic to take in. Watching the newly married couple dance, the family drink and celebrate. Everyone's so…happy. Well, there are a few people seated at the farthest tables who are miserable and drunk. Which is probably why they're seated in Siberia. But for the most part, the room is filled with laughter and joy. If I were still the girl, before the magical brownies, I might go all Maleficent in here and scream that it's all a lie. That their marriage won't last longer than it takes for the bride to change her name on her credit cards.

Can't say I'm a converted *believer*, exactly. Yes, I kinda-sorta confessed to Grant that I was in love with him. But that doesn't mean I'm sold on happily-ever-after, or that love conquers all. I still don't trust it not to go to shit.

"Weddings turn me on, so bad," Ashton confesses as we watch the couple cut the cake and feed each other.

"Are you sure it's not the three tiers of chocolate cake?" I tease.

"Well, that too. But it's so…romantic."

I try to hide my cringe.

"Really? I thought we conquered this phobia."

"Sorry. It's involuntary." Speaking of romantic phobias. "Where's Brendan?"

"Valeting." Her eyes brighten. "I think I need a fifteen-minute break."

This time I don't hide my cringe. "Please bring sanitizer wipes with you."

All of the servers are signaled to go back into the kitchen. "Need everyone in the kitchen for cake service," I'm told by Nancy, the event manager.

I pass the room off the dining room where the bar is located. Stefan and Grant are behind it, serving and chatting with guests. Grant looks up just as I pass and smiles. I don't know how he knows, it's like he can sense when I'm nearby or something. I beam back at him, because…I'm an idiot.

I *can't look at Ashton* too long when she returns, not without making the most revolted face ever. She's seriously glowing, and her eyes are even sparkling.

"I want to be a good friend and ask about you and Brendan, but at the same time, I don't think my stomach can handle it."

"What's with you two, anyway? You act like children around each other."

"He's just…" I stick out my tongue in revulsion. "Gross." She laughs.

Grant appears behind us. "Hey." We make room for him to stand between us, adhering to the "don't turn your back on the guests" rule that has been drilled into us all night. "So Nancy offered to cut me, and I told her I was giving you a ride back to school." I glance up at his mischievous grin. "Want to get out of here?"

"Can I?" I ask Ashton. She picks up on my concern. I don't have a chaperone, aka Lance, to do whatever he's supposed to do when he's chaperoning. Which is basically yell at me when I punch douchebags and laugh at me when I get high. So he's useless, and I'm more apt to do the right thing when I'm with Grant than any of the Harrison boys. I've basically just talked myself into leaving with Grant.

Ashton thinks for a minute. "I'll have Brendan text you when we leave," she tells Grant. "That way you can arrive around the same time we do. We'll just tell them you had to stay a little after to clean something. I don't know. Brendan's better at this, but we'll lie."

"Thank you." I hug her. "You're my *favorite* liar."

"Bring sanitizer wipes with you," she calls after me. I make a face at her and follow Grant to the computer to clock out.

"What does that mean?" he asks. "Was she making a sex comment?"

My cheeks flush. "Sort of."

"I don't really get it," he admits.

"It was a bad joke," I tell him.

"Do you want to go back to the firefly field? I still have the blanket in my car."

"Only if you let me drive."

"Uh, do you have a license?"

"No. But I know how to drive."

He hesitates. "You don't know how to swim, but you know how to drive?"

"Do you really want to know how I learned to drive?"

"Was it illegal?"

"Yes."

"Maybe I shouldn't know. Not yet." And with a heavy exhale, he pulls out his keys. "How's your hand?"

"Sore but fine. Won't affect my driving, I swear," I reply eagerly.

"And you know how to drive stick?"

I nod, my eyes twinkling. He sets the keys in my hand, holds on to them for a contemplative second, and finally releases them. I throw my arms around him and squeal like Kaely.

"Why are you two still here?" Nancy asks. "If you don't want to be cut—"

"We're leaving right now," Grant announces.

"I'll meet you in the parking lot," I tell him as I enter the event locker room to change.

Grant tries to remain calm when we pull out of the parking lot. It takes me a few gear changes to get used to his clutch. He traps his commentary behind pursed lips with every grind of the gears and jolt of the car. But I figure it out fast enough, and we fly through the wooded roads, the day settling into twilight. Grant probably wouldn't have agreed to let me drive if it were already dark.

He soon figures out that I need more notice than a "turn here" if he doesn't want to be forced to grip the outside of the door as I squeal around the corner. When we finally reach the firefly field, he visibly exhales like he hasn't been breathing the entire car ride.

"Who taught you to drive?" he asks, stepping out of the car and taking another deep breath to settle his nerves.

"Um, I did," I tell him. "You want to know the rest?"

"Give it to me," he says, bracing himself.

"One of my best friend's brothers used to steal cars, just to take them on joy rides. Sometimes we were with him. And sometimes he'd let us drive."

"You had a very interesting childhood, didn't you, Lana?" he replies, trying to make light of it. I can't tell if he's honestly this easy-going about my illegal escapades or he's hiding his shock really well. I still question if this much honesty is good for him. Or me.

"Maybe you shouldn't hear too much more about my colorful life," I tell him. He retrieves the blanket from the trunk and takes my hand to walk out into the field. "Grant, you realize you and I are from complete opposite worlds, right? I mean, they write stories and stupid movies based on characters like us. We couldn't be any more cliché if we tried."

He spreads the blanket on the ground and sits, waiting for me to join him. "Why? Because I come from a stable home, and yours is a little more…free-spirited?"

"That was the nicest way of describing my insane life that I've ever heard," I say, laughing. "Then again, it's kind of what Ashton said when she called us unrated."

He gives me a questioning look. "Basically the same thing," I tell him. "My mother and I don't have the typical parental relationship. Maybe because she was so young when she had me. Or maybe because I pretty much grew up overnight." I shiver.

Grant swaths me in an embrace and rubs my arms to warm me up, thinking I'm cold.

"I had to help pay the bills after my grandmother died, so it's been a crazy few years. And my tendency to get into fights hasn't helped with the crazy."

"But you have people who care about you, right? Your mom? Your friends?"

"I do. My mom is a kind and generous person. I worry about people taking advantage of her. I love her, so I do what I can to protect her."

"Shouldn't it be the other way around?"

"Maybe in your story. But in mine, we look out for each other. And since I tend to be more cynical and distrusting, I end up protecting her from herself."

"What do you mean?"

"My mother's curse is *Belief*. She believes true love will find her. But that's never going to happen. I've watched her believe she's found *the one* so many times. But he ends up breaking her heart, leaving a little less of her behind each time. Eventually, there's not going to be any of her left to give to anyone."

Grant is quiet.

I wonder if I've finally said too much. But he did say he prefers honesty… even if it's unfiltered.

"So these curses, they're the thing we want the most?"

"Essentially. It's the virtue we value above all others. *Honesty* is my curse, so I can't lie, but I don't trust easily either. Yours is *Integrity*, because you always do what's morally honorable."

"But why are they curses?"

"Because they're also our weaknesses. For example…Maybe someday you'll be forced to make an impossible decision that challenges your integrity. But then that choice is hard to live with."

"And you…other than not trusting easily?"

"The truth is already ruining my life. It's the reason I'm at Blackwood." I quickly add before Grant can question me, "Please don't ask me about it. I can't tell you."

"It's that bad?"

"It's one of a few truths I need to protect. Hopefully not always, but for now."

"Protect?" he ponders, almost to himself. "So it has to do with someone else." I remain silent.

"You don't see the world, and probably don't even live it, the way the rest of us do."

I strip a blade of grass from the ground and suddenly find it riveting.

"That's why I'm so drawn to you, you know? You're honest with who you are. No apologies. No excuses. You're different than everyone I've ever known. You said you have a colorful life, and that's just it…you *are* colorful. Every single one. I don't know how else to describe it." He laughs. "You told me you're more honest with me than anyone, and I'm not sure why that is, but I *want* to hear your truths."

"For now," I warn. "Grant, knowing the truth isn't always a good thing."

He contemplates this for a moment. "But it's not the wrong thing either."

"Did you lick the batter from Squirrel's brownie bowl? Because you're opening up a whole other conversation that I may need another brownie to participate in."

Grant laughs. "I just mean, it is what it is. Either you accept it, deal with it, forgive it…or you don't. It's pretty much that simple."

"You really have been hanging out with Squirrel too much," I tease.

Grant dips me so I'm facing him. "I trust you." I stare at him, dumbfounded. "What?"

"I trust you." He lowers me so my head is on his lap and I'm looking up at him. He runs a finger along my cheek, sweeping loose hairs away.

"Where did that come from?"

"I don't know. But I needed you to know." He smiles down at me. "So you really don't believe in true love?"

"True love? What does that even mean? I can barely even say the word love without vomiting in my mouth."

Grant laughs. "Wow. Okay."

I sit up to really connect with him as I explain.

"I don't know...I don't think *true love* exists. It's all an illusion we're sold in bookstores and movie theatres to keep us hoping for our own happily-ever-after ending. To convince us that love is all we need."

"Are you going to start singing?" He chuckles.

I shove at him playfully. "Anyway, I didn't believe in it."

"Didn't? And now?"

"Well...after the magical brownie ride, I heard what Squirrel said. His explanation made more sense, and I can't believe I'm saying *that*. But it did. More than anything else I've been fed. When he said love isn't something we're given outside of ourselves. That we don't need anyone else to experience it, because... we are it—I understood that. I just wish he could have called it something different. Because everyone else's *love* gets all tangled up in romantic gestures and waiting for someone to come rescue them. I've seen what that can do to a person."

"Your mother?" he asks quietly.

I nod. "I won't be her." I let out a slow breath. "True love is bullshit."

Grant's deep, raw laughter, that I adore so much, rumbles around us. "Then I'll just remain an idiot." I smile at him. He glances at me affectionately. "If it really bothers you, I won't say it."

I swallow. "Doesn't this feel like it's happening too fast? We've only known each other a few weeks. How can we know it's real?"

Grant looks out at the fireflies and watches them for a bit. I fear I've been *too* honest again. I don't want to dismiss whatever is happening between us, because I know it's *something*. I'm overcome by it, and even though the word *love* drives me insane because of its commercial misuse, I know that's where this connection comes from. But…it's only been a few weeks, so how is it possible? How can I honestly believe it'll last? How do I know it'll be strong enough to withstand anything? Even something as simple as the start of the school year?

"How long have you known Ashton?" he asks, still focused on the fireflies.

"As long as I've known you."

"And you tell her things, right? You trust her with your truths?"

"Most of them."

He turns toward me. "But you care about her. Feel protective of her. If you used the word, you maybe even…love her?"

I nod slightly.

"It's the same amount of time as you've known me. So why is it different? When you're connected to someone, time doesn't matter. It can feel like you've known them forever. And even though I don't know your details, like when you lost your first tooth, or your favorite ice cream flavor, I know *you*. The rest is just…well, details. The most important thing is that feeling I have that lets me know that I can trust you. That you're a good person. That allows me to see through your cynicism and recognize that you really do believe in love. You just don't like what other people have done to abuse it.

"We're connected, Lana, and despite where we came from, who are parents are, or what we were doing a month ago, it brought us here…together. And that's pretty fricken amazing if you ask me. Because I didn't know you even existed until a few weeks ago. But the moment I met you, it was like you've *always* existed in my life. You always belonged there. So we don't have to say love, but I *feel* it."

My chest is thumping so hard, I wonder if he can hear it.

His words linger in the air between us. They come from a place so real and honest, it's like I can reach out and touch them, hold every letter in the palm of my hand and believe in them.

"I feel it too."

I don't just say the words, I give them back. I want him to hold them too. To believe as much as I do.

I reach up and brush my fingers along the sculpted lines of his jaw, over the definition of his cheekbones, and through his hair. He blinks his eyes closed, absorbing it. I lean in and taste his lips. Gentle and soft, a breath of a kiss. He inhales a broken gasp. His hands cup my sides, leaning me into him until I have to adjust, placing my knees on either side of his thighs. His eyes ease open as if he's been dreaming—they look into me, through me, beyond me.

My heartbeat has taken over my entire body, pulsing and thrumming through my core to my toes. Our eyes remain locked for a slow inhale, then I close mine and find his mouth again, pressing harder, running my tongue along the tender give of his lower lip. His hands slide across my back and cradle me like I am the most precious thing they've ever held. I can feel his pulse pounding in time with mine. His lips skim along the sensitive flesh of my jaw to my neck, nipping at the beating under my skin. My hands slide into his hair and I move into him, closer, tighter.

He lowers me onto my back, gazes down at me, observing, admiring, searching. I am exposed beneath his stare, but I don't shy away. I let him see me, because this is the truth. And as he said, it can't be changed. His mouth captures mine, our pace increases. Our wanting becomes need. His hand skates along my hemline. He pulls back before he removes the fabric. "Is this okay?"

"Yes."

He lifts it over my head. And before he can ask, I remove the bra as well. His hands are warm; his tongue is gentle. I reach for the edges of his shirt and ask, "Is this okay?"

He grins and answers, "Yes." So I pull it over his head. He is smooth and hard lines, dips and grooves. I run my hands over every inch, and then my lips follow. Our mouths meet in our exploration. His heart covers mine, flesh to flesh, beat to beat. I swear they are talking, communicating, conspiring, belonging. Light pumps through them and into every cell of my being.

When I reach for his button, I hesitate, seeking permission. But before I can ask, he answers. "Not yet." Instead, he lays beside me and cradles me against his chest and I listen to his heart pound against my ear.

"I trust you too," I tell him and kiss the spot where his heart tells me the truth.

Chapter Twenty-Two

As the beast lay dead upon the forest floor, Thaylina bent down over his body. She did not see a handsome face, or a charming smile. Only the truth of what he was, a horrific monster. She lowered her mouth to his deadened ear and hissed, "I wanted this."

I **groan at the annoying beeping,** wanting to stay lost in my dream—flashes of fireflies and…well, Grant.

Please come to the front office of the administration building immediately.

That's not a good message to wake up to.

Within a second, my thoughts jump to my mother. That she's hurt or sick or something bad has happened.

I scramble out of bed, still disoriented, and start throwing on clothes. With my shirt half over my head, it occurs to me that maybe they have my drug results. My movements slow. Isn't it too soon for the results? I've never had a blood test before, but it *seems* fast.

Whatever the reason, I'm pretty sure it's going to suck. And as soon as I enter Dr. Kendall's black and white throne room, I'm positive it will.

Seated in front of her desk is Niall. And standing off to the side, looking miserable with his arms crossed, is Mr. Garner. His eyes flash to me quickly before continuing to scowl at the floor.

Niall stands when I enter, his expression stoic and controlled as usual. And Dr. Kendall has her lips pursed, accentuating the expression lines around her mouth, cracking her plastic veneer.

I look from one to the other and am tempted to walk back out of the room.

"Have a seat, Miss Peri," Dr. Kendall instructs, her sugary demeanor cast aside.

Crap.

Niall remains standing until I'm seated. I shift uncomfortably, waiting for my world to end.

"Let's get right to it," Dr. Kendall says, folding her hands on top of her desk. "It's been reported that you were off-campus without the required chaperone last night."

I close my eyes and silently curse. Seriously?! I just had the most amazing night of my life, and I'm getting punished for it. What the hell, karma? What did I do to deserve this…this time?

"We understand that you were released early from work, but instead of coming directly back to the school, you were…somewhere else for several hours."

"But I returned at the same time as everyone else," I say in weak defense. "And I didn't do anything wrong during that time."

"That's up for interpretation," she snaps. "You are given specific guidelines to adhere to for your safety. And one of those stipulations is that you are not to leave campus unaccompanied except when you're at work."

I want to argue that I *was* accompanied, but bringing Grant into this, no matter how stellar his character, isn't the best idea. The last thing I want is to get him into trouble because *they* believe I need a fricken babysitter. And that sitter actively violates the code daily. But Lance isn't at fault either. It's their stupid logic that's to blame.

"Right," I say. "I screwed up. I left work. I didn't come directly back here. I wasn't with an approved chaperone. But I also didn't steal, take drugs, have sex, or get in a fight. That's an improvement, right? I'm sure Mr. Garner will agree that it's a huge step in the right direction for me."

Mr. Garner clears his throat to smother a laugh. Dr. Kendall shoots him a scathing glance. Niall just breathes in deep and releases it through his nose.

"The fact that you didn't get arrested or impregnated is not a victory, Miss Peri," Dr. Kendall scolds.

"Are you sure? I'm pretty impressed with myself," I say with an arrogant shrug.

Dr. Kendall's face turns as red as her hair.

"Lana, this might be one of those times to practice the silence you're usually so good at," Niall advises calmly. "Dr. Kendall, I understand why the guidelines are in place and respect them. But Lana is admitting she made a poor choice, and she didn't participate in any transgressions while unsupervised. We have a reputable individual who can account for that, if necessary. So, what can we do to rectify this situation?"

I stare at Niall, my brow raised. Mr. Garner appears just as awed.

Dr. Kendall runs a hand over her skirt, composing herself. "All off-campus access will be denied, including her work program, for the rest of the month."

"What the—"

Mr. Garner has come around to stand behind me and places a hand on my shoulder, easing me back into my seat. "That's fair."

She glowers up at him. "And I suggest you better acquaint yourself with our life advisor script, Mr. Garner. I hold you directly responsible for her actions."

He presses his lips together and nods. "Of course."

I *am* going to get him fired. Shit.

"Thank you, Dr. Kendall," Niall says, standing and ushering me to the door. Mr. Garner is just as eager to escape, striding alongside me. "I'm going to speak with Lana before I leave. I'm confident this will be the only time we'll have to address this or any other matter."

When we reach the foyer, Mr. Garner turns to Niall. "I'm so sorry, Niall. I know you entrusted me with Lana's care...I don't know what to say. Other than, I'll keep a better watch over her."

"It's okay, Isaac. You can only do so much. Trust me, I know." Niall shoots me a side-eye glare.

I fight the urge to roll my eyes at them both. "I can take care of myself."

"No you can't," they say in unison.

"I'll be in touch," Niall tells Mr. Garner. Then to me, "Lana, a word." He walks toward the doors of the sitting room. I follow with shoulders bowed.

"I know you're used to having your freedom and doing what you want, but that's also the reason you're here. You have a lot more freedom here than you would in juvenile detention, and you know it. So I suggest you start abiding by their rules. Blackwood has a very limited tolerance for insubordination. You already have a list of minor infractions, and now a major one, within only a few weeks. You have to be more responsible, Lana."

"I really didn't do anything wrong last night," I say earnestly.

"I know who you were with, and I know the Philips family. Grant's a responsible individual, and I can only hope that he's more of a positive influence on you than you are a negative one on him."

I open my mouth to take offense when he says, "I approve of him, Lana. He's good for you. And if you can do what's expected of you until school starts, I'll request that he be allowed to escort you off-campus."

Hearing him *approve* of Grant, felt...fatherly. It definitely didn't sound like my lawyer talking. And now I don't have any words. None. I just stare at him with my mouth gaping open.

Niall gives me a rare smile.

"Um," I say, regaining my ability to speak. "Have you heard from my mother? I keep missing her. I want to make sure she's okay."

His eyes shift down solemnly.

"What?" I hold my breath.

"She fainted at work the other night. But she's okay. Olivia's arranged to take her to see her doctor next week to follow up."

I close my eyes and sigh. "So she's *not* okay."

"We don't know that for certain. She says she feels fine. Blamed it on not eating."

"She's lying," I tell him.

"That's why Olivia is going, to make sure she keeps this appointment. I'll let you know if there's anything to be concerned about. For now, do what you have to do. Stop messing up, Lana. There's only so much I can do to save you."

There's a knock at my door within seconds of hanging up from my nightly security check-in.

"I'm here to break you out," Brendan announces, stepping into my room. I know his timed appearance isn't a coincidence. Our government seriously needs to hire him, before another country's does—because if they get him first, we're screwed.

"You know?" Then I shake my head at my stupidity. "Of course you do. I can't get caught leaving my room."

"I won't let that happen."

As much as I don't trust him, I do believe him. "Where are we going?"

"My room. Roundtable meeting with the middle Harrison prince."

"You did not just equate yourself with a knight, did you?"

"I am rescuing you right now, aren't I?"

"Or kidnapping me."

"Hey, you don't have to come. You're the one who wants answers." He hesitates a second before adding, "But I have to warn you that this passage is long, narrow and really dark. I have a flashlight, but I'm not sure if it'll be enough."

I study him. His face doesn't reveal anything, like maybe he's genuinely concerned about me. But the fact that he's warning me about what could happen if I go with him, says enough.

"You can squeeze the shit out of my hand if it'll help. But just don't punch me. You hurt."

I release a small laugh. He holds out his hand and I take it.

Brendan pokes his head out of my room, checking the hall in both directions before he pulls me out after him, having taped my latch open so it won't click shut. We walk briskly to the end of the corridor on my side of the grand staircase. In the few seconds it takes for me to check over my shoulder and turn back to him, a section of the wall has swung open.

"Ready?" Brendan asks, giving my hand a firm squeeze. I nod. He turns on a flashlight and illuminates a steep, narrow stone staircase. I step down to allow him to close the passage, then grab his hand again. This stairwell is as narrow as the one that led up to the Quiet Room; the wall is so close I can feel my breath bounce back. My chest is heaving by the time we reach the next small landing. "How are you doing?"

"Distract me," I rasp, my forehead prickling with sweat. "Tell me something about you. Anything, no matter how stupid."

"I love how you assume anything about me will be stupid."

I laugh, or wheeze.

"Did you," I take in a couple short of breaths, "ever leave Nantucket before here?"

"Save your air, Princess. Don't want you passing out before we get to my room. And to answer your question, yes. I didn't remain trapped on the island like my mother. Mostly went to Boston or New York. Flew to London last summer. My grandmother is protective but trusting. She caught on early enough that I wasn't someone to be contained. So she pressed some morals upon me and hoped they'd stick."

"They didn't," I mutter.

He stops and pulls my arm so I'm right up against him. "But I make up for it in morale. I'm very good at everything I do."

I shove him forward. He releases a menacing chuckle and continues down the steep staircase that turns at sharp angles. I know we have to descend five floors, but it feels like we're entering the bowels of hell the farther we go down. The air becomes colder and feels so heavy, it's like I can taste the decay with each labored breath.

My body shivers when the frigid temperature collides with my damp skin. "Are you sure you're not going to murder me and leave me down here with your collection?"

"No. You're too fun to play with," he answers. "Stay close."

I grip his forearm with my free hand and huddle up against him.

"Talk to me," I beg, tripping over my feet which refuse to move properly. I want to close my eyes to stop the spinning, but then I know I'll fall. I don't want to be down here. I'm not sure how much more I can take before I'm lost to the panic again.

"You're a pretty fascinating person, Lana Peri." I can hardly hear him with my pulse roaring in my ears. My shoulder scrapes against wet, slimy stone and I bite back a scream. "With everything life has thrown at you, you know how to take care of yourself. Hell, I wouldn't want to be trapped in a dark alley with you." He laughs. "Oh, wait. We are."

I punch his arm.

"Dammit, woman! Stop punching me. You're a hell of a lot stronger than your little spritely size might indicate."

"Then stop saying stupid things," I choke out.

Finally, we start climbing up a different set of stairs. My body is racked with the shakes. I have to stop.

"Hold," I draw in air, but it's like I'm breathing through a straw, "on." I bend over, trying to inflate my lungs.

Brendan lifts me up and throws me over his shoulder. "Let's get you out of here." I don't try to resist, even though having his hands on me right now is causing my body to quake. I fight every instinctive defense that's screaming at me to kick and punch him. So I squeeze my eyes shut, clench my fists and concentrate on the sound of his footsteps.

He's swift, easily moving up the confined stairway as if I weren't slung over his shoulder. I can feel the sinewy muscles along his back, taut and lean. Guess eating like a middle-aged man pays off.

He sets me down on a cool, supple leather surface. When I open my eyes, black circles float before them. I sway in the seat, afraid I might pass out. Bending forward between my knees, I concentrate on breathing.

"Here, drink this." Brendan holds out a glass in front of me. I shoot it down and cough instantly. The fiery liquid burns the entire way down.

"Thanks," I say between coughs. "I didn't need my throat."

"You going to be okay?"

I lean back and wait for my pulse to return to normal. My eyes slowly shift up to meet his. He's standing above me, dressed in dark slacks and a grey shirt, looking like he's ready for a GQ photoshoot, not like he just emerged from a dungeon.

"Yeah."

"He's dead, you know."

I don't have to ask who he means.

I study him, waiting for an explanation that doesn't come. "How do you know what happened?"

He shrugs casually and leans against the counter, crossing one foot over the other. "Wasn't hard to figure out. The police in Sherling aren't the brightest, are they?" When I only stare at him, he continues, "I read the police report detailing your grandmother's death. I know you refused to talk to them, never answered a single question. But you did tell everyone what happened."

I swallow, an acrid taste rising in the back of my throat.

"Wolfe. Morgan Wolfe. Hell, you pretty much named him in the story you wrote."

"How did you..." I croak, unable to finish.

"It was submitted to Blackwood as part of your admission file, along with your transcript. You're a talented storyteller. A bit dark and twisted, but good."

"Why do you care so much about my life?"

"I told you, the truth is much more interesting than the lies."

"Do you know this much about Ashton? Or is it just me you're obsessed with?"

"I wouldn't call it an obsession. That sounds so…creepy." He grins, and I glare at him. "It's intriguing, really. Putting the pieces of a person together, to better understand why they are who they are. Probably has to do with understanding my mother's suicide, but I don't care for psychoanalysis."

"And Ashton?" I persist.

"I'm not going to talk to you about her," he says sternly. I see a flash of something hard in his eyes. Is he…protecting her?

I decide not to push him about it, even though I'm becoming more concerned for her by the second. "Fine."

"Aren't you curious?" he asks. I narrow my eyes, not following. "How he died? Your *beast*." I remain silent. "He was stabbed in a bar fight, about a year and a half ago. Strange, right? That he died just like in your fairytale, by a blade."

"Why do I get the feeling you know more than you're saying?"

"Don't I always?" Brendan smirks like he is a vault of secrets, and has swallowed the key. "Is it better, knowing he's dead?"

I shake my head. "Doesn't bring back my grandmother. Or erase what he did."

"I'm sorry about your grandmother," he says sincerely.

"She hated lying, more than anything." My voice is weak when I first speak. I glance up at him quickly, then back down at the floor. "We made a promise to never lie to each other. And she said breaking a promise was worse than a lie, so I never did. Even when I wanted to. It doesn't mean I always told the truth. But I never lied to *her*."

I swipe at the tear that snuck out of my eye. "That night…it was the last time I ever lied, to anyone. I chose to keep the truth to myself instead. And maybe that's worse, I don't know. It's what I do. I either tell the truth or keep it trapped inside. But I never lie."

"I know," Brendan replies, like this all makes perfect sense. After a weighted silence, he says, "I would kill him for you if he wasn't already dead."

I snap my head up and stare at him, questioning if I heard him correctly. He tilts his mouth into his notorious smirk and I shudder.

A knock breaks our connection.

"Here's one of your sworn protectors now," Brendan announces. As he walks to the door, he continues talking. "These Harrison men have all vowed to protect you, haven't they, Lana? It's a little strange if you ask me. You have your own legion of knights, all within one bloodline."

Before I can react, he swings the door open. "Sir William. Please do come in."

Joey enters, shooting Brendan a suspicious glance. When he spots me, a tantalizing, dimpled smile ignites. A jolt of electricity stirs in my gut. I know it's a lie. But my body doesn't seem to care.

I stand, and he walks toward me. "Hi."

"Hi," I say, looking directly into his brilliant blue eyes. I'm trapped within their gaze, unable to look away.

Joey brushes a hand along my cheek, and I inhale sharply.

"It's like you can't resist," Brendan observes in complete fascination. "It's a little disturbing."

The arrogant lilt of his voice breaks us apart.

"Uh, so." Joey clears his throat uncomfortably. "What is it you wanted to show me?"

Brendan retrieves the photograph from a hidden compartment beneath his roll-top desk. He hands it to Joey silently, like he's anticipating how he'll react. I figure there's a reason for this, but then I remember Brendan has a thing for theatrics.

Joey examines it for a second. "Um, so, what am I looking at?"

"You tell me," Brendan insists. I roll my eyes.

"We don't know who everyone is," I explain. "We were hoping you could tell us."

Joey scans it again. "Well, you know my dad, my mother, and that's Parker." He points to each of them. "That's my Aunt Cassandra," he indicates the woman we didn't know, the only one who doesn't appear to be pregnant. "Um, I'm not sure who this is next to your mother." Joey looks up at me.

My gaze switches to Brendan. He nods, granting permission.

"That's Brendan's mother. She grew up on the island."

Joey directs his attention to Brendan. "Your mother?"

Brendan nods. Joey appears confused. Join the club.

"What about the other two?"

Joey narrows his eyes, like he's trying to place them. "Um, it's hard to tell who the woman is. The guy looks familiar. I've never met him, but…I know I've seen him before. Maybe in other pictures." He pauses in contemplation. "I can't place him. Sorry."

"Do you know where this was taken?"

"Our family estate on Nantucket. My great-grandfather built the main house, and then my grandfather added houses for each of his children, so we could all vacation together."

"What are you, the Kennedys?" There's an undertone of hostility in Brendan's voice that draws my attention. Where is *this* coming from?

"Brendan," I say in warning, not wanting him to piss Joey off and keep him from cooperating. Brendan walks to the bar and pours himself a shot.

"Drink?" he offers Joey.

"No thanks," Joey replies.

"Do you know who this guy might be, the one cut off, running to get into the picture?"

Joey presses his lips together in contemplation. "It could be my Uncle Kaden. His house is on that side of the property. And it would make sense considering."

"Considering what?" Brendan demands impatiently. I shoot him a look, silently questioning his irritation, and he shakes me off. What is going on with him?

Joey pulls out a folded envelope from his pocket. He smooths it out and removes a small stack of papers, along with a photograph. He hands the photo to me.

"That's my uncle," he tells me quietly, like he wishes he didn't have to say it.

In the image, my teenage mother is sitting on a guy's lap. He appears a little older, maybe early twenties. His face is tucked into her neck, kissing her. Her tranquil blue eyes are sparkling and her smile is so bright. She's so...in love. I've only ever seen her this happy with Nick.

"My mother was dating your uncle?" I ask, trying to digest this. My eyes widen at the unspoken conclusion. "Is he..." But I can't say it.

"Your father?" Of course Brendan can. Joey flinches. I think I might throw up.

Joey and I stare at each other for a moment. "That can't be right," I gasp, swallowing against the bile in my throat. There's no way I'm related to the Harrisons...no way.

"Would explain a lot," Brendan remarks. "Except the incest part."

I glare at him. He laughs like this is the most amusing thing he's ever witnessed.

"Maybe not," Joey finally says, but still not sounding all that confident. He spreads out five pages on the coffee table. We bend down to examine them. They're DNA tests, more specifically paternity tests. My eyes flick between them, my brain too freaked to comprehend what I'm looking at.

"I found these in my father's office. I made copies. They were in a hidden locked drawer, kind of like yours." He looks to Brendan.

Brendan picks them all up and shifts through them. "There aren't any names. Only patient numbers."

"And?" I demand, my heart racing and my palms slick with sweat.

"These three," he stacks them on the table, "all have the same father. And these two, aren't a match to the donor."

I swallow.

Brendan lets out a heavy breath, like he's preparing himself. "Was your aunt pregnant at the time this picture was taken?"

Joey does a quick calculation in his head and nods. "She was like, four months pregnant with Lily."

"*She's* Lily's mother?" I gasp. Joey nods again.

"So, there are five pregnant women in this picture. And five DNA tests. Anyone want to take a guess who the kids are, and more importantly, who their fathers are?" Brendan flips through the pages again. "The tests were for three boys and two girls." He holds the pages up to the light. "The birthdates have been redacted for some reason. I'll have to search for the originals to tell us when each was born."

"How?" Joey asks.

"You don't want to know," I tell him. His mouth rounds in a silent, *Oh,* understanding it'll be illegal.

"The two girls are you and Lily. And there's no denying you're a Harrison," Brendan says, his eyes shifting to Joey. "So, one guy impregnated three women in like, what, six months? What was he thinking not wrapping it up?" Brendan lets out a humorless laugh.

My brain finally starts connecting everything he's saying.

"If Kaden's my father then that makes me your cousin." I give Joey a quick glance. My throat constricts like it doesn't want me to say the rest out loud as I face Brendan. "If not, then I'm *your* sister." Even Brendan appears disturbed by this revelation. My knees buckle. I collapse in the chair with a heavy plop. "Is there any chance Lily may be Brendan's sister?"

"Cassandra married my uncle a month later. I always assumed it was because… he was the father." The pause leaves room for doubt.

"But he might not be?" Brendan asks, queuing in on the same hesitation. Joey shrugs.

"This is fucked up." Joey runs a hand through his hair.

"Undeniably," Brendan agrees, finishing another shot. "Good thing you didn't give in to temptation and sleep with me." He winks at me.

I make a disgusted face.

"Why do you even have this picture," Joey looks at it again, "from Labor Day weekend…" Joey's face pales instantly. He shakes his head like he's hoping whatever it is isn't true. "I didn't recognize him because I never met him. He *died* the weekend this was taken."

"Who are you talking about?" I demand. Joey stares at me with wide eyes, like he's silently apologizing. "Whatever it is can't be worse than finding out I made out with my cousin, or that I'm…Brendan's sister." That was so hard to say.

"I know who that man is. Which means, I know who the third boy is."

Brendan and I stare at him, willing his mouth to move. But as soon as it does, I wish I had stapled it shut.

"Vic."

Acknowledgements

This story was determined to be written, even after years of writing and rewriting the first four chapters. I learned a lot during those years—mostly, that I needed to be kind to myself, even when I felt like I was failing. Especially when I felt like I was failing.

My journey in creating this story was much like Lana's discovery of love—I discovered what it was to be a writer again. To live within my words and not want to let them go, even as I typed the last letter. Lana's journey isn't over, and neither is mine.

I am surrounded by the most wonderful and passionate women. They were there to remind me of just what I'm capable of accomplishing. They never once stopped believing in me. Their love helped me fall in love with writing once again. It was a long four years, but here we are. And I am very much in love.

This story is for all of my friends who talked me off the cliff or screamed right alongside me…

Elizabeth – You have endless patience. You taught me how to keep swimming. You sacrificed for this story, not because you had to, but because you love me and what we do. I love you and couldn't do this without you. We are capable of miracles—truly beautiful magic. You are the other half of my love for writing. Together, we are one.

Kim – You listened. You read. You advised. You encouraged. And loved. If I could give you a hug of love and gratitude every day, I would!

Kathleen – You encouraged me. You guided me. And you were always there to listen, even during the times I questioned everything. You are the voice I search for when I'm lost.

Tarryn – Your love of words. Your passion. Your love of me. There's a madness to being an artist, and you get my crazy.

Jenn – You answered every time I asked, "What the hell am I doing?" You understood the frustration, the pain and longing to be in love again. And you didn't give up on me. That was exactly what I needed.

Dina – You offer unwavering support, no matter what I choose to do with my life. Because you know exactly who I am and love me all the same. You are my truth.

Thank you, **Kate, Leah** and **Paola** for being the friends every woman deserves. I am grateful to call you mine. I trust you.

I was supported by a full team of patience who cheered me on until the very last second. Thank you to **Nina, Ellie, Janet, Nadege** and **Regina** for taking this story and making it brighter, for everyone to see. I mentioned the endless patience, right?

I write for me. But I am an author for all of you. Thank you to **every reader** and my **Dolls** who have allowed me to do what I needed to create this story, no matter how long it took. I'm enveloped in your love every time we meet. You make my heart sing! I will always find my way back to you, I promise. ♥

About the Author

Rebecca Donovan, the *USA Today* and *Wall Street Journal* bestselling YA author of **The Breathing Series** and **What If**, lives in a small town in Massachusetts with her son. Influenced and obsessed with music, Rebecca can often be found jumping around at concerts, or on a plane to go see one. She's determined to *experience* (not just live) life. And then write about it.
Follow along: www.rebeccadonovan.com